D0843474

Beautiful Soul

An American Elegy

Spuyten Duyvil New York City

ISBN 978-0-923389-58-1
cover: *I Like America and America Likes Me* by Joseph Beuys,
used by permission from Artists Rights Society

Library of Congress Cataloging-in-Publication Data

Corey, Joshua.
Beautiful Soul : an American Elegy / Joshua Corey.
pages cm
ISBN 978-0-923389-58-1
I. Title.
PS3603.O7343B43 2014
813'.6--dc23

2013047381

Henceforth and forever I am my own mother.
Roland Barthes, *Mourning Diary*

1

Film for the New Reader

BLACK SCREEN. A FLICKER. THE LETTER:

In the heart of the night the new reader lies awake with the lights turned off listening to the rain tapping on the skylight. If she opened her eyes she would see the darkness of the ceiling and a differing quality of darkness above her, a rectangle gradually reorganizing itself into a gray filmy gleam, glassy surface blistered by streetlamps, and the little shudders of water whose shadows she can feel moving across the bedspread, her husband's sleeping body, her own face. Like hieroglyphics or Hebrew letters they form and squiggle and dissolve almost legibly before her closed eyes. The letters are falling on her roof and the roofs of her neighbors: they fall invisibly into Lake Michigan, that vast unplacid text, and coat metal and glass and asphalt from Waukegan down to the Indiana border. Others too are awake reading the weather, establishing degrees of correspondence between internal and external states of being, between the past and the present, what they expect from the day and what they are incapable of anticipating. She thinks of other bedrooms, other couples, men and women lying awake while their partners, women and men, sleep soundly. Alone, straining after significance, for signs and portents, reading clockfaces, windows, glowing screens, magazines, books. Her book is on the night table where she left it, face down, straining the binding: she reaches with her hand and feels the rough skin of the spine, its slightly crumpled edge like a lip, and then the pages dividing reluctantly under the gentle pressure of her fingertips. Under the covers, the pages marching together, many folds, many pages, the words she has read and the words she has yet to read. The book is mine while I read it, for as long as I keep turning the pages, and once I am finished it dies to me but lives in the hands of other readers, and we might meet in a cafe or the supermarket or on a bus or in a hospital waiting room and discover, without title, that we share the same blind insatiable need for print, ants at the picnic, words printed on the insides and outsides of our eyelids, passwords, like canceled checks bearing signatures negated by the loss of value, the transfer of energy from beginning to end, unceasing until the book drops from my hand, I close my eyes, the rain spools, lurches, stops. Let me live here ever. She is dropping to sleep, a few hours from dawn and the baby's cry, as her husband breathes evenly, wordlessly. The rain carries on past consciousness. The bed is a boat for strangers.

Sleepwalking she might arise and dress and drive in the dark to a wedge-shaped building in the heart of the city. In simple gray slacks and a white blouse under a tan raincoat, watching the elevator needle swing. And find herself in a granite hallway, in the loud hush of the janitor's floor-polisher, knocking on the pebbled glass window of an office door with letters on it: S. Lamb, LLC.

Sit down.

He does and does not look the part, as she, dreamer, puckering crimson lipstick beneath a black bob, fails to resemble her limp-haired daytime self. The office is small, with a metal partition separating out the heavy desk and file cabinet from a waiting area with sofa and armchair and a table with magazines (a yellowing assortment of copies of *The Nation* interlaced with *Guns & Ammo*, an issue of *Field & Stream* poking out from underneath a stack of *Psychology Todays*) and a water-cooler gurgling discontentedly to itself. With the side lamp and the magazines and the unopened box of tissues it could be the therapist's office it so exactly resembles: the office of Rita Rattman, MSW, where Ruth and Ben spent one awkward evening per week for three months before Lucy was born. Rita Rattman, MSW had long curly fraying hair and an oblong horsey face and sandals that slipped distractingly on and then off her long-toed feet as she curled in the armchair across from the sofa where the three of them sat: Ben and Ruth and Ruth's belly, the future made flesh, taut as a drum if drums swallowed sound, swallowed inchoate possibilities of the life that Ruth had imagined before the morning she'd opened her eyes knowing she was pregnant, the evening before she'd peed on a stick, the sleepless night turning beside Ben waiting for the right moment. It came or failed to come in the small hours, perhaps three in the morning, to shake her boyfriend awake and say the words to him, studying his sleep-smeared face for the least hesitation, the slightest sign of doubt, horror even, all reactions she would have taken for signs of intelligence, would have let her release a little breath, feeling herself for one moment to be less alone. But the insensitive bastard had only smiled beatifically into his pillow and reached out a hand to caress her belly, for the first but not last time touching not herself but past her, like one who pushes a revolving door and travels with it for only so long as it takes to pass in or out, to where you were really going. Her knuckles whiten. The tears come.

How can I help you.

Watching, in three-quarter profile, profile, waning, turned entirely away. A mass of black hair, too vivid to be natural, tentacular, gone.

Did she speak? Has she spoken? Did she hand over, across the featureless surface of the table, the manila folder he now leafs through, with its documents, letters, photographs? Where did it come from? Is he repeating back to her what she told him?

The photos.

He pushes the magazines aside and lays them out on the coffee table, one next to the other. Three women, or three photos of the same woman, or two photos of the same woman and the photo of a different woman, or one photo of a woman and two photos of a woman trying to look like the first woman, or two photos of different women and one photo of a woman trying to look the platonic ideal of the woman the first two only resemble. The possibilities are not exhausted.

The same woman. Not the same woman.

One of the photos is black and white, one is in color, and one had once been in color but has faded. The black and white photo shows a slender young woman with long dark hair looking full at the camera, features placid, but there is something of an angle, a subtle arch to her eyebrow, that creates the impression of barely suppressed laughter. It has the dimensions of a passport photo but is about twice as large. She wears a plain blouse of a pale wheatlike color, almost no color at all, and no visible jewelry. If there were a hand, for instance, wearing a ring, it does not stray into the territory that the photo so sharply delineates. For identification purposes only.

The color photo shows a slightly less young woman with dark hair, cut shorter than the hair of the black-and-white woman, in profile, bare of arm with pink palpable flesh, leaning her elbows on a railing looking down at water. The landscape bends behind her, raises obscure buildings: a river or a canal, a palace or a church. The profile is pensive, but the presence of the first photo on the table sets up a sort of vibration, a call and response. The lip of the profile the color photo doesn't show might be quirked upward, as the eyebrow of the woman in the black and white photo suggests a bitter hilarity. Her hands are folded in front of her over the railing over the water. If she's wearing a ring the ring is hidden.

The faded photo, a Polaroid, shows a woman older and heavier than the others, with dark shoulder-length hair. This is a candid shot, whereas the others are manifestly posed. She is sitting laughing on a blanket in what looks like a park or meadow. There is a basket, there are plates, there is a bottle of wine and a plastic cup in her left hand. A plain metal band—the fading makes it impossible to say whether it is silver or gold—adorns the fourth finger of that hand. The other hand reaches down around the shoulders of a small girl, perhaps three or four years old. She is dark-haired like the woman and her eyes are squinted shut and her mouth is round in an O. She could be yawning or yelling. She is certainly not laughing like the woman who holds her lightly, laughing hard, doubled over slightly, as though she has just been tickled or poked. The image is poorly framed, for it shows most of the head and body of the woman but the girl's body is cut off. She is a yelling or yawning head with a single disembodied hand outstretched in protest toward the sky.

The man rearranges the photos in reverse order. He stacks them in a pyramid. He puts them in a line again and flips them over and studies their backs. One photograph's back is blank. One has the words "Venice 1972" in blocky print along the bottom. One has an indecipherable scribble. He flips them back over one by one arranging the faces side by side, crossing their gazes.

"The skill of police artists is to make the living appear dead."

He looks at her, we see her face as though over his shoulder: the dark circles and fierce beak, full lips stained bright and bloody.

You want to know something more about her: what she ate, what makes her smile, what she is looking at in the photograph in the white dress like a bride's, in three-quarter profile looking at a river you can't place—the Hudson, the Thames, the Seine, the Po, the Danube. Your question is always the brute one, the necessary one: Did she love you? Whatever the answer, you will not be satisfied with it. Whatever the answer she will elude you, as water eludes, flowing through her memory that can never be yours.

My mother is dead.

Dead.

But she sends me letters. I have them here. Touching the manila envelope sticking out of the top of her purse. Didn't she already hand it to him?

Legs curled under her on the sofa. When did she take her shoes off? They lie discarded like patient animals under the plain pine table with its magazines.

The therapist sat with her legs pulled under her in the armchair across from the couple on the couch, shielded by the low table, by the box of tissues, by an expanse of cream-colored carpet. These were night sessions, and the room was inadequately lit by a single lamp in the corner opposite where the therapist's armchair was. A bright lamp in a dark room makes strong shadows. It lit one half of Ruth where she always sat, her right arm and right earring, if she wore them, sparkled and reflected in the dark window opposite. Ben at his ease in the fuller dark, right ankle on left knee, his wristwatch and glasses glinting whenever he moved or spoke, which was not often. The therapist sat cross-legged in her chair making sudden grotesque gestures with her large ringed hands, subsiding, looking up at the ceiling with the whites of her protuberant eyes showing while she gathered her thoughts, or fixing Ruth orbicularly and nodding with exaggerated attention. Ruth, hands folded on her belly, swelled up with right words that did not come. The words that did make an appearance were stupid and obvious. The therapist gestured for Ruth and Ben to face each other, for one to speak and the other to listen and to repeat what she or he heard. Some words went unspoken that were neither wrong nor right: *job, jealousy, abortion.* Ben said something about Ruth's mother and she heard herself say, like a character on TV, Leave my mother out of this. But that hadn't been what he'd said at all. You'll be a wonderful mother said the therapist, referee, recording secretary. Not her words, not Ben's. But she'd been looking right at his mouth. She knew what she'd heard.

The listening man is dressed neatly, monochromatically, in dark suit, white shirt, and dark tie. But where are his shoes? She tries not to stare at the mobile toes in thin black dress socks, kneading the carpet.

Answering a question. She hoped she hadn't misheard. Almost three years.

And no contact since then?

Except for the letters.

When did they begin to arrive?

Three months ago.

Real letters?

On paper, yes.

Handwritten?

Some. Some are typed.

You mean printed?

I mean typed.

Stamped? Postmarked from where?

Europe. Different cities in Europe.

Where?

Paris Rome Vienna Venice Budapest Berlin. Trieste.

Trieste, he repeats.

Trieste. The far edge of Italy. There's a sea there, or a river. The sea is warm, the river cold. Rivers remember the places they pass through. The sea is blank and unmemorable like a sunbather in dark glasses, prone, dead, on a beach strewn with hundreds of other inanimate bronzed bodies. Germans, most of them, or Austrians. There are no Americans here, Elsa. Just like home.

A stray line comes to her, a wandering sentence from a poem: *Do I not withhold the penetrations of red from you?*

She puts down the letter and shuts her eyes for just a moment. But to shut your eyes inside a dream is only to open them more widely.

And you want me to find her?

I know where she is.

Where I last saw you, where you were supposed to be. A field. A small oblong stone set in the earth among others. A bronze vase inset that can be inverted and filled with flowers.

In the halftone room the man leans toward her, vulpine, unsmiling, patient, takes a cigarette out of a pack from the drawer, leans back, produces matches, lights one, lights the cigarette, tosses the match into a glass ashtray. Each action leaves behind it a little shimmering trail in her sight, like one of her migraines. No one smokes any more except in the movies: smoke creates texture, the illusion of depth, pulls focus. He leans back, plumes it up and outward, makes a little indescribable generous gesture with his hand. The blinds slat the wall with light from a streetlamp. It is all more perfect, more familiar, than she could have hoped.

These letters lead back to someone. I want you to find him.

Not her then. Who?

My father. My real father.

How many fathers do you have?

Call him Papa, patient companion of her years, with his mustache, his glasses, weak kindly eyes. Sang me to sleep, held my hand at crosswalks, brought me to his classroom where I played in the hollow of his desk while he delivered his lectures on mathematics. He was always there, trying too hard to make up for a more singular absence: hers. Also his.

I couldn't come from him. It's someone else. My father. She left him, too.

Who is writing the letters, then? Your father or your mother? Or some third party? To what advantage?

They are... He is... She stops to think of the word, eyes lowered. Raises them, unwavering, into the black gathering hollows of his face. Complicit.

In the drained toplit room of shadows there comes a pause. There they are, framed as though from some third person's point of view, hovering spirit, a person with a camera, silent, not to be observed observing detective and client, doctor and patient, animus and anima. Headlights from the street track up the wall, gleaming obscurely on panes of glass concealing photographs, certificates, diplomas. He's got a drawer open, two glasses, pouring shots of rye. She holds the small hard heavy glass he hands her in her lap watching him knocking one back and pouring another. It's what you expect, what you wish for. You pay for this. For the disciplined derangement of the senses, disarrangement of false reality. You pay him to enter your dream, your nightmare. So you can wake up. The fall guy, the sacrifice. She notices, as if for the first time, the long seam of the stockings on her legs, leading suggestively ever upward, and the undone buttons of her blouse. It's me. The fatal one.

It may get expensive.

I'll pay anything. I want to know who she was.

I thought we were talking about your father.

It's the same thing.

Thy mother's spirit. Doomed for a certain term to walk the night. The glass in her hand protects her palms from her curiously pointed nails.

He makes a small horizontal gesture with his cigarette hand.

It's your money. So to speak.

The king died, then the queen died.

How do dreams end? She sees a man kneeling in a narrow room, as though at prayer. She sees the man in black enter with a gun in his hand. The body kicks out as the life leaves it, falls prone. She can almost see his face.

Men take and take, her mother had told her, until there's nothing left. They can't help it, it's in their nature. They're babies, all of them.

The baby, rooting.

She swung her legs out of bed (Ben grunts, his

body jackknifed, burying his head more deeply in the pillow) and stepped into her bathrobe, passed Lucy's closed door and passed through the room that Ben calls her office out of misguided courtesy, located the pack of Marlboro Lights tucked in the back of the top drawer where it's been keeping company with dried-out pens and bent paperclips for more than a year, and treaded softly down the stairs and passed through the kitchen and out through the sliding glass door onto the deck with the red firestarter Ben uses for the grill in her hand, feeling the cool humid pre-dawn air pressing itself against the parts of her the bathrobe didn't cover, and in a gesture that has never failed anyone propped a cigarette between her lips and lit it, holding the handle of the firestarter away from her as though it were a blowtorch, and blew grateful stale smoke up and away from her in a cloud toward her neighbor's silent black backyard, rising past the second floor windows she imagined, moment of panic wondering if her daughter's window was open, decided that it wasn't, imagined Ben's nostrils whiffing the smoke and turning again in the bed like the bore of a drill deeper into some quietude where she can't, won't follow, and the image of her mother's face when she was young (which "she") rose unbidden before her eyes, its planes and curves, the dark bulging slightly startled dark eyes like Ruth's own, the hair like woven strands of coal and glitter (even at the far side of middle age), lips like hers perpetually narrowed to mark the imprint of irony like a kiss, like the burning coal of Moses, like memories carried like treasure in a box that's never been opened, is it the treasure that's so heavy or all that iron and lead and hollowness and the burden of not knowing what is precious, what is dross, never dropped, buried at sea.

Lay my burden down. In front of the kitchen laptop casting its frail glow on her face, saucepans, the night. She types a few words and clicks Send. And drifts back toward bed, where she lies sleepless, searching the backs of her eyelids until dawn.

Produce a match. Was that her goal?

Why do we insist on a plot for our lives?

Dark curling hair in the oldest photographs. When I knew her short severe and flat, grayed gamine, bobbed. Tracked back in time from heavyset to voluptuous to slender: can it be the same woman? Produce the body. Sits in ashes, listening to the voice thunder: Where were you when I laid the foundations of the earth? How a woman suffers. I hope you never have to suffer the way I've suffered. Drama: bangles tilting on a wrist, the bob a little longer, A-line. Thrift shops, colorful voluminous fabrics at her heaviest. Her breasts, ample, tucked away, one breast, swaying heavy that time in the bath, and then, none. The years between cancers in which she grew up. Was I breast-fed? Is she accountable? Like me she hated her ankles and short waist. Dark large heavy-lidded eyes quivering with hurt or scorn. Arched eyebrows she used to pluck. The elegantly hooked unignorably Israelite nose that answers mine in the mirror: Shulamit, shalom. She was proud of her strong arms and shapely calves. Her lips like mine of an exaggerated fullness, particularly the lower. Dimples. I never wore bangs again. Eleven years old in the locker room of the Jewish Community Center, white of cheek, wadding a towel between my legs that I threw out later, in the dark. *You're like me, I also bled early.* Matter of fact, I almost said matter of fat: the endless diets: she was contemptuous of daytime TV and slick magazines and self-help books, lived in a self-imposed bubble of the most elevated culture, the operas whose scores she studied, *I, Claudius* on PBS, tunneling every weekend to the city for doses of theater, ballet, visits to the Met: but somehow she always knew about and followed the latest diet, the latest fad: liquid, raw food, low-carb, no-carb. I always had to diet with her but not Papa, she insisted that he eat what he liked, she cooked separate meals for him and for us; staring across the table at his plate of paprikas swimming in sour cream and down at my own plate where half of a single seared chicken breast kept company with cooked carrots. He was decently embarrassed about it and took his dessert into his study, a dish of ice cream or pastries she'd baked that afternoon, sometimes I'd find the plates and lick them. Then when I went to college she gave it up and ate what she liked. Her voice, I'll think about that later.

Produce a comparison: I'm two inches taller, my hair is lighter, my boobs are smaller and so, oddly, are my feet. Her shoulders slope slightly, I'm wide as a linebacker, played for the volleyball team. Her skin is milk pale and mine runs to sallow. We both feel the cold. The last time I touched her in New York, an awkward hug, lips brushing one another's cheeks. The last time I sat in her lap, the last time she held me in her arms. The last time we raised our voices at each other. The last time she approved of something I'd written. The last time she saw my husband, *never*, the last time she saw my daughter, *never*. The last time she expressed her disappointment. The last time she expressed her disappointment with me. The last time the three of us were together, a week before she departed for Europe with Papa, never to return. An Indian restaurant on the Upper West Side. On the phone with Ben in the ladies room, crying. The awful bitch, I said. How dare she? The awful cunt. Ben at his best then not saying anything, just breathing on the other end of the line. I don't know what I'm crying for, I said. I don't need her any more, I've never needed her. I'm a grown woman. She's dying, Ben, do you understand? She's dying and now she'll really be gone. Fuck her. *Fuck* her.

She's going away, but she'll come back. Of course she'll come back.

I wish I knew, I said. I wish I knew if she were telling the truth. About anything, ever.

Papa glancing up at me for just a moment with his

dark sad brown eyes, dropping then his gaze to study his glass of Kingfisher. On his side of the table but sitting apart, regal, solitary. Fixing her make-up, as I had been doing moments before in the bathroom, erasing all trace of grief, self-contempt, homicidal rage. Smiling for both of us.

We ordered the saag paneer, she said. I remembered how much you love it.

Produce the evidence, all of it damning. Shards of a life, her life, in me. What do you call a mother who is not one? This compulsion to repeat.

Touching my belly then, not yet showing. In six months I'd be a mother. In ten months I'd be married. Within a year she'd be dead. She was cheerful about it.

Call it a vacation, she said. A long vacation. I want to see them again, all the places I loved. Papa does too. The old country.

Shrugging, embarrassed, meeting no one's eye, least of all that man, almost invisible from embarrassment.

No one knows how to die in this country. As if she knew.

My baby.

We'll be home in time for the baby. Of course we will.

Of course, Papa echoes.

You should stay. The doctors…

I'm done with doctors.

Then you're done with trying.

Trying? I have tried, Elsa. I've tried my whole life. It's time for a new life of not trying.

Ruth is my name.

Of course it's not so easy to find good curry on the Continent, she says dreamily. At least it didn't use to be. You have to go to England for that.

And where do I have to go? Swallowing the words.

But this is not the conversation. These are the gestures and countergestures, the motions of forks and glasses, the perfectly ordinary congratulatory words and details of a trip long dreamed of, the trip of a lifetime. Without her.

Smiling, reaching a hand to stroke my cheek. I suffer the touch but look away. Couples, families, eating. The sky's traffic. The city.

I'll write you, she says, motherly, faraway.

Eaten behind the eyes, both of us.

Produce a threat.

The image of Elsa Ruth, sixteen years of age, rising listlessly into view of the full-length mirror in her mother's bedroom. Outside it's the suburbs, New Jersey, birdsong and acid rain. Empty Saturday afternoon, the well-made bed. Tears for Fears playing somewhere. Plucking at her shapeless nightshirt and shapeless skin with thumb and forefinger, watching red marks fade on her neck, cheeks, arms. Without bothering to shut the door moving to the bureau, opening and shutting drawers, the dressing table where elaborate earrings hang from a sort of tree, glint of the silver and turquoise New Mexican jewelry her mother favors. Passing over a photo on the nightstand of a young woman in off-white, another somewhat older posing with a man and little girl, this woman in a gray suit next to a big placid bespectacled man with a daylily in his buttonhole, the little girl like a solitary bookend between them holding a little basket of daisies, the background bare and institutional, a courtroom Ruth remembers, no not a courtroom, just an office, a judge's chambers, a long time ago, a hollow in the grit of the matchstick decade of her birth, New York. Drifting out at last down the upstairs hall, listening for voices from below, the radio mumbling in the kitchen, a few sharp scrapes of cutlery on a plate. Into her own room, shuts the door. Lies down on the bed, arms and legs outstretched and stiff, sweaty, clutching the strip of paper in her palm, wondering if her mother knows, down there in the kitchen, why doesn't she call me, how doesn't she know, is there still time to get out of bed and brush my hair and come down smiling, like none of it happened, return the paper to its hiding place in her mother's nightstand. The door was opening. Eyes squinted shut, the sun was on her, her mother leaning in.

So?

And when Ruth says nothing:

You're sick? You do remember that it's Saturday, don't you? Being sick isn't going to get you much.

Steps in briskly to put a cool hand on Ruth's burning brow. Ruth's hand holding the piece of paper relaxes, opens, like a flower inviting the wasp. Creak of bedsheets.

It's that time of the month, is it? her mother croons softly. You stay in bed then if you want.

It's not that, Ruth manages to say, though of course on top of everything else it is that, that very thing. The cramps churning at the center of her body like the lobsters she's seen in the tank at the supermarket, trying to unclench their rubber-banded claws.

You don't have a fever, you're just hot, her mother decides. Take a bath, that always helps.

I'm fine.

Her mother shrugs. Suit yourself. Remember we've got Papa's birthday dinner tonight, we're going to John's. I do hope you at least remembered to buy him a card. If not, take one from my desk and sign it. I'm off.

And she is off, leaving without having noticed Ruth's paper or closing the door after her, a terrible habit of hers. Ruth waits a long moment then leaps out of bed, slams the door histrionically, dives back under the covers and waits. But there is nothing. No: the garage door opener is shaking the house with its prodigious yawn, how many times has Ruth reacted to that signal, her parents coming home, stubbing out the cigarette or the joint, urging the boy back into his jeans and out the back door as fast as his skinny deer legs will carry him. But now she is still. The car starts. Her mother driving away. The sun begins its long trek down the wall as she lies there staring at the ceiling. Closes her eyes for just a moment. She must have slept, her eyes open to the sun striking full on a poster of Morrissey inscrutable and dead-sexy in his chaste removal, his aerie. After a while she gets bored listening to the neighborhood, the radio still mumbling downstairs (she never turns it off), her bedroom stereo singing tinnily to itself at low volume *every body wants to rule the world.* I do so have a fever, she insists weakly. She reads the paper again with its dates and numbers, its signatures, its blank spaces for missing names. Feels the raised indentations of the notary's seal. It's thin paper, waxy, inflammable. Why did you keep it? she asks her silently. Keep me. Keep me twice. She considered the possibility that somewhere sometime there had been another daughter with the same name, a secret sister who'd died, and she, Ruth, is the hasty replacement, a bridge over the river of grief. My sister Elsa, beyond the sea. She can see her, just fifteen months older but infinite in her experience, wearing the short tulle skirt that her mother had scorned to buy her, made-up, sitting at the end of Ruth's bed. More developed than Ruth, heavier breasts, hips wider, lighting a joint with practiced aplomb, offering it to Ruth after taking her own deep appreciative drag. Slightly hunched, sitting up in bed, searching the shadows of her eyes. Where is my father? Give me my father. What is he like?

Kind. Steady. Honest. The other says these words with her mouth twisted, as if she intends the opposite. Mocking the question.

This paper says you were never born.

Elsa shrugs, blows smoke. Here I am.

My papa is kind too. But sad.

Our father isn't sad, beyond the sea.

He's European?

Of course.

Is he French? English? He's not German, is he? Where does he live?

Very far from here.

Can I go to him?

He's in the dark, Elsa says mysteriously. She's up now, walking around Ruth's room, looking at her things.

You mean he's dead?

Elsa picks up a record album. No deader than I am.

Is he good-looking?

He's not handsome if that's what you mean.

What I mean is…

His face?

Yes. What's his face like?

He eats too much. Sometimes he wears a beard.

Does he know about us?

If he did, he'd come looking for us.

But you live with him, I thought.

In the dark.

She puts the record on, turns the volume up. Immediate voices, harmonizing lonelily.

So he is dead. Or he never existed, like you.

I was never born, Elsa says. It's not the same thing. Anyway, of course Father exists. You're here, aren't you?

I'm here.

Well, that's your problem.

Singing along with the record, eyes shut. *Hey now, hey now, don't dream it's over. Hey now, hey now, when the world comes in.*

She didn't hear him come in. A knock on the door. Elsa?

Open the window, turn on the fan, get the smoke out. One minute!

Your mother says you're sick, says Papa through the door.

I'm much better now.

Can I come in?

Spritzing the room, spray droplets hanging in the sun. Yes.

There is Papa, his face like a moon swelling over his gray turtleneck, wincing slightly at the loudness of the music. He turns down the knob.

I just wanted to ask if you were coming to dinner. It's getting late.

Yes of course I'm coming. I just need to get dressed.

Awkward, hands in pockets, smiling. If you're sick of course you should stay in bed. I'll bring you something. A doggie bag.

Woof. No it's all right, I'm coming. Do I have time for a shower?

You must hurry.

Papa, wait. Can you do me a favor?

Of course.

He is not a big man and she has shot up in the last year. It's possible by now that's she's more than an inch taller.

Can you call me Ruth from now on? I don't like Elsa.

But that's your name.

It's not. It's really not.

Wary, shrugging, unsurprised. What does he know?

All right. Ruth.

Thanks, Papa. Happy birthday.

Thank you, Ruth, he says, trying it out. He walks away down the hallway, almost singing it in his deep voice. Ruthruthruth.

When she shuts the door Elsa is there. No, she's gone. Elsa is gone.

She sings it softly to herself down the hall to the bathroom to the shower. *Don't let them win.*

Following the figure of a man, her man, ours, his back, walking away from the camera and taking our vision with him. We want to look at a man looking at the Alps, a battlefield, the sea, the sublime cityscape, an image consuming itself. The scene that includes him does not include us, and that is its perfection. We see him as part of the landscape, landscape defined as that portion of terrain that the eye can comprehend at a glance. And if an itch crawls up his spine to tickle his neck and the head hunches, snaps backward to peer over his shoulder, accused or accusing, what will he see? We are the audience. We are not there.

Poet or assassin, we follow the man. The camera is a gun, the gun is a microphone, the microphone is a pen, the pen is a telephone. Calls in the small hours, between two and four, gone straight to voice mail. In the morning she deletes them without listening, noting only the times and the country codes. Two fathers, one father, then no fathers at all, no mothers any more. M. Tense and alert before the page, the phone downfaced on the bed beside her, on vibrate. Her husband sleeps.

Fathers are depressing.

Mother of invention, asleep or awake, she dreams him, Lamb: a black-and-white man in a simple lineless suit, gray raincoat over it, a fedora, out of the airport, out of a cab, pulling a black wheeled bag behind him over the cobblestoned streets of a nameless European city. Call him anything, she did not pay for his name. She quit smoking so he still smokes; she rarely drinks so a bottle stands by the bed in they small dry hotel room, where a single window overlooks a trellis or an alley or a canal or a blank whitewashed wall. Tethered to her by cords of time: the mother, the daughter: she needs a man without appendages, masculine and alone. The camera is close enough to smell the back of his neck: tobacco, cornstarch, bay rum. On audio: waves' scumble, foreign voices, a kicked ball, shouts, a busker accompanied by electronic orchestra, handclaps, bumblebee scooter engines whistling and whining. He sits with his back to her, us, smoke drifting from his left hand, its bandless fingers. The right hand, the writing hand, the knowing hand is still. Rests tarantula on his knee. If we look closely at the back of a man's head, whose face we have only seen in a dream, seeing only the skin of his neck and the pattern of hair (black flecked by gray) and the two ears standing wide astraddle, and the barest movement, fleck of tension. Is he listening. Is his breath, in exhale, part of the mix.

A woman's fantasy. A man.

He goes out and takes care of things.

Exterior. A narrow street, black ribbon in a yellow canyon of blank-faced apartment buildings. Too narrow to be an American street, too few cars. Lamb in medium shot, seen from behind, wearing a black-brimmed hat, someone's idea of the eternal past. His pace is unhurried, almost unmodern: he slouches, he ambles, like a man with no destination or agenda. But he has the crucial thing, a knowledge he bears in his body: how to ignore the camera that follows his every move. As he walks or shambles along there's a rasping sound, a grating noise, and as he shrinks in the frame we can see the plain black rolling suitcase that bounces and drags and skitters on the pavement as he pulls it behind him. Something paper in his hand, completing the image of a lost tourist. He pauses at a doorway, a wooden door with flaked green paint, a brass mailslot like a tarnished mouth. He folds the map and slips it inside. The map is a letter. The letter vanishes.

Interior. A woman in a severe black dress, in late middle age, bends down with a little grunt and picks up her mail where it lies scattered on the ragged tile floor. The strange envelope doesn't register at first because she flips through the letters looking at their right corners so that the postmarks blur by, and the hand-delivered letter of course has no postmark, and no stamp for that matter. Tight shot of the bundle of mail in her hand as she goes back up the dark wooden stairs, and drops the letter on the mat in front of a door, and keeps climbing. The camera retreats suddenly, staggers back like a drunkard and points up the stairwell to the next floor where another woman, also in black, stands watching. It could be the same woman, climber and watcher. We hear a door shut and the sound registers in her eyes.

Interior. A simple apartment, finely if anonymously decorated in muted feminine style. Closed French doors, a sofa, a vase offering a single tulip, a lamp.

Doorway to a kitchen, to a bathroom, to a bedroom. Tidy, silent, but for sounds from the street.

Meeting no other men with hats the solitary man continues dragging his suitcase down the narrow street. Does he wear it unselfconsciously? To scratch his bald spot does he raise the hat with his free hand or do his fingers creep under the brim? How can we know about his bald spot? Close in, encircled, like a tonsure, like Henry Miller. He pushes (he pulls) on his way.

The apartment is empty. No: there is a breeze. It stirs the curtains. There is a whistling kettle in the kitchen. Extreme close-up of a smudged tall glass that fills with boiling water, with black particles that rise and swirl to fill the screen, touching the water with their color. The plain pewter kettle replaced on the stove with a clank. The specks like sparrows entering a black cloud, suddenly pushed down and pressed out of sight. Ceramic rattle, cube of sugar in a chipped cup. The coffee streams out of the French press into the cup and presses down on the sugar cube, breaking it down but not utterly: a sweet residue underneath the bitter surface. The cup is carried out of the kitchen.

The envelope on the table by the tulip. It is a bill, *billet doux*, it is news. Perhaps it's news from some man gone to fight in the war. The camera is always before the war, never after or inside it. The camera is still, it's a wide still shot, but our eyes are drawn irresistibly to the empty hatrack. A shout in the street, can't make out the language, ricochet of a soccer ball off of someone's stoop, a short barking laugh. We are Americans and we call it soccer and there is a woman who is of an age, a fadedness, a resilience we don't have a name for. Something Mediterranean or Semitic in the angles of her face, the prominence of her nose, the darkness of her eyes. The hair shimmers with its blackness, the beautiful gradated blackness of a silver gelatin print. Alone she holds her beauty before her like a mask or a microphone, in one untrembling hand, so that we can't see what the other is doing. When she turns her back to us we are blind. Is she weeping? Is she whispering? Is she judging the time of day by the angle of the light? There are no clocks in this room. The envelope, torn.

The old reader sunk in her English cozies while the new reader is up to her neck in noir. Meeting only once on a twilit sofa a hundred years ago in the afternoon of a fever together thrilling to Grace Kelly in *To Catch a Thief*, her alien blondeness like fate itself co-piloting Cary Grant's little convertible along the twisting mountain roads of a Technicolor Monaco. But she shuns her mother's library, curls up on the floors of chain bookstores with shiny American paperbacks in her hands on the trail of serial killers, mass murderers, conspiracies that go all the way to the top. The new reader favors the cipher, the hard face, Eisenstein's principle of montage: intercut with happiness or sadness the face is happy or sad, though the eyes never move, though the mouth remains the same, level and transitory as a hyphen, a wink: Harry Lime vanishing in the Viennese fog. Missing man formation. Paradise alone of M walled in on herself, *Murder on the Orient Express*, Paris to Istanbul, open the first-class compartment: the lady vanishes. The new reader follows mean streets to the city's edge (*My Business Is Circumference*) where a desert opens in front of her like a map of blankness. Meeting the man, landscape of a man's face half-obscured by sunglasses, confronted like an object of increasingly durable celebrity: Gabriele Ferzetti, David Hemmings, Richard Harris, Jack Nicholson. Navigating the face to a lonely place, a precipice with a view of the vast conspiracy that includes her, us, the secret to which she herself is the key (*I'm not in the business; I am the business*). In the heart of the mountain reclines M languid with the old world pages, inside the locked room with the Colonel and the Countess and the Doctor and the Housekeeper and the Scion and the Mistress and the Dowager and the Lame Footman and the Reformed Burglar and the Lusty Squire and the Poetess and the Inspector with his pipe and his precarious infallible chain of clews: "I knew it all along," sniffs the Countess. We knew all along that it had to end this way: in this drawing room this hunting lodge this tramp steamer this prop plane this stable this abandoned warehouse this by-the-hour motel this funicular this fishing shack this philosopher's forest hut this fire lookout this Duesenberg this nightclub this country road this burning barn this suburban ranch this first-class stateroom this hospital ward this churchyard this cattle car this lonesome prairie this dilapidated greenhouse this twilit empire this retreat from Moscow this siege of Leningrad this Sarajevo motorcade this occupation of Paris this Ukrainian nuclear facility this march to the sea this grave of narrative that demands only death to start its dominos and only death, perhaps a symbolic death, perhaps a birth in disguise, to restore the uncontradictable order that rescues us, that decrees What Was and Shall Be, that foils novelty and sells novels, that denies all possibility of aerial views, from the precipice the locked room the womb. The new reader in sleep reading on, effortlessly converting text to moving images, restoring words to the purity of their referents, the things, as the novel gives birth to cinema, to a narrative launched by the immobile visible inspecting face of a man who has made his deal with the devil, the man who never compromises, the man who is well paid to navigate and pull taut the disparate threads, to shuttle in black and white, among the multitudinous cities incarnadine of Europe the only colorless thing, cutting like a slender blade to the essence between frames. Riding for days on a train, on a horse, on a camel, walking blind, bound for the locked room, to the desert, to the pyramid of skulls, to find her standing there on her naked native ground, heart stripped bare of secrets, and the man, guided by a love he himself will never feel: a speaking knife, a spear, a plunging tongue.

The camera clings to him, practically hanging on his shoulder, as he turns onto an avenue. There are cars now, there is traffic. He passes a group of schoolgirls in blazers and skirts, chattering to themselves in a language without subtitles; we understand that these are schoolgirls on the near side of puberty, talking about what schoolgirls talk about: boys, or rather not boys but those other schoolgirls not present, schoolgirls who are with or have been with those boys and what they've done or might be willing to do with those boys. Lamb lowers his head and pushes through them without looking back, and the camera doesn't linger either, but maybe he swivels his head a quarter-turn to the right, a little twist; blink and you'll miss that infinitely complex appraisable line or fractal territory suggesting a nose's wing, a heavy black eyebrow. A little farther and he pauses in front of a window, turns fully, one hand still on the long handle of his roller bag, and the camera turns with him, so we can see something of his reflection in the spotless picture window, nothing to deter our sense of the fundamental monochrome atmosphere that follows this man like the lens itself, passing through a halftone world into which color, now, is starting to creep. Flashes now behind him of a red car, a green skirt, a blue policeman pausing to fill out a ticket, his face a depthless shadow under the brim of his cap. Lamb studies an array of jewelry, nothing particularly expensive, without moving much, his face as invisible as the policeman's under the brim of his hat, but we can make out the outlines of a dark tie against a light shirt behind further layers of darkness: a suit coat, an overcoat, too heavy for the weather. There are watches, bracelets, brooches, necklaces, earrings, pins, ankle bracelets, chokers, armbands, wristbands, breastplates, or so it seems to the tourist and so it must seem to us, marveling now at the neatness of the trick, for we seem to be standing directly behind him and yet there's no camera or cameraman in the reflection, just the streaks of light that resolve themselves into cars or pedestrians and the twin pillars of darkness, the man staring unresolvedly at the many watches (no one of which shows the same time) and the policeman, head bent over his ticket book, scratching away.

Terrain of sounds. A long scraping noise. Indistinct voices. Foreigners. Small engines, tires on macadam, whine and wheeze of a bad fan belt, receding. A motorbike's burr, dopplering toward us, getting louder and more aggressive, then its reflection whizzing past in the window, then dopplering away. In this film our man is closely miked: we hear his slightly heavy breathing, the soft movements of his clothing, his footsteps, when he lights a cigarette we hear the heavy snap of the lighter and the audible combustion of the first strands of tobacco, hear him inhale, hear the smoke pouring down his windpipe, scratching up against precancerous polyps, hear him cough shortly, a bark, hear his blood and heart agitated by the nicotine, starting to beat louder and more quickly, hear his pupils dilate, snapping wider with an audible click, hear the dripping sound as sweat glands above his hairline gather moisture and salt to form beads of sweat to be absorbed by his hatband, a kind of reverse sponge-squeezing sound as that no doubt already stained ribbon of cloth takes on a further burden of the very essence of his tourist's anxiety, if he feels anxiety. We have, we hear, so much and no more. Lamb is almost a palindrome, almost a blade, petit mal, blam. He carries us toward what comes next.

She sits on her sofa staring into a compact, fixing her make-up. It's discreet, made visible only by her application of it, or by her repair, for there's a little black streak of mascara under her left eye that even now she wipes away with a bit of cotton. She studies herself in the little mirror and sighs, not quite audibly, then bends again to her tools. As she reapplies her mascara we are struck by the absoluteness of her concentration, of her utter presence to herself in the mirror as simply a face, a severe beautiful face with lines at the brow and at the corners of her eyes, and slightly sharper edges around the cheekbones, the curve of the mouth. She gives herself the kind of scrutiny our films don't give to women her age, older than thirty, older than forty or fifty, an American unperson's face still lovely in its mobility, though just now she's holding it steady, as steady as any starlet or woman holds her muscles when not being looked at; though a woman is never not looked at, so if she smiles or frowns because of that she does so invisibly, under the skin so to speak. She bears our looking, she wears our desire, masculine and feminine, men and women desire her, that still firm and erect body, though past middle age, a desire she herself cannot feel but understands abstractly, as an astronomer's most sophisticated instruments help him know about distant bodies without seeing them, that understanding of desire that she holds at a distance because of what we call age, what we call experience, like a second skin, and that hides the smile or frown, though it cannot, quite, hide her tears.

And if the letter were blank? A single sheet of white paper, unmarked save for a pair of creases? And if the woman, austerely attired, made up, not a hair out of place, were to sit down now with it at the kitchen table, with a pen? If she looked for a while out the window as her cup of coffee grew cold? If she took up the pen? If she looked at the paper then away from it again, as though searching, looking round at the kitchen, the apartment, like a place she had never before seen? If she applied pen to paper? If she began to write? If she wrote for a long time, immune to our eyes, the whispery crinkle of pen on page (she has filled one side, turns it over, begins the next side), clink of a ring on her finger on the coffee cup, sipping mud, putting it down again, applying herself, bent low, one manicured hand holding the paper in place, the other moving swiftly, fluently, without pausing for thought? If she stopped writing at last? Refolded the map, now become a letter, and replaced it in its envelope? Taped it shut? Addressed it? Searched a desk for stamps, found one, applied it? If she stood now, in the center of the room, hands at her sides, tapping the envelope against her leg, deciding?

Screening and absorbing print that isn't print: newspapers that leave no stain, feuilletons that never pucker the skin but only the seeking, restless eye. She reads old media on its way out the door to new media, photos in motion over changing captions, acting as though there were use in a center—*The New Yorker* and *The New York Review of Books* and *The New York Times* washing over the transom in sloppy paper waves. She reads mommy blogs, political blogs, book blogs, cooking blogs (but she rarely cooks, it's Ben who's at home in the kitchen, who can relax there, whistling his way through the slightly old-fashioned menus he favors: pot roast Provencal, filet of sole), sex blogs and advice columns, blogs by women about being women, blogs by men about everything, blogs by people in countries we have bombed, blogs by peoples in countries we've yet to bomb. She follows celebrities and comedians and authors and academics and smartasses and cleverdicks and drunkards and addicts and her brother-in-law the author of thrillers on Twitter. Everyone speaks English if they want to exist, but never too much of it at a time. She reads searchingly, with bitten lip and anxious eye, trying to break out of the bubble, to extend her breath's reach outside the shallow mainstream of American life in which all of us regardless of nationality are supposed to live and thrive for all the beautiful days of our ignorance. And yet this discourse—wry, intellectual, ineffectual—somehow slips by her trained and desperate eyes, so that when she closes the screen with a headache it's long past bedtime, Ben with a pillow over his head against the light, or Lucy crying in the afternoon, a naptime squandered, a vein throbbing so close to Ruth's left eye it might as well be the eye itself, hooked deep into the brain, a chain of pain leading from the light into dark and unfulfilled hollows of her skull. Unsolaced, unappeased, almost frantic with loneliness: the mind of the reader without print, without the stable march of characters, same today as they were twenty years ago in the mass-market paperbacks she devoured as a girl now solitary as sardines in basement boxes, on yellowing paper with split spines, the books that made her a reader, that she fell into and climbed out of as easily as a Channel swimmer, greased like a seal, creature made for that sea. So with laptop extinguished, with her husband breathing steady beside her and the barest flicker on the bedside monitor assuring her of Lucy's midnight silence, she reaches out once again for the book that's been waiting for her—the book no one asked her to read, that is party to no discussion group, that no teacher or talk show host recommended, that was patient it seems for years since she read the first chapter standing up in the town's last bookstore, yes years ago, that joined a stack of books propping up the frame of her lover's futon, the year she thought she was pregnant every month and every month read the single uncrossed blue bar of the pregnancy test with blank disbelief, saying nothing to her lover or her mother or her friends but firmly believing in her own changed life metastasizing inside her, years before Ben and forgetful striving and Lucy, little yolk with legs. The book was waiting. Not like her mother's books, grim and watchful on the shelves of the den, shadowing ordinary nights of television, books with pictures and without, objects of an impersonal terror inseparable from M's never-to-be-spoken sorrows, unthinkable documents of an unthinkable past that M carried mutely into the present, in the tense pose of her body at the kitchen table, in the spiral of cigarette smoke. Papa's books pleased her more: orderly rows of print or specifically riven with white space, the science fiction novels and popular histories and even the dense lightless volumes of mathematics; these pleased her, simply to touch them, rocking them back on their spines to feel their heft in her hand. The best of them were never on shelves but spread profligate throughout that house, as now in her house: scattered on tables and under chairs and on top of both stereo speakers and piled high on her bedside table so that there's scarcely room for a glass of water: more books even then that, stacked in the basement on shelves and in boxes, some perched precariously near the sump pump, the oldest books in her life, the thickest and most lightweight, scanned with a flashlight under blankets prickling with static electricity so that the hair on her arms rose in the aftermath of a thump on the door and a voice shouting Lights out and the battery dying with her still reading, still a girl, and life on the horizon in the form of the raked distant skyline, clouds imported from Europe, the destiny written decades ago waiting for her to collect it.

But the letters are real: documents. Someone wrote them, bought borrowed or stole the unremarkable paper they are printed on, or written on. The letters change. Some are printed, coldly stippled in black by the head of an inkjet, streaked. Some are handwritten, in a sometimes erratic but always legible script, with broad looping L's and G's striding across the paper. The ballpoint pen leaves a groove in the stationery that her fingertips can almost read when they brush its surface, the papers stacked against her knees in bed or tucked surreptitiously underneath it, where Ben never goes. The ink is dark blue, almost black; the pen in question is not generous enough to dot some of the hastier I's. One letter was typewritten without the benefit of correction tape and some of the letters are crossed out with small or capital X's. Only the signature does not vary: at the bottom right corner of the last page, almost in the margin, the rapid illegible squiggle that resembles an M. M with a dash in front of it: M and em dash: M as interruption. The pages are folded and carefully matched with envelopes without return addresses, each stamped or labeled Air Mail / Par Avion. It is this latter French phrase that moves her lips, each time, a kind of mantra as she folds or unfolds each letter, perusing its surfaces for clues since the words, she knows, are all lies. Par avion, par avion. It sounds to her like the name of a long-limbed bird, a crane, unfolding itself for flight across a marshy plain, a riverine landscape, suspended for a time over the cragged Atlantic, and then tracking the waterways, up the Hudson River Valley as far as Albany, following the nap of western New York along the Susquehanna, up to Buffalo with the snows and then another slow plunge across wide waters, Lake Erie, Lake Ontario, Lake Huron, and the dash across the state of Michigan to Lake Michigan before beginning its final descent into her city, her Chicagoland, her home, where at any time she might wake from uneasy dreams to find another letter neatly folded and sealed in its envelope, another missive from across the sea, from the country of death. Under her night-stand blank paper, a sheaf of envelopes. Tucked into an old day planner, a ballpoint pen taken from the Grand Hyatt on Wacker Drive. In her office, squat and ugly on its stand, the inkjet. In the basement, by the disused sewing machine, an old Selectric that makes a droning hum when switched on. It is a strangely soothing sound. If she finds herself in the basement among the unfinished dresses and tatty tablecloths and cardboard boxes unpacked from law school days, she might idly switch it on and listen for a while to the urgent whir of analog machinery, while the little planet of the ball waits for a keystroke to call it into action, almost faster than the eye can track. To make its mark. Eyes inward. A call or cry from upstairs so she leaves it running, it stays on for hours, until her husband comes home that night through the garage, stops wearily and warily for a moment at the urgent familiar hum; then silently, without imprecation, reaches down and pulls the plug.

Like a sightseeing bus pushing slowly through in-undated streets. That's how he moves, deliberately, lugubriously, like someone who has rehearsed this path a hundred times before without any appetite for the destination. Yet there's something or someone that he carries with him for whom it's all new, and so once again he patiently treads past the cathedrals and plaques and statues and fountains and squares and shops, pausing occasionally to discharge or take on some other passenger seeking novelty, a shade of distraction, something to photograph for the express purpose of forgetting all about it. As though tourist and guide were one. The guide remembers for the tourist, but if he too has forgotten all about it he has a script he can follow in one of several languages, and if this script has been repeated often enough he's free to think about other things, to daydream or worry or remember scenes from his own life, his own history, forever unnarrated except by himself to himself: a native to this place, let's call him Marco, thinking there's the flower shop where I bought her roses when they were out of those magenta daisies she likes, and she laughed at me, with real scorn I thought, for my unoriginality; there's the auto shop where Hector works, who never looks me in the face any more since I saw him one night with his trousers down in the alley behind the bar with another bloke kneeling in front of him, and Hector's eyes were closed and he opened them and saw me seeing him, but all he did was close his eyes again; there's the school where the nuns beat me black and blue but mostly black, black around the bone, until I thought I was becoming a nun myself; there's the office building where my sister was a secretary for just one little month to that bastard she married before he knocked her up with twins and knocked her down when he was drinking and then took her and the twins (Luis and Ramona) away forever to some fucking Spanish island, where they've never invited me to so much as visit; and all the time this secret narrative is unfolding, or jigsawing, through his mind there's another narrative coupled to it: the history of the city, the layers of centuries peeling and disclosed to the bored, avid ears of the picture-snapping listeners on the upper deck, above it all, while all around them swirls the ordinary traffic and weary populace of the city of now, each of them unfolding or jigsawing the private narratives with which this ancient history has only apparently very little to do. Thus Marco, thus the private invisible stream making its pressure felt to the viewer, indirectly, in the length of the shot, the minutes uncut. So Lamb, weaving and waving his way down the high street, halting occasionally to tug his bag's wheels loose from some snag in the paving stones or a curb's edge, edging, it's clear, with steady trepidation toward his ultimate goal.

What he, Lamb, has to go on. Very little. A client's scantly documented claim. The folded letters. M.

He turns his gaze from his reflection or the array of watches or the policeman's reflection (blue back to him now, putting the ticket book away in his hip pocket and looking at the sky reflected in his sunglasses), tips his roller bag from a vertical to a diagonal position and begins once again to move. We follow him into more crowded streets, now thronged with traffic, stoplights and gridded lines mazing the intersections and crowds of shoppers and tourists and idlers, men and women, really more people than you'd expect in what had seemed such a small and sleepy town (is it the same town or is it a geographical atrocity committed by the filmmakers, splicing together two or more places with superficially similar architecture and light, a sign of their commitment to a global audience implicitly ignorant of the difference, a rejection of local knowledge in favor of the spectacle intrinsic to film and film editing's capacity to get along without visible parentheses), and there's no mistaking now the sticky overlay of modernity coinciding uneasily with that stone miscellany, the flagstones and paving-stones, because there are people with cellphones pressed to their ears in the crowd, and a line of Japanese motorbikes the color of hard candies in front of a café, at which a young woman is briefly visible at an outside table tapping on the keyboard of her laptop—flash of her eyes as she looks at the man and his hat passing over the tops of her designer shades, but he takes no notice and walks on bent and leaning as though into a wind, free hand loose at his side like some sort of slow sea creature eddying past a slower one, whistling in the dark, prey and predator. She slides off the edge of the visible world as the camera tracks the man in the hat in profile, riding on parallel rails, the man's face shadowed in the hat's brim and his monochrome clothing and most of all the hat itself sustains a sense of his sliding somehow on the edge of time, outside our era, so that he belongs to the early Sixties at the very latest or the early Thirties at the very earliest, though his suitcase is the very mark of the modern cosmopolitan, dense and compact and massy, allocated to the last centimeter for an airliner's overhead bins. Then he passes in front of another shop window, sheer reflection this time, just a glint of red—velvet? meat?—and again the whole street beheld behind his mirror image and no camera or tracks or crew in sight, miraculous perspective, that puts us into the scene and removes every trace of spectatorship. Just looking, not seeing. Just telling, never showing.

We accept trompe l'oeil as the truth of looking: we accept the deceit of appearances in the name of a higher truth. If the camera follows a man we discover what he discovers a beat after he sees it, registering how to see it in the assumption of his stance: dully ambling, ambitiously striding, cautiously skulking, or bridled to a short, shocked stop in the face of what must remain literally obscene, the world of the off-screen. If the camera precedes him we never see what he sees except what's reflected in his face: Lamb reacts to a reality we infer, the necessary fiction that when he looks at us, into the camera, he sees something that is precisely not us, and yet we are his reason for seeing it: each of us in our seats are the stand-in for the beautiful woman, the blood trail, the nemesis, the dead end that at last receives him, that births no further mystery. Like a bad conscience Lamb penetrates the visible on our behalf, always two steps behind the truth right up until the moment it's too late. With rigid grace he navigates the labyrinth that he and we can see: mean streets, the planes and angles of treacherous faces, a fat man's wiggling wattles: he's nobody's fool and so the biggest fool alive, taking for granted as we do that there's a skull beneath the skin that will ultimately grin out at us, as skulls grinned from the spines of the books lining my mother's shelves when I was young: Agatha Christie, John Dickson Carr, masters of the locked room, the fresh kill, the cozy horror. Does he, Lamb, our American man, squat down now by that same green door, that same brass mailslot, and glance around to see if he's alone? Does he take out a pencil and use it to poke open the lid and peer inside? From his point of view we see only the dim shabby foyer, the dark stairs climbing upward. And then a shaft of light illuminating where the letter had fallen, and the letter is not there. We don't see his face, we must glean his satisfaction or lack of it from the set of his shoulders and his slight grunt as he gets back to his feet and takes hold once more of the handle of his rolling suitcase.

But by now some people in the audience will have walked out. After a start that promised a degree of intrigue and the pleasures of vicarious tourism, it has become evident to the discriminating that this is going to be a large bad picture, a pretentious attempt to translate certain American genre codes into the anti-vernacular of neorealism in a fundamentally uninteresting effort to present one man's investigation of a past in which he has neither stake nor existence. The shamus is a blind man proud of the keenness of his sight, whose narrative begins innocuously and yet from frame one he is already in over his head. For the rest of the film he will collide, vertiginous body, with the violence of facts, the implacability of the past, discovering his entanglement with a conspiracy too vast to defeat or survive. And without his innocence he ceases to exist. One more American crouched before the monuments of Europe, lacking a sense of scale, of his own relative size in regard to a thousand dollhouse churches, castles, palazzos, parliaments. Lying down each night in a fresh bed of innocence in penziones and hotels, rising each morning to put on his layers of protective coloration, impregnable behind the screen he carries or that we carry for him.

Shamus or cowboy: if the shamus bears his innocence before him like a shield the cowboy wields his like a weapon. He penetrates the landscape, squint-eyed, the better to protect his pitiless vision. He is, his posture insists, a force for righteousness, and so will commit any crime in the name of his disinterested goodness. He dies obediently and rises again, returns as an old man to the beaches he renamed in his youth: Utah, Omaha, Pointe du Hoc: Dog Green, Easy Green, Fox Green. The cowboy is there to be seen, not heard: a living monument silhouetted against the historyless sun. Over the next rise stand the numberless unrepresentable: natives, Americans, women and children. Can a cowboy be a woman, can an Indian be white? Under his buckskins? But his eye, like the shamus's eye, is caught looking. The shamus's eye takes in the corruption, the conspiracy, the henchmen arranged on spider strands leading toward the unbearable unrepresentable truth. The cowboy's eye reflects, dauntless and unwavering, crinkled by faux epicanthic folds, refusing light, revealing an empty soul or no soul, till it extracts a flinch from the opposed searching eye and closes it forever. Diagonal, simultaneous, men, the cowboy and the shamus dwell in the same foreign element, bearers of the fascination that leads them, us, hinges on which adventures and investigations turn. They are here for the purposes of the darkened theater of enthrallment. Those who remain, isolato or in couples, testify by so doing: No matter that we've seen it before, done better, fresher: we are not children, we understand we can never again see those films, those celluloid bandages over our wounded and regenerating innocence, for the first time. Yet we are undaunted and unblighted so long as we—though fewer and fewer—still gather with strangers in the dark and speak together the terrible affirmation in the open eye, following the gazes of straight-bodied men with faces in profile or in shadow, men with guns or cameras to kill the objects of their vision, to sacrifice, to gift our eyes. Down these streets we must go, ourselves accompanied by ourselves, seeing how far down innocence can go before dissolving into air, into thin air. We will go deeper yet. A hand dangles, the gun falls, the credits roll. Let's sit still for a moment longer under white lights before the white screen. Close your eyes. Listen to a voice, a man or woman's voice, recount what he or she has seen, what we will never see ourselves. That story, appendix to seeing and antidote to innocence, is what this bad and peculiar film is after.

She wraps a shawl around her shoulders, drops her keys into a simple black purse. She's going out. She deposits the letter into her purse and shuts the clasp with a click. Then she stands there a moment longer. Then she turns decisively and marches toward the door and opens it a little too hard so that it swings open and bangs into the wall—there's a dimple the knob has made—and we see her lit from below going down the stairs, her back and her shoulders and her head and then just a band of diffuse light, and around this time the apartment door swings shut and just before it shuts we hear the street door open, and then the apartment door shuts and we're alone in her living room. Straining our ears we can just make out her heels on the pavement below but they quickly fade. Yet we linger a bit longer in this sparsely decorated room, with its uncomfortable-looking sofa and single easy chair, a watercolor or print of a watercolor over the sofa that looks like a negative Monet, and the tulip with petals continuing in their process of blooming, of parting, of drying, of desiccating, of dropping to the table and to the floor and the simple rug at the center of the floor, off-white, the color of an empty page.

Sometimes I feel like a motherless child.

She walks quickly, taking short swift steps as her knee-length skirt requires, the short heels clacking down the little street to a corner and then up a little hill, like a little Montmartre, for there's a church hunched on the hilltop framed by gray chopped clouds. The few people she passes are young, with the scattered affect of students, moving in pairs and threes, some with headphones and earpieces, even as they maintain a desultory conversation that's live there on the street. She seems to be headed for the cafe on the edge of the plaza that belongs to the church, where a little gray fountain splashes or rather seeps, just barely contained by its plain smooth square rim—an abstract fountain, curiously modern, all right angles, an atonal intruder in the very lap of the Romanesque church, a rectangle in deadly opposition to its ancient roundness. But at the last moment she swerves left and into a doorway under a sign that reads, simply, *Poste*. Inside an antiseptic space, linoleum, row of mailboxes, the counter, an old woman in black stands arguing in what sounds like Italian with the long-suffering middle-aged overtall clerk folded down with his elbows leaning on the counter, eyes almost closed, absorbing his customer's untranslated wrath. The woman with the shining black hair takes a key out of her purse, steps up to one of the mailboxes, opens it, slides out a few letters, a folded newspaper or broadsheet, snaps the door shut again. She opens her purse, puts in the new mail, takes out the letter. Slips it casually into the slot of the letterbox on her way out the door. We want to follow her: maddeningly the camera remains fixed on the blank face of the letterbox, its single slit the only expression, while in the background the old woman in black's harangue goes on and on, interrupted occasionally by the clerks' world-weary half-whispered repetitions of *Si*. As if roused from slumber the camera lurches away now from the letterbox, stumbles almost out the door into the sunshine of the square, handheld suddenly canted casting about to the left and right as though questing. This woman's pair of legs or that woman's, walking away from us: not her. Surging up to the tables at the outdoor café where couples murmur and solitary old men read copies of a newspaper called *Il Piccolo*; not there. Swerving back the way it came, back up the hill, taking in the view of the cathedral with its face nearly as blank as that of the letterbox, coming to rest finally on her door, on its own mail slot, even more mouthlike under the nose of the doorknocker and the pair of eyelike windows. Resting there. Sounds on the street. We've lost her. The image remains.

The apartment. Nothing has changed, but everything is changing. The sun has crossed the street sufficiently to blaze in through the windows, to send dust motes sparkling and rippling like a second, heavenly set of curtains. The tulip is in ragged bloom; gap-toothed, it discloses its stamen shamelessly, as death has crept an hour further up its severed stem. A phone begins to ring in another room, an ancient phone with an actual bell powered by an actual motor triggered by an electrical signal that travels through twisted copper wire from an analog elsewhere. It rings nine times. Each time the phone rings the tulip seems to tremble a bit in our vision, the curtains seem to vibrate, the dust motes seem to shiver in time to the summons. We begin to notice that the frame is shrinking, the camera is dollying in, so that we lose the doorframe, we lose the French doors, we lose the tips of the curtains, we lose the dust motes, we lose the lamp and sofa, the tulip is larger and larger, but moving out of the center of the frame, and as the seventh ring comes it is abruptly bathed in voluptuous sunlight, afire with red depths and pink shallows. With the eighth ring the tulip is almost gone and we become aware of its pale shadow. With the ninth ring we see a little bell of color in the shadow's head begin to glow against the wall. As the ring dies away we see the tulip's shadow born into color, a red patch on the white wall, a tumescence, a little cauldron, bubbling away its living secret in shadow form on the wall: that no one can see. That only we can see.

In the mornings now Ruth wakes alone. Ben has taken up running again, so before dawn he slips as quietly as he can out from under the covers and pads downstairs to pull on his shorts and a pair of running shoes he's had practically since college, though they're falling apart and bad for his back. She's asked him a million times to take his keys with him and he says that he does, but at times like now she lies awake knowing in her heart that he's left them behind—how do you carry a set of keys when you're running?—and the front door is unlocked, and anybody could walk in, with her and her daughter sleeping upstairs. She burns, quietly, thinking of this, gripping her pillow. Ben walks fast, limbering up, passing a few other joggers and dog walkers following the same path as him, drawn ineluctably as though for a ritual to the lakeshore and the sunrise unfurling there, the sky streaking with pink scissor-cuts. She lies still, waiting for Lucy to start crying or for feet on the steps that may or may not belong to her husband. You're being ridiculous, she tells herself. She sits up in bed and turns on the lamp. The book from last night is lying there face down, its binding creased. She's never fetishized books, any more than she's fetishized food: she treats them casually, roughly even, dog-earing pages, smearing them with jam or spaghetti sauce, tossing them on the floor. It appalls Ben, not because he's any sort of book lover but because he's a sanctimonious neatnik. She rolls the words *sanctimonious neatnik* off of her tongue and realizes that she's in a rage, pointlessly. Lucy isn't up yet. She throws over the covers and stalks out into the hall, where a few of Lucy's toys are scattered—a little wooden car is perched on the lip of the top stair, ready to make a racket or break someone's neck. The white noise machine that Lucy's slept to since she was an infant trills softly behind the closed door, rolling its r's. Ben is running now, easily, still breathing through his nose. Dark houses, mansions really, on his left; the sun's disc brightening the lake on his right. Sometimes he encounters friends on these runs, men he'll encounter later on the train platform; the sort of not-quite-friends you never seek out, never have to seek out, your paths just keep crossing. There's a set of chin-up bars by the tennis courts and he stops to do a quick set, then jogs off again. It's autumn and his feet crunch the leaves. A power-walking woman with a shitzu scrambling behind her on its lead gives him an efficient smile as he passes her. In forty-five minutes he'll be showered, shaved, dressed, and riding the train southbound to his job in the city manager's office. In the kitchen he's started a pot of coffee and she sips a mug of it black and sweet after firing up her laptop—she has to move a stack of catalogs and junk mail to find it. The house is a mess, which means Ben's having one of his periodic moments of resignation in which he doesn't dervish around cleaning up after her and Lucy, which itself reminds her of a kind of ragefulness, which takes her back to her own inexplicable sense of having been ill-used, even violated in some unmemorable unforgivable way. There's a new e-mail. Ruth doesn't click on it. She closes the computer and puts down the coffee and drifts to the front window overlooking their street. The plants need watering. She puts her hand to her cheek and looks at her fingers. Tears. Ben has circled the university campus, is pounding his way back now. He's thinking about the day's projects, about the upcoming election, about Lucy, about her, Ruth. Anything but himself, she thinks bitterly. And upstairs, Lucy starts to wail.

She sits in the armchair nursing. Lucy's hand strays up to grasp Ruth by the chin sometimes with surprising firmness; Ruth moves to grab her wrist and Lucy giggles, her lips still fastened around the nipple. At moments like this what Ruth thinks and feels seems strangely separated from everything else about her—her bent posture, her arms cradling the baby, the cooing sounds that come from her throat or from Lucy's, it's hard to tell. Only that sweet sharp tug of Lucy's mouth on her nipple—that pain in which she takes a sober delight—unites her sense of distraction with that rootedness in the moment she usually only recalls afterward, nostalgically, even when she's wishing for a moment's peace, or thinking fondly, guiltily, of the time before Lucy, before Ben, before Ruth was Ruth. She hears the door open and shut downstairs, hears his heavy breathing. She thinks about Ben's life, which impinges on and shapes her own. His blank-eyed fondness. His toil, his sacrifice. His hard, lean body, so different from that of the softer man she had married, with long hair she used to tousle, like a boy's. On the brink of forty he's all grown up. And where does that leave her? She tenses—something in Lucy has coiled, her back, her lip—

Don't bite! Lucy...!

Lucy bites. With a little cry she yanks the baby upright and stares at her. Lucy stares back, a trickle of blood visible at the corner of her mouth. Ruth's whole breast throbs.

Lucy!

Lucy starts to cry. Ruth, not knowing what to do, opens her mouth to call Ben, but nothing comes out. Lucy keeps crying. She puts Lucy's mouth to the other breast and Lucy sucks. Somewhere a door closes. She breathes deeply and lets it bleed.

Legwork. Montage of faces, closed or partially opened doors, fingers pointing out of doors or out of windows or poking Lamb in the chest; a montage of hotel rooms, cigarettes, furrowings of his brow in front of his laptop, receiving messages from concierges and desk clerks, sitting in cafes alone with a pen and notebook or the *New York Herald Tribune*; a montage of stakeouts, from the backs of cabs and from alleyways and rooftops, snapping photographs of license plates, men on streetcorners, old placards and posters, railway schedules, lit windows in the rain behind which a woman's silhouette can be glimpsed, descending. A montage of monuments: Big Ben, the Eiffel Tower, the Prado, the Piazza del Campo in Siena, the Brandenburg Gate, the Chain Bridge in Budapest, the Vienna Staatsoper, the campanile of the Basilica di Santa Maria del Fiore in Florence, the blank faces of rivers (the Danube, the Po, the Rhine, the Seine), the Brandenburg Gate again, the Eiffel Tower again. In Paris, outside La Hune with a book under his arm, meeting a furtive contact; in London, touring Samuel Johnson's house with an unusually forthcoming guide; in Hamburg, strolling the St. Pauli quarter in Hamburg with a talkative old sailor; in Berlin, standing under an awning in Kreuzberg in the rain exchanging a few tense words with a Turkish man in a leather jacket and pink Mohawk. A hotel bedspread, frigid with anonymity, on which documents appear: the three photos, the letters, hospital bills, official certificates, passports, currency, a driver's license, more letters, more papers, until the bed is covered except for a square in the middle, filled then by a photo, a face, massive head of an old man with heavy jowls and brows, nearly bald, small eyes pouched and folded, meeting the camera's gaze with ineffable humor and sadness. Smoke. Lamb, standing in his shirtsleeves, arms folded, knees pressed against the bottom of the bed, a single harsh lamp, through the window, considering, and a city, any city, pressing up against the surface of his meditations, the dank heavy paws of the night.

Time has passed, or shifted, unguessably, fading in on a kind of open hangar, *une gare*, *stazione*, or *Banhof*, where suited, hatted Lamb sits at one of three metal tables beside an oil-drenched falafel stand, just a few meters from platform 7. Sitting across from him is another man, thirty or forty years older and many pounds heavier than the man we have come to identify with as the bearer of our voyeurism, our agent, our Lamb. He's the man from the photo, with craggy gray brows and a few extra bobbling chins and an improbable cap of thick white bowlcut hair, a rheumy gaze, a paper cup of espresso and a folded newspaper with a cellphone on top of it squared in front of him. Lamb takes off his hat and perches it on the upright handle of the black roller bag standing sentinel beside him. A garbled announcement over the loudspeaker, people hurrying by, little leisure at the train station. The fat man is asking a question, he's speaking English with a heavy accent, a generic European accent to our ears, but clearly enough to be understood without subtitles. The gangster question. She got the message?

Yes. A pause, then: What did it say?

What did it say.

Our man Lamb leans forward with an appearance of desultory curiosity and speaks again in his flat American accent, the newscaster's accent of imperial nowhere, clear and intelligible enough to bind us to him incrementally further, to further our investment in him, a narrow middle question mark of a man whose subjectivity, we understand, is to be viewed transparently by us and for us, as we see might see a stranger approach the window of a café where we sit writing or talking and step across the invisible barrier to press his forehead against the window, shading his eyes, searching as if for us, and we stop our fingers on the keyboard, we stop the cup from reaching our lips, we half stop our breathing waiting for him to move toward the door, to become a destiny, a man in a long coat and a colorless expression, or else to drift past, to rejoin the long crazy stream of humanity past the intelligible, the acceptable, the corporate comfort of numbers in the darkened theater. But for now he speaks for us and to us as we look him full in the face for the first time: handsome but not too handsome, middle-aged but vigorous, world-weary but bristling with perceptivity, dark hair flecked with gray, dark eyes with a luster to them, eyes that see too much, windows to our own weary souls, wise as we want to be, a suitable mask for our own willed naiveté, an Everyman of exceptionalism, American by default like the audience itself imagines and wishes itself to be, of the immortal twentieth century where all imaginable futures still live.

You do not send letters for her, Lamb says. On her behalf.

I?

You are her husband?

Till death do us part! But actually, no.

It takes some work to find you.

Do you have a question for me, monsieur? The *monsieur* is a deliberate affront.

I have one question: the letters. You deny all knowledge. But then you present me with a letter of your own. You know where she lives. You ask me to deliver it, since we have met in the city where she lives.

I don't like email, the man says, shrugging. I don't trust the post. If I write a letter, I prefer that it go by hand. Which means I can't be the one you're looking for.

No, you can't. But I found you anyway.

To find before seeking, the fat man says. That's a motto, isn't it? Sounds occult, like something from one of those thrillers you Americans love, about the secret history of everything, some conspiracy of old men in a star chamber that runs the world.

People are always hiring me to uncover conspiracies, says Lamb, leaning back. It's my job to show them that it's all in their heads. It's understandable. You feel caught up in something larger than yourself, that you can't control: a machine, a system, an establishment, your life. You want to believe that someone out there has the answer, even a malevolent one. Even someone plotting against you is better than there being no plot at all. The hardest part of my job is showing people that life is simpler than that. They want proof.

Sometimes, I imagine, the pressure to give them what they want must be hard to resist.

It is.

But then you give them proof. Are they satisfied?

Not really. Enough to pay me and let it go. I'm not a priest.

But you hear confessions. You are here to hear mine.

If you like.

I would like to hire you, actually, the man says.

You can't. Conflict of interest.

Yes. Because the question I have is a simple one. Who is your client?

You know I can't tell you that.

But I can guess.

Guess away.

Not here, the fat man says. Not now. He gestures up toward the loudspeaker, which has just garbled an announcement. That's my train.

Where, then?

Not here. Not now. The fat man rises, dwarfing the seated Lamb, the table, old but formidable, taking up his hat. Lamb smiles lazily up at him.

You think you can just walk away?

Do you propose to stop me? Mr. Lamb. The woman is dead. There is nothing for you to learn here. Go back to your client, whoever she is, and tell her so.

How do you know it's a she?

Be seeing you, Mr. Lamb, the fat man says, saluting.

That's right.

Watching him walk away, down the platform, carrying no luggage. Boarding the train. Lamb, he studies it, the sign for a moment. Picks up his espresso and sips it thoughtfully. *Venezia.*

Time, enough.

Hang up the phone now. Now. The new reader is almost here. Not an electronic book, not a heads-up display, not a cybernetic prop for reading, but a brand-new reader, organized by, for, the page. She does not compile, she does not calculate probabilities, she is no search engine. She is found wherever readers are still found: on buses, under trees, in grimy break rooms, in beds beside sleeping husbands. She props the book on her knees and worries a ragged thumbnail with her teeth. The book is hushed momentarily under her gaze, a cat with arched spine and ruffled pages. It is the new novel, always the new novel, the one that everyone who still reads is talking about, the one landing on important desks in Los Angeles and New York, an old-fashioned paper brick, surprisingly heavy. It doesn't matter who the writer is (but it's a man). It doesn't matter that everywhere old readers are gathering in front of television sets and computers and podcasts to hear the book discussed by other old readers. It doesn't matter that in the academies the oldest readers of them all scoff at this book and its readers, then turn themselves and their bored charges back toward tending the classics, the immortal beloveds of literature, bricks in the picturesque ruins of our civilization's self-image, held up not by other bricks but by hands and backs, bent, having grown deformed and nearly human under the strain of bearing its colossal weight. The new reader is coming. She grips the uppermost corner of the recto page, ready to turn it, but does not turn, lingering over the last lines, shining black in the matte white sea of rectangular space. What is the nature of her pleasure, reflected in dilated pupils, in the blush response, in breath ever so slightly roughened in contrasting tempo to her husband's even breathing? Whatever its nature, she takes her pleasure from that page, that arrangement, that musical score so perfectly attuned to the syntax of human synapses that have been evolving for thousands of years toward this moment, this pleasure. *Lux, calme et volupté*—she remembers, the new reader has an imperfect memory, an ordinary memory, a random-access memory, that lights brilliantly like a landing strip when touched by an incoming stimulus, a word or phrase or image or character's gesture or rhyme in the plot that activates the blazing network, that stirs vivid sensations in half-remembered languages: Madame Follet's eighth-grade French class, for instance—a contoured plastic seat, a jagged replica of the Eiffel Tower (made by Mr. Bund, the metal shop teacher, rumored to be sweet on Madame Follet), the chocolate eclairs on behalf of which her mother descended from her air of rarefied sorrows for an afternoon to help her prepare for Foods of France day, the irregular verbs between being and having, her bitter disappointment at coming down with chicken pox three days before the class trip, the milder disappointment mixed with amusement when she finally sees Paris in the springtime a dozen years later, strolling the boulevards on the arm of her not-yet husband, not yet the father of her unconceived child, who won't put his camera down even in their hotel room (only incidentally erotic, the lens pointed outward in a doomed attempt to capture the quietness of a quiet street of the Marais, the naked pear of his body photographed by her eyes in her memory from her prone position on the hard, undersized bed), the framed photograph of her lying back in her overcoat with her eyes closed on a cold sunny morning in a chair in the Tuileries, the fight they had in the Rodin museum, the image of her husband pouting in the sculpture garden while she gazed down from the second-story window, stiff shape of the back of his neck and shoulders, the rigid inverted U of his arms as he lifted his camera, framing tight lips, a stubborn chin, an Adam's apple, the *Bande dessinée* shop they paused in on their way back to the hotel (to make up, to make love), the comic-book adaptation of *Les Fleurs du mal* that she glanced through, the eighth-grade French which she hadn't needed once the whole trip, not even to order a glass of wine, suddenly suffusing her consciousness, so that when the new reader encountered *«L'Invitation au voyage»* she was able fully to accept, guided in part by the black-and-white images the artist had chosen to illustrate, no to accompany, the text: a languid arm pocked with needle scars dangling down from a bed, a needle rising to meet it that is really a ship's mast, a ship's mast that is really a gigantically erect cock thrusting from the hips of one grinning sailor into the eager sucking mouth of another sailor, a mouth that is really a cave lit from within by phosphorescent crystals, a cave that is really a grave straddled by a waif-thin woman in a black raincoat, wearing sunglasses from under which tears are streaming. She took all this in—the artist's melodramatic conception and the innocent poem—in a single glance, or so it seemed, as her husband approached the register carrying a Tintin book, *Objectif Lune*. Murmuring to herself silently now—a split now, at once in that hotel room on the Place des Vosges and in that bedroom in a soft Chicago suburb—*Tout y parlerait / À l'âme en secret / Sa douce langue natale.* All illuminated, as in a flash of scarlet, by three words at the bottom right corner of the page she holds between thumb and forefinger, not even the end of the paragraph or the sentence, syntax incomplete and yet luminous: *the invitation to....* The rain falls on the skylight window. The new reader is always a stranger.

2

Letters from M

HOTELS. HOW I LOVED THEM. The intoxicating combination of anonymity and privilege, as though living in an American city could be made somehow portable, bearable. There were times, of course, when I needed that feeling, that departure. Midweek, in the unreal interval after my diagnosis, I would find myself on a train or in a cab wandering without luggage into the lobby of an old hotel, out of the chaos of unmade decisions into the cool echoey atmosphere of marble and steel, the lobbies with their heavy upholstery and mirrors and chandeliers and fresh-cut flowers winter and summer and the silent tread of the uniformed employees and the laughter of temporarily unrumpled businessmen and visiting wives as they traipsed in and out to the cabs or over to the elevators or across to the winking comfortable cavern of the bar. Sometimes it was enough for me to sit, just sit on one of the sofas by a white telephone, as if waiting for a call, and to read the newspapers and brochures I'd find lying there, or even the occasional discarded paperback. Skin on my neck prickled against the possibility that I'd be discovered, asked to show my key, asked to leave, but it never happened. I looked like a traveler, I suppose, or less flatteringly, like a tourist. Other times I'd walk right up to the front desk and ring the bell, if necessary, and some cleanly young man with brilliantined hair or a dignified older man with a carnation in his buttonhole would assume the proper distance from me to be heard without shouting, to assume the friendly impersonal intimacy of hotels, and I would take bills from my purse and place them on the counter between us and he with a faint formal gesture of precisely calculated embarrassment would pick up the bills as though they were litter and make them disappear in a drawer, and he would hand me a key, that is to say a card, a little plastic rectangle with an image, as often as not, of the skyline printed on it, or the hotel façade, or an ad for a nightclub. With prize in hand I'd deflect the suggestion of luggage, but accept the accompaniment of a bellboy to escort me to the elevator and we'd be carried up up up (I always asked for the highest floor I could get) and the door would open onto a whisper-quiet carpeted hallway with its glowing sconces, a kind of silence and antiseptic grace over everything, and the bellhop would lead me to the room, bearing my key in place of a suitcase, and use it to open the door to what was invariably a small, almost cramped room with a single queen-sized bed and an armoire (rarely were there closets) and a television and a window, and he would busy himself drawing the curtains or lighting the bathroom or pointing out the telephone while I stood there breathing in the pure, false, expensive air, until at last a small bill would find its way from my hand into his and he'd step out with a little bow that reminded me thrillingly and fearfully of the uniformed men of my childhood and close the door behind him with the quietest of clicks, and I would stand in the window for a while looking at the city from an angle unavailable to my apartment, a taller bleaker more brilliant city than the sleek fat domestic cat of a city that lies perpetually purring with its tail of suburbs wrapped around it; or I'd lie on the bed fully clothed after carefully removing the bedspread (it's there you'll find the bedbugs and all varieties of dead matter, the maids never wash them until they are vigorously and permanently stained) looking up at the ceiling, listening to the faint sounds of traffic and the occasional timbrel of sirens from below, or the muffled voices in the next room (the finer the hotel the thinner the walls), sometimes accompanied by the creak of furniture, or the empty high-pitched whine of a television, or of course, more frequently than not, the sounds of people making love. I remember once coming into the room with the bellhop while my neighbors were at it, a comic opera of bedsprings and low moans and lumping thumps that shook the large bad painting over my own chaste bed, and the bellhop, who was very young, perhaps not even eighteen, turned scarlet to the roots of his hair and rushed out of the room without so much as unhooking the drapes or extending his palm—it probably didn't help that I was laughing loud and hard and painfully and for so long that I imagine the lovers could hear me, for they quickly subsided without audible climax and

I went on laughing until the tears came.

What would I do afterward? Almost nothing. Listen to the radio or turn on the TV. Take a shower. Sit in the single armchair by the window listening to the hotel breathing, to the city grumbling and grating to itself, to the small sounds and movies of my own body as it turned against me. Sometimes looking at the door where no lover would appear, comfortable in the knowledge that one would appear if I so chose, if I ever wished to surpass the possible. But then again there is no surpassing the possible: the actual is cheap, experience has taught me that. Too often I'd gone to see for myself and returned disappointed in the oldest sense of that word: an appointment that was not kept, a messenger that was only a man with an empty envelope up his sleeve, a maddening sort of helpless shrug, a compassionate distracted glance over the tops of spectacles, a woman with a red face. No, look at the door, a solid rectangle of wood with its brass-covered peephole that I might lift to survey the fishbowl the lens made of the hallway, which was empty: it was emptiness I paid for. It would end with me in the bed, bedspread folded and tucked into the bottom of the armoire, lying on top of the blankets, fully clothed, listening. Dawn waked me, not with sunlight (even the highest hotel windows in the city rarely offer an angle by which the morning sun might penetrate) but by the change in tone, an impalpable waking presence of life in the streets, the gurgle of pipes feeding showers, the sober murmuring of adjacent solitary guests talking into phones. I'd wake dry, in a wrinkled dress, underneath my coat if it had been cold, a taste in my mouth, the stale sick self I hadn't after all escaped for a single moment. It would have been simpler to take up drinking. It would have been easier to forget. But for a few hours I'd been, not your mother, no one's wife, no singer or survivor, no one's daughter. Only no one. And I knew, as I slipped out the door like a woman fearful of waking her husband on her way to meet her lover, that I'd be back again and again, until at last I took flight, to find my final home, to tuck the tail of my life into its beginning, in Europe, in the past.

Yesterday is dimly starred, the day before a blank, the days before that blank but bright, like a projector run out of film. I can only remember yesterday, Elsa, can remember this morning and the first part of the afternoon, can remember everything up until the moment I discovered it: the letter. Now it's a blur; this page is a blur. Yesterday I didn't work, as I haven't worked for what feels like a hundred days, but I rose early all the same and took myself down to the café where I like to have my roll and coffee, watching the traffic thicken. It's impossible to find coffee to go in this country, you know, so no matter what you have to sit there or stand in one place while the caffeine charges you up. By the time you start moving again you're already moving. It was like that, still early, me with no particular place to go, so I wandered down in front of the Hotel Verdi and as it happens the tram had just stopped. Without thinking I got on and we began to move—there was hardly anyone else aboard because the tram was heading back up the big hill, to the houses—everyone coming into town to go to work had already gotten off. The tram is wooden, prewar, and it doesn't take very long for it to creak above the main buildings and become surrounded by trees. There are some low, heavy pine branches that have been trimmed just enough for the tram car to pass, so that if you look forward through the driver's window it looks like you are entering a tunnel with a bright point of blue at the end—that's if it's a sunny day, which it usually is if it's not winter, we are so blessed here, Elsa, it's so unlike that terrible cold city you insist on living in. Out of the morning sunshine into darkness, so that for a moment I could hardly see anything. Gradually I became aware of the shadows of leaves dappling the floors and seats, the back of the driver's thick neck, and the back cover of the book that the only other passenger, a woman in her seventies in a pillbox hat, of all things, was reading. I couldn't make out the title but just at that moment she looked up from the page at me and I had to look away. I told myself a story about her, the inverse of my story, a widow from the hills who had come down into the city that morning to do her shopping—there was a tote bag on the floor by her feet—and was already returning home again. But then I thought again about the lipstick she was wearing—freshly applied—and her makeup. She really was quite beautiful, for all her being seventy, even seventy-five, and so then I thought that she was going home after having spent the night in town with her lover, a much younger man perhaps, in his fifties perhaps or even younger, who was passionately in love with her, who had perhaps loved her when he was a child and she was the adult, his teacher maybe, or just a local beauty whom he'd imagined speaking to time and time again as a man speaks to a woman but dared not to, who grew up and lived his life as a species of waiting, biding, while she went on with her husband, having children probably, living a bourgeois life in this little city on the edge of Europe, and then one day her husband died and her lover swooped in, so to speak—no doubt he was tactful, no doubt he could wait a few weeks or months if he'd already waited for so long, or perhaps he'd gone away, tormented by his proximity to her beauty, had made a life for himself nearer the center of things and had come back one day out of nostalgia, to walk again these quaintly cobbled streets, to partake of the town's peculiar combination of age and historylessness once again, and there she'd been, at the flower market perhaps or sitting at the café, as beautiful as ever in his eyes, and he'd gone up to greet her, and in the course of mutual reminiscences he'd learned that her husband was dead. Then and only then did the banked fire blaze up in him, and forgetting all his old bashfulness he would tell her that he was staying at the Hotel Verdi, and staying alone, that he himself had never married, that he'd made a success of himself in the great world and come back again for her and only for her. And she would have gone with him, out of pity perhaps, or boredom, as if in a dream, into the hotel lobby and past the prying eyes of the concierge without a care, into that creaky and tiny old elevator they keep so that already they would be in dangerous proximity to each other, and she would discover that even at her age she could permit the blood to flow and permeate her body with warmth, to remind herself that she was a woman, to accept his kiss, and when the elevator opened she'd take the lead, holding his hand, pausing at each door and turning to smile at him, radiantly with the question, This? and he'd shake his head and they'd pass on to the next door and again she'd turn and ask This? and he'd shake his head once more until finally they were at the correct door, and his trembling hand would barely be able to manage the key card so that her own steadier hand would have to take it from him and swipe it once, and they'd hear that little switch of the lock. And they'd go inside together, and it is from that moment, that assignation that would have been his lifelong dream, but for her more like a gift, an unsuspected fantasy, a blazing realization that life wasn't done with her yet. In truth she hardly remembers the younger man, may not in fact have recognized him at all—may simply have assented to the mad desire of a stranger because his misdirected passion had gone and stirred her own, and made her forget that she was a widow, forget her marriage, forget the life of disappointments and small resentments that most of us women are left with on a fine morning such as the one on which I saw her. By this point her gaze had safely returned to her book and I was looking to the left, like a child would, straining to catch a glimpse of the sea that I knew was there. And we came out of the tunnel then and the world was blind and blinding. She got off at the next stop, moving with some diffidence, older-seeming than she had when she was just sitting and turning the pages. The driver had to help her. Finally we reached the end of the line: there was no one waiting to board the tram, but we had to sit there for a while anyway. The driver got out to stretch his legs and smoke but I just sat there, on the hard wooden seat, smelling his smoke and a little sea air and the pine branches practically protruding their fingers into the windows. I had no book myself. And when the driver got back into his place he looked back at me for a moment without expression, not puzzled or curious or disapproving: I was only something to look at that wasn't his tram. I was a passenger. And then together, slowly at first, we began the ride back down the mountain.

The camera perfects experience, shrouds it with a fine flexible skin. So cities, so filmed. As even virtual streaming maps with their street views and glimpses of actual life—a woman leaping over a puddle, a man with a dog staring at the camera—these images falsify our street level jars, false steps, paranoid whisperings, smells of baking bread or urine, suppressed, caught but not preserved in pictures of us, we trippers and askers. Even falser the tourist's city, even and especially the blank streets off the beaten path, uncolonized, with or without a native informant. But falsest of all is the city you've known all your life seen afresh at the movies, as strangers see it, as it is now traversed by cops and gangbangers and housewives and Batman. The camera is a prophetic voice stuck in neutral, it declares only that this is, that nothing else shall be, it is the enemy of every future. We depend on the soundtrack for a hint of that other, unseen world: footsteps, sirens, voices, music. The light changes, the people cross. Things speed up and slow down, but there is no true future. *Ex cathedra*: from the seat where your posture matters not at all. *In camera*: in the room. We are sheltered. We are struck.

Lamb in the station. Lamb on the train. In a compartment while a landscape slides by, dappling in sunlight and purple shadows. Lamb giving the eye to a young woman, long of torso and limb, sitting across from him with legs crossed, her boyfriend stubbled and asleep with his head on her lap, her fingers in his hair. Looking frankly back at him, at Lamb, a man, unspoken and sexual exchange the camera can capture. Lamb in the washroom, throwing water on his face, looking at it in the mirror, studying its planes and angles so that we can study it too. At the movies mirrors pass for narration, we watch him watching himself looking to discover what goes unspoken, motivation, scars, marks of the past, signs of what's to come. Music under the looking, the moving train. If the door slides open behind him and she appears, serious under dark brows and lipsticked mouth, and advances to kiss him, he kisses her back, roughly, the door slides shut and she's already hooked her underwear with her thumbs, pushing it down, he has her by the waist and hoists her up onto the narrow sink, pushes his face into her neck, her fingers working at his crotch, thrusting into her, watch her open mouth, *Oh*, the two of them rocking with the train, fucking, the movies give us fucking, its futurelessness, alone in the dark in the static electricity of watching Lamb, our surrogate, even if you're a woman it's his skin we're in, and the tight shot of her hand gripping his shoulder, nails digging in. Then the cut, back to the compartment, where the young man sits up, yawning, passes his hand over his face, looks around, confused. The door opens, Lamb comes in, he closes it, sits down opposite, picks up his newspaper, nods. The door opens, the young woman comes in, adjusts her skirt, sits down next to the young man who puts his arm around her automatically, she nestles against his chest, her face hidden. The young man's nostrils flare, his pupils dilate, he looks down at her, touching her hair tentatively, he looks across at Lamb who is staring at his paper, he looks out the window where the sea is flashing by. He opens his mouth and closes it: we see him deciding, as they say, to let sleeping dogs lie. There is only this train, this stillness in motion, this compartment bound over the sea, westward. Only the set of his jaw remembers. And Lamb takes his laptop out of the top of his rolling suitcase, for writing is an aid to memory and he, Lamb, is the writer.

From her high chair little Lucy looks up from her bowl of oatmeal as the train vibrates past the house as it does a hundred times a day. "Choo-choo," Ruth says to her, pausing with the spoon in midair. Lucy concentrates. "Dada," she says. Ben's life is the train, whether he knows it or not. The train he rides at this moment, that he rides every day, is an arrow; the suburb and the city are bowstring and target. What defines Ben but this coming and going, that straddling of his own existence? Where he lives is not where he comes to rest: the train itself, sitting alone on the upper deck as she knows he likes to do, laptop open, coffee in hand, taking on the business of the day before the business day proper starts. Many men, women too, more and more, south at the start of the day, north at the end of the day, to and fro, their computers and smartphones like the hooks of lines they pull themselves along toward all their frantic responsibility, their indispensable arcs, home and away. Is he ever seized by the desire to arrest that suspension, that illusion of forward progress or backward regress? Has he ever stood up, snatched his briefcase, and stumbled out before the train reached its terminus? To wander streets and neighborhoods where he has, in every sense, no business: Rogers Park, Ravenswood, Wicker Park, Wrigleyville? How easy to transfer him in her mind from his perch on the commuter rail to a perch in the ballpark or in a movie theater, still neatly dressed in one of the suits Ruth chose for him, wearing one of the printed ties his mother, with faultless taste, selects and sends to him each birthday, Hanukkah, Father's Day. Or in a strip club, in an artificial night streaked with hot lights, motionless in a chair as some woman more than halfway to a whore writhes and gyrates against him. She can picture it so clearly, it's as if she's seen it—as if she's been that woman, trying and failing to get a rise out of him, in any sense. Ben is still, calm as glass you've mistaken for water, unruffled, faintly smiling, looking out from his experience and giving nothing away. Nothing but his devotion to the train, to going away from her and coming back, but never completely, gone or here, he lingers in the sympathetic vibrations of the house, the rattled windows, dented pillows, Lucy's face. Ruth gives her another spoonful of oatmeal, her left breast throbbing—she has put a bandage on the nipple, a blood-touched plastic pasty. She looks into her daughter's eyes and sees neither herself nor her husband, only the stranger looking out. Lucy takes the spoon from Ruth's hand and thrusts it into her mouth. She takes the spoon out and raps it once on the tray in front of her, hard. Dada! she cries. Dada, Ruth says back to her soothingly, and pries the spoon from Lucy's fist. Lucy cries.

An hour later, alone as usual in the kitchen streaked by sunlight, she touches her husband's name on her phone, an impulse she regrets the moment the name lights up, but it's too late, he answers on the first ring. The baby's not sleeping, she tells him. And: I miss you. He is grateful, wary, silent. She paces the kitchen, her robe hanging open, left nipple on fire. She can hear Lucy alternately babbling and wailing in her crib upstairs.

What's wrong, he says.

Does something have to be wrong?

She can feel him, see him, his posture canted slightly from the desk, one hand covering his brow, the other holding the phone, so that only part of a cheek and his nose and lips are visible, and his smooth chin. She can smell his aftershave or something like it, a brusque antisepsis, so different from her own unshowered funk, the sour smell from her armpits, her greasy hair. It's just so much sometimes, she tells him.

Too much?

That's not what I said.

He exhales loudly, a little windstorm in her ear. She is playing him, pushing him, she knows, into the unfriendly emotion of sympathy, a step or two from pity. She is making herself a burden. She knows it's unfair and tries to pull it back.

How's work, she asks. He starts to tell her and she tries to listen, but really it's just a release valve she's inserted into the conversation, a way of playing for time. He says something about his boss, about where he's going for lunch, about plans for a meeting with the mayor's chief of staff that afternoon. He stops talking and she searches for something to say. You do good work. Silence. You're doing the lord's good work, she repeats. She represses a giggle.

You should maybe try to get out of the house, he says finally.

I'm doing that, she snaps. I'm canvassing this afternoon, remember?

Oh, yeah.

She bit me, she says suddenly.

What?

Lucy bit me this morning. Hard. Just before you left.

She's succeeded and she hates herself for it. He sighs again. She can see his fingers pinching the bridge of his nose, see him turning finally completely away from the desk, getting up to close his office door.

Do you need me to come home?

No, of course not. I just.

Is it still bleeding?

I put a band-aid on it.

They both find this funny, she knows, although nobody laughs. When he speaks again the tension has lessened.

I can pick up dinner tonight if you like. You've got enough on your plate.

That's all right, she says. So do you.

Another long pause. You've got to go, she says.

No. No, it's just.

Well, I have to go. She's crying.

I'll call you later, he says. She wants to tell him, Don't call me. She wants to tell him, Take care of yourself. She wants to tell him, Deal with your shit and I'll deal with mine.

Okay, she says.

He hangs up. She is alone again with Lucy and Lucy's needs. Alone with herself. She takes her robe in both hands and opens it wide for a second, feeling the slightly chill air of the kitchen prickling her skin, the soles of her feet cold against the cold tile floor. Then she closes the robe and ties it and begins to move toward the stairs and up toward Lucy's room, toward stammering cries, guided, as so often, by an inchoate voice. *I didn't ask for this.* To which another voice answers, *Liar.* Outline of M in the doorway, mothering shadow that withdraws.

But the new reader too has a skin, transitioning from degrees of tautness to degrees of looseness, folds approximating experience, if not wisdom. She has eyes with imperceptibly thinning corneas over dark brown irises, modified by glasses, spectacles; but she is nearsighted, she puts them on when she rises from bed in the morning and goes forth to be in contact with the other bodies for which she creates a context: a husband's body, a daughter's. In the evening, alone with sleeping bodies like buoys in the darkness of the house, she folds them and sets them on the night table, then lifts a volume and props it on her knees and reads, and the moon like her family is an invisible watchful presence through the ceiling, through the clouds. She has given birth, has been wrenched from one ecstasy to another, has felt the crush of the growing fetus on her bladder, has felt less and less pretty and more and more beautiful: the word not the feeling, *beautiful*, the word her friends used, that Ben used, and they even said You're glowing and she nodded, feeling it, hands straying again to the rise of her belly, elapsing half-life of herself as an adult with some place in the world outside of nursing, meeting needs, biting her nails, reading. Now the baby is no longer a baby and the husband is only a husband and she is neither beautiful nor pretty, only now in the night of books is she not someone's object, in bed, just reading. I'm somebody's mother she thinks, wondering if her mother thought the same, concluding instantly No, she was no one's mother, not in her mind, maybe in her heart but no. She was indignant to be a mother, a minor character, blamed backdrop for someone else's story. And so I have no story to call my own, she gave me everything but. But she did read. She can close her eyes at last when the night gets old and see her, the old reader, at the kitchen table when Ruth came home from school, still in her bathrobe maybe, with the cloud of black iridescent hair voluminous around her shoulders and eyes blanked by glasses (the old reader never removed them, she saw what there was to see through heavy glass lenses of the Seventies and Eighties), always smoking cigarettes, menthols, and a cold cup of coffee, holding some heavy hardback encased like a sausage in the public library's cellophane, murder mysteries (the series with the little silver skull grinning at the base of the spine: Agatha Christie, John Dickson Carr: the old reader loved a locked room) but sometimes nonfiction, feminist keys to all mythologies (Gloria Steinem, Susan Brownmiller) and then the books she never actually saw her reading, the ones she owned, haunting shelves otherwise innocuous with thrillers and policiers: the books of the vanished and the murdered, the oldest readers of them all, the books that set Ruth on the first false umbilical trail when her mother began her disappearing act, right there at the kitchen table, a process of years, long before her actual body up and vanished, magnificent in its age and volume and remoteness (she was glowing, wasn't she, before her books like a cat by the hearth, soaking and storing away heat), its death-haunted beauty (memory of Ben kneeling in the first weeks in the doorway of the old apartment to kiss Ruth's still-flat belly, looking up at her wet-eyed and she smiling down, bemused, fingers nesting in the vigorous black thatch of his hair), in flight all those years from little Ruth's hungry incurious gaze, on fire to be elsewhere, now achieved, that vanishing, not a reader any more to Ruth's knowledge but a fugitive to be pursued down paths of memory, through questions asked of oneself in the hard small hours when one can read no more, when one longs only for facts, figures, dates, reports in the best objective style, one wishes for a procedure, an agent, a white or black knight in pursuit of the quarry, sleep, so long denied her, a woman reading late and long into the life that's passing her by. Somnambulist, self. She closes the book and snaps off the light and the darkness rushes up to greet her. The el clacking by. His breathing. Lucy, learning to dream. Ruth in the alien corn once again, hugging herself, waiting for her story, sorrily, to begin.

This impossible possible. To write this past. To live it. To be a woman. A man. It is the most serious of games, in which taking the time to read the rules means you already have lost. Given birth to the ending. This is the moment, like every moment, in which you choose to follow, or do not. Close the book: if it has an off-switch, use it now. Or else, write with me: a story, this story, of the original snake in the garden, that tempted a woman, that forgot so long ago its own tail, ours, mine, at the root of the tree: the tail. Which it had swallowed.

Dear Elsa,

Summer shakes loose its hold so slowly here. Like a woman putting up her long hair in reverse. The days are still hot—the sun, from its strange angles, still manages to shine in every window and doorway I enter, and my back burns when I wear black, like I'm wearing today. It's stuffy in the apartment, I go out seeking relief, I sit at a table outside the Caffe San Marco to write this in the shade. But the nights are chilly, the cold comes creeping up from the water, so when I wake, suddenly, at four in the morning, my window is like an icy mouth and the sheets are heavy and damp. The hot flashes, I never got to experience them, but it's so easy to imagine, a sudden heat flaring just beneath my skin, a burning that goes to my bones without warming, having been cold nearly all my life. Papa used to laugh at me for wearing sweaters in summer, which was cruel, I thought. But now I can see how absurd such a thing as body temperature is, the absurd multiplication of differences between bodies that are fundamentally the same; now, that I am never really hot nor cold. Elsa, I shouldn't be going on like this, I should be asking how you are, or more to the point, apologizing, begging even for you to answer these messages, to read them at least. But I'm not going to do that. I will continue to insist instead that we remain connected—that you are my daughter—and these letters affirm that, even if you never read them. These impossible letters. You demand them from me. Admit it's true, wherever you might be, perhaps with your own daughter beside you. She must be walking by now. She must be saying Mama. You're the mama now, Elsa, and I'm just an old woman in an old country, with an itch she can't scratch. Oh, I can hear you now in your strange accent: Don't be disgusting, Mother. Where did you learn to call me "Mother," to be so formal, so cold? Did I teach that to you? Was it Papa? He was always so courtly, so formal: he had the real old world manner. Not like your father, of whom I never spoke. Yes, we ought to be able to talk about such things now, especially since we aren't really talking, since this is just the thing we aren't talking about—our little secret. Which is what Papa and I called you, sometimes, when you were small. Papa. He never complained or whined, he just did what was necessary, like turning down that thermostat after I had cranked it up too high, and if I moved to say something he just lifted his hand as though to say, Enough! I admired that. A man should be forceful, to a point. He should know just where his power begins and ends. Certainly I resented it, his solitude if not his sufficiency, that tightly wound and overly precise mind deciding his destiny and incidentally mine too; but I was relieved at how little he seemed to need me. Not in the ordinary ways—he was a man, after all—and he needed me on his arm and in his bed and even to talk to, many evenings, about his bosses and his ideas that they'd taken credit for and his new work as a sales rep for which he was so spectacularly ill-suited. But fundamentally he kept his own counsel, and I was glad ultimately to just come along with him and not ask too many questions. It was lonely sometimes, but it was also a relief. You never forgave us that, did you? Maybe now that you have a husband and child of your own, you'll understand. Life seizes you sometimes by the scruff of the neck and gives you a good shake, and if you're not broken by that you just look for a place to land. Any place, it doesn't matter. And for me if not Papa, this twilight is that place.

Words without pictures lying fallow in the dark. The new reader lies awake on her side, a question mark to her husband's exclamation point, the imprint of their bodies palimpsesting the covers, his bare feet protruding like commas, his dark sleeping head a full stop. Sometimes she sits up awake and stares at him, head or feet, shimmering in the dark with the fullness of his rest, the head with its short hair tunneled peacefully into its pillow, the feet firm and shapely with high smooth arches, a runner's feet. Every day he runs his miles, varying only the distance, so that the weeks and months add up in a series of monotonous clauses varied only, she thinks, by their duration and the weather. He is not a reader in any sense, old or new—on his nightstand you'll find only a tablet computer and a few books about investing, on the tablet he sometimes tries a novel or a presidential biography but over his shoulder she sees how easily he gets diverted by email, by puzzles, by little videos at which he laughs soundlessly, discreet earbuds in so as not to distract her, though she can't help but be distracted by his waking presence, its permanently refracted acts of attention. Reading in her sense is for him a thing in the past; I used to read, he says, but I just don't have the time, and it's true she remembers when they used to read together and talk about what they read: novels and biographies and poetry, not just his endless manila folders and the parenting manuals in a guilty heap at the foot of the bed. Like her he had acquired the appendage of a liberal arts education, but time is a thing of the past, just a few minutes before bed with his machine, flicking restlessly between images with impatient sweeps of his forefinger, seeking what he calls relaxation, dissipation, frittering away what she accumulates with her book, those droplets or droppings, spots of time, before lights out on his side, turned away from her, he never complains about her light, he can sleep through anything, she thinks, her resentment by this time dulled and rote, all the other mothers say the same of their husbands, men in general, it's why they rule the world, a friend once said, not joking. For Ben words and stories and facts are all the same, in the same category as YouTube videos and sitcoms, smaller and larger chunks of data to be collected and sorted and perhaps briefly savored before being filed away in a process as good as forgetting. There was a time, in law school and her years afterward working at the firm, when she'd been almost the same, when her days, which often became her evenings, were so filled with print of the driest variety that there was nothing possible for her at night but television, HBO, *The Sopranos* and *Curb Your Enthusiasm* and *The Wire*; these things sustained some capacity in her, what she supposed you'd call her imagination, kept a dormant self alive in what had proved to be only a long transition between the old reader and the new. At home now with the baby, doing next to none of the work she had trained for, reading had changed for her: it was the nearest thing she had to an identity, if it's possible to have an identity that goes unrecognized by another living soul. Identity's probably not the right word for it; it's only her center, the still point around which her now hopelessly ephemeral and other-driven life revolves. She is the addict, not Ben who has the job, who snaps off his own light every night at exactly ten o clock and is up before her and the baby while it's still dark for his run, no matter the weather, while she is still trying to gather up the fragments of her interrupted sleep. He turns out the light and turns away while she goes on turning pages, trying to do it silently, wincing at the gossipy crinkle of paper or the nearly inaudible creaks of a hardcover's spine. She is certainly tired, she's exhausted even, the night stabs at her body with little twinges, demanding unconsciousness; but her eyes run ceaselessly over print, absorbed in story, phrases, guided by syntax, like a blind woman whose fingertips' contact with a line of braille is more than a substitute for sight—it is her only means of transcending distance, of bringing what's far away close, of locating in a landscape her otherwise hopeless immured and provincial body, buried in motherhood, wifehood, the Midwest, confined to understanding only what it can itself grasp, enfold, entwine. The halogen lamp presses its long finger to the page, diffusing only a little light into the underwater corners of the bedroom, outlining in shadow the volume of her husband's submerged sleeping body, cold and lifelike in the dark. If she were to put down her book and shut out the light, turn toward her husband and stretch out her arms, gather him to her in search of warmth as she had so many times in the past, would he remain stiff and asleep, would he fold with her, two questions in the bed, journeying together to the end of the night? The shadows sharpen, the line of his body leaps away from her, instinctually his feet find the covers and disappear like a pair of divers without a splash. Her finger follows the light down the page, her lips move slightly, she plunges into the only river that will receive her, until finally it all blurs overmuch, she lets the volume slide from her hands, hits the switch that plunges the room into darkness, settles back on the pillow, feels her husband shift beside her, stares at the ceiling, closes her eyes, opens them, closes them, until the night itself is asleep.

The recurring dream:

In from the yard, suburban dirt covering my knees, hands, face. There she sits at the kitchen table under a blue corkscrew of smoke. The coffee cup stained by her lipstick. The stack of books I'd later take from her shelves and page through with their sentences, statistics, first-person accounts, photographs in grainy graphic black and white. The spell of the halftone, tumbling bare motion made still. The foreign familiar names, I won't repeat them, names of unmaking, cancelling like stamps the other, equally foreign names. Photographs of bodies with all the color bleached away. It's a cliché even to me because I grew up with it, in the shadow M carried with her everywhere like a torch, like a strange pride, up to the very moment she put it all away, married the man I call Papa, moved on. The thick academic books on the kitchen table replaced by thinner and broader pages, by musical scores, as she reclaimed, at forty, her singing voice. It's in her already, the cancer, waiting, lurking, undetected, inevitable. Meanwhile memories of a suffering not quite hers, certainly not mine, linger for me like a rumored inheritance, a birthright, the deed to a property one has never seen in a country one has never visited, whose laws might not ever acknowledge the deed's validity. Meanwhile the photographs of bodies, for the books had come to live with me. Surveying these materials, composing a rhetoric to meet M's silent speech. She will not speak of these things, these books she'd read and abandoned to me. Her silence captures me when I open those books while she opens her mouth only to sing. An anorectic silence fills her song with terrible pits and echoes only I could hear. Photographs of countless emaciated bodies. She stands on stages and in church basements and at weddings and funerals and sings the German songs of Strauss, Schubert, Kurt Weill: German, the language of evil, an evil language, harsh and seductive, evil in itself and as an accent in the mouths of the movies I watched on television, mouths of men with slick hair and black uniforms clicking the heels of their polished boots. German was the language of my worst dreams, twisted into something beautiful when my mother stood up and sang. A cartoon language that my mother takes inside herself and hones into the pointed instrument behind which she puts all her velocity. A language, she says, she doesn't know and will never learn: she sings phonetically and with perfect pitch. But this mishandled memory is only a scar, a negative identity, dry and imaginary as the seas of the moon. I never studied Hebrew, I wasn't bat mitzvahed, we planted no trees in Israel. In this way she tries to stand apart from the wound she had spent so many years making her own, which later I took up like a barbed and bloody instrument. But sometimes, oftentimes, she can not stand. So many mornings she doesn't get out of bed, at all. Papa emerges from the bedroom freshly rumpled for his workday, shutting the door behind him with exquisite tact. Papa standing at the kitchen table spreading butter on an English muffin, saying to me Your mother's resting. By this I understand that I won't see her until lunchtime, and that lunchtime might not come until one or two or even three o' clock in the afternoon. I understand that I an on my own. It's summer. I go upstairs, go inside my room and shut the door. I sit at the desk under the single window through which sounds of traffic filter through the waving green leaves of the maple tree that edges our postage stamp of a lawn, and look at the heavy spines on the shelf propped up over the desk that Papa made for me with his own hands. I take down one of the books and open it on the desk and out it all spills. A crime scene. A name for the nameless affliction that we all feel, heads bent at the breakfast table and one empty chair. The clean ashtray. Countless photographs of countless emaciated bodies spilling—the photographs are spilling into ditches and rivers all over the Europe of my dreams, the Europe of depths, black Europe I read about, read into, whirlpool of my mother's unspeaking, into which I fall.

Dear Elsa,

When I came back down from the mountain I didn't quite know what to do with myself. With time on my hands, I found myself drifting further downward, until finally I was by the sea, on the edge of the Piazza Unita, looking out at the long quay that pokes like a thumb into the eye of the Mediterranean. The sky had turned gray and the sea had a hammered look like it sometimes has on hot days, though it was cool that morning. Cars went by. I looked back at the long piazza, hedged on three sides by hulking buildings in the imperial style. There's nothing Italian about this city except for some of the people and the language (but that's not quite Italian either). And the strikes. But that's what Papa loved about it—he called it the quintessence of Europe, this strange city like a hinge between east and west, forgotten but scarcely forgettable. His words, you remember them. This was as close as he'd let himself come to the real heart of things, the open wound, the city of his dreams and nightmares. It was like home without quite reminding him of home. And it was the sea instead of the river, the terrible river that flows only one way. In our year of retirement we would stroll along the waterfront, which seemed frozen in amber then without quite so many tourists as now. He never looked inland at the lights and buildings but always out to sea, toward the south. But he never broke free of that other city. Even in the hospital, when I opened my eyes and saw him standing at the window, looking at the sea, I knew his thoughts were directed northward, to the Danube, to the dual city of his heart. It was the week before his birthday and I decided to surprise him. One of the last good days when I was strong. We went to our favorite trattoria, a seafood place, and he was drinking his coffee—never cappuccino like me, he used to make fun of me for doing that, no Italian does that, it's a breakfast drink he said. But as I like to remind him, this wasn't quite Italy, and anyway I had no interest in passing as a European. The moment had come, he was in better spirits than I'd seen him in since we came here. I didn't want to ruin things. But they were already ruined.

No more treatments, I said. We agreed.

He sipped his coffee as if he hadn't heard me.

I'm done with them. I'm ready.

You are ready, he repeated. And what if I am not ready?

I took an envelope out of my purse and put it in front of him.

What's this?

It took him some time to put on his glasses, and more time to produce the little penknife he always carried and to make a neat slit in the short side. The single ticket slid out onto the tablecloth, where he stared at it.

First class to Budapest, I said to break the silence. And I got you a room at the Gellert. You used to tell me about how you loved going to the baths there.

He looked at me. I will never forget that look, over the tops of his reading glasses. Not anger, or even disappointment, what he might show to one of his students. A measuring look, I'd call it. The look you'd give someone that you suddenly discover has become a stranger.

I kept talking. I couldn't stop myself. About how beautiful it was supposed to be in autumn, and the stories he used to tell me about riding here and there on his bicycle—on the flat side, Pest, when he was young and climbing the hilly side, Buda, when he was older and something of an athlete. About how we could find the house he'd been born in, and perhaps even that other house, in the old ghetto, and his school—

He put his hand down on the table, flat and hard, making the glasses jump. Eyes turned in our direction and I looked into my cappuccino cup and blushed like a girl.

It's not possible, he said. And then: You should be ashamed.

It's not me. It's my time. My time is up.

That's not for you to decide.

If not me, who?

You should go home while you still can. See your cousins. Settle things.

I am not leaving without you.

Yes, my darling. You are.

He got up then, blind as a bull, scraping back his chair suddenly. The other diners stared. He put some money on the table and turned and walked out and left me sitting there. I felt ashamed then. I knew I was trying to intervene in a personal matter, the most personal matter of all, my own death. I knew I had wounded him. But the real wound was outside and beyond me. What my death represented. What I, his dying wife, had ceased to represent.

What we forget about inside a marriage, Elsa, is at least as important as what we remember. You ought to know that. There is a margin, call it forgiveness, or privacy, that must be respected at any cost. And I had trespassed on that margin.

I gave the money to the waiter and went outside. It had been raining but the rain had stopped, and I looked out at the Piazza Unita and it was like a sheet of heavy black glass had been laid across the stone, and all the golden lights of the double-headed eagle were reflected in it, and then came the margin of the road where headlights were passing, and then the real blackness, the tumbling broken monolith of the sea. I walked in that direction, carrying my shoes in one hand to save them from the puddles, and found him at the railing looking out. I came up beside him and touched his arm and felt it tense under the sleeve. Then he lifted it up and over and settled it onto my shoulders with a long sigh and I leaned into him and thought We're safe now, for now we're safe. Even then he was slipping away into that privacy that my death was trying to take from him, that I wanted to save, even at the cost of my own. He would leave me, as I left you. Making it possible then, somehow, for you to find us both. Though you will not write me back, though my time is over, still I know you will find us, in that black margin. Find. Surrender.

Theory of the gaze: no one's in particular, anyone's eyes borne on the back of a stranger the camera selects for delectation, identification, man or woman. And when a woman watches a man who watches, a man with eyes under hatbrim or behind sunglasses prowling streets, pacing under windows, listening to a hotel phone with his hand over the receiver, setting down his briefcase and picking up another identical briefcase, asking for and receiving messages from the desk clerk, standing absorbed in museums before Dutch masters, smoking cigarettes, dining alone, pretending to read newspapers in railway waiting rooms, studying a sheaf of photos and setting fire to them one at a time dropping each still flaming into a metal trashcan, ambiguously wandering the red-light district, encountering resistance, thugs, dead ends in alleys and apartments and restaurants and graveyards. A man can be a search engine. A woman can see through his eyes, can pay for his time sorting endless individual beads of data, can follow his path on a map of Europe and see more deeply into the past. A woman, cool as a blade, under crocodile tears, finds a sap, an agent, an icon, to conduct an investigation identical with burial, and tamps down the dirt around the body of her man. To look can be a way of not knowing, of bearing down on mystery. A film by itself is evidence of nothing but your desire to see. See without being seen, voyeur, collect the pieces of history that are yours, that do not belong to you. The woman you won't speak to is in back of all this searching. She smiles wryly, enigmatically, from her seat in the front row of the theater, so close to the screen that the images are almost meaningless. Light, shadow, noise of a zither. Who made me and why. There has to be a purpose. There has to be a story, in back or in front of this screen. Another search term, another Boolean operator. Trying not to read the subtitles. Trying not to feel the sticky human residue gluing your feet to the floor. She closes her eyes to be pulled forward forever. She opens them and falls back into the page.

Pitiless sun blazing on stone, a watery shimmer that reveals itself to be actual water, a single trudging figure with suitcase rumbling behind him. Pull back a little and buildings and awnings and jostling fringing tourists appear: the center of the Piazza San Marco, with water pooling in the center, a second layer to the image in which wavering man and campanile and the cloudless sky appear and reappear. Refracted, dosed with lens flare, the camera opens wide to convey the briny heat of summer in Venice, sun amplified by the city's long swoon of decay, heat that forces every unshaded eye to squint and burn. Sprawled on the big screen the black figure at the plaza's center ripples toward us, but the lens must be long for he seems scarcely to move as he moves. There is nothing on the soundtrack but the sound of lapping water and an incoherent hum, as of voices, as of bees.

Eyes cannot adjust so quickly: from the blinding rectangle with a spot of black at its center a black room with a single lozenge of white, a window that gradually spreads what can be seen before us: the tight little lobby of a penzione, sagging with dusty velvet furniture. The man with the suitcase accepts a key from the bony, mustached clerk, who speaks a few words of Italian to him. He nods in response, then begins the long trudge up the wooden stairs with a worn strip of Turkish carpet for a runner. Cut to a shot from the top of the staircase, looking down, mazy cored apple, with that hat and suitcase occasionally slipping into view, breathing more harshly, thump and thump of the rolling bag's wheels as he drags it step by step. Cut to a simple wooden door with an elaborate glass doorknob, which turns to admit the American and his rolling bag to the sort of cramped, dingy room that bespeaks budget travel, so small it must be a set with cut-away walls, there's no room for the American and his suitcase and our gaze in such a space, unless we peer in through the window, let our body be the dazzling one and his the native of anonymity and murk. There is a little brass bedstead and bed, a single chest of drawers with a mirror propped on top of it, a half-folded plastic screen behind which a combination toilet shower and sink has been ingeniously lodged, like something you might find on a ship. Lamb drags in his case and closes the door behind him and locks it with the key. He takes off the hat, moves to toss it on the bed, thinks better of it, hangs it on a bedpost. He is perspiring heavily. He takes off his suit jacket and loosens his tie. He wedges himself into the little bathroom and runs the tap for a while, then splashes water on his face and washes his hands. He turns off the bathroom light and sits on the bed with its threadbare lace coverlet; the springs groan. After a while he gets up and goes to the window and opens the curtain. He leans out and opens the shutter. The camera leans out with him and looks down into a backwater canal, black water which only intensifies somehow the impression of great heat. There's a little marble bridge over the canal where a fat woman in a tube top and short skirt smokes a cigarette. Shadows fall here and there, and we can just glimpse the beginnings of an alley past the little square that the bridge gives way onto. The ambient churning hum of voices suddenly and violently returns.

Night shot of a vaporetto churning up the Grand Canal, the San Marco campanile visible in the background. Pulsing house music comes in heavy. Lamb in a courtyard surrounded by elegantly dressed people holding slender flutes of Prosecco and Champagne. Tiny white lights are strung on the balconies and balustrades, reflecting off the large gleaming metal fountain streaming at the courtyard's center, streaming what looks like water but is actually paper-thin metallic streamers animated by hidden fans, an effect somehow cheap and expensive at the same time: some of the streamers are made from gold leaf, some are tinsel. The camera can't know this, like the caravan in the proverb it passes on, circulating around the courtyard observing salient inhabitants and features. A low stage against a far wall seemingly pocked with bulletholes, upon which a short blackclad person of indeterminate gender with a tall plume of feathery white hair and an enormous set of headphones is DJing—insistent, deafening music to which no one is dancing except for a slender man in a white three-piece suit and a black feather boa, his shaved head glistening, wineglass in hand, right in front of the speaker stack to the DJ's right. A long white tableclothed table with two young men in black T-shirts and black jeans behind it—the bar—visible occasionally as flashes of deft white hands and arms, bobbing subdued faces, through breaks in the continual scrum. Ringing the courtyard, as in an Escher drawing, a stone staircase with no handrail that marches from one balcony to the next—four flights in all—and, contrasting with the ancient stonework and the mottled, ruined plaster of the walls, a simple black arrow on a dull gold background pointing upward at an angle. And the arrow flickers, it's actually an image on a flat screen TV anchored diagonally to that wall, and becomes a woman in profile who steps forward to inhabit the otherwise blank screen and purses her lips and raises a wand to them and blows soap bubbles, and then walks off screen leaving scarcely visible crystalline spheres in her wake, and the arrow returns. There are many such screens placed at random on the walls, not all of them level, cycling through images akin to road signs followed by men and women, of diverse ethnicities, all of them beautiful, making repeated gestures that manage to appear childlike and pornographic at the same time: a bare-chested Turkish man unwraps a candy and pops it into his mouth; a European woman dressed as a Catholic schoolgirl jumps rope in slow motion; an African man with a shaved head blows kisses at the camera and smiles with heartbreaking guilessness. Passing the other people at the party clustered in two and threes: the men in well-groomed middle-age, the women young, showing lots of skin under expensively artless hairdos. The camera seems like a stranger here, an outsider: it pauses for a few seconds at the different groupings of people as if just long enough to ascertain that it knows no one before passing on. Two men stand next to one of the screens holding drinks: the image of a red circle with a white hyphen inside it fades into the image of a heavyset man of Slavic appearance, nude, flaccid penis prominent in its nest of pale blonde hair below his swelling gut, eating a chocolate bar and smiling

What is that? the first man asks, and the second man answers, definitively, It's brilliant.

Names swirl and circulate as the camera makes its rounds: Hockney, Emin, Chapman, Hirst. Faces montaged in varying conversational attitudes: laughter, raised eyebrows, squints, protruding tongues, scowls, lidded glances, bland smiles.

Lamb climbing the stairs, passing more screens, some with viewers, most without. The bass diminishes and faint strings make themselves heard as he climbs, getting louder and cleaner as the other sounds fade: a Schubert string quartet playing in one of the brighter neighborhoods of A minor. The camera pushes past him in a sudden urgent rush, up the stairs and straight up dizzily into the pearlescent evening sky, swivels down to capture a pattern of rooftops, dotted here and there by lights, and then two blazing strips with the black ribbon of the canal dividing them, a ripple of negativity, water by night, lined with crumbling, brilliantly illuminated landings and palaces. The rooftop erratically lit by a few colored Chinese lanterns where a few people term and team while the

Schubert carries on without a source. Coming up to the back of a woman in a short sharply cut cocktail dress looking out over the city. Lamb's voice folds into a conversation already in progress.

It's like thinking about the piece is more interesting than the piece itself.

Yes, of course.

The woman, one arm folded across her chest, the other holding a highball glass, with a large Louis Vuitton bag dangling from one shoulder. Sharp angles and planes to her face, which has a Mediterranean cast; thick coarsely curled black hair with a white streak at the right temple, wearing a hip-hugging black dress with green horizontal stripes that not very many figures could pull off.

I just don't see why we can't think and feel at the same time, that's all, Lamb says. Art is physical, I am physical. You are physical.

They are leaning on a railing, looking out over the Grand Canal, beyond the Palace of the Doges where the lagoon begins and history, from which the city stands recused, resumes its course.

We are divided between pleasures, and all pleasures are of the flesh, the woman says. Riot and renunciation, there's really no difference, no difference between multiplication and subtraction; either way you lose sight of yourself. If I taste, suckle, supple myself to another, that is pleasure. And astringency, denial, abstraction, diets, refusing sweets, that too is pleasure, though of a higher sort.

What's higher about it?

Because denial is always itself and also the thing denied. It is the pleasure of anticipation deferred.

I think you just enjoy feeling superior. Isn't that what the Biennale is about? What Venice is about? All of fucking Europe, actually.

But the other sort of pleasure is purely positive, the woman continues. It is mortal. It leaves no trace. The only thing it leaves behind is itself. The deadliness of repetition. One needs higher and higher doses. The law of diminishing returns takes effect.

He has her, she has him. They are alone at the center of the party.

One must continually increase the level of stimulation, she says. Finally the organism can no longer take it. Something breaks down. The capacity for pleasure, for living, breaks down.

You could say the same thing about denial. You can get addicted to it. It works backwards, doesn't it? Needing less and less until you're hardly there at all?

She's throwing herself at him. Is it all words? Bought and paid for?

It depends on what you deny and why, she says. Denial can be a secret fullness. I go to a restaurant—a charming café. I sit outside, it's springtime. There are lovers and baby carriages and lecherous old men in beautiful bespoke suits. The waiter is a dark lean and handsome young man from the East, Greek or Estonian, Turkish perhaps, an immigrant, but cocky, with a long fall of straight black hair curling at his collar. He doesn't hand me a menu, he knows me, he brings me an espresso without my having to ask. I ask for a pastry to accompany it, he smiles knowingly and withdraws. The people pass. The pastry, something slightly vulgar, let's call it an éclair, is brought to the table with a folded linen napkin, a fork, a little glass of water. I pick up the napkin and spread it across my lap. I pick up the fork, and press its edge into the rich chocolate, it splits and the cream comes out. I raise the fork to my lips and extend my tongue, I take a single taste—not even a lick—of the bit of cream and chocolate adhering there. Then I put the fork down. I do not take a bite. I do not pick up the pastry with my hands as I did when I knew nothing of pleasure. I sip my espresso. The world goes by. I open my purse and take out a single bill, I spread it flat on the table. I use the laden plate to weigh it down so that it is not carried away by the breeze. I stand up and I walk away. Do you understand?

What pleasure! What pleasure! The voluptuousness of it. Do you understand?

It's stupid, Lamb says.

Pleasure is information, she persists. And seeking information. Is the pleasure in the seeking or in the having? What happens when you cannot solve the case? When the trail goes cold? What then?

There are no unsolved cases, Lamb says. There are

only cases that I haven't solved yet.

So you do understand.

You are exquisite, Lamb does not say to her. Your denial is like a sculptor's chisel. You are the artist of yourself.

She smiles at the water.

Your reticence hides you from me, she says to him. But does it hide you from yourself?

These questions don't interest me.

Let me tell you another story. One rainy afternoon in Rome I hailed a taxi pulling over where I was standing at the curb getting soaked, trying to keep dry holding a shopping bag over my head. It's a one-way street so that the passenger who's in the taxi got out on the opposite side. I didn't get a good look at him: he was a large heavy man in a raincoat, he unfolded a black umbrella and hurried away. I got into the taxi on my side and gave the driver my address. The rain beat down on the thin metal roof, it was very loud in there, and the driver was playing pop songs on the radio so I could hardly hear myself think. And then just as the taxi was pulling into traffic I notice a briefcase on the floor where it's half tucked underneath the driver's seat. At first I assumed that it belonged to the driver, or maybe I was just thinking about something else; it was getting dark, it was winter in Rome and it gets dark early, and the rain was heavy and wet, and I felt damp and wanted to be home. Then I realized that it couldn't be the driver's case, if only because the driver had a bag of his own, a big canvas satchel like a postman's that was sitting next to him on the front passenger seat. Besides, the briefcase was too expensive and well-made to be a taxi driver's, well beyond his resources if not his taste. I tried to tell him that his previous passenger left his briefcase behind but he didn't hear me or he didn't listen. We were pulling up outside my building; I told myself the cabbie would find the case at the end of his shift, or some other passenger would be more successful in calling it to his attention. But then I had an impulse. Having paid the driver, I grabbed the handle of the briefcase and pulled it out from where it was wedged and took it with me. He didn't turn around, he drove straight off, I hurried to get out of the rain. In my apartment I examined the case for clues. Smooth soft leather, a narrow profile, a little calfskin monolith or obelisk, no monogram or other distinguishing features. There's a combination lock set to 7 7 7, I try the tab and it opens. No one's looking, I told myself, and I lifted up the lid to look inside. And what do you suppose I found?

A gun? Money? Drugs? Passports?

I can tell you this. There was no evidence of the owner's identity. Not a business card or a mobile phone, not a scrap of paper with a name on it. Nothing. The case might as well have been empty.

But was it empty?

I held onto it for a day or so, the Mediterranean woman says. Then I decided to advertise it. On Craigslist I placed an ad that read FOUND: Black briefcase in a taxi on the Via delle Sette Sale outside the Banca di Roma. I renewed it every day for a week. At the end of the week, on a Friday, someone responded. That Saturday at eleven in the morning I waited at a café, the same café I mentioned earlier, with the briefcase sitting next to me for company. A man approached me, a large man in late middle age, handsome in a rough sort of way, with the face of someone who has seen much of life. He introduced himself and sat for a while, flirting with me a little out of politeness, before asking to look at the case. He opened it and looked inside, the back of the case to me, moving his hands around purposefully as though looking for something. He took something out of the case and slipped it into his jacket pocket. Then he closed the case and looked at me. It's not mine, he said. Oh, I said surprised, but you did leave a black briefcase in a taxi on the Via delle Sette Sale outside the Banca di Roma. Yes, he said, it's very strange, but it's not mine. And it was raining, I said, when you got out. Yes, he said, and I hurried inside to conduct my business, and then I felt stupid when I realized I'd left my briefcase behind, but it was too late, the taxi was gone. And you didn't see me, a woman taking your taxi. No. And you waited a week, why? I didn't wait a week, I was frantic, I went to the police, I called all the cab companies, I tried everything, it was my secretary who thought to look online, I don't use computers you see, she does that for me. How luxurious, I exclaimed, how wonderful, you mean you don't even use a computer for email? No, he said, I don't, I write all my correspondence by hand on a yellow legal pad, there's quite a lot of it actually, and my secretary types it up for me, she's a treasure, I'd be lost without her. And the briefcase? It's not important anymore, he said, it's unfortunate but I was able to make the necessary adjustments. So why did you come? Curiosity. Thank you, Signora. I must be going now. Let me pay for the coffee. He put a large bill on the table, far too large, enough money for a month's worth of coffees, nodded to me, and left.

What is the point of this story? asks Lamb.

What is the point of a briefcase, the woman sighs, or a suitcase, or any appendage that we drag along with us? When we know what's in it it's like a prosthetic, it's just part of us, we don't think about it, we call it our luggage, a necessity. But when we don't know what's in it, or what it's for, or whose story it is part of, it changes. We can try to find out, but sometimes discovery is impossible. Then it is something else, it is metaphysical, it reveals itself to us—a briefcase—and conceals itself—what is in it, what does it mean? Like a stranger, like your own face in the mirror when you catch your own eye unawares. We are always masked. Your profession is to unmask, isn't it, you call yourself a seeker of truths. The truth is out there, as they used to say on the television. But it is not possible. You should be more like me, Mr. Lamb.

Put what you think you know in that suitcase you've been carrying around, and lose it in a taxi sometime.

But he took something from the case, you said. Something that did or didn't belong to him. Either way it's suspicious. Unless it's something that you planted there, for him to find, but not to acknowledge.

Perhaps the original owner left it for this other man, the Mediterranean woman says. I think often of him, the way he just got out of the taxi and hurried away. I don't think he was heading for the Banca di Roma at all. He had an umbrella but I imagine him rounding the corner and discarding the umbrella too. Letting the rain spill down on him, plastering his thick white hair to his head. Lifting his face to the sky, grateful and anonymous, drinking the falling water. With the light heart of someone who's left it all behind.

You sound envious.

What does a mask look like from the inside?

It doesn't look like anything.

The Mediterranean woman leans forward suddenly and gives Lamb the softest and gentlest of kisses. Her soft lips meet his rougher ones, both give a little under the pressure. The night surrounds them like a halo. You have what you need, she whispers. He closes his eyes. when he opens them again, she is gone.

Lamb stands at the edge of the rooftop for a moment longer, surveying the patterns of light and darkness, and the larger darkest surround that is the sea bearing La Serenissima up toward the stars or down into the drowning abyss. These are your thoughts, accomplished cinematography, iconography of a lone man, a seeker, poised at a height, a figure that orients space around himself, point of reference, spectral and incapable. He reaches down and picks it up, where she left it leaning against the wall. A black leather portfolio. He takes it in both hands to carry it in his arms like a child and turns and redescends into the ongoing tumult of the party, holding his upper body stiffly, arms cradling his burden.

Detail asserts itself just when I want a picture, the moving image's atmospheric density of immersion, worldness, *Stimmung*. Realism is a temptation, nearly fatal. Lamb is not a character but the stilly turning point of the viewer's axis, the camera's ally and no more. Looking's limitations impose themselves on sentences and paragraphs that offer up the camera as agent, as that which follows whatever action is to be found beyond and between their flow. Sting of mediation conditioned by the real, which is that drive, that motion, carrying Lamb and the camera and these words through stories, streets, cities, a tourist's information about loss, recovery that resists the image, that wants to be multiple, his and hers and his stories, now in a city devoted to looking, which has no economy but looking, no cars or readable maps, propped up on thousands of soggy pilings and sinking by the day, a metropole that makes nothing, that births no natives, electronic art cheek by jowl with columns, pediments, porticoes, domes, massy and unimportant, relics of a lost centrality, of so much as a working port or fishmarket. When I was there I had an injured foot and limped down streets that were also alleyways, getting thoroughly lost in sweet sticky heat, crossing bridges, passing mossy stairways descending blankly into water, dead-ending suddenly into the hazy blazing edge of the city, the lagoon leveling away, the sheer improbability of it all compossible with my real staggering sweating stare, pain in the ball of my foot, wondering which way to the Arsenale, which way to the Giardini, which way to the Grand Canale, which way to my hotel. Hotels are the essence of this travel, this circulation without pauses that will be meaningful beyond one's own precarious memories and snapshots: I bought little, sold nothing, have nothing to make of my experience but a simulacrum seeking to be unlike itself, not a record or imitation but something true to the fundamental experience of passage, passing on and through and by, passing intransitively as something I don't feel myself to be, a citizen of the world, an American man, a self-sufficing seeker after what further thing might suffice, clumsy solitary limper (wife decamped for Crete after a fight, eight weeks pregnant) scribbling notes to himself and to the unborn, awash in consequencelessness and possibility. Lamb in snapshots he must have taken of himself: eating gelato, standing in front of the Bridge of Sighs giving a thumbs-up, sitting at a table in one of the cafes on St. Mark's Square wearing squared-off sunglasses listening to dueling orchestras, drinking a Peroni at Harry's Bar. In motion again, reclining in a gondola wearing his hat, the black rolling case perched at his feet, seen from above, slow ripples surrounding his head, his black eyes, the gondolier foreshortened into a straw hat, a red band, a pair of hands, an oar. Passing slowly under a bridge, the whole vanishing for a moment, re-emerging, the gondolier alone and singing, horseless horseman, pass by.

Under the linden trees Ruth walks with toddling Lucy, who repeatedly throws out her hands and falls into a froglike crouch, then lifts head, body, arms and toddles on again down the sidewalk just a few yards from their front door. Lack of sleep has Ruth descending, it seems, through layers of consciousness, so that phenomena are less and less distinct, more and more surprising in their combination, though she doesn't really have the energy to be surprised. Lucy tries words. *Kah*, car. *Tway*, tree. *Huss*, house. *Buhd*, bird, she says, pointing to a robin on the sidewalk, and then cries, quite distinctly, *tweet tweet*. See now, Ruth says to herself, how you lurch from boredom to fascination and back again. The sheer drab ordinariness of her life, her street, her leaking breasts, oppresses her, and then as though stepping through a shaft of sunlight for a moment she's dazzled by her daughter's continual opening and flowering, as though Ruth could see through the not-yet-closed hole in the top of Lucy's skull and behold all the colors there ever more brilliant, illuminant, in greater and greater correspondence with the bright poisoned world that rises now to meet Lucy who falls to earth and rises, falls and rises, sometimes to clutch her mother's finger, sometimes tumbling ahead, hands and elbows raised, out of the sunlight into the trees' shadow. The daughter that made Ruth a mother, that tore her out of one life and deposited her in another, a life fuller somehow, more three-dimensional—when she thinks of the days before Lucy with Ben the images are sharp but flat, and further back, to her single life, it's like she was just a point moving on a straight line, or a long curve that must eventually become a circle, a circle interrupted by Ben, Lucy, her mother's e-mails, a circle contradicted by an ending faintly in sight, more strongly felt in this moment, the vanishing shadow of past lives, even Lucy's life, out of whatever story Ruth can tell of herself, to herself, about herself, a story that will not end properly but will simply stop years from now or tomorrow or this afternoon. She shakes herself mentally, like a dog. M can always do this to her, will always do this: make Ruth question herself, her decisions, the shape of her story. As though Ruth were a novel and M a ruthless (ha-ha, Ruth says aloud) critic who disagrees with everything, starting with the novel's premise, a woman unmoored from her career, caught in a continual continuity error—even its title, the name Ruth always hated that she could never dissuade her mother from using. (Who is the woman who walks beside you, eyes downcast, flat-bellied, bare feet barely brushing the suburban grass.) A form of critique, a rewriting, or insisting that an earlier and as it were unpublished manuscript should somehow supersede the published book. As though Ruth were merely apocryphal, a wavering author's concession to a tradition that M had simply ignored, as imperially as she had ignored Reagan's election, the fall of the Berlin Wall, 9/11, refusing to let these contingencies alter her own story of one woman's triumph over the treachery of men and time—of history itself. Ruth, on the other hand, has made history her specialty, in college wrote an honors thesis on the leadership roles assumed by women in the Warsaw Ghetto, had once aspired to be a lawyer in The Hague prosecuting the world's war criminals before settling into the mundanity of contract law, before letting that slip too to be a mother and glorified part-time paralegal—each step on this trail in its way an affront to the memory of M, what she remembered and what she chose to forget, what she took as a woman's right and what she set beyond the pale. But something has changed, something has muddied the clear waters of M's repose, from beyond the grave these letters to Ruth are arriving, once a week or so, from different European cities where Ruth has never been but tending, always, east. It's Papa, she thinks, it's her stepfather, there is no father, no origin, there's no need for any Lamb. But she doesn't want to think of that just now, she wants to be here in the moment with Lucy. In the moment, where Lucy lives, without remembrance or expectation, discovering grass. Ruth says the word to her where she's plopped down on the neighbor's lawn pulling up great handfuls and spreading them on her lap, and Lucy responds, quite clearly, without a lisp, *Grass*! Through the picture window Ruth sees her neighbor, a woman in late middle age named Margaret, pushing a vacuum through a living room that Ruth has stood in once; a room chiefly distinguished by its paleness, the spotless white shag carpet and bone-colored leather furniture, a clear sign, if any were needed, that children make up no part of Margaret's life. She looks out the window now at Ruth and Lucy on her lawn and waves without smiling; Ruth, after a moment's hesitation, waves back. She's tired. She would like to sit down on the grass next to Lucy, to lie down in the sun and go to sleep. It's such an attractive vision that for a moment she believes she's actually done it. Then she bends down, scoops up Lucy (still crying *Grass! Grass!*) and carries her away, back home, back to the flawless trap of this moment in both of their lives.

What does she need, the woman she leaves behind, who waits there prone, sun hammering closed eyes? Her violent desire to connect, to penetrate, but at a distance, requiring what? A new reader, a new verb: *to extimate*. Mr. Lamb. Be my eyes. Wear this skin for me.

She feeds Lucy: Greek yogurt with hard little frozen blueberries embedded in it and a piece of day-old cornbread cold from the refrigerator. It's a terrible lunch, slack and uninspired. Lucy chows down: picks up her spoon by the wrong end and drops it casually onto the floor, plunging her fingers in, picking out the blueberries and spreading yogurt on the front of her onesie in a broad Rauschenberg smear. Ruth picks up the spoon and slumps back in the Shaker-esque kitchen chair watching, picturing Ben's lunch. A sandwich at his desk, most days, but today she imagines him on Michigan Avenue in the brown pinstripe suit she chose for him, without the messenger bag he uses as a briefcase, hair rippled by the wind, striding purposefully down the street and then turning smartly as a soldier into some little sunlit bistro, sliding into a booth across from her. There is no woman, she knows and believes; but if there is no woman why can Ruth see her so clearly? True, she changes shape: sometimes she's the conventionally beautiful thin long-haired blonde that Ruth is not and sometimes she's the unconventionally beautiful zaftig brunette that Ruth also is not. But today the smooth-looking blonde sitting across from Ben in Ruth's mind has no name, just a big bright smile of the sort Ruth herself can rarely summon lately, one more beam of sunshine for her husband, but with tits. Lucy is banging on her half-empty dish now with her spoon, like a prison inmate in an old movie. It's a bright fall day: after lunch Ruth must find the energy to take Lucy outside again, even if it's just to the park down the block. Or to the lake, retracing Ben's jogged steps that morning. He's out there and she's in here: that's the point that Ruth sticks on. And he's surrounded, it seems, by the infinite varieties of feminine allure, while her own flesh is tired and flaccid and her own skin has to her a strange smell, scorched, electrical, like insulation melting on a wire. Lucy throws her spoon down on the floor again and yells, mouth wide open: Ruth yells with her. Lucy's mouth is still open but no sound comes out, she stares. Then she giggles. Ruth giggles too and the evil vision is dispelled. Ben's back at his desk, a paper napkin tucked into his collar to protect his tie, eating soup and crunching numbers, as cut off from light and air as she herself. But no longer. Come on baby girl, she says to Lucy, removing the empty bowl. We can't stay in here.

The lake has a leaden cast to it, ambiguous cirrus clouds refracting a gray piercing light that makes Ruth wish she'd brought her sunglasses. She pushes the stroller along the path that winds alongside the rock wall that separates it from the water, eyes on the young couple a few yards ahead of her, hands in each other's hip pockets. He's got a shaved head and a tattoo of the astrological sign Libra on the back of his neck; she's got a purple ponytail and what she's heard is called a sleeve, a complex web of tattoos that completely cover her bare arm from shoulder to wrist: mostly Ruth is fascinated by the spiderweb tattoo on the girl's elbow, on which the spider, with the face of Betty Boop, is only visible on the downswing of the girl's arm. Ruth pushes the stroller in which Lucy sits silently swinging her feet and wonders, rolling her eyes a little at herself, if she was ever that young. The occasional cyclist passes, runners, a small gray woman wearing a headband and sweats chuffs along in a kind of shuffle-run. Almost everyone has earphones on, though not the tattooed couple, who are conversing in a desultory way about their plans for the weekend. He says something to her and she pulls away and hits him in the upper arm, in a playful way; he pulls her back to him (she's a whole head shorter) and they stop dead in the path to kiss. Ruth should just pass them on the grass but instead she stops dead and waits for them to finish. The girl opens one eye and sees her there, and she gives her boyfriend a push. They get out of the way and the girls says "Sorry!" in a brightly scrubbed voice that belies her punkish exterior: a nice Jewish girl from the western 'burbs, after all, and he's probably not much different (though judging from the Asian cast of his eyes not Jewish, or at least not wholly so). It's a bad habit of Ruth's to always identify people by their Jewishness or lack of Jewishness: she knows

Ben doesn't think that way, and anyway a lot of the Jewish people they meet here don't actually set off her Jewdar: it's not just facial features or curly hair she looks for, and it's certainly not the religion itself, it's mostly the voice, its grain texture and speed, an East Coast voice she's homesick for and rarely hears here, a voice with toughness and mockery to it, a voice that shrugs, that pushes and pulls its listener; the opposite of the broad and bland voice that almost everyone she meets in Evanston, even people she calls friends, people who go to shul and light candles on Friday night, speaks with, a voice that carries heavy boredom into even the most interesting things someone might say. The voice or voices that she now hears ringing ahead of her, having left the young lovers behind to approach the playground at a bend in the water up ahead, where women mostly ten years younger than Ruth are sitting or standing while their children riot adorably on swings and slides and play structures—what used to be called jungle gyms but aren't, somehow, anymore. Lucy says "Whee! Whee!" which is her word for the swing, and Ruth obliges, unbuckling her and lifting her up and depositing her in the baby swing seat and giving a push. As she does this her eyes scan the faces of the other women, recognizing most but only putting names to a few—there's Katherine and there's Yasmin, each talking to other women that Ruth only knows by sight. The tattooed couple she can see are standing not far off watching the children play, or at least the girl is; the guy's face is in his cellphone, texting away. The girl's face has a simple open longing look to it which makes Ruth smile to herself: as she envied her so does the girl seem to envy Ruth and the other women, the mother-women. It must be so, she's far too young to envy the children, as Ruth only occasionally does, she's too close to their world now to be sentimental about it; she knows that children are fierce desiring machines moving constantly from anticipation to anxiety so that you can hardly tell the difference, and babies Lucy's age are devoid of empathy, looking blankly at others that cry or have hurt themselves (though there are exceptions: Ruth has an acquaintance whose child Thomas bursts into tears whenever he sees another child crying, tears that greatly exceed in volume and intensity those of the template, so that the original crier generally stops and stares; the parents are worried enough to take the boy to a psychologist though he's not even fifteen months yet; standard deviations are to be expected, Dr. Einmann says, but who makes the standard? Ruth she knows errs in the opposite direction, assuming all of Lucy's freaks to be normal, leaving her husband to worry that she shows incipient signs of this disorder or that, ADD or autism: let him do it, she has enough to carry just getting through the ordinary day). Ruth watches the punk rock girl as she pushes Lucy on the swing, unable for the moment to remember what she herself was doing and whom she might have been with when she was the girl's age—no older than twenty-two, surely. Ruth had been more goth than punk, really: she had favored black clothing, which she still did, come to think of it, except her blouses and skirts were now fashionably cut and generally accented with a single color, generally red or purple: she had loved, still loved, The Cure and Morrissey, Sleater-Kinney and Hole, and had gone to industrial parties and raves trailing a string of boyfriends as well-kitted out with piercings and tats as the tall Libran boy, always in search of aliveness, that feeling of intense and physical presence; and yet hanging back too, never as wild as her other girlfriends, clinging to lucidity, wanting to think and talk her way even through Ecstasy trips, and the boys hadn't been much different, she still kept up with a few of them and Ricardo with the safetypin in his left nipple was now a labor lawyer and Kenneth the bass player worked in public television in Atlanta and Louis her last boyfriend before law school, with his thrillingly nasal and sardonic voice, a drawer of underground and filthily funny comics, had also become a lawyer but was no longer practicing, he'd had some kind of breakdown and was living with his parents in Sun City. Ruth's boys had cleaned themselves up, cut or grown out their hair, and the few tattoos visible were simple generational markers scarcely worthy of censure or comment once paired with a business suit or polo shirt. Ruth herself had no tattoos, though she'd always been drawn to men and boys who had them (and Ben, in fact, had a single simple tattoo on his right upper back of a DNA strand, a relic of his days as a pre-med student at Brandeis, and she had once loved to touch it, in bed but also just out in the world, a secret sexual touch to an assuming shoulderblade rendered permanently erogenous to her fingers), but she'd been brought up with the Jewish prohibition against so marking the body and although she'd broken almost every other law she'd been raised with, often deliberately, this one had somehow maintained its hold, and her skin was unblemished by ink, though blemished in other ways by moles and wrinkles and cellulite, motherfucker and alas. If I had a tattoo what would it be? A Star of David, maybe. Cretan paradox irradiant with irony.

Tattooed. Her mind drifts to the forearm of her grandfather Istvan, a series of numbers, an inscription as cold to the touch, she imagines, as Ben's strand is hot. The last time she saw her mother's father was in a decrepit nursing home in Queens with the grimly ironic name of Hopeview Manor. Among the half-alive hulks in wheelchairs he had been bright and alive with his flashes of humor and bitterness, the crumpled suit he carefully dressed himself in each morning, and the liver cancer he saw as a black joke (I was never a drinker, darling, that's the shame of it. I should have drunk! I should have drunk a martini every day with the life I had). She had been able to extract a scant minimum of stories from him, halting and halted narratives of that life-in-death, the fragment of history his body was: the extra food he obtained from a Polish guard in exchange for the string of pearls that had belonged to his wife, her grandmother, and which he'd concealed somehow and given away one by one, just often enough to maintain strength, cunning, life; how he'd gotten a job in the camp barbershop—he'd been a trained hairdresser in Budapest as well as, she'd gathered from other sources, a gambler and rakehell, perhaps even a thief or fence—and the single indelible image he'd painted for her of him standing erect behind a barber's chair with the commandant seated in it, stropping his straight razor to administer the cleanest possible shave. How did you do that? she asked him. How did you not cut him, kill him, draw your razor across his jugular, take your revenge? And the answer, simple and true and unsatisfying: I wanted to live. And he did live, had lived, had survived the camp and survived the death march from Poland to Germany and survived the chaos of the war's end and made his way back to the city where his daughter, her mother, was waiting for him, along with his own parents, who'd escaped deportation thanks to false papers and a neighbor who'd acted from a mixture of benevolence and greed, a mixture she's all too familiar with from the hours and days she'd spent reading the grim unilluminating details of testimony that had been at the crux of her thesis, her exploration of the role of women in the Warsaw Ghetto. But the Budapest Ghetto, which had no similar history of resistance, and she'd had no call to interview her grandfather for her work, and as for her grandmother she'd died long ago—"She died before she died" had been M's enigmatic phrase. How Ruth wished she could talk to her, ask her questions, hear her story—her grandfather had never wanted to talk about it, had shrugged her most persistent inquiries away—"It was luck, pure and simple," he'd said, referring only to the fact that her grandmother had happened to get into a cab driven by one of Istvan's cousins, who'd gotten him similar work upon his arrival in the previous year—she couldn't have guessed that he'd changed his name to Freeman from Freitag, the name her mother had reclaimed for herself and for her daughter, who'd kept it into her marriage. Luck, pure and simple—but that only explained (it explained nothing) Istvan's New York reunion with his wife, it said nothing about her own wildly improbable survival, given what everyone always said about her frailty and nervous disposition. Klara, that had been her given name: Grandmother Klara to distinguish her from Grandmother Marta, her grandfather's second wife, whom he'd married just eight months after Klara's death from a perforated ulcer in 1967, less a woman in Ruth's memory than a red wig, an accent, and a cloud of cigarette smoke. She'd divorced Istvan when he was in his seventies and moved to Florida, and he'd stayed on in the basement apartment of the building on Kissena Boulevard in Flushing where for twenty years he'd kept watch over a tetchy boiler and carried older tenants' groceries for them, until finally he got too sick to stay and wound up in the Hopeview, sharing a room with an elderly black diabetic double amputee (the legs) named Raymond who watched soaps all day and never said a word, a room with a view of the Unisphere over which jets thundered at all hours of the day and night.

The first and only time she had visited him there he showed her the room with a sweep of his arm, then, grinning faintly, opened the blinds so she could see the big dumb steel softball coruscating in the afternoon sunshine. It was hot and the ancient air conditioner under the window labored to cool the sticky air with its tang of rot. She sat on the bed, he sat in the oversized chair, holding the one cigar per day he permitted himself to carry but not to light, at least not until after he'd taken his dinner in the dreary basement cafeteria with the bare fluorescents and stained acoustic tiles that crouched claustrophobically over the diners' nigh-moribund heads. This in spite of the rasp in his voice, in spite of the portable oxygen tank perched next his chair, a clear tube running up to meet the piece on his nose, where it blended weirdly with the white hairs of his walrus mustache. The awfulness of the place had stunned her into silence and banalities for the first hour of her visit, as he showed her what little there was to see, a tour of green hallways and gray carpets, human hulks slumped in chairs with wheels and without, the upsetting and unforgettable vision of a sunken-chested gray-faced man slouching slowly through the hall in a hospital gown, his full colostomy bag dangling from a hook on his walker, gown parted to reveal the shagged slumping flesh of his buttocks. Now, in the room, the small talk about her studies had ground to a halt. He seemed to read her mind.

It's all about money, darling, he said, with a kind of a K poking its head out of the G. This place takes the Medicare, which is all I've got.

She couldn't help herself. But Mom….

He waved the cigar dismissively. Let her lead her life.

You haven't told her? She doesn't know?

Of course she knows. Darling, it's not so bad. It's not so far from the old place that I can't still see some friends. Your Uncle Jozsef has been taking me to breakfast almost every Sunday: he comes in the car and takes me to the diner, and after that we walk around the neighborhood a little bit and talk. Well, we used to walk: now I mostly sit on the bench. And I say we talk but it's me, you know Jozsef, it's like talking to a wall, like he never learned English and yet forgot all his Hungarian too. Maybe I should try German on him, who knows.

Has she visited you here? When he shrugged in reply, she flared: Then she doesn't know what this place is like!

I tell you darling, it's all right. Wait until you meet my girlfriend Charisse—a looker! And she looks after me better than either of my wives ever did. No disrespect, sweetheart, on your grandmother, but she was never the same you know. After the war.

Ruth at that moment felt sunk in guilt, knowing and wishing to say what seemed the obvious thing: if Mom won't rescue you than I will. But she was only a student and had no money that wasn't borrowed and spoken for. And she lived in a small apartment in a cold upstate town that was all hills, miles from any place that could provide proper care; she didn't even have a car. She pushed the guilt and excuses both out of the way with the help of the opening he offered. Tell me about her.

Charisse?

No, Grandma.

What's to tell? I met her during a football match, on Margaret Island in Budapest. We were down one goal to zero when I spotted her watching from the sidelines, a small simple girl with a kerchief over her head looking all the world like a frummer except for the lipstick she was wearing. What a beautiful face, I'll never forget it. That's when I knew we had to win the game and I had to win it. The very next time the whistle blew I just went charging down the field and sidestepped the guy with the ball, he was slow, and I got inside his guard and then the ball and I were both moving down. I could have gone for it but my pal Almos was open and I could somehow already tell, just from that face, that she'd appreciate an assist from me more than me shooting it in. So I passed it to Almos and we tied it up, and when we came running back to defend our own goal I could see she was watching me. It came down to the last few minutes and everyone thought it would go into overtime, but the evening was coming on and I was afraid she'd leave. So when the ball went again to the same guy, who was not a small guy, by the way, I went after him again, and this time when he saw me he just lowered his head and stepped right, I stepped left, boom! Down I go with this shmuck on top of me, knocked all my wind out and bruised my ribs, I can tell you. Well nobody calls a foul—it's a rough game, we're all kids, even the umpire—and play resumes after a minute and this time the situation's reversed, it's Almos who sends the ball my way, and I can hardly run my ribs hurt so, but I run, and I do a header—this is a long time before they were doing headers, let me tell you, I was ahead of my time, heh, you like that? And the ball goes in and we win the game and I won it. And afterwards I look and this girl is gone, but I hang around a while with the chaps and then, this is right before curfew, I see her all alone by the fence waiting. And I go up and I say my name is Istvan and she says my name is Klara, bold as that lipstick. And that was it.

I remember that story. I love that story. I wish I

could have heard her tell it.

She would have told you everything the same as I told you. Because you can only tell the truth one way.

But what she was like, really? Bold you say?

Bold, yes, but sneaky. I mean she always looked like a good girl—she *was* a good girl. But if she wanted something, even something her parents or her friends told her she shouldn't want, well, that was it: she would go after it. She wanted to wear that lipstick even though nice girls didn't do that. And she wanted me, who knows why. So that was it.

There was a photograph Ruth saw only after her grandfather's death, in the moldy album that had been among his few effects, of himself and Klara on their wedding day. It had been a simple civil wedding and he was wearing a striped suit and she wore what looked like a gray dress and a cloche hat and held a small bouquet in which daisies figured prominently. He seemed much sharper and nattier than she did with his zoot suit and the mustache (thinner, trimmer, blacker) and the gleam of pomade in his hair. Of course what drew the eye immediately, before taking in the slyness of his smile or Klara's curiously neutral expression, were the Stars of David affixed to their clothes. It was 1943 when they got married and they had less than a single year of together to look forward to before their violent separation, unimaginable ordeals, and dramatic reunion in America. Back in the Hopeview, voice straining from talking over the wheeze of the air conditioner, she wants to ask an even more impossible question: What was it like? What was it like to be singled out for a part of yourself that may or may not have been important to you, to be prohibited from working or from eating where you liked or from living anywhere but in a tiny island crammed to bursting with others whose affinity with you was being imposed from outside, by the state? And what was it like not to know, as she did: always she'd read the endless hopeless stories of European Jews who'd refused to believe in what for her coming after was the simple factual abyss of murder; who'd said fearfully to one another as the latest outrage came down the pike, Well, let's see, things could be worse, and were probably still saying that to each other in the cattle cars carrying them to their deaths. But the question goes unanswered, and anyway her grandfather had moved on to more general conversation and the question of dinner: of course she desperately wanted to do something for him and dinner at least she can do, but he wouldn't go anywhere but his usual diner, a grimy coffee shop that's kind of a long walk for a man with emphysema but they did it, stopping frequently in a way that marked them as other even in the churning oddball streets of Queens where a crowd of Puerto Rican men were camped out listening to a boombox in front of a bodega, where they must dodge two men carrying a very large sheet of glass down the sidewalk with no frame, not even so much as a bit of cardboard to absorb impact; where a dark-skinned woman in white moon boots and a flamboyant pink weave was stepping into the traffic on 111th Street talking on a cell phone and looking neither to the right nor left as cars screeched to a halt and drivers shouted curses at her. In all that noise she still felt conspicuous, a girl in a gray felted dress and glasses shuffling alongside an old man with tubes in his nose, pulling a green oxygen tank behind him with difficulty but refusing absolutely all offers of help. It was even worse in the diner, a place the color of a cracked saucer, with cigarette burns in the Formica tabletop and a sullen bottom-heavy waitress with no name badge who resisted all of her grandfather's charming if automatic efforts at flirtation. She felt sad for him, but he didn't seem to notice, even when the woman forgot or deliberately omitted the ice cream he'd asked for on the gelid slice of apple pie he had for dessert. She pushed some food around and drank awful coffee and tried to fix him in her mind. How handsome he still was, in spite of the thin greasy grayness of his skin that showed too much of the skull: he still had a full head of white wavy hair but this had the effect of making his actual head seem smaller, bobbing atop what had never been a big body but was now assuredly a wasted one, with his Adam's apple bobbing up and down behind his tie like an elevator without a building. He was winded from the walk so there wasn't much conversation until the food was all gone and he was staring down into his own coffee cup, into which he'd poured what seemed like six tablespoons worth of sugar and no cream or milk.

Listen, Grandpa, Ruth said, not quite impulsively. You don't have to go back to that place. You could come home with me.

He didn't seem to be listening. He was humming tunelessly under his breath, eyes on the spoon with which he was stirring his coffee, making little clinking sounds.

I don't have much space, but you could sleep in my bed until I find someplace with two bedrooms. With your Social Security we could afford it.

That's very sweet of you, darling, he said at last, looking up and nodding. She felt guilty relief, understanding his refusal.

She has to take you, then, she burst out, as if they'd been discussing M the whole time. She doesn't know what that place is like, she can't. She has the money, she must. If she won't bring you home she can at least afford to put you somewhere nicer, with a private room for God's sake.

That's not going to happen, darling.

Why not?

Your mother, Istvan said, and began to cough, a prolonged, hacking, convulsive series of coughs that turned his face bright purple. It seemed to go on and on: people at the other tables were looking, an old woman frowned and put her hand over her mug of tea, as though to protect it from germs. The waitress, who stood at the end of the short counter jawboning with the cook, looked over at them but didn't move. Istvan coughed some more. Ruth slid out of her side of the booth and bent over him, touching his back hesitantly, feeling the slight hunch there. He waved her off, so she just stood there tableside and watched him cough and cough into a handkerchief on which the monogrammed letters OF were just visible. Finally the coughing subsided enough for him to drink some of the water Ruth pushed at him. He sunk and sighed.

Grandpa....

Sweetness, he said loudly, addressing the waitress. She shuffled over.

You want some water?

The check please, sweetness, but don't rush, Istvan told her. Do you want more coffee, darling?

No, Grandpa.

The waitress smiled sourly, took the check out of her apron, scribbled something on the back (Ruth discovered a moment later it said "Have a nice day!" and "Marie" with a heart to dot the i), and put it on the table. Istvan took out his wallet: a thick, worn, patched leather monument to the man her grandfather had been, a man with a place in the world though not one of consequence, bulging with business cards and shoppers' club cards and folded papers, very few of them green.

Let me get this.

A man doesn't let a woman buy him dinner, her grandfather said hoarsely. He carefully extracted a pair wrinkled twenties and smoothed them on top of the bill.

She swept up the bills and went to the register to pay, glancing back to see if he was watching her, but he was staring at the cable again. She handed her credit card to the slack-jawed sallow-faced man who served as cashier, trying to think of how she could slip the money back to him somehow. For a moment she thought her card had been declined, but then the cashier handed her a receipt to sign with a gravelly and distant thank you.

When she returned to the table her grandfather looked up at her as if startled and then smiled: it was not a sad smile, she thought either, certainly not a happy smile. It was a *patient* smile.

Your mother, Istvan said, and again, more softly, your mother, looking into Ruth's eyes so she could see his own, brown and rheumy. She wants to help. She tried to help. She sent me a check, even. You want to see it? Before she could answer he'd taken a folded slip of paper from his wallet. He handed it to her and she unfolded it just enough to make out her mother's signature and some zeroes and the date. She looked at him.

This is six months old. You haven't deposited it?

No, darling. I have nothing, do you understand? Her only inheritance will be what I don't take from her. I want her to spend it on herself. Or on you. Look at this.

He'd extracted another piece of paper from the wallet: it was a Polaroid, folded and curled at the edges. He held it in his hands and slowly opened it like someone drawing open a curtain, to reveal a picture of Ruth as a baby toddling with her hand tucked in Istvan's. They were walking away from the camera toward the waves—it was a beach shot, and her grandfather looked tanned and strong in a pair of Bermuda shorts and an unbuttoned shirt. The setting sun heliographed in her hair, which had been a reddish blonde until a little after her third birthday. She tried and failed to remember what it must have been like to be that little girl, tiny smooth hand in his large rough one (but his hands strike her now with their mottled smallness, their delicacy), sand burning the soles of her feet, and who had been the photographer? She tried to picture Papa with the camera and dismissed the image immediately: he would have been under an umbrella somewhere with one of the thick volumes of military history that he used to devour on vacations. It must have been M, young and beautiful, in that two-piece suit that tied at the neck she used to wear, fully made up with lipstick and mascara even though it was only a daytrip to the Jersey Shore. There were books and books in the apartment filled with the pictures she'd taken of little Elsa, mostly Polaroids—they suited her brusque impatience in the long-ago age before digital photography, and Ruth could easily picture her standing there waving the undeveloped photo back and forth as though fanning herself.

Did she take that? she asked her grandfather.

Istvan seemed surprised by the question: he took the photo back and looked at it. I thought Louisa took it. She liked to take pictures. This is Jones Beach, summer of nineteen seventy-three. I remember because it was the day your mother told me she and your father had gone and gotten married that day.

Ruth remembered this story: they had lived together in common-law fashion for several years before and after her birth. It was only when she was three or so that they had decided to make it official with a trip to City Hall. There was another photo somewhere of the two of them in a picture eerily similar to the one she remembered of Istvan and Klara's picture, except that this one was in color and standing very small between the happy couple was Elsa Ruth, the only one in a white dress—M had worn a shade of blue that the passing of the years had rendered a muddy turquoise.

Were you surprised?

Her grandfather had taken the cigar out of his pocket and was clenching it between the second and third fingers of his right hand. Nothing your mother does surprises me, darling. She was always her own girl. You're the same.

I'm not the same, Ruth heard herself say, but her grandfather doesn't respond, for the waitress was bearing down on them. You can't smoke in here, she declared. The grandfather looked up at her with an air of injured pride.

I can't smoke anywhere, sweetness. I'm dying in the lungs. Probably be dead before I haul this out the door. He gestured with the cigar at the oxygen tank crouching at his feet like a surly pet. The waitress' mouth opened and then closed. She looked at Ruth as if for help, but for once in her life Ruth didn't apologize for anything, she just gave her a level look. The waitress retreated without saying anything.

They're trying to kill me, he said to Ruth. Let's get out of here. It's time to go home.

Some home.

Ruth took her grandfather's arm and slowly, painfully, bumping the tank wheels down the short flight of steps from the dirty glass door, they stepped out together into the humidly teeming July evening. Step by step they made their way to the end of the block and around the corner to where the Hopeview dankly loomed.

We have to get you out of this place.

I've been in worse places.

Yes, I know. I wish you'd tell me more about your experiences.

There's nothing more to tell.

What if I came back with a tape recorder, Grandpa? Would you tell me then? It's history. People ought to know.

It's enough, darling. It's another life.

You don't remember?

That's right. He stuck the cigar in his mouth, as though to plug it.

It was summer in the city, sticky, infernal. She squeezed his skinny hand in her own. By autumn she'd be sitting shiva for him in the old over-airconditioned house in New Jersey, where polite conversation was fueled through the night by endless cups of coffee until Ruth was nauseous in her belly and sick in her soul. He's buried now and I never heard his story, she thought. I never really touched him. But she remembered then returning him to his room; he'd wanted to say goodbye in the lobby but she had insisted on accompanying him up the antiseptic peeling elevator to the room he shared with a frail snoring black man with tubes in his nose, only a plastic curtain between their beds. At least she'd turned down the roommate's television and sat there for a while with him, and he'd taken out a bottle of some sort of medication.

It's for my eyes darling, perhaps you could help me with it. I have to sit in the chair.

He sat in the chair and took off his glasses and leaned back. She studied the thin gray skin of his face, bunched at the ears and neck, the turkey neck folding loosely above the white hairs sticking out from the top of his undershirt. His eyes were open, looking up at the ceiling, not registering her, little tremulous orbs. What these eyes have seen. She positioned the dropper over first one eye and the other, just a couple of inches. He blinked tears and she touched, for a moment, the sparse oily hair of his head and felt the warmth of his scalp.

Thank you darling.

Gently replacing his glasses on his face. Holding for one more moment that papery hand. I would see for you, Grandfather, if I could. Still dressed, he lay down with difficulty in the bed, stretched out with a sigh, rested his hands on his sternum and smiled his goodbye. At the door she looked back, saw the light from the TV reflecting in the lenses of his glasses. His eyes were open or they were closed. She shut the door.

The past is a succession of Russian dolls, each smaller than the last, with finer features, fainter colors, receding into something, many somethings, that's too small to hold, cascading through open fingers like water or sand. Lucy on the swing, riding gently back and forth, singing the words mommy and daddy to a tune of her own invention. The lake heaves and simmers in the autumn breeze to Ruth's right. To her left the other mothers are clustered by benches and strollers, exchanging gossip and childrearing advice: they look absurdly young to Ruth, none of them a day over thirty. Ruth's eye is drawn to the only other woman here standing apart: quite tall, of Slavic appearance, with reddish blonde hair and tight designer jeans, silently assisting her silent toddler son up onto a metal horse mounted on a spring and then, with an open-hipped and masculine gesture, rocking him on the horse with her foot. She's the youngest woman there but seems somehow older than the rest: something clings to her, a preoccupation that isn't distraction, there's a special slowness to her, like royalty must have, a woman used to being looked at, with enviably unlined skin that Ruth guesses is not the result of Botox. The woman notices Ruth and simply looks back at her for a moment without changing her expression; Ruth drops her gaze. Up, up, Lucy demands, so Ruth picks her up and perches her on the slide, a bit nearer to the woman in jeans. She hears herself addressed finally.

How old is yours? says the woman. The accent is Russian, maybe Ukrainian.

Almost two, Ruth says, suddenly relieved to speak to someone, hoping against hope that the subject won't be cloth versus disposable. She remembers, with difficulty, to ask about the woman's son.

Two and a half, the woman says, giving her son's blond curly head a kind of pat that Ruth's familiar with, a touch that doesn't communicate affection so much as presence. His name is Boris. His father's name is also Boris.

Ruth doesn't quite know how to respond to that. That's Lucy, she says at last.

A very beautiful girl. Like her mother.

Ruth feels the heat in her cheeks. Um, thanks. I

don't think I've seen you here before.

We moved here recently, the other woman says, up from the city. My husband thought it would be better for Little Boris. Better for Big Boris too, I suppose.

Is it better for you?

The woman shrugged. I like the water, she said. And there are many trees here. But it's dull. Don't you think it's dull?

Sometimes. The city's not that far off, but it seems like I never go there. Except sometimes on weekends the three of us will go downtown or to Lincoln Park. Or when visitors come, we go to the Art Institute and things like that.

Do you work? the woman asked. My husband doesn't want me to work.

The matter-of-factness of the statement momentarily displaces Ruth's anxiety about the question. How many times has Ruth had that conversation with other women who themselves had either given up or sidetracked their careers or who still doggedly and with a distinct air of superiority continued to follow their bliss as lawyers, Realtors, administrative assistants? But this woman came from another world, an older world. She took a breath.

I'm an attorney. But I'm not practicing right now. I mean, I do a little bit on the side, edit briefs and that sort of thing for my old firm. A glorified paralegal, really.

What sort of law did you practice? the woman asks

eagerly.

The boring kind. Corporate contracts. I wanted to do criminal, actually.

Criminal?

Yes, I wanted to go after the bad guys, Ruth says, smiling a little at the absurdity of it. Actually, I wanted to work for the International Criminal Court, in The Hague.

Interesting, the woman says, in a tone that makes it impossible to know if she truly finds it interesting or not. Myself, I have no profession. I am still getting used to America.

The sun is shining, children are shrieking, the wind off the lake stirs Ruth's hair and plays with the collar of her blouse. Why, then, does the strange woman's presence feel like an intrusion from her old life, when she was free, like cold water pricking and stippling Ruth's skin into wakefulness?

Boris has climbed off the metal horse and has moved a short distance to the slide, impelling his mother to follow him; Lucy is clamoring for Ruth to pick her up. She follows the Russian woman to the play structure, where she's holding her son's hand as he goes down the slide.

I'm Ruth.

Nadezhda is my name. You can call me Nadia. Everyone does. She studies Ruth for a moment. Why The Hague? You do not have enough American bad guys?

Oh we do, for sure. It's just, ah. I've always been

interested in European history. My mother came from there.

Conscious of the imminent reveal of her Jewishness. Ruth rarely thinks of or directly encounters anti-Semitism, but Nadia's coolness, her foreignness, has her antennae up.

Her parents were in Auschwitz. My grandparents I mean.

How terrible, Nadia says simply.

Yes.

So you would like to go after the Nazis then. But the Nazis are all dead.

No, Ruth says, shaking her head. There are always Nazis.

Nadia stares past Ruth at the waters of the lake for a moment. It is why I agreed to come to America. Why I am standing here talking to you with my American son. Because of what my own grandmother told me. She survived the siege of Leningrad. You have heard of this?

Yes, I have.

And in my own country there are bad things. I wanted to live somewhere that wars don't happen. Somewhere normal.

I can understand that.

Bad things happen here, says Nadia as if to herself. Terrible things. But they do not *mean* in the same way. You understand my English?

Nadia's eyes are a pale and crystalline shade of blue

that makes the pupils startlingly dark. Ruth smiles, reflexively, and looks away.

Perhaps you can. Americans are so, so comfortable mostly. I have noticed this.

Ruth smiles with one corner of her mouth by way of acknowledgment, and Nadia laughs suddenly, a snapped-off sound.

I like you, Ruth. I hope I see you again.

Likewise, Ruth says, astonished at what has been said, at what she feels in the air between herself and the stranger. Contact.

It can be tough in a new place, Ruth hears herself say. She fishes around in her purse; she still has business cards, sat down one night with a permanent marker and crossed out the office number on each one, leaving the cell number intact. She extends one and Nadia takes it between her elegantly manicured fingers.

Nadia murmurs something into Boris's ear, and he immediately holds up his arms to be picked up. She places him in the stroller (an expensive model, Ruth can't help noticing, a couple hundred dollars fancier than her own), nods to Ruth, and rolls away without another word.

Hungry! Lucy says. Snack! Except *snack* in Lucy-speak sounds just like *cock*. She shouts it, loudly, so that the other mothers turn around: *Cock! Cock!* Ruth gives them all her most beatific smile. She lowers Lucy into the stroller, fishes a Graham cracker out of the diaper bag to hand to her, and wheels the stroller around to head home, in the opposite direction Nadia took. It looks like rain, she tells herself. Her skin is flushed. Her ears are burning.

Certain ideas of Europe closely held by a reader. The American configuration: hostility, curiosity, indifference, contempt, fascination, prurience, a persistent sense of inferiority, lewd speculation, exploitations, saturation, colonization. We are new and they are old. Except for history and the conditions of history's procreation, America owns the New. She dreams of a new Old World in which her own hidden history lies embedded like prehistoric gases awaiting miners to bring about their detonation and release. A Europe of babies and old men and women and nothing in between. Europe of scholars, bearded men with peyes and spectacles, picking up fallen books from bombed-out shelves and kissing them as one does a dropped infant. Europe the furnace of horrors, untold accumulated sedimentary beauties of history heaped and strewn and doused with coal oil in the ashy fields of Poland, the former Czechoslovakia, the former Yugoslavia, the once and future Lithuania, Ukraine, Byelorussia, Hungary. Burned: the Paris of the East and the London of the East and the Venice of the East. Not burned: New York, Philadelphia, Pittsburgh, Rochester, Cleveland, Chicago. As the line between the two Jerusalems smolders, incommensurate fires burning in Ramallah and Tel Aviv, fire of the citizen, fire of the subject. One stands or sits down in these reflections, quite at home. In search of a path of resistance to the downward drift of entropy and forgetfulness: dream, reverie, reflection are her methods. Above all, as though distracted, she decides. She does or does not turn the page, does or does not pick up a ballpoint pen with which to carefully underline words, phrases, clauses, sentences, whole paragraphs; does or does not grip the pen close to the tip so as to create marginalia: five- and six-pointed stars, asterisks, a word or two, or the most eloquent marks of punctuation: question marks, exclamation points, while a simple period marks her *nota bene*. In so doing she emends the quiet of reading, brings greater proportions of noise to particular rows and blocks of black signals, oblique semaphoric signs. Other paragraphs, pages, and chapters are passed over in silence: the reader leaves no sign of her passage. She looks in from the outside of her own experience as half-understood text written by collectives of anonymous authors: her Jewishness, her whiteness, her femaleness (not to her own satisfaction achieving womanliness), her status as an immigrant's child, her relative prosperity, her degrees. Tearing off strips of paper in her mind (in reality motionless), she says: It is a fact that more men survived than women. It is a fact that the killings of and by men are better documented than the killings of women. It is a fact that the widespread rape of women, then and now, has been poorly and inefficiently documented. It is a fact that some women collaborate or try to collaborate with their oppressors, even their murderers, in continual attempts at the survival of themselves and their children. It is probable that Sophie never had a choice; it is certain that Sophie was fictional. It is probably that such concepts as "agency," "personal morality," "mercy," "justice," "mere decency," "humanity" have been put under such extreme pressure by the events of the past century that they are no longer fit to be used. It is probable that our appetite for news of these events is inversely proportionate to our appetite for what is called "reality." It is likely that a patina of something we dare not call "nostalgia" clings to our collective memory of these events. It is a fact that old men who have been soldiers in a war speak of wartime as the best, the only real time in their lives. Subtract "best" from "real" if you like, it makes no difference. To describe is to affirm, to tell a story is to say, You should have been there. The wind rose, rain swept in: you should have been there. I miscarried my first child after seven months of pregnancy: you should have been there. I dropped out of the life I knew into someone else's life, a placeholder life: you should be here. Stuck here in someone else's idea of Europe, an American woman with an American child, secure and comfortable and never for a moment free from fear of losing all security, all comfort. There are certain activities that occupy the entire foreground of one's capacities—movies, music, reading, writing—while leaving the dark background to metabolize, metastasize, to grow tentacles, so that when you put down your pen, your book, your instrument, you emerge into the dazzling matinee sunlight and find that the background has seized your life and you will never be quite the same. As when you stand by the graveside of a loved one, your grandfather for example, and think, "The stage is set," and "The coffin is being closed," and "Here I am at the graveside of my grandfather," and "Here I am heaping a shovelful of dirt onto my grandfather's coffin," and "Inside that coffin under the earth I put there my grandfather is lying with his eyes closed, wearing a ticking watch, wearing the same suit he married his second wife in thirty years ago," and none of these thoughts are to the purpose or affect in the slightest the real work going on in the background, the work of being alive inside a wound, pain dimmed by the narcotic haze of self-consciousness. You did not choose this wound, you did not give it a name. It's only a background from which you emerge, like a paper doll cut from a newspaper. The shape of the doll does not affect the news, the contents (front page, advice column, obituary, editorial, book review, advertisement), and yet it is inseparable from them. That is the essential story: daughter of the daughter of a survivor, herself a kind of survivor, once married to a kind of perpetrator, my father, my fathers. Everything else is symptom.

So why pursue it? What could be more absurd or pathetic than a paper doll straining to read herself? Indecipherable text in which I take root. So compelled, I owe a debt unpayable. I go forward, to wring blood from stones.

The city is brilliant under layers of sun and cloud. A train arriving in a palace of glass, a level pan across the skyline. Conurbation on a plain, historyless from a height. But there, iconic, once sinister, the eye of the East, now beloved and harmless and as absent in its omnipresence as the city's other totem, a bear: the tower, at the base of which hunkers a Starbucks where Lamb is using his laptop. Snaps it shut now, passes out among the hipsterati, the punks, the tourists, out onto the blank bare face of Alexanderplatz, rolling his suitcase, to another train station, to ride the S-bahn. Of the Italian portfolio there is no sign: perhaps it has been swallowed entirely by the rolling bag, never so anodyne or sinister as now, lugged heavily up the steps to the train platform where they are massing, the Germans, coming and going, easting and westing, with studied casualness. Now he is walking again in sunlight, coat billowing behind him, into the deepest past the city now has to offer, under and through the Brandenburg Gate, crossing the ex-death strip, passing on doggedly down Ebertstrasse, looking neither to the right (trees in the gentle breeze, green lung, vast acreage edge of the Tiergarten) nor to the left (the field of stelae, the memorial the film we are watching uncharacteristically and melodramatically captions with its full and actual name: MEMORIAL TO THE MURDERED JEWS OF EUROPE). His head is bowed a little, only his feet meeting his eyes. Further and farther to Potsdamer Platz, impersonal assemblage of skyscrapers proclaiming their shaky fealty to the Euro, which is only the Deutschmark in sheep's clothing: mute, defiant, they reflect only the sky. Under a dazzled postmodern canopy like the biggest of Big Tops, by a reflecting pool or fountain sandwiched between chain restaurants he squats again with his laptop, again uploading or downloading what's necessary, the updates, the tweets, data. We have not seen this man with a phone. Onward, exhausted Lamb, who has forgotten that trains exist, crossing the bridge in late light with the etiolated yellow geometry of the Philharmonic Building behind him, over the canal and into the old city, the West Berlin that was: island, white showcase in a sea of red, costly bauble of the postwar economic miracle, ground zero when that phrase had another meaning, when Berlin rehearsed perpetually the end of history, tanks facing each other across land mines and barbed wire, the end of the world as we once knew it, suffused now in kitsch the very phrase that was born here, World War III. He is under leaves and trees now, in a quiet prewar neighborhood, strollers and gay couples, a Swedish furniture store, bakeries, restaurants, cafes.

He comes to a flagstone plaza with a brick church at one end of it, an outdoor café at the other end with scattered tables and chairs. He is weary now, rolls up to one of the tables and sits down, a bit slumped, as the evening shadows begin to catch in the buildings and treetops and young boys, not all of them white, kick a soccer ball at the church end of the square. A waiter approaches, listens, withdraws, returns with a pilsner, withdraws. Lamb takes his laptop again from the rolling bag's outer pocket, opens it, checks for a signal, shuts it again. In his eye the amber evening. He reaches inside his coat and takes out a slightly crumpled white tulip and sets this on the table. Takes a sip of beer. Waits.

It is dark, which is to say light: the lamps have come on and the square is more lively than before, a mostly young crowd settling in at the surrounding restaurants and bars for an unforced and lively evening. Lamb is sitting with another man who sits bent over, shoulders practically between his knees, necktie hanging down, as though trying to catch his wind after getting kicked in the stomach. A large man, swarthy, carefully unshaven, with heavy black brows, in his forties perhaps, in a polo shirt and black jeans and motorcycle boots. A manila folder is on the table by the empty pilsner glass, the tulip resting on top of it. Lamb is listening. The man is talking, steadily, compulsively, to the ground it seems, someone getting something off his chest, confessing something of which he is ashamed, glad to say it once and once only and completely to a single other soul. Only Lamb's eyes move. What does the man say. I had forgotten that all this time, all of it, from the first moment of the train, the first moment we caught sight of him, our man, Lamb, to reorient us in the plot, in Europe, in Berlin, from the Fernsehturm to now, we have heard nothing, no street sounds, no dialogue, only music, strings at first, for quite a long time, and now, as Lamb is listening, as this man, who is somehow his victim, is speaking, pouring his heart out, we are hearing only the lyrics, the voice, of a woman, in a language you very likely do not speak:

Meghalt a szeretet!
Meghalt a szeretet!

A pure song, a song of despair, a song of suicides. As Lamb or someone like him would say to you, without irony: I could tell you, but then I would have to kill you. But I cannot kill you, you are only a spectator, here to be pushed or pulled by the spectacle of failure, my failure to understand, my failure to communicate something ineffable, something that goes beyond the privacy of grief: though it begins there, and ends there, in its universality, the inevitability for each of us of real irrevocable personal excruciating loss. It is Lamb's song, Ruth gave it to him, I found it for her. It is the song of the reader. It is the last song, of M.

A letter never sent, from herself to herself:

A mother is no saint. A mother is sheerly myth. When she's there, she's not there. When she's not there she's everywhere. The moon is new. I don't need to read her messages because I read. Dowry of myself to myself, wedded to the word. I have her in the mirror, when I linger with the newspaper while Lucy calls my name from another part of the house. When my husband's eyes slide past mine to Lucy's, birth a smile. Once I thought she wanted me to accomplish something. To finish what she never quite started. But I am the one who's unfinished, who lacks the finishing touch of a blessing. So I read the books, I studied the testimony, I stared at incomprehensible black-and-white photographs of children waiting to be beaten, gassed, starved, shot. The heart of her heart of darkness. Mother's unintended. Granddaughter unknown, extrapolate what she knows of my character, Ben's. No lineage. Dead-ended in some shtetl, under somebody's boot. Cossacks. Spectacles on my eyes and autumn in my heart—that's Babel. Am I a mother before I'm a woman, a woman before I'm a Jew, a Jew before I'm a daughter, a daughter before I'm nobody? There's a pair of us. Meanwhile I've put my own heart under surveillance. Moving image of a man, a shamus, sharp shadow in an indistinct world. Europe of mistrusts. Space stands in for time: easting, easting. Poised between tourism and graverobbery. Autumn, mulch, winds, decay. Whoso has no house now will not build him one. House built on quicksand. It's not the photos that are incomprehensible, it's the expressions on their faces. Blank, quizzical, even smiling. Very rarely contorted into a grimace. Very rarely registering pain. A father strokes his sobbing son's hair. They are naked, waiting their turn to be shot. The father points upward, he is explaining heaven. That image, not even an image, just three short sentences, seared into my memory and erasing my own childhood. A rainy afternoon when I was ten or eleven, under the kitchen table with my mother's books. Rainshadow on the floor, on the table above my head with its immaculate lacy tablecloth. Surrounded by solid blond legs of the furniture I'd known all my life, secure in our apartment like the astronauts in their space capsules, I felt the gravity of the world let me go. And I've never been fully recaptured. Her key in the lock, my throat seized by a scream. I left them there, the books, some with photos spread open, ran to my room and shut the door. Heard her enter, calling, then silence but for her heels on the hallway's parquet. She walked out of hearing for a long time—me face down on the bed, back arched like a cat's, pressed against the rapidly warming pillow. Walked back, past my door, then returned without pausing, passing on the way to the kitchen. A half hour later I found her there with a glass of wine, chopping vegetables for ratatouille. Her beautiful face calm and blank as the children in the photos. Through the archway to the dining room I saw the books were gone. She asked me no questions, I told her no lies. I picked up a second knife and helped her chop the vegetables. We spoke of inconsequential things, the radio playing softly from its berth over the refrigerator, both of us looking at the clock waiting for my father to come home. And he never did. Because reading that story, seeing that gray sky and ravaged landscape and wasted fruit of naked human bodies and the coats and hats of their killers, also human, taught me something I'd always suspected. I do not know who my father was. And I knew my mother all too well. But M. What was she.

Like shattering glass filmed in reverse, the pieces, integrating into a picture. Hotels. Lamb sitting in a chair by a rain-streaked window, back to us, wearing headphones, hunched, listening. Lamb on top of a bedspread, no jacket, shirt untucked, ashtray balanced on his sternum, looking up at the ceiling. Lamb in the shower. Lamb standing at the window—a new window, the same window—looking out at the city, suitcase packed and erect next to him, ready to go. Lamb at the hotel bar looking into his glass of whiskey while a slender woman with ash blonde hair and a green dress stands at his elbow, talking. Legwork. Lamb pulling his bag down a street, landmarks signaling behind him, brute signifiers, like a painted canvas spooling behind him, so that we take it on sufferance, indication: Madrid Paris Rome Budapest Vienna Berlin. Berlin. The generic café, sitting at a table looking out at the passersby while informants come and go: bureaucrats soldiers cops academics prostitutes old men, leaning in to fill Lamb's ear. Leads. Fanning the photos under the noses of bartenders, hotel clerks, coroners, pimps, reckless divorcees, librarians, janitors, junkies. Exchanging envelopes, currency, significant looks, shaken heads. Lamb's notebook, Moleskine of course ("of Chatwin, of Hemingway"), with the elastic to snap it shut creating an aura of decision, finality, a new link in the chain. Berlin, he's back in Berlin. In the men's room of the train station two men come up from behind, offer no words, but one hits him in the kidney and grabs his arms and the other shouts questions, pummels him in the stomach, slams his face against the mirror, slams his body into the toilet stall, shoves his head down into the bowl, flushes, shouts abuse, leaves him there: Lamb, survivor, offering no resistance, limp. Bandaged Lamb on top of a bedspread, no jacket, shirt untucked, ashtray balanced on his sternum, looking up at the ceiling. Lamb gingerly in the shower. Lamb standing at the window—a new window, the same window—looking out at the city, suitcase packed and erect next to him, ready to go. The man with the heavy brows looks up shocked as the stockroom door splinters open and Lamb like an avatar comes lunging and coldcocks him, lays him out, administers a technical and righteous beating. Bends down to the broken and bleeding form, shows him again the photos, listens. Lamb stands, brushes his hands against his pants as though to clean them, walks out.

A new hotel, the same hotel. Are there any messages? Lamb pulling his suitcase behind him, tape over his right eye but no more swelling, turning to face us as elevator doors close. Lamb at the door of his room with key card in hand, hesitating. Silent ambient breathing of an anonymous carpeted corridor lit by florescent sconces, the only window at the hall's end overexposed: Lamb washed out darkly, kneeling by his bag, glancing at us, taking something out, standing. Lamb with a gun. Lamb opening the door.

Bland, a room, bed bureau TV desk and chair, floor to ceiling window with the smoky gray day outside, quasi-industrial the view, the long asphalt ribbon of Karl-Marx Allee stretching into the dark of the oncoming evening, East, perdition. The man in the chair, a big man, an older man, back to us, in a good suit, looking out the window. Swiveling to face us, Lamb, the man, ballooning at the belly, the waist, eyes smiling, sinister, benevolent, completely bald, slightly ashamed. Looking up under lidded eyes, standing now, smile widening. Lamb shuts the door. With his left hand reaching into his jacket pocket and thumbing them out, the photographs. Fanning them on the bed where the man can step forward to see. Looking down, takes them in. The smile fades, changes, comes back. Look at him. Look at his human face. He is a big man in his seventies, imposing, huge even, and well bruised. Spreading his hands.

You've found her.

Dear Elsa,

What I never told you, what I kept from you. What if it doesn't exist? Because you hate me, perhaps with cause, but will always be my daughter, and always be my Elsa, no matter what you choose to call yourself. And so it's almost time for me to tell you about your father, and my father, and this awful world that fathers have made. But not yet. Before I do that I want you to picture me as I was this morning, before the letter arrived. I was at peace then. Or if not at peace, at quiet, settled, at rest in the way an object is at rest, like a stone at the bottom of a puddle that does not know that puddles evaporate, that things can change again after so much change has already gone by. Husband gone, the old life gone, America most of all gone into memory. And me in this strange old city, here on the edge of Italy where I thought I could be reasonably confident of never or at least rarely seeing another American. A city more German than Italian, more Slavic than German, written into and out again of the margins of history, a city that crossed national borders almost routinely, as eastern as it is western, an excellent place to disappear because it was always itself in the act of disappearing like a magician's mute and beautiful assistant. Alone but for a few distant friends, I had found a pattern for my days. I walked the streets, I worked in the shop, I read again the same poems I'd loved when I was young, Rilke most of all, taking strength if not comfort from those lines I'm sure you've also never forgotten, lines whose advice I follow now:

> *Wer jetzt kein Haus hat, baut sich keines mehr.*
> *Wer jetzt allein ist, wird Es lang bleiben,*
> *wird wachen, lesen, lange Briefe schreiben*
> *und wird in den Alleen hin und her*
> *unruhig wandern, wenn die Blätter treiben.*

Such beautiful words make loneliness bearable. And this is becoming a very long letter indeed, and isn't it strange that the German for "long letter" sounds like "long brief"? But it was not a long letter that came to break my peace this morning, that I could hear even from upstairs by the creak of the mail slot, a slip of paper that slid between the brass lips of my locked door and came crashing down on this life, my afterlife. I went down the creaking stairs which have always served to warn me in the past of my neighbors' comings and goings, and now they—the old Signora on the second floor, the young Signora on the third—might have heard me go down and then come back up again, as if I were indecisive about leaving. I went inside, I closed the door, I picked up the old ivory letter opener your Papa had brought back from a long-ago trip to South Africa, I opened the envelope. And what did I find? A blank page. A blank page confirming what I knew already in my heart: that he who now has no house will not build him one. That he who is alone now will continue to be alone, will write and read long letters, will wander the streets and alleys as the leaves fall, remembering. Remembering in this case my own death, that is to say, my life. Who sent it to me, this page, the page on which I write this, that you may or may not read? Was it your father? Was it you?

In this life I do not expect pity, Elsa, from you or anyone else. I expect no response. I don't expect you do anything but to read this page, and I know that I cannot even really expect that. I do not know what you will feel or what you will want to do. I'm writing to tell you simply what you must already know, that I am going, or gone. So if you have anything to tell me, even in your mind, you might as well tell me now. I have come to rest. Each day I walk. Sometimes I walk very far, all out along the coast road to Miramare. Have you heard of it? It is a castle, the second famous castle on this coast. The first of course is Duino, I've been there too, to listen for Rilke's angels, but I heard nothing except tourists snapping pictures of each other. Miramare is different. A hundred and fifty years ago it was caused to be built by Maximilian, the sailor, future Emperor of Mexico, younger brother to Franz Joseph who was then midway through his endless reign. It's a strange blocky gray building, more house than castle, dramatically situated on a promontory thrust out into the water. I've heard the tour guides speak about it so frequently I could be a guide myself. The story is that when Maximilian was serving in the meager naval forces of the Austro-Hungarian Empire, his ship was blown by a storm into the Gulf of Trieste and nearly sank within sight of that promontory. As a way of giving thanks, perhaps, or just struck by the beauty of the spot, he returned there in after years and had the castle built. He was never happier than when he was at sea, so he had his rooms in the castle done up to look just like the cabin of his ship, the *Novara*, in which he had sailed around the world in the years before the castle was built and which would carry himself and his wife to Vera Cruz a few years later, in 1864, where they became Emperor and Empress. On the instigation of Napoleon III a picked delegation of Mexican aristocrats had come to visit him at the castle, persuading him that an election had expressed the will of the Mexican people that they join a new empire in thrall to the interests of France and Austria. He must have loved the idea: that in one stroke he could step out of his minor role in a minor empire and into a more paradoxical empire denominated by democracy. Once in Mexico he alienated every constituency: the liberals wanted nothing to do with a monarchy, while the conservatives who had dreamed up the empire were displeased with Maximilian's progressive ideas, which included a limited monarchy and the elimination of a system of serfdom that had virtually enslaved his native Mexican subjects. Three years later he was dead, a benevolent but naïve imperialist executed by republicans outraged at the very idea of an Emperor of Mexico, let alone a bewhiskered adventuring Habsburg who spoke not a word of Spanish. They say his last words before the firing squad were "Viva, Mexico!"—which shows a kind of touching, stubborn loyalty to the fiction that had overtaken his life. His poor wife, Charlotte—the Mexicans called her Carlota—went mad afterward; she had returned to Europe seeking help for her beleaguered husband when the republicans were at the gates: no one would help or could help and she spent a few years after Maximilian's execution in seclusion here, in this impossibly lonely and isolated castle surrounded by the sea, surrounded by artifacts of the couple's brief reign over the land of the Aztecs. Her own quarters were on the second floor, but perhaps often she wandered into her dead husband's nauticalized chambers to stare out the porthole-shaped window at the Adriatic, the castle almost shaking in the strong wind, imagining herself once again on the voyage to Vera Cruz, or more pathetically on the voyage home, in a womblike wooden room that must have all but smelled and tasted of the body of Maximilian, whom she had truly loved. Eventually she was too much of an embarrassment for the Habsburgs and was shipped back to the country of her birth, Belgium, where she wasted away as the Empress Dowager in another castle for long decades, outliving not just her husband but his empire, while her cousin Leopold used her money to pillage the Congo.

It is a strange, haunted place, redolent not just of the nineteenth century but of how the nineteenth century imagined itself; a kind of mirror like its name, a funhouse reflection of mingled idealism, strategically ineffectual politics, and cruelty. I wander from room to room, I walk the grounds, which are extensive and beautifully landscaped, and the sunshine all but banishes the ghosts that walk alongside me. On the very tip of the promontory, before the great windows of the castle, one can indeed feel as though on a prow of a ship, thrusting forward through the water toward a sublime or ridiculous destiny—it hardly matters which, the illusion of motion is the point. I persist, you see, in thinking I'm alive. Don't you do the same?

If you will not meet me in this place, this margin, what will I do? What I have been doing. I will wander the reduced and palpable streets of my former life. I will read. I will write to you. I will imagine that I have a grandchild who knows my name, who knows what I look like, who can recognize my voice. I will imagine, without expecting or deserving, your forgiveness.

3

Pavement

PERCHED on a mannequin head, coolly observing them both, the white wig, heavy as a swan. Gustave shoots a glance at it, then rises to stand with his arms at his side, to face the intruder with his level, curious gaze.

Why have you found me again?

Not *how*. We're past that now. On the verge of story. Lamb looks at him.

Because you know something about her.

Who?

Don't play games. Lamb lifts, pinched between thumb and forefinger, a photograph. The heavy man's face, as though struck, reaches for it, wondering. The gesture is all he needs. Lamb pulls the photo away and tucks it into his pocket.

You were involved with her.

Involved is a good word, the other man says at last in his nearly accentless English. Devoted is a better one. In the religious sense.

Then tell me about your devotions to her.

We are speaking of the same woman? *The* woman, as Sherlock Holmes might say? Of M?

The American shrugs.

I wish you would tell me something of your client. I have no rights there, I suppose.

None. Let's get on with it. Your story.

My confession, do you mean?

Your side of things. Do you mind if I use this? Holding up a small black oblong. A digital voice recorder. And this? A camera.

Do you know Gertrude Stein?

Who, the writer?

The writer. She was an American, like you.

I've never read her.

You don't read Stein, not really, the man says. It's pure grammar. Like pictures of sentences. You spend time with them. I've improved my English a good deal spending time with Miss Stein.

What's your point?

"Fathers are depressing." An observation of hers. A warning.

Let's get on with it.

Very well. Are you recording now?

Yes.

This won't take long, the man says. He steeples his fingers, closes his eyes for a moment, opens them. Looks right into the camera, unsmiling. The camera cradles his face as you, reader, demand this story.

In 1967 I came to Paris as an art student. Naturally I submitted to the mania of the times, felt that simply to look out the window was to have my eyes peeled open as though I were being born, and this happened dozens, even hundreds of times every day. We all felt it, all the beautiful young men and women, plus me, a coarse unlovely youth from the provinces, whose accent was mocked by the professors and bureaucrats of the university where I was one of the students, plus one. I had come up in the fall of '67 from the little village on the Rhine where I grew up, where from an early age my drawings had won me a degree of infamy, for I drew what I could see, and, universally ignored except for the occasional good-natured offhand beating, I saw everything: drunkards beating their wives, wives who took in boarders and fucked them while their husbands were at work, the field west of town where with a dog's help you could turn up bones they said had belonged to collaborators executed by partisans during the war. Once I climbed a mound of coal outside the window of the house of LaFleur the barber and saw him sitting at his dining table with the business end of a revolver in his mouth. Startled, I slipped and fell, scattering the coal and marking my clothes, feet and hands with black dust. He came out the door a moment later but I had already made my getaway, down to the riverside where I tried in vain to scrub my sooty clothes clean. I let them go, they drifted blackly downstream toward the Mediterranean, and walked naked in my shoes back home, where my mother bent over me sorrowfully, scrubbing at my shoulders and cheeks with a rough towel until I howled. LaFleur hanged himself a week later; he never fired a shot, I don't know why. I drew the things I saw on foolscap stolen from my father's office—he was a kind of country barrister, originally from Lyon, who'd met and married my mother right before the war, gone to the Line and been captured and spent the next five years in a prison camp, then came drifting home again in '44 to find me, just four years old, his son. It was known to all without needing to be said that I was German, that my mother had accepted or given comfort to one or more of the Wehrmacht passing through. Or had it been a fellow citizen, reclaiming temporarily his pure Germanness in the bastard's brew that was Alsace-Lorraine, his pride in the thousand-year Reich leading him to my mother's bed, and then carried away again by duty or defeat back to Germany, or back into frightened Frenchness, silence, anonymity. He must have been a large man for I was large, even at birth, more than four and a half kilos, an astonishing size in that time of universal malnourishment. My father, a slightly built man, accepted my existence dutifully, as though in the spirit of a legally binding agreement to which he'd stipulated, though by all rights he could have walked away from my mother and me, returned to Lyon, regained his dignity and lived a different life. Instead he stayed on in that little town, the butt of jokes, the hairs on the back his neck bristling every time he left a room as though he could feel by static electricity the sign of horns that some yokel—his own client, like as not—was even then making to the sniggers of others. Pitiable, really, even in his rages, taking me behind the outhouse no matter what the weather to beat me with a bit of rope he hung there for the purpose, so that the neighbors might listen to me squirm and scream, though in fact even by the age of eight I was large enough to put up a stiff resistance if I so chose. He was good at least for paper, and high-quality inks and pencils, for he loved to write by hand and had the most elegant script, which I only later learned was a mark of his own provinciality and lower-class origins, for the aristocrats, the grande ecole types, have always prided themselves on their sloppy handwriting. I was considered slow, and a bastard besides, but I was in this one way only fortunate in my size, and the other boys learned not to pick on me, if only because their kicks and punches went nowhere, it was impossible to do me visible damage, I stood and panted with the excitement of violent contact and covered their faces with my breath until, embarrassed, they dropped their fists and stepped away. Besides, my drawings were in demand, especially the lewd ones that for a couple of coins I'd draw inside of your notebook—I was careful, you see, but I got caught anyway, only I was lucky enough to be caught by Father Juneau, what you'd call the principal of our only school. He was a little like my father, a stranger in our little provincial town, having been exiled from the capital for some indiscretion or other. He was a sallow, slightly built man, bald on top, with a pot belly poking through his black robe, and long fingers that he drummed unhappily on his desk when we were brought before him for the usual transgressions: shouting, cursing, fighting, stealing, defacing school property, maybe a bit of buggery in the toilets. I'd been caught doing something a little rarer, giving half my earnings to Genevieve, a lanky blonde dairyman's daughter with protruding ears and gap teeth and a long braid she said had never been cut, who in exchange for my few coins in her father's barn would slip out of her coarse cotton dress and pose naked for me, the blades of sunlight that shone through the slats in the walls cutting across her white belly and breasts, blinding me. How well I remember those afternoons after school when I would come by and find her at the milking stool, her hands firm on the udders, and without more than glancing at me she'd lean back, take a pewter ladle off the wall, dip it in the pail, and hand it to me, and I'd drink the sweetest milk I'd ever tasted or will ever taste. Then she'd stand up from the milking stool, much taller than I was, and look me full in the eye and—what's the English? not scowl, smirk, she smirked at me, and in a single motion bend down and pick up the hem of her dress and pull it over her head, and the smell of milk and cowshit and straw and rust, the cows lowing softly, chickens scratching just through the walls—they were paper thin, you could hear everything, her mother Madame Toux clucking just like the chickens as she scattered the feed—and in response to my nod, as I produced my writing tablet and pencil from my knapsack, she'd move to where the bands of light were striping the strawpile and stand there, arms at her sides, awaiting my directions. Then I would think always of the saints and martyrs in stained glass I'd seen in the church and they would tell me to tell her what pose to strike—left arm outstretched, right arm bent at the elbow, eyes toward the roofbeams, or sitting on a crate with a bit of sacking on top to protect from splinters, cradling a broomhandle like the bony body of Christ, or as Mary, holding to her breast one of the puppies that were always underfoot (her father owned three big bloodhound bitches that were always having litters, all of which he drowned, but he'd take his time getting round to it). Sometimes afterward, dressed again, she'd sit with me in the sun-drenched corner and leaf through the drawings and giggle, and I would paw her a little, out of politeness mostly, for her pale raw body was in no way erotic, or at least I didn't find it so. But it was in our favorite pose, Mary and the infant Jesus, in which we were caught one warm September afternoon, when I'd been laboring to transform not the dog into Jesus but Mary into Genevieve, a Genevieve with the intelligent and queenly eyes and head of a bloodhound, and so intense was my concentration, and hers too perhaps, that I didn't hear her mother cease to cluck, or the noiseless hinges of the door (little did we know that they'd been oiled in anticipation of haytime), and only looking up, eyes squinting at the sudden light bathing Genevieve's whole body, and her little ecstatic cry of shame, and I remember particularly the blonde blaze of the fine hairs on her arms as she lifted her hands to cover her face (how strange, I thought at the time, that she didn't cover her pubis, which with its darker hairs was like a little coalfire, bright at the edges and ashed at the center), dropping the dog which squealed as it tumbled to the straw washing up like sand around Genevieve's blunt dirty feet. Her mother was a sober woman and didn't scream, in fact she had her wits about her and quickly shut the door, for her husband was about and his rage would have been terrible. She told Genevieve to get dressed, and then she turned toward me. I don't remember what happened next, but somehow I was outside, my shirt torn, running pellmell for home. It must have been the loose board in the wall that I could just barely squeeze through if I sucked in my gut. I began to breathe easier and walked the rest of the way, was able to elude my own mother and get upstairs to change my clothes in time for supper, and it wasn't until that night, lying in my bed, that I reached for my drawing tablet under the mattress and realized that I had dropped it in my flight. A nameless horror gripped me for a long moment; then, I relaxed. What can they do to me? I asked myself. I'm already a whoreson, a freak. In a way, I was glad that finally my drawings were going to come to light. I had a larger audience coming than that of the dirty boys who paid me a few sou for sketches of half-naked nuns to beat off to. I closed my eyes and went to sleep with a light heart. The next day, all was normal as before, until I looked out the window, day-dreaming, while Father Juneau was teaching us algebra, and saw Genevieve's mother striving purposefully down the dirt road, my tablet in both of her hands like a hymnal. Then the panic seized me again: I began to sweat, my mouth was dry, my palms went cold. She came in through the front door—all eyes turned curiously toward her—and strode up to the priest, who was stiff with surprise at the blackboard, chalk dust on his soutane. He asked her what she wanted, and she turned and pointed at me. Gustave? Father Juneau said blankly. Then the spell broke and he put down his piece of chalk, put Felix the head boy in charge, and whisked the madame into the little closet off the main room that served as his office. Of course Felix and his odious confederates flocked to the door, jostling each other in silence trying to overhear what was said, leaving just me and a few of the slower and weaker boys at our desks, staring down at unsolvable proofs. All was quiet save for the low vibration of Father Juneau's voice (felt in the floor) and the higher vibration made by Madame Toux (felt in the light globes). Then Felix's jaw dropped and he turned toward me and pointed. Pervert! he announced, with just a shade of admiration. The class snickered and hooted. I kept my head down. Then suddenly the knot of boys at the door exploded like sparrows after a gunshot, and Father Juneau was standing in the doorway, beckoning to me. In his office Madame Toux stood by the priest's desk, composed as a nun in her town clothes; the tablet lay shut on the desktop. Father Juneau ushered me in, with a certain respect I thought, and then continued to hold the door open. He looked at Madame Toux. When she didn't get the hint he coughed slightly, and again, louder.

I think it might be best if I spoke to Gustave alone. Man to man, as it were.

Madame Toux tossed her head a little—I wouldn't have guessed she'd had it in her—and trotted out.

Father Juneau waited until her footsteps had receded. He took papers and a pouch of tobacco from his desk and began rolling a cigarette. My drawing tablet lay open before him on the gigantic metal slab that served as his desk. I tried not to look at what was drawn there but paid attention to the view out the window over Father Juneau's shoulder. It was gray. There was a weedy meadow, and beyond that a drainage ditch, then the trees started. Father Juneau smoked and leafed through pages. He glanced up at me standing there.

Sit down. These drawings. They are yours?

I looked down at my shoes, then up into his face. It took a moment to recognize the line of yellow teeth he showed me as a smile. He was looking at my bloodhound Madonna. He gestured with his cigarette.

You have an eye, he said. An eye for sin, to be sure. But an eye for form as well, for line and volume and... character.

Thank you Father, I said wonderingly.

And well you should thank me, he murmured, turning the pages of the tablet, lingering here and there. He lifted the tablet to show me an older drawing of Genevieve, in which I'd given her the head of a horse, viewed from the front, with her small left breast nearly on a level with the horse's right eye.

Have you ever heard of Picasso, my son?

Something my mother had said once flashed across my memory. A dirty old man, I said. A pervert.

Father Juneau did not smile. I think it's time, Gustave, that you received a proper education. Something to accompany and complement the very improper one you've so far carved out for yourself.

And that is how I became, in a manner of speaking, Father Juneau's apprentice. Every day after school I would follow the priest home to the rectory of the little church in the center of our village, where his housekeeper Madame Lustig, a widow with a neat little mustache reminiscent of Hitler's, would serve us tea and loudly berate Father Juneau for the shag tobacco cigarettes he rolled and smoked, one after the other. Then we would retire to his study, a miniature shrine to art, for Father Juneau had a passion, illicit as all passions are illicit, for modern painting and sculpture. The shelves were piled with books, the walls were lined with prints—except for the obligatory crucifix over the door the entire space was consecrated to Picasso, Miro, Matisse, Giacometti, Chagall.... I told my mother I was going to be an altar boy and she crossed herself and lifted her eyes to the heavens in gratitude. My father only shrank a little farther behind his newspaper. But in fact I spent nearly afternoon in Juneau's company, as he divulged mystery upon mystery to me: modeling, perspective, color. And also the history of painting, his passion: he'd pull down the heavy volumes one after the other until they stacked high upon his desk, where I sat in his chair and he hovered over my shoulder, pointing with his brown finger: Greek sculpture, manuscripts illuminated by monks, the Byzantine, the Gothic, the Italian masters, baroque and rococo, the neoclassical travesties (his word) of the French Academy, English landscape painting, the Impressionists (he worshipped Van Gogh with a touching simplicity, and I believe he styled his own austere bedroom on the famous one at Arles), the German Expressionists, the French Cubists, Picasso and all of his periods up until the war, at which catastrophe his knowledge of the history of art stopped dead as if he himself had died, for I eventually inferred that that was the moment he had gone underground, so to speak, the moment in his own life in which one sacred calling was superseded by another, and though it was perfectly easy for him to order new books and prints, and even perhaps to visit the galleries in Strasbourg, if not Paris, once in a while, for him the glorious world of European art came to an abrupt and appropriate halt with the Guernica of Picasso, which he had a print of that he did not display on the wall, but instead leaned in its frame mixed with a pile of blank and botched canvases that he kept for some reason in the rectory's tiny attic, a crawlspace really, into which he crept one day so as to retrieve the print and show it to me, wordlessly, his bulging pupils flickering over my face as I took in the appalling image, and only downstairs again in his study, before cups of tea brought by a disapproving Madame Lustig, did he explain to me what Guernica was and where it was and what it meant. This went on for months and months, with all the passion and clumsy secrecy of an affair, though in spite of what other boys whispered he never laid a hand on me; or rather, if he did, if he placed his hand on my shoulder while showing me the sketches of Leonardo and massaged quietly and insistently at my collarbone, if he insisted every time on my evening departure that I wash my hands of the chalk or oils that he'd had me sketching with, and stood in the doorway watching me with fervent, furtive intensity; if in fact on more than one occasion there'd been brandy mixed with the tea, and afterwards he'd sit beside me on the little settee in his study which offered the best vantage point for contemplating the only real painting in his study, a ragged impasto of a barley field with a single startling gray streak of paint in the middle of it, like a dull knife or wing in all that burning gold, which he had never quite admitted to having painted himself, if as I say he sat next to me on the settee and rested one hand on my knee and massaged it, and then perhaps the thigh, and then so upward, what of it? His real crime, we both knew, was his love of art, which was a merciful distraction from the idiocies of life in a small rural parish, but a distraction all the same, and a sin, a mortal sin that far exceeded the venial sins of his flesh, for in his love of art was concentrated all his mingled pride and despair, his hopeless unrequited love for what was not god, nor even the image of god (he showed no particular feeling for specifically religious art, instead constantly calling attention to the modeling of the flesh of Christ's thighs in a painting of the Deposition, or to the interplay of shadow and light on the ribcage of Caravaggio's John the Baptist. Next to that passion for form, for light and line and color, how could a few furtive little caresses and soft insincere words compare with that greater crime in which he and I were co-conspirators? I had never before considered the possibility that for every grim and foolish face in my village there was a past, a beforetime, an imaginary peak from which each of them was forever tumbling downward. Father Juneau had not always been Father Juneau; he had been Jean-Paul Juneau, a son of *la Belle Époque*, not a Frenchman at all but a Belgian who'd been a soldier in the Great War when he was only a little older than I was then, who'd seen terrible things, who'd lost, it was intimated, his one first great love in that war (face of the lute-player in a black-and-white image of a Frans Hals painting in a book, *Les Maîtres Néerlandais*, that I sometimes caught the good father lingering over, cigarette ashed and forgotten in his fingers), who after the Armistice had not returned home to his destiny as the son of a mercantile lawyer in Brussels but had boarded a train to Paris, from which he disembarked and, bearing in his hand a letter of introduction that he'd had from the superior officer who'd admired his drawings (another beauty, no doubt, and no doubt killed in action like the lute player), a letter of sufficient import to permit his immediate matriculation at the Ecole des Beaux-Arts, where he began, as he too colorfully put it, "to run down the Muse," to pursue art with a maniacal hunger, not only for himself but for the two dead men he'd loved, slaving day and night to master technique, following the instructions of his teachers to the last degree, absorbing uncritically their freaks and opinions, their wisdom inseparable from their outbursts and tantrums, worshipping with his whole soul the very sawdust on the floors of the studios, feeling each day as he entered the grounds of the Palais that he was again wrapped in *le rêve sacré*, the sacred dream that had been his birthright and from which it had taken a world at war to awaken him (he was given at times to bathos, but I too was young, I too was uncritical, I too was at that time possessed by dreams, and I let much go), standing before nude young men and women, before bowls of fruit, blood blooming in his mind, under the skin of the nudes, under the skin of the fruit, but rendering only their perfect surfaces, that is to say the truth of nudes and fruit, and no one would look his classmate Claude in the eye, Claude who painted with his left hand only in jagged, ungainly stabs of the brush, because the right arm had been taken off at the shoulder at Ardennes, Claude who once turned to Jean-Paul in the w.c. with his cock hanging out, asking for help zipping up again after pissing, or maybe he was asking for a blowjob, it doesn't matter because Jean-Paul turned away in horror (of what was missing? of what was there?), and Claude was found with his throat cut, inexpertly but sufficiently, in the studio the next morning, not in front of his easel but sprawled on the little pediment where the nudes were accustomed to pose, and Jean-Paul left the studio, he went out into the streets and cafes, and he discovered the terrible secret of art—his exact words, *the terrible secret of art*—which was that it can't, won't, be taught in academies, or by masters to apprentices, or at all, yet it must be learned somehow, and he saw the paintings that his teachers sneered at, if they acknowledged them at all, by men just a little older than himself, men who'd given miraculous birth in the years just before the war to what we all now universally acknowledge as the modern, and he met the Americans who had begun to arrive as he had, after the war, men and women who seemed the very children of the modern, birthed by the war, stained in its blood and yet innocent, so innocent, and he began to move in new circles, circles that rippled inward rather than outward, with famous personalities at their centers, personalities that dazzled with the cruel completeness of their gestures, personalities that seemed to need no one and that everyone needed, that were surrounded naturally by accretions of imitators and lovers and models and sycophants, as a glacier carries the earth with it on its travels down from some incomprehensible north, and leaves that earth behind when it withdraws just as inscrutably, in its own good glacial time, and so the years fled and Jean-Paul labored in nearly perfect obscurity, making paintings that sold just occasionally and often enough to keep him from starving, not that he was in much danger from that, as he still received remittances from time to time from his loving mother, without his father's knowledge (I am, he'd said with a smile, a Father disowned by his father, or did he say a Father disowned by the Father?), and so he suffered inconsequentially up until the thirties, when he and everyone else began to suffer in earnest, the remittances stopped with the failure of his father's business and his mother's dementia and death, the market for talented amateurs (that's how he referred to himself, aggrandizing and deprecating at the same time) dried up, and everyone in starved Europe began to gorge themselves once again on an appetite for epic, for big history, but Juneau's hunger led him elsewhere, back to the Church, the masses he'd attended while still a student in the church of Saint Germain des Prés, which he once again began to haunt in spite of its being a long walk or a short Metro ride from his digs in Montparnasse, the church's Romanesque architecture no doubt attracted him as a total antidote to the modern which was once again threatening to leave him high and dry, a spiritual amputee, the winds of a new war stirring his thinning hair, and he became a lay brother of the Dominicans though by temperament he was surely a Jesuit, but no, he was a Dominican, and then took his vows three weeks after the Germans began their offensive, and it was not long after that he was in his black cassock high up in the north tower of Notre Dame watching the Wehrmacht swagger over the Pont Neuf, and thus he entered a dark territory of which he never spoke, from which he never fully emerged, of which only flashes are visible in his slightly hunched back, his chain-smoking, his brown nervous fingers smoothing and smoothing pages or his surplice or what was left of his hair. Then after the war he began his rise, administering masses in the great cathedral, writing sermons and editorials for *Le Figaro*, a posting to Rome, but all the time he nourished undying the flame of modern painting in his heart, and continued to paint a little himself, on the sly. And in 1950 he had his downfall—something political, no doubt, an impolitic word overheard by malicious ears, but the way he spoke, or didn't speak, of the matter somehow persuaded me that it was his passion for art that had been his undoing, that some superior had caught him in flagrante, so to speak, with proscribed books in his rectory or paying some young Italian to model for him, nude of course, which made us brothers under the skin, another cliché he tossed around with ambiguous irony: You and I, Gustave, we are brothers, aren't we, brothers under the skin. Which is a very strange thing for him to have said, since he was old enough to be my grandfather, but perhaps my youth inspired him, and after all it was true that art had brought the both of us nothing but trouble, and it has also brought us together, which was another form of that same trouble. And so it came to pass when I was seventeen (but I looked older, no matter how often I shaved my jaw was blue, as it's gray now, and I stood before Father Juneau in the suit he'd bought for me for my journey to Paris and asked him how I looked and he told me, a convict), when I was seventeen I came to his study and he had a bundle for me (the suit and about a hundred francs in small bills, held together with a paper clip, and also his old brushes, and a tarnished badge or medal that he didn't identify, with a crown at the top, the ribbon long decayed, subsequently determined to be his Croix de

Guerre, signifying either bravery in the face of the enemy or else mere endurance, persistence, duration, I don't know which) and also a letter which he'd written, which he handed me with an ironic twitch of the lips, and then he told me or rather filled in the outlines of the story of his own life, which I've just done for you. And that very morning I left the village of my birth forever for Paris, incomprehensible city which I nevertheless knew better than Strasbourg from Father Juneau's stories and the books and maps we'd pored over, explorers planning a last assault on a lost kingdom populated by hostile natives, and from the Gare de l'Est I made my way on foot, goggling and no doubt goggled at, a giant in a too-small suit and a pair of clogs, and arrived as Father Juneau had done at the gates of the Ecole des Beaux-Arts with his recommendation letter held tightly in my hand. There I was, a creature from the nineteenth century, or maybe even something older than that, medieval, Hugo's hunchback, in Paris, an art student, 1966. Two years later I was absolutely modern, absolutely in love, with a beautiful woman, absolutely beautiful. If I now, an old man, take the most convoluted route possible toward contact with her, toward reminding her of those times, with a message delivered by a messenger unknown to her, to another messenger she may never meet, it is only because I am still at heart that coarse young man, but one who has learned to live, to fit his skin, in spite of everything.

Watching the screen, after midnight or in the haze of late afternoon, when the world is dead, his mouth moving. Like a clean streak in a dirty window in which everything gets reflected so dazzlingly that your chances of seeing through the window are reduced to almost zero. That's what it is like listening to him, the foreign man, the fat man, Gustave.

The new reader has an hour while the baby sleeps. She should clean, she should eat something, she should answer e-mails, above all she should sleep herself. But as she climbs heavily into the unmade bed her hand reaches out as though of its own volition to pick up the hardcover she'd closed far too late the previous night. No bookmark, her finger finds the exact place she left off, the book springs open there of its own accord. Settling into a sleeping position except for her neck crooked uncomfortably against the headboard, telling herself she'll just read a couple of pages before sleep takes hold of her. It is not a novel, it is not a book of poems, it is a book including poems but not of them. She reads a poem—if by *read* we mean passes her eyes over words and sounds them in her mind, subvocalizes them in her throat. The poem is a page long in French and a page long in English and she reads both versions with similar incomprehension. She is or will be the new reader but she is tired tired tired. It is enough for her in her tiredness to sound the language, to ring each word with the little muffled mallet of her tongue, though her lips don't move. The new reader is happy on the surface of words; like her baby she does not think to open the plain or colorful box with the toy inside, but the box itself is her toy. And yet with repeated scannings the box begins to fray; roughly handled a seam splits here and there and something can be heard rattling and jingling underneath. Not the poem, now, but her reading of the poem, and not that either; her misreading, for without quite meaning to the French is becoming English: *Sur mon crâne incliné plante son drapeau noir* becomes sermon crane inclination plants on Japannoir, that's not a word but it ought to be, she thinks drowsily, early Kurosawa, Mifune in a cheap suit, tormented gunsel, there's a word that ought to be in a poem, *gunsel*, like Hansel and Gretel in one body. Is it the new reader who thinks these thoughts or does she occupy a space, a moment, through which these thoughts can pass? Her eyelids getting heavy, the book heavy on her chest, the spine pressing into her sternum, the poem pressing into the wet receptive meshwork of her brain handing off consciousness to unconsciousness, to networks of association, cells associated with rapidly dwindling exterior senses (but her upper lip itches and she must scratch it), rapidly approaching interior ones, recombinant memories, sensory data attached by the slenderest and most mysterious of threads to strong emotions, fear envy lust hatred deprivation anxiety depression curiosity punctuated by outspread patchwork joy. She is sinking and rising, held back by the certain knowledge of the baby's waking, like a balloonist hanging on to a stray rope—in another moment she'll be too high to let go, she's in it for the duration, till the short sharp shock of her plummet to earth, but for now gravity's reversed itself, and on her mind's eye certain images are imprinted:

Ben's face ten years younger, shining below her white belly as he meets her eyes, his mouth on her cunt.

The face of the man she'd always thought of as her father, lined and white as his thin straggling hair, glasses folded and unused on the bedside table, deflated body pillowed on a white sheet stained slightly yellow, masked by plastic and oxygen and doubt, this man she'd loved a stranger to her in more than one way.

A figure in a white robe and hood, masked as though for carnival with a long terrifying nose that curves out like a sinister albino banana, leading her through a riotous crowd by the hand, turning back to glance at her as it pulls her into an alleyway, its face a blade, pulling her hands up to its chest where she feels breasts.

The view out her backyard one night two winters ago when she was pregnant, hand on her belly, looking out at the moonlit snow where a single brown rabbit squatted transfixed in her view till she tapped once on the glass and it spasmed, it hopped, in elemental terror it vanished.

The new reader is sleeping. Her baby is crying. The new reader fights her way up through layers and layers of perfect white sheets on which words are printed, words in elegant typefaces, unreadable, like words that Internet bots come up with to detect other bots, that only humans can pierce, words masked by static, by gridlines, by nonsense.

May sixty-eight. A legendary inscription. As if the floor of the sea had swapped itself with dry land and all the usual creatures—students, cops, judges, booksellers, waiters—had been replaced by their deep-sea analogues: seahorses, sea urchins, sea-snakes, sea-lions. Exactly the same underneath, but our skins were radiant and new. The elements had shifted.

Those of us who were not political—I especially, a lump of Alsatian clay—nevertheless had to learn how to swim in the political. It was not the air we breathed but something more fundamental—the water we swam in. I sprouted gills, my hands were like fins, from any situation I could wriggle my back and be free. Yes there was music and yes there were drugs. But it was, as I say, water. It had to flow somewhere, and we flowed with it, oblivious to the truth: that water will always seek the lowest possible point. I was in love. Not with a woman, but with Charles, my flatmate. He was the shark who taught me how to swim. Lost in my classes, dreaming through the studio hours, I occasionally drifted south to the Sorbonne to attend a lecture that I had heard my otherwise aloof classmates buzzing about: for the most part incomprehensible talks on Marx, on psychoanalysis, on revolutionary consciousness. On a rainy afternoon I crept in steaming to a darkened amphitheater, a vast, overheated space in which it seemed hundreds of bodies were slumbering. At the bottom of the amphitheater the tiny figure of the professor strutted back and forth, while overhead, on a rippling screen, images of statuary flickered into being and disappeared, one by one. The lecturer was saying something about the decline of the Greek spirit; I was fascinated by his big belly, a brilliant white convexity at the center of his abstract figure, and the gleam of his spectacles as he stepped in and out of the path of the projector. There was a haze of smoke in the room, not all of it tobacco. I stumbled into the first empty seat I could find and was immediately confronted with a glowing roach, handed to me from my left. That was Charles. In the sunshine breaking through the massy clouds afterward I was stunned by his beauty: the waving honey hair he wore nearly to his shoulders, the clarity of his skin (myself a mass of pimples and scars), and the way he wore his T-shirt and Levis on his long, sloping body—he was always leaning against something, hips cocked, looking like one of those Greek statues that the lecturer had just been going on about, one whose armlessness seems integral to its beauty. I had seen him before, in the hallways outside the ateliers at the Ecole des Beaux-Arts: he read philosophy but came to art school to score: he said the art students always knew how to find the best hash and they appreciated (said with an unnervingly straight face) his own efforts at consciousness-raising: you artists, he said companionably, you're such dopes, Plato was right to be suspicious of you. And as our friendship began to unfold, I began to understand how very much further from the center of things I was than I had suspected. His friendliness, his openness, seemed genuine and ironic at the same time. Certainly he acted by conviction, for he was a Marxist, the sort that spoke scornfully of the "official" Communists and glowingly of Castro and Che; I meanwhile was unmistakably a product of the working class, or even lower, so that I must have had as much glamour for him as he had for me. He asked me endless questions about the oppression I had suffered at the hands of the state and the Church. I did my best to oblige him, but I could tell he found my stories disappointing. When I tried to tell him about my benefactor, Father Juneau, he refused to listen until I told him Father Juneau was homosexual. Of course, he said, smiling, all those priests are faggots. That's all right then. I understand it all. What he understood, or thought he understood, I didn't dare ask after that.

I had only known Charles for a week before I found

myself living with him: for a flat he had to himself the entire, barely furnished floor of a crumbling former hotel on the Rue de Mézières. All the walls that weren't load-bearing had been knocked down (Charles had knocked them down himself, and proudly showed me the sledgehammer); it was a vast open space out of which Charles sometimes composed rooms with paper curtains that aped Japanese screens but were closer to the ward dividers in a hospital. Every Saturday he would rise late and groom himself in front of the full-length mirror he kept near his bed; then in just his shorts or sometimes nothing at all lead himself through a series of exercises, based I think on yoga but largely invented by himself. Sometimes I would join him and we would stretch and bend and hiss together, like a pair of shadows. On Sundays he woke morose, threw on yesterday's clothes and headed straight out without so much as brushing his teeth, returning only late in the evening; I learned this was the day he visited his parents in Poissy, and was undoubtedly given his allowance, for he would burst in on me as I was painting or reading and recruit me to come out to a rock show or the bars, buying all the drinks and all the drugs, staying up as long as possible, so that neither of us ever made it to our Monday classes. He had lots of girlfriends, of course, in a variety of shapes and sizes and even ages (I was once only a little surprised to discover the henna-haired woman who ran the corner tabac perched primly on the toilet one weekday morning; she couldn't have been a day younger than fifty), but he favored most of all a type he called the Swan: long-necked, small-bosomed girls with long hair like Bardot's or cropped hair like Jean Seberg's. These beauties haunted me, quite literally, for as I said there were no real walls in our flat and so time and time again I'd open my eyes in the dark and, from my mattress, catch glimpses of these naked apparitions gliding to and from Charles's bed. Once in a while, out of curiosity or pity, one of these girls would come to join me on my own mattress on the floor, but not knowing what to say or do, I would just lie there petrified until she withdrew, confused and offended. I recall one particularly humiliating adventure, the morning after one of these encounters: I was in my life-drawing class and as I began to rub charcoal on the paper, I realized that the model was Charles's latest Swan, the same girl who'd come to lie next to me just a few hours before, whispering filthy nothings into my ear and groping for my penis while I had tried to express my diffidence by turning away. It made no difference, she pressed her breasts against my back and reached around to fondle me so that I was forced to grasp her wrist and squeeze it until she cried out. Motherfucker, she said, and stalked off. Now in the studio she sees me by my easel and smirks, then abruptly shifts from her neoclassical pose (a virgin cradling an imaginary jar), ignoring the instructor's protests, and gets down on all fours and thrusts her buttocks in my direction and looks back at me and sticks out her tongue. The electricity in the room shifted suddenly in my direction, though not a soul looked at me; I heard someone laugh once behind me as I stared at the blank blackened tablet, my face burning, my peripheral vision overwhelmed by the dark tufted cleft I dared not confront directly, itself a grin of perfect insolence, and I seemed to hear that laugh a second time (but it was not so, everyone was silent, concentrating, working earnestly to capture the new pose) and I knew that it had belonged to Charles, though he was not enrolled in the class and should not have been there. And now comes the most humiliating part: not the humiliation itself—not the compromised position that Charles's Swan had put me in, nor Charles's own easy contempt, but the fact that I was now excited, intent, and hard as a stone. I began to sketch, using just a rubber eraser and my fingers, working with tremendous rapidity to lighten the charcoal veneer in the right places, so that curve and volume and depth began to make their appearances, each globe of her rump taking shape, and the grimy soles of her feet, the valley of her spine leading down to her angular shoulders like white outcroppings in a black bay, the black mass of hair and the sliver of visible face and just the tip of her tongue now panting between the white rows of her teeth, and then picking up again the stick of charcoal and working with intensity to deepen and blacken the profusion of pubic hair, which in my drawing seemed like the outer layers of a vortex leading into the null space, the utter darkness of her asshole and cunt, I couldn't see them with my eyes but the charcoal could. My hands completely blackened, I stepped back and almost bumped into Charles, who had stepped away from his own drawing to study mine. He said nothing. But that night, in our usual café, where some awful folksinger was the center of attraction so that we had the sidewalk nearly to ourselves, in spite of the November damp, he jumped to his feet and moved into the crowd and returned with the same Swan on his elbow. She looked at me unsmiling, her cornflower eyes kohl-rimmed under the sort of glasses John Lennon had made famous.

I thought I ought to introduce you two properly, Charles said. Gustave Lessy, this is Simone.

Enchanté, said Simone drily. She had an English accent.

I looked at Charles, but he just winked at me. He made a show of pulling Simone's chair out for her, then turned his own around and straddled it. Simone asked me for a light and I took out my lighter. She leaned forward and cradled my fist, eyes meeting mine. The flame flashed sardonically in her glasses.

Charles says you're not really a faggot, she said, blowing smoke.

He's a virgin, Charles explained.

Virgins, faggots, she said, no difference. Is that

what you are?

I blushed my answer.

Right, she said in English. She looked at Charles and they both laughed. I pushed back suddenly from the table, which screeched. People looked at us, at me, towering clumsily over the beautiful ones.

My brother, Charles said easily, smiling up at me.

Rough customer, Simone said to him. It's all right, she said to me. She smiled at me, warmly this time, but still with a hint of a taunt in it. Come back to my place, eh?

It was all arranged, apparently. Simone put out her smoke and moved around the table to put her hand on my shoulder.

You're very strong, she said. Statement of fact.

We went back to the flat she shared with a roommate on the Boul' Mich. The roommate was sitting on the sofa, by a lamp, absorbed in a book; other books, papers, and pencils were scattered on the low table in front of her. She was short but wonderfully shaped, a true hourglass, not a Swan at all. She wore jeans and a peasant blouse and no makeup that I could see, her bare feet tucked under her. Her skin was nearly translucent, her face a glowing oval in the frame of her dark hair. She looked up distractedly at the jingling of Simone's key.

Hey, she said. In English, with an American accent.

Have you seen Louis around? Simone asked, as

though they'd only just been discussing him. The other girl shook her head. Simone led me by the hand to a closed door, opened it, then seemed to remember something.

Gustave, she said to the girl, indicating me, and then reversing, said the other's name.

Enchantée, I said, meaning it.

Yeah. She looked me up and down and then raised an eyebrow to Simone, who shrugged.

No good deed— Simone started.

Goes unpunished, finished the other. She cocked her head wryly and gave me a little wave. Go to it, then. *Bonsoir.*

Bonsoir, I said, turning for one last look at her as Simone pulled me into the bedroom and kicked shut the door with a bang.

But does it not appear that our view of things just then, in Gustave's dark backward, stands outside his own possible point of view? We remain for a lingering moment with M, her hair shining under the reading lamp, the slam of Simone's door dying away, guessing what it conceals. The truth and verity of the camera: it shows only what can be shown. How then are we to receive Gustave's narrative? Do we follow him back into time by means of flashback, seeing what he describes? Show don't tell. But what I show is what he tells. Gustave framed by the blank sober wall of the hotel room, lit from the side by the window through which the lights of the city radiate. Imperceptibly, excruciatingly, the camera zooms in, millimeter by millimeter, as he tells his story: medium shot of his torso and head, close-up of the great gray slab of his face, dyed slick hairs on top, chins waddling below; further close-up into the essential features, his eyes and eyebrows and nose and cheekbones and moving lips; extreme close-up of a single feature, but which? The eyes alone, a single eye, the pupil darting, contracting, dilating, a tiny Lamb, our camera, in the center? Or the wet lips lit occasionally by the tip of the pink tongue, his white dentures and gray gums churning grotesquely? The words, the words. To accommodate them must the camera start ever further back, tracking in from street level into the hotel, riding a baggage cart in subtle slow motion, passing through the expensive hush of the lobby and under the mild indifferent gaze of the concierge into the elevator, confronting the closed door as the floors ring off, and when it opens, gliding out into the carpeted hallway and down through the soft glow of tear-shaped sconces past the numbered doors to a particular door that swings open at the last moment to reveal it, the bed, the television, the telephone, the other camera posed between the two men seated before the window? Must we travel even further outward, ever upward, until we take in the entire horizon of the city—spread out on its vast plain, divided by the snaking river, no visible gap between east and west except perhaps in the shapes of architecture, the east more rectilinear, the west fractal in its conformation to the vast park and, at its edge, the black shimmer of lakes, while to the east nothing is visible beyond a more fatal blackness, hinting at forests, at nothingness. Taking in the widest possible scene, at the limits of intelligibility, then swooping down like the world's slowest bird of prey toward the city center, its *Mitte*, down to the black featureless rectangle of the roof, and somehow through it, as if it were peeled off to reveal the cellular life of the separate rooms in which people sleep and fuck and stare at screens, focusing now on the singular cell from above where are grouped the lucid geometries of bed and desk, lamp and table, and two black heads, two bodies, one camera on its tripod with red LED glowing steady toward and into which we finally plunge, oblivion of sight that we meet with the moment Gustave's story returns us to the present? Or must space expand still further, so that the camera flies from yet another great Western capital—Vienna, Rome, Zurich, London, the Paris preserved by Gustave, antecedent to the city of now—flies from a crumbling high monument of the present eastward into Gustave's past? From Paris itself, Paris of memory, overlay or underlay to the Paris briefly wandered and scrutinized by the new reader, then the Paris of the twenty-first century, the lens streaked with oily rain obscuring our view of the expected (the bridges, the churches, the Orsay, the rhinestone sparkle of the Tower at dusk, the men in shabby clothes sleeping with hats over their faces on the quays of the Seine, the faces of Sarkozy and his wife, the fires in the banlieues, the overturned cars, the graffiti, the exploded schools) so that the Paris of our fathers' time can flicker into sight—Gustave's past, a generation's past, the exuberant troublemakers with their pale faces and red banners, cops with short combs on their helmets like embarrassed roosters, the tear gas then joining hands with the tear gas now, the hurled stones, Algiers under everything (*sous les pavés le pavé*), Paris of revolutions, now and always, what goes around comes around, sticks around, comes aground. Drunk on the violence of recollection: Gustave's eye, Gustave's mouth, Gustave's confession, Gustave's Paris—these things are now ours, the camera gives them to us, memory becomes sensation, to thrill us for once and to be forgotten for all.

Blind austerity of men and women at odds. A failure to communicate comes of communicating monologues (in the sense of communicating rooms: the door exists but who has the key?). They look into one another's faces but not at them. Seeing is a poet's prerogative; readers are just looking. Talking past each other: even when we practice active listening, repeating everything the other says and affirming what was said, the mind wanders, leaving little trails of thought, word, desire, like smoke dispersing in the air, like extinct fish no one will ever again catch.

I thought only of M, he said. I would see Simone now and again still, at the flat. I would be lying on my mattress with a lamp, reading, half-listening to the grunts and cries. After a while Simone would enter the circle of light, wearing only Charles's white shirt, smoking a joint and weaving slightly. She would sit cross-legged on the floor and talk to me of her life. There was no more cruelty from her, but I could tell even after that night something about me amused her; I could hear it in her voice. I would listen to her talk because sometimes she would mention her flatmate. M was the daughter of an American diplomat who had worked in Saigon, and it was there that she began her study of French. Her father had lost his post—some kind of scandal, Simone didn't know the details, though she dearly wished to—and returned to the United States, but his daughter had gone to Paris and was studying French literature at the Sorbonne. She was a very serious girl, Simone said, but they mostly got along, and anyway she could surprise you. For example, one cold and rainy evening in February M suddenly decided she wanted to go dancing. It was the middle of the week and there wasn't much on, but M just pulled on her raincoat and took Simone by the hand and took her to the nearest bar—a workingman's place a few blocks south of their apartment. Even Simone had to pause in the entrance as she took in the black and grimy floor of the place, the men with their rough clothes and stony faces, the total absence of other women. M just sauntered up to the bar and ordered a couple of Pernods. One of the younger men—he had dirty blond hair under his cap, Simone remembered—got next to M and said something to her, something offensive, Simone was sure. M turned away like he wasn't even there, handed one of the drinks to Simone, who was still just a few feet inside the door, and then stepped lightly over to the jukebox. I imagine her bent over its light, her shapely silhouette from behind as great a provocation to the bar's patrons as her American accent. It was mostly French pop, awful stuff, Simone said, but then she found what she wanted and pushed the buttons. She expected a rock song, Elvis perhaps—Simone loved Elvis—or the Beatles, who were already a bit of a cliché at the time in my opinion, Gustave said. But it was actually something slow and dreamy, Johnny Mathis I think, and M started swaying to that slow music, a hundred-and-one strings, all alone in that filthy tavern in the spotlight of men's eyes. I think Simone was afraid, though she didn't say so, but her way of being afraid was to bristle at every point, sharp, like a porcupine. So she started to dance too, in the now silent room, everything still but the smoke from cigarettes and the two women, who began to dance with each other, and M, who was a good few centimeters shorter than Simone, put her head on Simone's shoulder, and they danced like that, swaying to the beat for a few moments even after the song had died away. That broke the spell and a man approached the women, a little older than the others, and he looked Simone in the eye (M's face still hidden, pressed into Simone's chest) and said, It's time to go. I, who had been on my back listening, eyes half-closed, now rolled onto my side and saw Simone sitting there in the light reflected off the ceiling from the streetlamp, her face as beautiful as it was blank. She looked at me. Watch yourself, she told me. And then: She'll be at the party tomorrow night. And then with a kind of shrug rolled herself to her feet and retreated into the dark, and after a while I could hear her voice and Charles's, indistinct, and then their lovemaking would begin again.

The party took place late the next night in a Montparnasse art gallery which seemed at first to be empty, white walls, except for the people cramming the main room, packing it with smoke and dancing and drinking and talk. A reel-to-reel recorder had been set up and was playing what sounded to me like backwards music—I want to say it was The Beatles, "Revolution 9," but it isn't likely, that album wasn't released until November of that year, long after this story ends. It must have been Stockhausen or Cage. But let it be the Beatles—imagine the Beatles playing as I searched that gallery that seemed crowded with people and empty of art at the same time. There was a table piled high with pamphlets I browsed for a while in an attempt to get my bearings. The music was utterly undanceable but people were dancing. Over the heads of the crowd I saw a little space in front of one of the speakers where some women were dancing by themselves. I couldn't see M, but then I saw a bare, sinuous hand rise momentarily out of the pit of heads and bodies and gesture like a bird, or like Isis on the wall of a pyramid. I edged my bulk into the crowd and in a moment I was standing in front of M, who was swaying to her own private beat—it must have been, because the music that was playing had no discernible beat, the lack of melody was beginning to drive me crazy and I couldn't understand how all the others could stand it, could just go on talking with each other about Mao and what Godard had to say about the Nanterre revolt and how good the pot was. I myself had taken a few hits on a joint earlier, it didn't affect me, it was literally the atmosphere of the time. M's eyes were closed and I couldn't think of what to do but stand there, swaying slightly. I had to lean over and roar in her ear to be heard. Hello, I shouted. She opened her eyes slowly without looking at me directly. It's Gustave, I said. Simone's friend.

Simone's not here, she said, and gestured vaguely at another part of the room.

I know. It's you I want to see.

Why? she said in English.

I didn't know what else to do so I grabbed her by the hand—that bird hand. She pulled away from me.

Please let's go outside, I said. Panting a little, eyes unlidded.

We skirted the walls to avoid the crush. Outside on the street it was raining lightly. I took note of a police van halfway down the block, and three or five *flics* were standing around in the street next to it, smoking. We stood under an awning.

Gustave, she said, trying it out. Can I call you Gus?

I'd rather you didn't, I mumbled. Then, hastily: Yes.

We were quiet for a moment. She took out a packet of cigarettes and offered me one. I took it loosely between my fingers and let it hang there. She offered me the flame of her lighter and I shook my head.

Simone's told me about you, she said. She looked at me frankly. She says you have a gigantic dick. But it doesn't seem that big because you're so big. In fact, that makes it look kind of small.

Evasive maneuvers seemed called for. You study philosophy, don't you? I said to the rain.

I study philosophy, she echoed.

Plato? I said, knowing immediately it was the wrong thing, the wrong name or note.

All of philosophy is just footnotes to Plato, she said kindly.

Who said that?

His name was Whitehead.

I've heard of Sartre of course, I said. I've seen his play. And Beauvoir. Someone pointed her out to me on the street once.

De Beauvoir, she corrected. Yes, I like her. She knows the truth about women.

Which is?

You don't really want to know, she said, picking tobacco off of her tongue.

I don't read any philosophy, I said stupidly. Then, to compound it: I study graphic design. I want to study art, but I study graphic design.

She smiled up at me. I know.

The door to the gallery opened and a stream of young women and a few men emerged, giggling. The men, to show their bravado, began to shout at the cops down the street, calling them Fascists and so forth. The cops stood there, heads cocked to one side like curious dogs. I moved a few steps away from them, but when M didn't move, I came back. She didn't turn around.

Charles stepped out with a woman on his arm, a new swan, not Simone—this one had a cropped peroxide cap for hair and layers of white foundation to render her face sepulchral and ghostly. This place is dead, Gustave. I've got some hash—we're going to the cemetery. You and your friend want to come along? Before I could say anything M had said Sure, why not, in that sharp flat American way that cut through and mocked the very notion of hesitation. We began to trail behind Charles and the other woman down the Rue Huyghens toward the vast and silent expanse of the cemetery, shut tight for the night. When we reached the boulevard, we steered past the northern entrance and then ran through the parked cars, across the wet street, to the high stone wall. We'll never get over, M said. Charles looked at me and I went and placed myself spread-eagled against the cold wet wall, ivy tickling my face. He laced his fingers together and M, without hesitating, stepped into his grip and he hoisted her onto my back. I felt the soft weight of her for a moment, then she climbed onto my shoulders and to the top of the wall. The new Swan was next, then Charles himself. Charles and his Swan were giggling, but suddenly they stopped and Charles hissed at me to come on, someone was coming. I glanced to my right and saw a light streaking in the mist. Digging my fingers into the mass of ivy, I hoisted myself to the top of the wall, swung my legs over, and dropped to the hard ground below, where the others were waiting. We held our breaths, listening to the crunch of gravel on the other side of the wall, and then the crunching passed.

We were in the city of the dead. Rows upon rows of upright stone, some of it carved into angels with and without wings, some of it in obelisks, many crosses, many simple slabs. We walked down the narrow rows in twos, not talking much, passing a joint back and forth. Charles and his Swan were ahead of us—he was hunting for a particular tomb, Proudhon's I think. I was only astonished to be there, at the center of a silent universe with this beautiful girl who barely came up to my sternum walking beside me.

Do you think about death? she asked.

You're the philosopher.

I mean your own death. Do you think about it?

I don't, I said. I felt again that this was the wrong thing to say—that I was, as you Americans say, blowing it. But I couldn't pretend to think thoughts I didn't have. I tried to find a way to say this.

I want to be a painter, I said with forced loftiness. I'm interested in what I can see. I can't see death. Only decay.

Look around and you'll see both.

We were indeed surrounded by the dead, and by a dead darkness impossible to find in Paris. It reminded me of home, at night, but inverted: instead of a square of light surrounded by the dark (with the strong ceaseless life of the river felt rather than seen, never far off) we were in what I felt to be a vast field of blackness haloed by the city. Except that the tombs caught the light, wet as they were. The white marble ones in particular seemed to be on fire, but coldly. And the shadows were crazy, falling in all directions like chess pieces swept off the board.

Brancusi's around here somewhere, I said, stumbling. And Chaim Soutine. Do you know his work? He was a great friend of Modigliani. He painted carcasses that look like faces. And faces that look like carcasses.

M smiled up to me. Indeed this counselor, she quoted, is now most still, most secret, and most grave. Who was in life a foolish prating knave.

What does "prating" mean?

M shrugged. We had come to a stop at a crossroads between graves while Charles and his girl kept on moving ahead. They were leaning together as though drunk, barely supporting each other, like the shadows.

Simone says you're from Vietnam.

She said that? I'm not. Nobody's from Vietnam.

The Vietnamese are, I said stupidly.

We are all Vietnamese, she said. Quoting again

Aren't you an American?

I lived in America. Not anymore.

But you're not from there.

You're more American than I am, she said, glancing up at me.

What does that mean?

Nothing.

If you're saying I'm provincial, you're right, I said. You can't insult me with that. In fact, you can't insult me at all. Charles tries sometimes. He doesn't understand what it is to come from nowhere and have nothing. But Americans are rich. I'd like to be rich, but I'm not. So you shouldn't say I'm American.

She smiled. You're kind of dumb, she said. I like that.

I thought she wanted me to kiss her, but it seemed ridiculous. Standing like that, in the wet cemetery (the mist had gathered itself into a proper rain at this point, streaking her dark hair into commas on her forehead), I felt as I've felt so often the grotesqueness of my height. She was so far away.

Gustave, mon vieux, big old man in a bespoke pin-striped suit, pear-shaped shadow on a flimsy chair, dust motes dancing in a last shaft of sunlight pouring past his shoulder, nearly caressing his empty scalp. The listener is occluded, there's only us, the eaves-droppers, the voyeurs, still trying to grasp the picture that his thousand words are composing. Still talking in other words, his fingers laced together, looking steadily into the camera, violet glints in his gray-blue eyes.

I began to see M more often, yet there was no question of anything between us. For one thing she had a boyfriend, a Vietnamese student named Ly Cam. I asked her if she only dated Vietnamese men, and she said Yes the way she sometimes did, not to mean yes but to tell me I should stop asking stupid questions. And that's how she answered all the questions I asked her that were meant, in my clumsy way, to open up a path between us for the kiss I'd wanted to give her in the cemetery that night. One evening we were in a café and I was drunk and I asked her if she wanted to know how strong I was. Yes, she said looking down. But I was drunk enough to ignore the real meaning of that yes, and so without pausing I scooped her up in my arms, spread my legs apart, and lifted her over my head like she was a dumbbell. Everyone was looking at us and hooting, applauding, mocking me. I am strong! I bellowed like a gored ox. I am strong!

Please put me down, M said in the gentlest voice I'd ever heard, and so after a moment I did.

In spite of this behavior M continued to tolerate my presence, in the halls and courtyards of the Sorbonne, at the seedy bars she favored, in the apartment she shared with Simone. I was far from the only moth drawn to the flame of those two women, fundamentally similar as women are, yet with completely different capacities for imagination and for danger. Often enough I'd find Ly Cam there, bearded like Che, sitting cross-legged on the floor strumming his guitar and singing Woody Guthrie songs in his own private melange of Vietnamese, English, and French. He was half my size, smaller even, exactly M's height; if I worried him he gave no sign. And really I gave him no reason to worry, in spite of my clowning: I was simply built on a different scale than he and M, so very less fine-boned in body and in mind, so that he couldn't have foreseen any connection more profound than curiosity. Ly Cam was very popular: the French students sat at his feet and asked him questions about the war and his sufferings; plus it was reputed that he had access to the best drugs. He played to their sympathies, talking about national liberation and the heroism of Mao and Ho Chi Minh, though M had told me he was the son of an ARVN officer, a personal crony of Diem's. She said this with an indifference that puzzled me.

Doesn't that make him a hypocrite? I asked her one rainy afternoon when I had her to myself, except for Simone and one of her boyfriends shut up in her room, from which occasionally a low growl would emanate.

He thinks he's sincere, she answered. Who am I to judge? Do you know who my father is?

But you sleep with him, don't you?

She looked at me pityingly.

How can you sleep with someone who represents himself one way but is really completely a different way?

It's in the past, she said. Who he was in Saigon, who his father is—that doesn't tell me who he is. And neither does what he says, or what he believes.

What's left, then?

She gave me a direct look. It's his smell.

You're serious?

Yes.

So what you're saying then, I said, getting angry, is that the sex is so good it doesn't matter that he's a liar. A fake.

No.

Well?

I don't just mean his smell, that just seems like the best word for it. It's his feel. I can feel him. I look at him, I stand a few inches from him, I touch him, and I just know he's a good person. Plus he listens to me.

I listen to you, I said. You will notice as I recount

this conversation I do not spare myself. I did not spare myself then either. My own sense of dignity, the peasant's reserve with which I greeted the strange kaleidoscope that was the Paris of my fellow young people, always seemed beside the point when it came to M. I let myself hang open with her, like a tongue hangs out of a shoe.

She shook her head. You don't listen. You're not listening now. You devour, but you don't listen.

A long, steadily rising cry caused the door to Simone's bedroom to vibrate. Neither of us looked away from the table where our empty coffee cups were. We could both all too easily visualize what was going on in there.

So what do I smell like? I asked. She sighed.

Like the river, she said. Not the Seine, but a river in the country. Like silt. Earth and water. Paint, of course. Turpentine.

A good smell? I asked.

Actually I can't smell much of anything these days, she said. Too many cigarettes.

Quite a philosophy you have there, I said with some bitterness.

My open door is my philosophy, she said. Anyone can walk in. Even you, Gustave. And if someone doesn't belong here, sooner or later he'll walk out again.

Well, I'm not going anywhere, I said a bit too loudly, folding my hands behind my head and kicking out my legs to make the point.

She smiled sadly. Yes, Gustave. You are.

She was right. Things fell apart, or fell together. When the time came Charles was off like a shot to the marches and speeches at Nanterre—the deadly dull suburbs he used to complain about were suddenly the center of the student universe. But I kept going to class and doing my figure studies and showing up at all hours at M's flat, where she continued to tolerate my presence. The door was never locked, so sometimes when I showed up nobody would be there, or it would just be Simone and one of her boyfriends, and by this point Simone had decided I was completely uninteresting so they would just ignore me. Or M would be there with Ly Cam, and they'd both be wearing thin robes and smoking hash and Ly Cam would be playing his guitar, and there'd be an odor, I almost want to say a stench, rising from their bodies, a hot dank smell, and only then would I be so depressed I'd just turn right around in the doorway and go home again. Otherwise there was no insult, no gesture of indifference that I wouldn't put up with—I was like a dog that licks the hand that beats him. Though truth be told, M was never cruel, at least not deliberately. She was just forgetful—it was part of her beauty, part of what made her seem so intensely *there* when she was there, when her mind wasn't drifting as it so often did like a cloud over forlorn landscapes, like the rice paddies and burning jungles we saw every night on television. If she did bring her attention to bear on me, as she had that night in the cemetery, it was like drinking electricity. She was the first to ever listen to me, and so I learned to talk from her, to her, as I'm talking now, though I'd spent most of my life up to that time locked in the silence of looking, brute slab of a boy that no one looked at, who lived in his eyes.

Speaking, Gustave's eyes are shut, smooth eggs in the heavy trapezoidal slab of his face, with wrinkles at the edges evocative of epicanthic folds. So, he says, lips twitching beneath his mustache, and again, so. He opens his eyes, gray unrippling pools meeting the camera.

So finally May came, the May you've heard about. Up came the students and the workers, marching, filling the streets and squares. The famous slogans appeared, the paving stones were pulled up, the barricades that are a part of the French legend, that every French child secretly imagines himself standing upon like Gavroche, daring a phalanx of soldiers to fire; they were erected, they came to pass. I also took part, following Charles lead to march with the rest, to shout with the rest, to hurl bricks at the police wearing a bandanna soaked in Coca-Cola to ward off the tear gas. In the Ecole des Beaux-Arts I and the other art students were deputized to create posters, stencils, propaganda, working all day and long into the night in shirtsleeves, listening to the increasingly panicked music of radio reports as the Latin Quarter caught fire, red and black paint on my hands, arms, face, clothes. For one day even I spoke for the movement: Charles's Sorbonne groupuscule deputized me to go to the Citroen factory in the 15th to meet with the young workers there. My class background, Charles explained, made me an ideal spokesman and go-between: I was a sort of centaur, half-student, half-worker. In fact I couldn't have had less in common with these sons of smoke and metal, but my appearance I suppose was authentic enough: the size of my body, the size of my hands. From a glassed-in office that had been hastily vacated by the managers I was briefed by some of the foremen and union representatives, then led out to the factory floor where hundreds of young men stood in coveralls shouting, a terrifying spectacle, I had no experience with public speaking, I was led out to a sort of catwalk above them, flanked by other beefy men, the pressure of their bodies on my own reassured me and I said to the workers, Strike, and they shouted Yes; I said in a louder voice, not reading from a script but remembering what Charles had told me, The students and the workers are equally oppressed, for the destiny of the students is to become capitalists, your masters, and they refuse to commit this crime, to be accessories to crime or to take any part in crime, and the young workers (who were French workers, after all, and who'd no doubt read much more Marx than I had) did not see this as strange or condescending or contradictory, they shouted *Vivent les étudiants, Vivent les travailleurs*, as though they were the same thing, and waved their red banners in the air so beautifully, in long streaks the pennants crossed and recrossed the air above the factory floor where I haltingly but then with growing confidence addressed them with a megaphone that had been handed to me, becoming louder and more strident, until one of the other men tapped me firmly, almost a punch in the upper arm, and I yielded the floor, leaned perilously against the narrow rail gasping from the effort, the exhilaration of being a movement's mouthpiece. Intoxicating, this enlargement of the ego but of the space it usually occupied: I had become a vessel of something, a spirit or a power, that was quite beyond my comprehension. For hours and days it seemed I'd been listening to Charles or M or even Simone (who'd cut off all her hair in a revolutionary gesture that sublimated her medusan sexuality, that transferred all that smoky energy from the hair that had shrouded her gaze and neck into her lips and fingertips and hips, so that I wanted to sleep with her again, it somehow brought her closer to M, to M's M-ness, but Simone wouldn't sleep with me again and M would not sleep with me at all; as for Charles, he'd come once to my bed late after a party with nothing but a copy of *Paris Match* over his blonde crotch, grinning puckishly, and without thinking I threw back the covers and invited him in and we spooned for a while, not saying much, my lips on the back of his neck and my cock nestling between his hard firm buttocks without quite becoming erect, and we fell asleep like that and in the morning he was gone) talking or even reading to me directly from essays, books, and pamphlets, and I'd read some of these books and pamphlets myself: Sartre and de Beauvoir, naturally, and Mao's *Little Red Book* (Charles's favorite), some English poems that M loved, and the prison writings of Gramsci (I remember one lazy afternoon lying on my stomach in M's apartment while she patiently explained to me the difference between state power and civic power, the coercive power without versus the coercive power within, and I listened and drew her, as had become my habit, but with the left hand so to speak, for I was listening to the hum of her voice and also through the open windows there were already at that time shouts and songs and sirens on the street pulsing by, recurrent events of sound that gradually accelerated into the heart of May, all of which ended up in the swift lines and subtle crosshatching of the drawing, M pacing imitating Charles with one finger in the air), also of course there was much talk of the Situationists and the art of the happening, which I as an inveterate and incorrigible slave of the pencil and brush was curious about but could not in my peasant's heart accept as art, though I could full well appreciate the power of sensation, as I appreciated the sensation of the movies we went to, late at night, every night, we saw Godard Truffaut Rosselini Pontecorvo Pasolini but also American films of the previous decade, and I still remember sitting side by side with Charles and Simone and M with our eyes and skins shining in the dark watching Marlon Brando's sly and endless humiliation in *On the Waterfront* (curiously oblivious to the traitorous and counter-revolutionary reputation of the film's director), or Jimmy Stewart in the ecstatic vise of looking forever at the tumbling body of Kim Novak, or Rock Hudson cherishing the secrets of chastity in bed with Doris Day, or anything with Humphrey Bogart, especially *In a Lonely Place* where he's the screenwriter suspected of murder: as I say these films were for us like the happenings of the Situationists in that we could feel precisely or obscurely just how they pulled the skin off of reality, pulled off our own skins and made us raw with feeling and perceiving, and yet I could not call this art because for me art meant beauty and it still means beauty. And there is not much beauty in the story I have to tell of myself as a young man in love with a woman and in love with a man and in love with their cause, without ever really having understood woman, man, or cause.

Early in the course of the Events M said to me lightly, Let's go to the peace talks. A lark to the Right Bank to witness the arrival of the delegation of the Republic of South Vietnam at the Hotel Claridge. A crowd had gathered, small and peaceful by the standards that were currently being set in the Latin Quarter, held back by the humorless helmeted police, people straining their necks to see the front of the hotel, which was a dead zone, cleared for the arrival of the delegation in their limousines. A cop was shouting at a teenage boy who had climbed a streetlamp to see better, threatening him with arrest. Another boy, a young man really, no younger than myself, in sunglasses with a leather coat and his collar turned up moved among us pointing mock-surreptitiously at various people and objects, muttering the arcane letters CIA, CIA, over and over again. Perhaps he was accusing himself. Some people held signs: US OUT OF VIETNAM, etcetera. M was probably the only American in the crowd. She didn't chant slogans, or wave a sign; short, all she saw was a sea of shoulders. Then a ripple ran through us: the delegation had arrived, preceded by a pair of police on motorcycles. People pushed, straining forward: caught in an eddy, M and I were separated from Charles and Simone. The cops manning the line warned us back. The black limousines were opening their doors.

I can't see, Gus, M said to me.

I edged my bulk into the masses of young men and old Communists and forced an opening at the edge of the cordon, face to face with *les flics* and a few anonymous men in suits (CIA, I heard the young man in the leather coat mutter again). The sun glided onto the roofs of the long black cars. Her hand in my hand. The hotel doorman stepping back in a kind of salute. The voices behind us doubling in volume and intensity as men got out, slightly built men, no uniforms other than their business suits, old men with weathered faces, Chinese-looking to my inexperienced eye, circled around one tall austere-looking American man with straight slicked back graying hair and an imperial nose, the ambassador-at-large. At his appearance the crowd's frenzy heightened. M's grip on my hand became painful, she was standing on tiptoe, I unlatched her and moved her in front of me, without thinking took her by the armpits and raised her two feet in the air, like a doll, so she could see. She hung there looking, breathing, I held her motionless and steady, the crowd could not budge me. Flashbulbs, reporters were photographing the ambassador who smiled, one hand raised in benediction, turning so that everyone could get a view, while the much smaller men behind him, the Vietnamese, Thieu's lackeys, impassive, wearing sunglasses, while a second limo disgorged its contents. The tall American turned one last time to the crowd, no longer smiling, leaning down a little listening to something one of the Vietnamese was saying, intent, one hand on his shoulder, nodding, straightening up again, flash of teeth, acknowledging us, turning away.

Put me down, I heard M say. And in a lower, almost guttural voice: That was my father. Wherever he steps is American soil. American ground. Wherever he treads is bloody history. Paved with smiles.

I lowered her to the ground. They were all small

in the entranceway of the grand hotel, the second limo lurched forward to cut them off further from the crowd, they were turning, people were shouting, CIA yelled the leather-jacketed man, hey hey LBJ how many kids did you kill today, the men were walking the red carpet, were swallowed by ornate doors, were gone. My hand groped for M's but she had pulled away, was fighting her way back out of the crowd, Simone and Charles already gone, off to the next demo, I caught her sitting on the curb half a block away, staring at nothing.

That was your father?

She didn't answer, just stuck out a hand. Help me up.

I thought his name was Harriman.

Forget it, she said, looking up at me, dry-eyed, smiling. She patted my huge hand. Forget it.

And I did, until just now, here in this hotel room, with you.

Those were, as they say, the days. But it wasn't all tear gas and rock music, there were longeurs, still points around which the world turned, as the thing grew and leaped and metastasized from the complaints of students into a mass movement that had brought, as they say, all of France to its knees. We went to the movies, to lectures, we argued with each other in the Sorbonne and on the stage of the Odeon where spontaneous, sometimes very funny skits took place mocking DeGaulle, Pompidou, LBJ, the CGT, even our own leaders—I remember a tall boy with a pillow under his sweater and a red clown wig, pretending to be interviewed by an obsequious reporter. Committees, committees, trying to maintain some kind of order within the larger chaos, picking up trash on the Sorbonne grounds, fixing the toilets, organizing the donations of food that came in with astonishing regularity, like grace itself, from the grocers and shopkeepers and delivery men sympathetic to the cause. Money was almost meaningless, one committee was set up to investigate the possibility of a student-printed and student-administered currency to challenge the franc, the pound, the dollar. The Communists and the Socialists, grown men, serious men, came to visit us, to talk with the students but more often to be lectured by them, to do them homage, almost humbly, in awe of what we had accomplished, astonished and uneasy at the spirit that prevailed everywhere, the shaggy dog joke of the revolution waiting for its punchline, in the meantime everyone behaving as if liberation had already come, as if being young were enough. It almost was. We were never bored but there was still time, somehow endless time in a single month, between actions and riots and speeches there was sex and reading and movies and football and theater and art and even sleeping, people slept well when they slept, they fell down wherever they were, in ateliers and lecture halls and in the apartments of friends and strangers, angelic smiles on their faces. And the days went on.

And it seemed that reality, what we had once taken for reality, was well and truly suspended, permanent vacation, no future to worry about. I take my desires for reality because I believe in the reality of my desires. My slow fat heavy body was slower to take in this message than the others. But I began to feel it in my limbs. I was looking at her differently now, when she was listening to someone else, laughing, arm in arm with Charles and Simone, dancing in the streets, hysterical with joy. But still, if she caught me looking, I looked away.

But finally some alchemy of indifference and curiosity led her, one rainy afternoon when Charles and Simone were out, to agree to pose for me. It was a kind of dare she made herself that I was the vehicle for—I did not flatter myself that her willingness to be painted was different in kind from her willingness to tolerate my simple oafish presence. But she did admire my skills as a draughtsman. I had come dripping from the school where I had been engaged in my usual practice of poster-making, left my portfolio in the living room while I dried off in the bathroom. When I came back she had my drawings out on the coffee table and leaned over them, frowning, a cigarette burning unattended in the ashtray balanced on the sofa's arm. She looked up at me and gestured at a pastel drawing of a large woman with broad hips and low hanging breasts, posed so that she appeared all buttocks and thighs, but the head and hands were waifish and delicate, connected improbably but firmly to her lower half by a sinuous sway of spine and back.

Does she really look like this? Your model?

That's how she looks to me.

But would I recognize her if I saw her on the street?

Perhaps.

She lifted the sheet, a bit roughly, to expose the next drawing: a nude man in heroic posture, as if he had just won a prizefight, one fist in the air. His muscles were huge and exaggerated, like those of a comic book character, but his genitals were exact and ordinary—their ordinary proportions made the rest of him seem inflated like a parade balloon. She laughed and glanced up at me and a quick little spark crossed the smoky air between us, a spark I hadn't really felt since that night in the cemetery. She looked at another drawing, and another. Then:

You should draw me.

Truly?

Yes.

Have you modeled before? I asked. Conscious of an unavoidable sleazy lewdness to the question, I tried to make a joke of it by waggling my eyebrows, as if I were Groucho and she was Margaret Dumont.

Not for drawings.

Photographs? I asked, removing an imaginary cigar from my lips.

She just smiled. When can we do it?

Well...

Why not now? What do you need?

What if they come back?

Then they come back.

Well. I don't have my crayons with me. Or an easel.

Here's a pencil. And the card table.

All right.

She had stepped to the mono turntable parked precariously on a bookshelf and lowered the needle: a Bud Powell piano riff punctuated the air.

Where do you want me?

Producing a joint from her purse, lighting it, offering me a toke. When I reached for it she laughed and danced away. I tried to look severe. She danced back to me and held the joint to my lips. I inhaled deeply.

Behind the sofa, near the window there. No, don't open the curtains—that light is perfect. Stand right there.

She stood on the bare floorboards near the tall window, from which I could hear the occasional spatter of rain on the glass in counterpoint with the piano's cartwheels. She looked left and right, as though crossing the street, then began to unbutton her blouse.

You don't have to take off your clothes, I said stupidly.

She continued to unbutton as if she hadn't heard. I persisted in my folly.

You realize this can take a while and be uncomfortable? Modeling is hard work.

Simone says there's nothing to it. Sliding out of her

jeans.

Simone…

She said to me in English, Shut up and draw.

She was naked. In a glance I took in the salient patterns of lightness and dark: the skin of her belly, her thighs, the tops of her breasts, her face. And the black hair on her head and the shaggier hair between her legs, and the little tuft visible beneath her right arm as she bent it back to adjust her hair. The shadows played on her neck. As an art student, and before that, I'd looked at innumerable naked bodies of every shape and age. Old men with goiters came to pose for us, and middle-aged men who removed suits to reveal the hard round bowls of their bellies, their sunken chests. Many of the women were beautiful, but just as many were not, and indeed it was the ugly and ungainly ones who were the most interesting to draw. Strangely, it was not M's body, as enchantingly curvaceous as it was, that my eyes and pencil were drawn to; it was rather as if her disrobing had revealed her face to me for the first time. I put her through rapid changes, assuming the voice of command that up to now I'd only heard from my instructors: lift your left arm, bend your right knee, turn away from me, face me, squat on the floor, raise both your arms. She did everything I said, the features of her face unmoving, but a flush started in her cheeks and across the thin skin of her sternum as my hand moved rapidly, mechanically, sketching, getting a feel for how that face and that body could fill the blank space of the page, bear its whiteness, the viewer's gaze.

Are you bored? I asked her suddenly.

No.

Tired?

A little.

All right.

I turned one more page. Having broadly and rapidly sketched the volumes and masses of her body with the broad side of the pencil lead, I now concentrated the point on her face. Strong eyebrows made more pronounced by the pale clarity of her complexion, high forehead, a slight endearing chubbiness to the cheeks, a full, almost drooping lower lip and a thin bowed upper, a Mediterranean whisper of a mustache, like Duchamp's Mona Lisa's, under her nose, which was angular, almost broken-looking. A face that could be starkly arresting or beautiful, depending on the light, but never pretty, never *jolie*, and in her blanker moods—when a dark repose overtook her features and the light went out of her bright brown eyes and her thick hair hung lank around her ears and her mouth hung slightly open, the better to let smoke in and out—she could seem very nearly malformed and hideous. It was that face, to my growing alarm, that I found myself drawing—my pencil had subtracted the twinkle from her eye and rendered it heavy, dragged down by shadow, and the upturned corners of her mouth on my sketching paper tilted down toward the center of the earth. Her nose, a challenge in any case, had become a Picasso-esque wedge dividing the Red Sea of her cheekbones, which in any case I had somehow rendered bloodless though working in monochrome, even as a slow blush worked its way across her living face and the chill in the room stippled her nipples and the fine hairs on her forearms. With a frantic blurring motion of my thick fingers I put in her hair, not the closely shaped cap that she had in life but a jagged thundercloud that darkened and darkened until the pencil point broke with a snap.

Can I move now? she asked.

Yes, I said without looking up. I felt a vibration, a lurch, as when a train starts unexpectedly, the woman on the sheet and the woman by the window, both utterly alive, giving and losing reality to one another. I thought about her looking at it and was frightened. With a quick slap of paper I overturned the sheet and started again. When I looked at her, I saw that she was now in three-quarter profile, and that she had crossed her left arm across her torso, slightly lifting her heavy breasts. I started with them this time, carefully but quickly shading in their volume, getting a sense of their slight ripple and pliancy, the surprising red-brown darkness of the aureoles with a stray hair or two springing from their circumferences, a little red mole the size of the tip of pinky finger on the inside slope of the right breast, just above where her arm was hugging them together to make a cleavage of nearly parodic generosity—something the curl of her lip suggested she was fully aware of doing.

Should I move?

No. Stay there, please.

I felt now that surge of energy in me that was not only the surge of arousal—though it was surely that—but of attention, a kind of inward leaning toward the object of my gaze I had experienced from time to time when drawing or painting from life, which I was capable of not only when confronted with a beautiful woman (in fact it was rarely the case, for I summoned an excess of sang-froid in such moments to avoid embarrassment) but with men of strong physique who would flatly or twinklingly engage my gaze, and sometimes even when doing *natures mortes*, when I would permit myself to engage the full voluptuousness, color, and albedo of a plumskin, an apple core, a blue China bowl. It didn't last long. My hand moved more slowly and caressingly up the planes of her body to the face, then in a few sudden motions the picture was done. I stood there for a moment, hands at my sides, then lurched back from the table and sagged my head to the rainy glass, conscious of my burning cheeks.

Can I see it? She stepped lightly forward and around the table to examine the drawing. I couldn't see her face but was left to read the angle of her inclined neck and the fine hairs quivering there.

It's beautiful, she said at last. But it doesn't much look like me, does it?

I shrugged.

She arched an eyebrow. You've had your vision, is that it?

I shrugged again. She lifted the paper to examine the first drawing; I thought to stop her but then didn't, instead continuing to watch the rain streak down the leaded glass windowpanes. Lights and colors free of figure and form rippled on the pavement below. I heard her inhale quietly.

Is that what I look like?

To me. Today. Yes.

She was looking at me. Unwillingly, as though in a magnet's grip, I turned my gaze to meet hers. Her body was blinding, her eyes blurred. I tried to desiccate that gaze.

How you must hate me, she said softly.

Not at all.

My tongue was confused but I knew that I wanted to use those words I'd heard in so many songs and movies. *Non, je t'aime.* But all that came out was that *Non.* It convinced neither of us, I knew, but what would it have taken to turn that *Non* into a *Oui*? Maybe everything.

Can I keep this? she asked. She picked up the drawing and held it in front of her, that second self, homunculus, black with soft pencil and disclosure. Then she turned away and walked across the living room to her bedroom door. She opened it, paused, looked back at me. Men are all the same, she said softly. She closed the door behind her.

The second drawing was mine to tuck into my portfolio and take home, where it took its place on the wall among a dozen other anonymous nudes, what Charles called my jerk-off wall. He wasn't home that night; he was home less and less. I watched the shadows of the raindrops walk down each woman—ink or pencil or pastels or oils, in similar and dissimilar poses, so that the row of them resembled nothing so much as the letters in a ransom note, different and disjointed but fundamentally legible, living letters spelling out a phrase or two, a poem of nudes, a demand.

Lie of the linear; micrologic of sentences. The new reader gets past that by reading multiple books at once, by skipping the pages in which the killer's identity is revealed, by reading only odd-numbered pages, by reading poetry. The new reader wanders the text-torn landscape looking for something to surrender to. The new reader writes at odd moments, in odd places: the desk is too neat, sterile in its brick of light on the second floor in the corner of the guest room, where no books are stacked, where the laptop could stand pristine or the guest bed beckons the new reader from writing to napping, dreamlessly, recovering bit by bit the nights lost to the stack of unfinishable books by her beside. No: she writes in a black notebook, self-consciously, interspersed with lists that point back always to the objective life: errands, groceries, phone numbers, friends. In the kitchen, constantly interrupted by e-mails, links, YouTube, and by cooking, the child, the husband, the telephone, her own mind, somehow frenetic and lazy at once. She cheats an hour: Ben is home on a Saturday morning, she puts her laptop in one of his old briefcases and walks six blocks to Starbucks, sits down with a latte, far as she can get from the cozy chairs where the insane are clustering, opens the computer and is immediately lost in e-mails, links, YouTube, the telephone, her mind making rabbit tracks across the window, following passersby wonderingly: where can she be going in such a hurry, too young to have children; why does that well-dressed man move so slowly, will he yes he will reach down into the trash can, sorting and searching; who is that woman in the black SUV with the windows rolled up and the engine running, talking to herself and laughing; the barista calls someone named Bethany and she appears, a woman in her sixties with iron gray hair in a ponytail down her back, where shall wisdom be found, and she strides out the door licking a spot of cream from her wrist.

She types I am alone and stares at the words, floating mimetically in the white window of what is not exactly a page. Flicks the cursor, changes it: I is alone. *Je est un autre.* My own private Rimbaud. An erect figure, flat on top like a broad-brimmed hat, flat on the bottom: flatfoot. An image out of the detective novels she used to consume indiscriminately when she was younger. Not the English locked-room mysteries her mother favored; Ruth liked the hard-boiled Americans. Hammett and Chandler's morose and witty heroes, men talked out of breath (*Breatlhless*), making self-pity look as noble as it is inevitable. There were women too, hard-edged and wisecracking, V.I. Warshawski and Kay Scarpetta and at the very bottom or top of the list there was wide-eyed infallible Nancy Drew. It was the men who drew her, the Hardy boys outscheming the bad guys, Bogart tugging his ear empathetically as Marlowe or coldly, cynically as Spade. What saps they were, these guys, how easily they were taken in by a beautiful and heartless woman. It was not even the women who were responsible but the man's own narcissism, his "code," his chivalric idea of his own ruthless perceptions. A man like that of limited intelligence and ruthless cunning, sealed off from the world of commitments and distractions by pride, immense privacy, loneliness, drinking. A man like that might accomplish something, might venture, while a woman stayed home and did the necessary raveling of his legend, his shroud.

The I was blinking. She closed the laptop and hit mute on the buzzing cellphone, where she read Ben's name. Time to return home with nothing accomplished. But there's an emotion floating atop the expected dull rage, like a rainbow sheening a black parking-lot puddle. Anticipation, incipient aliveness. The old books are at home, the old adventures in handsome trade paperback editions, buried somewhere in the basement. She'll dig them up again and carry them upstairs, tonight, while child and husband are sleeping. She'll read them. She'll reread her dreams.

There were many days after, all the days of my life, but those first days crushed us with their emptiness. The waves had crested and found their level without, after all, having capsized the great unwieldy ship that was La France. Out of the dark, out of the smoke, humid summer air no longer stirred the red banners hanging from the Sorbonne and the Odeon and the balconies of St. Germain. The students still marched and met and made speeches and left ruin and beauty in their wake, but some irreplaceable tension had snapped or slackened. During these belated days of early June, M and Charles and I were inseparable, the more so since Thicht had left the city abruptly, for fear of being arrested and deported back to Vietnam. Simone, too, had scarpered, under silent moral pressure from M, who without effort had become the center of our little circle, and so one evening she climbed on the back of a motorcycle behind a young Algerian named Mustafa and vanished laughing into the red stream of taillights escaping the smoldering capital.

What followed were dark dull days like troughs between waves, neither revolutionary nor quotidian, into which volition vanished entirely or from which senseless schemes erupted suddenly into complete life, only to be eclipsed by apathy between midnight and dawn. I thought often of Simone and her Algerian, her arms around his waist, a new wind carrying her away now that history had blown itself out. So M gave up her flat and moved in with us, into the big high-ceilinged doorless furnitureless flat just streets away from the storm that had become all eye, all silence, in the Boul' Mich, at the apex of an imaginary triangle joining the two centers of the sputtering revolution, the Sorbonne and the Odeon. There we began to pass the time, bell jar days half-asleep, half-clothed, eating out of cans, listening and then not listening to the radio, to phonograph records, emerging only at dusk to roam the streets, together, looking for the revolution and finding only cautiously open cafes, packed moviehouses, streets aimless with youths and slogans without direction or center. The TV was drivel and hardly anyone owned one anyway; the radio was propaganda but necessary to track the convulsions and flailings of the state, increasingly comic and helpless giant, never did we dream it would catch up with us, once again incarnate La France, even if it was a corpse it was heavy enough to crush us. The city was still turbulent, garbage stacked up in neat hallucinatory piles higher and higher on the impassable sidewalks, it became natural for everyone, bourgeois and student alike, to move in the center of the street, day or night, marching or alone. People were still cramming the Sorbonne for lectures, discourses, extended carefully argued disagreements about the nature of the state to come. Cohn-Bendit was detained in Germany, there were no leaders but it was undoubtedly the case that without him things began to lose their shape, teeter and swell, like a hot-air balloon that could no longer lift its basket but sat there, billowing in whatever wind. The first sizable demo in a few weeks happened and we took our places in it, or meant to: Charles had already gone, one of the organizers. But half a block away from the Boulevard St. Germain M stopped me with a hand on my chest.

Listen to them, she said. Can you hear what they're shouting?

I listened.

"We are all German Jews," I said in English. "We are all undesirables."

But it's not true, Gus. It simply isn't true. Someone like Charles… And they're all of them, they're all like him.

A gesture of solidarity—

With whom? With the dead?

You aren't dead, I said. Or German. And you are very far from being undesirable.

Oh, Gus. Remember when I said that I liked that you were a little bit stupid? The word she used was *bête.*

Yes.

I take it back.

She turned around and walked away from me, wiping away tears. Trapped between exigencies, I could only stand there watching, as she and the disorderly parade of students, beginning to be pressed by police, passed me by.

We read and read: there were runs on the few open bookshops as people fled their boredom, their stasis, I read indiscriminately, passing each book as I finished it to M: the letters of Rosa Luxemburg, *The Count of Monte Cristo* (I had read it again and again when I was younger, and now, again), a popular history of the Commune, a paperback edition of Fourier's *Theorie des quatre mouvements*, the fourth volume of Proust, the third volume of Churchill's autobiography I found in our usual shop; someone had written in black marker on the inside front page in English *Memoirs of a Fascist* and underlined it three times. Charles too read everything, but what he cycled back to us was didactic: he was shocked that I'd never read Rimbaud, the key to the revolution is in here, he said, but I found it incomprehensible. It's true certain aphorisms floated up from the frantic murk and stuck with me, I found myself looking at the window reciting to myself *si le cuivre s'éveille un clairon, ce n'est pas sa faute*, if the brass wakes a trumpet it's not its fault, or «*Matinée d'ivresse*» which thanks to M's English I thought of as a sort of movie review of the revolution itself: *On nous a promis d'enterrer dans l'ombre l'arbre du bien et du mal, de déporter les honnêtetés tyranniques, afin que nous produisions notre plus grand amour,* They promised to inter in darkness the tree of good and evil, to deport the tyranny of respectability, so that we might bring forth our purest love. We have faith in the poison. We know how to give our whole life every day. *Voici le temps des* Assassins. I said that to myself again and again until it sounded like a train leaving the station, picking up tempo: *voici le temps, voici le temps, voici le temps des* Assassins. We then watched the film of that title, revived for one week only at a crusty little shoebox of a cinema on the Rue St. Jacques, eyes wide watching the hapless Jean Gabin (the face in other films of that sublime detective Maigret) undone by every woman in his life, one woman whipping another in a greedy frenzy until it all ends in blood by the banks of the Seine: we said it together leaving the theater joining the roving bands of students under cover of night, all of us thinking or muttering "Voici le temps des *Assassins*!" Charles grew more baroque in his demands on our time and attention, he suddenly forbade American films, then rescinded the ban when *Bonnie and Clyde* came to town (the cinemas were packed, none of them closed, throughout May and into June they had a special status, like monasteries in the Middle Ages in which any common criminal might claim refuge), then reinstated the ban. After every film he'd lecture and harangue, our flat for an auditorium, M would lay her head in my lap sometimes looking up at the ceiling while he talked, leaving me the task of following him with my eyes, trying to resist the natural impulse to stroke her hair, I compromised by resting my hand there, huge paw on her head, like a hat, she closed her eyes. What am I doing here, I asked myself, how had I, of brute Alsatian stock, come to follow this road, to Paris, the path of striving toward the respectability Rimbaud would deplore, throwing in my lot with my fellow-children, sons and daughters of the bourgeois, in their sleek well-fed skins, who'd been so good as to take me for one of them, who was I to refuse this destiny, to sink temporarily with the mass and then rise with it, the new ruling class in a society without classes, as Charles described it, for all his personal despotism there was an undeniable light in his eyes, it held us both, this intensity, was it my birthright too, would I too feel the sand under my boots, the Midi come to colonize the capital, the whole world, the paradise of Fourier's maddest dreams, the seas turned to lemonade, the arctic regions temperate, wild beasts spontaneously transformed into the glad servants of man? I had made their cause my own, though the "they" and the cause were splintering, had worked night and day in a fever to transmit telegraphed slogans of defiance and hope that seemed capable almost on their own of conveying us into the new, unimaginable reality.

But something had shifted, something had snapped. I was awake now, watching the dreamers, watching Charles, hurt like a child's sticking to his face. It was not his revolution I mourned, nor my own stalled destiny as an artist, which I saw so clearly to be finished before it began; I was a painter, perhaps, but not an artist, I lacked the architecture for that particular brand of madness, I was simple, binary, a keystone arch that ideas, things, people passed through, in and out, on and off. It was the woman in my lap, asleep now, dreams uncertain, in the revolution's orbit (or is that redundant), embodying the more-than-life that the others had passed from hand to hand in the lecture halls of the Sorbonne and down from the stage of the Odeon and most of all of course on the streets where we'd all been in the momentary grip of love, revolutionary love. But the vast majority of them, Charles and Cohn-Bendit and all the rest, they were little old men at heart, little old men before it began and little old men forever after: I saw it so clearly, as though already in hindsight, in Charles's stricken angry arguing face in the underheated flat on the first of June, forty years gone. Even when M awoke, and rose, and went to him, casting me out once again from the little circle of warmth, I knew enough to pity Charles and the others, the sleepers, who suffered the illusion of a destiny. Charles stood there in an embrace with M, remote as always, head tucked down under the fall of his blond hair, whispering in her ear, hiding from the death that was before them, us, behind me already it seemed, the death of youth. The old man's brute-hearted and calculating betrayal of his younger self. Oh, Charles, even now, I would shield you from such a fate if I could.

Gustave's brow and eyes and nose and moving lips. The back of Lamb's head. Gray blank backdrop of a room. Here and now. Then and there.

On the first day of the month of brides DeGaulle dissolved the Assembly and took off at last the mask, revealing a second mask that was the true face of the state, the helmets and gas masks of the CRS, black immobile plastic and metal, raccoon eyes unblinking, the men inside just meat in rigid light-absorbing shells, violent mollusks heaped up against our inchoate victory, that was dissolving now in front of our eyes. We were losing the workers, who discovered after all that they had much to lose, not just their chains: pay rises had been promised, working hours adjusted. It was the Communists themselves who turned out to be the most at home in the system, who prospered from permanent deferral of their platform, itself a deferral from what Moscow pledged, what Che and Fidel in their own reckless, ruthless beauty had seemed to promise. What remained? Only thousands of students with no leader or plan, broken into dozens and hundreds of groupuscules, as large as UNEF and as small as we three smoking and dreaming in the empty flat, looking for and failing to discover our true size in the long humid evenings, passing through empty or crowded streets where the trees and barricades alike had been torn down. In the papers we bought and strewed across the floor like a carpet the reflections and post-mortems were already being disseminated, the lightning bottled for reuse by melancholics and those who'd afterward claim to have been there. It was as if the horizon itself, the one we'd marched for, the line that had defined the world we'd found and which had come to seem so close, so crossable, had vanished into the sea of ordinary life. M looked out the window, quoting T.S. Eliot to me and Charles bored and stoned and spread out on the floor like stunned insects, lying on top of the newspapers and posters and flyers and ashes. I would not have thought death had undone so many. I would not have thought boredom could ever return, could ever become again the context and fiber of our minutes, our days. Yet it had.

I didn't care. M was near me. Jules et Jim, Gustave and Charles. And M. I knew they slept together, though silently. Charles never made a sound, he had left that to Simone and his swans, to make that ugly inhuman cry echo through the wall-less flat at any hour of the night. But M too was silent, so that I believed they might have believed I thought them chaste, except in the morning I would see them, in the gray cotton light of a Paris dawn, entwined naked, covered or not covered by a sheet. Sometimes I sat in a wooden chair a few meters of and sketched them, and left the sketches here and there in the flat, a gesture whose meaning I didn't care to scrutinize. M would find them and collect them; I assumed she threw them out, but later on, after the very end, I found them coiled and tucked into a discarded boot in the corner she'd used as a closet, fanned them out on the floor and looked at the black charcoal streaks of bodies in the aftermath of love. A love I bore witness to without sharing. I suppose that she did love him, easily, the way they all did, for his beauty and arrogance; but there was something else, a skeptical inclination of the head when I caught her sometimes looking at him while he was speaking fervently about Marx or Godard or the revolution, always the revolution, the center of history that had been given to him wrapped in a bow like a present, like M herself. We shared something, she and me. It was her little joke to refer to us both as *les americains*; Charles would stride in the street with his usual impatient quick steps, and M would fall behind a few paces and take my arm, saying After all, we Americans need to stick together. Or at the café with our copies of *Action* and *Le Monde*, with Charles cursing over the haplessness of De Gaulle's ministers and the perfidy of the PCF, she'd say to me, Well, Gus? We could use the American perspective on this affair. Or the times I'd be at the kitchen table with a piece of toast and M would appear, languid, nearly naked in a paint-spattered shirt she'd borrowed permanently from me, because on her it was large enough to be a dressing gown, her little hands twisting like marionettes from the ends of rolled sleeves. She'd turn a chair around so its back was to me and sit down, straddling it, a lock of hair lolling over one eye, looking at me the way I'd looked at her that day and so many mornings afterward, with a pencil or pastel in my hand. Not appraising, not judging, merely measuring. And I felt for once that my big flabby body belonged somewhere, I'd lean my elbows on the table with my toast and pour her a cup of the same crap coffee and we'd sit there, quietly, like married people, until Charles would bring his noise and his bluster into the airspace we called the kitchen, and the day would start again, the revolution would resume.

But these were as I say the waning days. De Gaulle was back, a querulous and demanding voice on the radio, and the whole city seemed to be waking from its dream. Charles, like a little boy, fought waking. And he wasn't the only one. Losing his audience, finding it harder every day to rouse his cadre, each of whom little by little was finding himself caught up once again in ordinary concerns, exams, the summer holidays, he hectored the two of us more and more, answering the silence in M's face and the boredom in my own with diatribes on anarcho-syndicalism and the Communists' betrayal of their own legacy and the misguided veneration of Trotsky—we must get back to the first principles of Marxism-Leninism, we must mobilize our own class privileges on behalf of the people, who do not yet realize that they are the people, when they do it will be a terrible day for the bosses and owners and politicians and Charles's own father, it cannot be helped, to make an omelet etcetera. M made a face at me when his back was turned and I tried not to laugh but still my face was distorted and when Charles saw it he became enraged, he pushed back from the table and shouted My God Gustave, don't you understand it's all for you, you are the People, you fucking peasant, you're the one it's all for, and it's all right if you don't care for theory but without theory there's no practice, you asshole, you fucking smirker, you shirker. To which there was no defense but to raise both my palms in the air, I surrender, while M looked up at the ceiling, stone-faced. She doesn't understand any of it, he grumbled to me one afternoon when M was out, she reads all the books and shouts all the slogans but she has no feeling for it, she's really an American, she doesn't believe, they're a generation behind us at least as far as class consciousness goes, it's a real problem. But she goes with you to all the demos, I said, she's right there up front, she's fearless, I've seen her. That's not the point, he answered, what makes me crazy is she's there but she's not there, she believes but she doesn't believe, I can feel her standing apart, looking down on all of us, on me, on you, on herself maybe. I didn't answer but thought of the two of them making love, how her eyes must slide away from his, faking it, or rather not faking it hard enough, not the orgasm but the illusion that one is really inside the other person or has taken the other person in, is truly with him, moved by him, rocked by him, living and dying in a single embrace. It's a little too obvious, isn't it, with M, that you are not her fantasy, her mind or something, call it soul if you like, is elsewhere, possessed but by whom, by what. M was his lover but she was my horizon. I knew in the breathless nights of their sex that he fucked her in vain, in herself behind the eyes recessive and untouchable as the revolution itself. Underneath the scorn and derision, or contrariwise the lit flame of passion, I saw something, something tucked like a bookmark into the illuminated text of her life, something I recognized. I saw her, how she looked at me and my pear-shaped pullet's body, my ill-fitting face and clothes, my Frankenstein freakishness, and recoiled in fear and recognition at something that reminded her of herself. The two of us were pushed or pushed ourselves to the side of whatever river was flowing, the current caught us up but only took us so far, on the banks of the waters of Babylon we stood or knelt and watched, only watched and witnessed. Charles, protagonist, could not understand us, tried to bring us under the umbrella of his own fierce subjectivity, enroll us as players in the drama of his own hang-ups, which he of course thought were universal, those were the only terms by which a mind so educated could play the hero's role, he had to be the hero for everybody, he wanted to be my hero, M's hero, and could not. For myself I wanted only to paint her, to reach beyond my own manifest limitations and touch something as genuine and as elusive as my own soul, the flicker at the corners of her eyes, her mouth, looking back boldly at me when I sketched her naked. Naked! No woman was ever less naked, or more like a nude, than M in our occasional sessions, when Charles was out or asleep, sessions never longer than a half hour or so, whenever the mood struck her to discard whatever she was wearing and stand or kneel or squat or recline for me, wherever she was in the flat, and I followed after with whatever tools I could scrounge—a bit of newsprint, a stub of charcoal, if I was lucky some pastels. Always I worked swiftly, trying to capture what seemed most ephemeral in the pose, the breath, the tug of her upper ribcage under the slope of her breasts, a lock of hair over her left eye that she blew away, impishly. Then we would hear Charles on the stairs and languidly, without hurry, she would roll away to the bathroom or to cover herself while I finished the sketch. I did not bother to conceal these sketches from Charles, he looked at them sometimes, cup of coffee in hand, without comment, an amused expression on his face. I was no threat to him. And sometimes she looked with him, poker faced, leaning on his shoulder. He'd gesture at one of the pictures, at the thickness and coarseness of the jawline, or the way one eye was manifestly larger than the other.

Look at Picasso, he'd say. Look at you, Picasso's mistress.

He makes me so ugly, she'd murmur, as though in agreement.

She went on posing for me, a way to break up the tedium, to exhale a little in those waning days in the tense, static city. But she would not pose for a full session, the hours I needed to paint her properly; and when I finally had stretched a canvas and set up an easel and had paints at hand, so that the next time the mood stuck her I would be ready, the mood ceased to strike. Anyway things were beginning to move, to come unstuck for the final convulsion. Charles was talking over the radio, we had to hush him, DeGaulle was speaking, calling for new elections, a victory I should have thought but Charles for once saw it clearly, It's all over if he can do that, they'll return him for sure, he said, fists clenched, he represents stability, order, everything they want, my father always voted CGT but he'll vote for DeGaulle now like every other petty bourgeois, it'll be a massacre, it's all over if we can't seize the moment. He stood up. I have to go to the Sorbonne, now, we have to organize, we have to show them. He held out his hand, invitation to a dream. Distracted, smiling a little, M took it and stood beside him. They looked at me.

I'll catch up with you, I said. I have some things

to do first.

Let's go, Charles said to M.

Feverish, as if I were the dreamer. I worked at the canvas, all the rest of that day, the sketches and drawings surrounding me offering different angles, moods, movement almost, like film stills, a few frames, enough to complete—I hoped—a gesture. The radio played in the background, news reports, the announcer speaking rapidly of events as they unfolded in the city, the marches and countermarches, the new brawls. Outside my window it was quiet, a gentle early summer breeze came through the open windows. I worked. My palette was basic: black for the police, heavy browns for the secret earth, dark green for the jungles of Vietnam, ashy gray for the sands of Algeria, into which murky death-haunted colors intruded life in the form of a little pink, a dab of light brown, a very little vermillion. A figure assembled itself, I preserved the panel effect, a touch of superannuated Cubism, why not, odalisque at length, discarded caryatid, the canvas large, nearly two meters at its base, one arm crooked out at the elbow to support the head, delicate smear of her face, black hair torque upward, reap the whirlwind. All day. At some point near dusk I stood back from it, looking with disbelief at the liberated canvas, its jagged energy, like a tunnel into something, raw, ungainly, anatomically irregular, unfinished, but I knew if I touched it with the brush again something would give, I'd lose the painting, lose M.

I lay down to close my eyes for a few minutes, exhausted, to regroup, when they opened again it was night, the streetlights burned through the windows, and there was a low sound outside, unlullling reverberate roar, like the sea. I got up, looked out.

The bodies of the students surged and broke on the seawall of the police. The tear gas rose like spume in a nature documentary, in slow motion. The cries of the crowd and the grinding engines of CRS vans churned the dirty panes of class with their vibrations. The slogans were muted but I moved my lips to them. I'd been reading them for so long, on walls and alleys, in men's rooms, in the Metro, at the Ecole des Beaux-Arts I'd stenciled posters by the dozens, sweating and cursing without rancor, in the joy of solidarity, high on turpentine and spray-paint fumes, handing stacks out the door into the arms of lithe young comrades, their Mao caps rakish, their trousers pencil-thin and impeccably creased. *Soyons cruels!* we cried, lashing out in our rage and joy. And I'd listened to the speeches and debates, had even taken part in a few; I'd shouted with crowds, I'd wedged my fat blunt body into the ranks of sitters and marchers, I'd raised my fist and shook it over the others, like a priest shaking out sacred oils on the congregation. So why then, that particular evening, the day of the counter-demonstration, the surge of Gaullists (the old folks, our parents, every one of them it seemed a Resistance-fighter, a martyr, and we their ungrateful children, drinking

Marx, reading Coca-Cola), why did I sit there in the darkened window, invisible to the history that was passing us by, watching the revolution dying by inches?

They were down there somewhere. Events, *les Evenements*, had thrown them together. In my mind the film we'd seen last weekend, *Bonnie and Clyde*, how they went out together, Faye Dunaway and Warren Beatty, alone on a country road, riddled with bullets. And who was I, I persisted narcissistically in asking myself, what was my role in their solipsistic drama? Part of the scenery, part of the violence—the response, Charles taught, to powerlessness, response as proper as poetry. So much blood, Technicolor red, spraying up and out at the screen in an Artaud fountain. We loved it, we loved the shock, we came out laughing like our laughter was a spell, protecting us from the knowledge the movie had carried with it, Hollywood wisdom, across the ocean bearing its message of the glamour of death. They were down there without me. Were they together? Was she holding the bottle while he lit the rag? Were they locked arm in arm with others, the avant-garde that had been left behind by the convulsive reaction of a nation remembering its nationhood? Was she crying from the gas? Would he vomit? Would they get their skulls cracked, methodically, at the hands and clubs and shields of the masked CRS men? Did they not themselves at that moment wear masks of righteousness and beauty, mirrors of each other, mirrors on the faces of all the young men and women, *les jeunes*, mirrors reflecting the arc lights of the cops and the neon of the Champs de l'Elysees and the smoky torch of cinemas showing the films of our actual, dreamed lives? I reached up and touched my own face, half-visible to me in the greasy glass, felt the stubble, my chins folding into one another, the pendulous nose, the flesh bunched around my eyes that made them appear piggish and small. The back of the canvas rebuked me. Where was my own mask of youth and beauty? Had M taken it? Or had she thrown it away? What I had pressed into her hands, the night I knew she couldn't love or pity me, but could only be there, in my gravity well, fellow American. It was out there, somewhere, the mask that had been meant for me, my moment in the waning sun of revolution, forgotten or smashed somewhere on the streets, youth's canvas, where her body lay. I went out into the counterrevolutionary night.

Windows follow me, Elsa, when I walk the narrow streets at dusk, making me feel more invisible, not less. Sometimes my life seems like one long disappearing act. And now that I, from your point of view, have actually vanished, you will read these words with disbelief, if you read them at all. Because I write to you not as your mother but as a dying woman, trying to say goodbye to you and to my life.

My time now is pared down to a few essentials, a

limited catalog of moving images. When I lie in bed at night with my eyes closed I seem to watch them on a screen. Very early I see myself awaken, the whites of my eyes showing in a room where dawn is reddening the curtains. A kitchen, a kettle, coffee. Though I quit smoking long ago there's a line of smoke unfurling from the cigarette in my hand or in the ashtray, doing its part to compose an atmosphere. A solitary woman of a certain age walking on a narrow street, sometimes into a shop then out again, like Mrs. Dalloway with no flowers to buy. Sometimes my steps return me to the vast truncated dancefloor of the Piazza della Unita, fronting emptily the empty sea. You will sometimes find me in a café or library with a folded newspaper by my side, fingers busily knitting. I make scarves hats and sweaters that I donate via the good offices of a pleasant pasty nun, Josephine, half my size and twice my weight, who administers a program for cancer patients at the hospital. Once and once only she put her large white hand on my own when I came in with a shopping bag of cloche hats in assorted colors, fixing her watery blue eyes on my own.

La signora si sente bene?

Si.

E'stato chiesto di te ieri. Il dottor Maggio.

That's very kind, I said. *Grazie.*

Signora. Ancora non prenere in considerazione il trattmento?

Grazie, grazie. I fled.

I did not return for three weeks, and when I did return, the incident was not repeated. She only turned her head on one side and smiled at me helplessly, But I do not know if I can bear the sympathy, the frank solicitude of those eyes, for much longer. I will go on knitting; I need to do something with my hands. But perhaps I'll just leave my creations where I finish them, for whomever wants it, or doesn't.

There was a time when I would have found this absolute solitude delicious. Before I abandoned or was abandoned by America, your father, you. It seemed that there was never time for me, just myself to be myself, to meet myself, except fleetingly—meeting my own eyes in the mirror while dressing for dinner, or in the waiting rooms of dentists and doctors where I felt myself released from the charge of amusing myself and simply waited, not even knitting, hands in lap. You remember the books, the endless mysteries I consumed, and before that my morbid research into a past as incomprehensible as it was unchangeable. You thought that was time stolen from you, but it was time stolen from myself as well. Now I never read any more; I sometimes allow my eyes to pass over the print of a newspaper or novel, but I take nothing in except the rhythm of sentences, a sort of white noise on the page. It passes the time when the hours are too full of memories; yet when I look up in the late afternoon, the sun having passed on to more glamorous destinations, I remember nothing, scarcely my own name or how I've come to be here, washed up on the fringe of Europe, where my American life—yes, American, in spite of everything—can't quite catch hold, even now that it's ending. I remember nothing any more. Then a dinner, not always solitary, for there are one or two ladies, neighbors, a widow and a spinster, who sometimes ask me up out of curiosity for a plate of cuttlefish pasta, a glass or two of wine. The widow, who lives in the apartment just above me has me to dinner every Tuesday evening, always attended by her middle-aged bald bachelor of a son, a foreman at the Illy plant who speaks excellent English, though apparently in Italian he's something of a stutterer. We sit, the three of us, a little lost at the large formal dining table that's been shifted out from under the yellowing chandelier so the table's tail abuts the window, open on a mild evening to the shouts and sounds of the street below. The widow is thin, nearly emaciated, and wears a thick pasty white make-up in a misguided attempt to smooth out her wrinkles; she's eighty if she's a day. Her son, not twenty years younger, sits next to her so that I feel fronted by a sort of tribunal: she gazing directly with a luxurious sort of charitable contempt, he with eyes lowered, lidded, only occasionally flashing upward to display a startling eagerness, even an ardor. It's uncomfortable and amusing, especially after a third glass of the sharp Terrano wine with a finish like the karst cliffs that line the coast where the Balkans begin. There is a daughter as well, I am told, married with grown children of her own, living in Udine, to the north. She never liked it here, the widow said through her son. She didn't like the wind, the noise it makes in the winters. Many of the young people go there. She never comes back, I have to go to her. But I'm getting too old.

I wanted to ask how she managed living in a fourth-floor walk-up at her age. But the answer was there in front of me. Her son was a constant presence, though he did not actually live there. Every day he brought up her groceries, newspaper, mail; every other day some flowers, a box of chocolates, or one of the paperbacks stacked haphazardly against the wall of the living room—for the bookshelves were all crammed with knickknacks, including one shelf devoted entirely to a set of glass and ceramic pigs. It was hard not to notice a resemblance between one of the larger and more whimsical pigs, dressed in a frock coat and monocle, and the heavy, jowled, delicate figure of her son, whose manicured hands moved carefully and precisely as he served the dinner he had, in all likelihood, cooked himself. It fascinated me, their attachment, the long tail of motherhood that had come so tightly to enfurl a grown man, even a boss of men. He had never married, though—this was said in Italian while her son was in the kitchen—there had been a girl once, many years ago, whom he had been engaged to for a year and a day (that was her phrase, un anno e un giorno) but she (or perhaps he, my Italian is very imperfect and I often miss genders) had gotten cold feet at the altar. In any case, she was no good, *non abbastanza per lui*, and he loves his mama who looks after him, *lui ama la sua mamma che si prende cura di lui*.

The son returned to the room at this point with his eyes lowered, oven mitts on his hands, bringing in a steaming bowl of mussels in white wine broth. His lips were pursed slightly—ironically? He was an excellent cook and took pride in being so.

The last time we ate together the widow made her excuses before the coffee was served, complaining of headache. I rose to go but she told me to sit, sit, enjoy—Bernardo had brought a strudel and I must taste it at least or hurt his pride. Knowing as I did that pastry was not among Bernardo's accomplishments, I realized with mingled alarm and amusement that the widow was trying either to set me up with her superannuated son or—less alarming, more amusing—I was being presented to the son as a sort of cautionary tale, an example of what to avoid, a feckless American. Either way, it meant my secret was safe, in the building at least. She could not know of my illness.

With no one to translate for, Bernardo was silent at first. He poured coffee from a French press without bothering to ask whether I wanted it or feared the sleepless hours it might bring, which I took as a tribute to my having been adopted as at least half-Triestino. My appetite had waned in recent weeks and it had increasingly become a chore to do even the minimal duty toward Bernardo's cooking that politeness dictates. I would soon have to stop accepting his mother's invitations, and my world would contract even further, the clock advance toward midnight, toward the moment I vowed would be of my choosing. Bernardo ate his strudel quickly, methodically, his eyes fixed on the window to the darkening street; it was easy somehow to imagine myself married to him, a solid man who had mastered the art of taking up little space. Yet I could not, would not play mother again, to any man. That's all they want, Elsa; you have no doubt discovered this. Even your handsome lawyer with the squared-off jaw, does he not in the still of the night tuck his face into your bosom with the rapacious helplessness of an infant rooting for the breast? They are incapable of seeing what's in front of them, what's before their faces. Bernardo at least still had his own, actual mother, which made him a bit more attractive: he had no need to serve me, was in fact in serving me really serving the only woman, I was convinced, he had ever loved. When she died he would sit here, in her apartment, in that very same chair, hands limp in his lap, waiting and listening as the city goes quiet around him, night after night. Should someone have the misfortune to marry him she would find him as I found him now, courteous and even affectionate but remote, attuned elsewhere, like a dog whose master has left him with a friend for months and years but whose ears nevertheless prick up at every scrape of a key in the lock, whose tail starts beating until the accepted but unbeloved form enters the room, at which point all movement ceases and the animal returns gravely to his accustomed bed. Oh, Elsa, these thoughts do one no good. I hope you will not indulge them. I hope your silence means what it says, that these letters go unread, straight into the fire or into a shoebox where they will remain until long after I am dead, past the possibility of a pitying reply. If I have been a poor mother to you, it would be past my dignity to ask that you, at the end, be a mother to me. I write these letters to you, but for myself. Never forget that simple truth of my selfishness, Elsa, which I hope you can learn some part of for yourself, for your own sake. They will try and take everything you have—they *will* take it, unless you don't let them.

It is kind of you to come to these dinners, Bernardo said at last in his overly correct English that reminded me strongly of a man I had never met. I know Mother appreciates it. We cannot be terribly interesting company for you.

I will always compliment your cooking, Bernardo, but not your subtlety. At this time in my life my appetite for interesting is much smaller than my need for simple kindness, and I thank you for it.

Your appetite is not so good, I have noticed. You did not like the mussels?

They were delicious, of course. It's true, I'm not

hungry these days.

Our eyes met, and I was surprised by the directness of his gaze. Suddenly he seemed less comical, less the humble servant, more like—a man. But my gaze did not waver; I've been fooled before. His eyes dropped again to his empty espresso cup.

Do you ever think that you'll return to America?

I do not think that.

You've made a home here, then.

Is anyone really at home in Trieste?

You are being romantic, he said, or you are having fun with me. You are not romantic, I think.

I've given it up, I said.

You should find yourself some occupation. Mother watches you—watches over you, I should say. She says you're lonely. You have no husband?

I have a husband. But he does not have me.

Very unfortunate for him. Did you know, he added, without segue, that I am part Jewish?

You amaze me.

It's true. Papa was half-Jewish which makes me one-quarter so. He was lucky to escape when the Germans were here.

Haven't the Germans always been here? Look at the buildings. Look at what you brought for dessert.

Ah! he said, the Austrians. That's not the same thing.

Hitler was Austrian.

I was a little surprised at the energy of his response,

as I was by the entire direction that the conversation was hurtling. I began to feel less confidence in his English, or in my own powers of understanding.

Hitler was Hitler. An accident of history, an abortion. It was not our fault, it was the *Anschluss.* My father was an Irredentist. Do you know what that means?

He was an Italian.

He was an Italian Jew who wanted Trieste to stay Italian. He felt safer with Mussolini than he did with Hitler. And he wasn't wrong. It wasn't until Il Duce was gone that they began to kill Jews here.

Why are you telling me this?

Because you are a Jew and you will understand.

My husband, I said, would call that an error in logic.

I would like to meet your husband, he said simply. I have not met many Jews. I would like to see what they are like.

There were many Jews here once.

In Trieste?

In Europe. But you must find me disappointing.

Why?

I am not very Jewish.

Ah, but you are an American, and that also is interesting. An American is so many different things.

I am not very American either. I don't feel American or Jewish. I can't help being those things, but I don't feel them. I don't know what it would be like to feel them.

Then we are not so different.

It felt, in spite of the clumsiness of his mother, in spite of his too-round, too smooth egg-like head, and the little mustache undoubtedly dyed black, like an offer of friendship. We smiled shyly at each other.

In this posthumous life I lead a friendship seems like something to risk. Do I want, I ask myself that night in bed with my eyes closed, waiting for the images to come, to restart the film? I am tired of being looked at, as Bernardo is probably tired of being ignored. He seems to offer some small, good ground of neutrality, in which I might wait out these last days before the disease makes itself visible and the film loses its poetry, turns into something maudlin, a weepie. Before that time comes I'll throw the switch, darken the screen. It is strange how I have never managed to fascinate an American man. My hope is that Bernardo is not fascinated. I would like to sit in a room with someone unfascinated for a change. Even to write these letters to you, Elsa, letters you don't read, I feel that pressure of eyes. Your eyes from when you were very young, locked on me like the eyes of Fate herself. I am as tired of the future as I am of the past. Bernardo has never started his life. Perhaps he can help me to finish mine.

I had another life, Nadia tells Ruth, as real as this one. More real, because it is complete, finished. Like a circle, like a snake with its tail in its mouth.

Sitting at the coffeehouse, the children sleeping in their strollers. Looking down at the perfect leaf of her latte. I had another husband. Another child.

For a moment Ruth can see them, like shadows, feel that vanishing presence of the afterlife. Are they dead? Please don't say they're dead.

I was born in 1989 and I was very young when I met him. Sixteen. He was eighteen and thought he was a man. I did too. He had a motorcycle and he'd take me on long rides through the hills above our town. Then I got pregnant and said to him, You must marry me. So he did. We were married twice, in fact, first in a courthouse, and then, to please his mother, in the Orthodox Church.

Vladimir couldn't find a job so one day he said to me, Let's go to Petersburg, my cousin works there. We went. His cousin was named Nikolai, he was fair where Vladimir was dark, he had pale feathery eyebrows and a blond beard and strong muscles from the work he did in construction, he had a job on a work site and he got Vladimir a job too, although Vladimir was smaller and much more delicate, he would have preferred to work at a desk but he had no education, he left school to be with me. We lived together in Nikolai's flat in a big building in a series of big buildings far from the city center, you only knew it was St. Petersburg because of the river rolling by heading north to Finland. I wanted to work but Vladimir was proud, like Boris is now, he said it wasn't good for the baby and I should stay home. I was bored, I watched TV, the doctor told me not to smoke but he was smoking a cigarette when he said it so I still smoked occasionally. I didn't drink though, I never liked it, I left that to Vladimir and Nikolai, in the evenings they'd empty a bottle of vodka and sing together on the little balcony overlooking the river while I was inside with the TV. Then it happened that they began to work different shifts, Vladimir wasn't good at his job but Nikolai intervened for him and they made Vladimir a night watchman, his only job was to walk around the site all night pressing buttons so his bosses knew he wasn't asleep. He'd come home just before dawn and crawl into bed next to me stinking of some chemical like formaldehyde they must have used on the site, though Nikolai never smelled like that. I'd have to get up then and to amuse myself I'd cook breakfast for Nikolai, who was just waking up. I made elaborate breakfasts for him, traditional Russian dishes like blini with sour cream and cold meats and hardboiled eggs and Turkish coffee brewed very strong. Then he'd sit there eating and smoking and talking to me like Vladimir never talked, he wasn't full of resentful dreams of the life he'd forsaken to be with me, he was living the life he'd chosen and was happy. Of course it was inevitable what would happen, with me bored all day, Vladimir snoring away in one room and me watching TV in the other, or wandering the halls of the building avoiding the old ladies and their gossip, or sometimes taking the little money Vladimir gave me and going out to buy something, anything, a cheap music player or a handbag, taking the subway or the bus to the Nevsky Prospekt where I could see a bit of life, the women in their expensive shoes and makeup and the men very sharp in their business suits, and the tourists speaking other languages, German and French and English, taking pictures of each other. Coming home to Vladimir, who'd yell at me for spending money, heating up something frozen for supper and then letting him paw me a little before he pulled on his boots and headed out to the construction site. He always left an hour or two before his shift, who knows what he was up to after all? Then Nikolai would come home, tired but exuberant, and pull off his own workboots and tell me about the day while I made for him his own special supper. No thank you, I'd say to him, I've already eaten, I'll just watch you, I don't want to sit down, I sit all day waiting for you. It was natural, it was human, what happened between us. I only had to remember in the middle of the night to be sure and get up and move from Nikolai's little bed to the larger one that Vladimir and I shared. I didn't have to worry about getting pregnant of course, I didn't have to worry about anything, that's what I thought. My belly was getting bigger, Vladimir didn't want to touch me anymore, that was fine with me, Nikolai liked it, he caressed my belly and spoke to it, he said the child might as well be his. You can leave him, he told me, we'll go away together, we'll go to America, I will raise your son as my own, or your daughter, it doesn't matter, I love you I love you. I looked into his eyes and saw truth there, he was no older than Vladimir but he was a man and he loved me and I loved him I suppose. I remember how his beard and mustache felt, kissing me.

Of course this story doesn't have a happy ending. It ends stupidly, obviously. One cold autumn evening Vladimir left for work as usual, talking as he always did about the need for us to find a place of our own. He was sick of being crowded and he didn't much like his cousin anymore, he said, he was a nice guy but a bit simple, he didn't have ambition like Vladimir did, Vladimir who tried to study economics in between pushing buttons, he still wanted to go to university someday, to make something of himself. We need our own place, something big enough for us and the baby, just us, our little family he said. I nodded, I didn't listen, I was thinking about Nikolai, he'd be home soon, with his beard and his big handsome hands, he'll take care of me, all I'd ever wanted was to be cared for the way he cared for me, and I had this now, why couldn't this go on forever? My belly was very big, it stuck out of my dressing gown, which was all I wore, my old clothes didn't fit me anymore and Vladimir was too cheap to buy me maternity clothes, he was saving for our apartment he said, and when Nikolai tried to buy me something Vladimir flew into a rage, It's none of your business, he said to him, out there on the balcony where they were drinking, and I imagined they would fight, absurd as that idea was, little Vladimir against giant Nikolai, Nikolai could squeeze the life out of him with one hand if he wanted, but he would never do that, he was so gentle. Vladimir left and I waited for Nikolai, I cooked him his favorite supper, a ham steak and boiled potatoes. The hour came and went, he didn't appear, I didn't worry and then I did, it was late, very late, when I woke up where I was curled on Nikolai's bed and Vladimir was sitting there beside me with his arm around my shoulder and tears on his face, I'm so sorry to have to tell you this, there was an accident today, I've come from the hospital, What is it, I screamed, what is it you are telling me, Calm down he said, you've got to calm down, you'll hurt the baby, Where is he, I screamed, where is Niko, where is my Nikolai, He's dead you stupid lying cunt he's dead I know you cheated on me with him he lost his balance and he fell twenty meters, he's dead, I got up screaming No, no, tore myself from Vladimir's shaking hands and hurried out into the hallway, clutching my belly where the pain had started, one of the doors opened and a pair of malicious black eyes peeped out, Shut the door you bitch, I said, it sounds much worse in Russian, very disrespectful, and then before she could shut it I said Please call the hospital, my baby is coming. He did come, I labored all night in the hospital,

Vladimir didn't come into the room but waited outside wringing his hands, he was filled with remorse he said, he came to me in the morning where I was holding little Josip and said Please don't be angry with me, I didn't mean it, our cousin is dead, let bygones be bygones. But I couldn't manage it somehow, I had to leave him, I went on public assistance and found my own place, and poor little Josip had been born with a heart condition, they tried to fix it, three operations, and the last one he didn't survive, the last time I saw Vladimir was at the funeral, we buried our little boy, not three months old, and I said to myself There are no more tears. But I didn't want to die, I wanted to live, and I was still good-looking though at seventeen years of age I felt fifty or sixty, I made myself up and went on the Internet and met Boris, he was already living here, he came to court me for one weekend in Petersburg and showed me life, fancy dinners and dancing and a suite at the Hotel Astoria, he is not a handsome man but he makes me laugh, he tells good jokes, he is a Jew in fact like you, I saw you hesitate before you told me, it's all right, I am married to a Jewish man, though he's not the least religious and though my father and grandfather blamed the Jews for every evil in the world, besides he has his own business, he's ambitious, he works as a computer engineer in Chicago, so when he asked me to marry him at the end of the weekend I said yes, there was no problem with the divorce, Vladimir I think wanted to forget everything and he was happy to sign the papers, last I heard he had moved to Moscow to enroll in university there. So six months after the divorce was final Boris flew me here and a little less than a year after that we had Boris Junior, my American son, and I have nothing left to wish for but for these memories I have just related to you to lose somehow their hold on me, there's a terrible sort of feeling that comes up when I think about that other life, though not when I tell it to you, Ruth, with your kind eyes. Your eyes tell me I ought to forgive myself, like the woman doctor Boris pays for, she tells me that every week. Yes, I might as well admit there are days I find it difficult to get out of bed. The worst thing I've ever done is to lie there while little Boris screams for me, he's alone in his room and the door is shut and he can't get out, he screams for what seems like hours, and the worst moment of all comes when he stops screaming, all of a sudden like that, like a light switch, and only then in the silence does the guilt and remorse flood my spirit, giving me the strength finally to rise and go to his room and open the door where he is only asleep on the floor, pink and innocent like I was innocent in my love for Vladimir, my love for Nikolai, my love for Josip, buried now like Nikolai in a faraway country that I can't forget. You are very lucky to have been born here, Ruth, you are lucky to be a real American. Even tragedies are cleaner here, they aren't really tragedies: yes, sad things happen, even terrible things, but everyone just forgets as soon as they can and goes on, you are all so optimistic, don't try to deny it, I see it in your eyes, you believe tomorrow will be better than today, that's your birthright, and I want it to be little Boris's birthright, as it can never be mine, because somehow it has the power of coming true. Even big Boris is somehow a believer, I don't know how he managed it, because he is a Jew perhaps, he is more American now than Russian, though my English is already much better than his, he is on fire for this country, where there are no oligarchs, no one-man rule, no Putin and Medvedev playing ping-pong with the presidency, no gangs except in the bad neighborhoods where nobody goes, and where more than money there is hope, endless hope. I am not yet a citizen, I cannot vote, but I wish that I could vote for this man, this black man who wants to be President, I can tell by looking at him he is a good man, a compassionate man, an educated man who wants the best for his people, even people who don't look like he does. Boris hates him, he says he is going to kill the American dream, but I do not hate him, when he comes on the television I always watch and listen. I am even thinking of going to door to door for him, canvassing, although I cannot vote. It is my way of feeling a little American and making a better life for my son, who I hope will never know anything about his brother or Vladimir or Nikolai or Russia or the woman I was before he was born.

It is so kind of you to listen to me. But Boris is

awake. I must go.

Ruth, saying nothing, eyes wet, wants to hug Nadia. But even after these revelations she feels something in the younger woman holding her stiff and apart. Only her own brimming gaze affirms the peculiar connection that Ruth herself feels with this strange Russian woman: as though they were mirrors of each other, as though Nadia in all her scarcely imaginable intimate losses represented for Ruth a kind of destiny, though she has never lost and God willing never will lose a child, or a lover, only her mother, she thinks, her mother. Something of mother here, she realizes, watching Nadia go, something reminds me of her. She knows something I don't know, that's the feeling I've had my whole life. Secrets, my mother's secrets, and Nadia's. Somehow the capacity to retain the feeling of a secret, though she has apparently disclosed all.

Her own phone buzzes. Time to go. The sun is brilliant overhead. There are mothers, mothers everywhere, pushing strollers, holding tiny people by the hand, waiting patiently at crosswalks, wiping stains from little mouths. What did she mean, is it somehow American to have children, crazy thought, but it's true, there's a kind of blind optimism or denial or expectation in these parents, some domesticated wild hope for a life lived that's entirely potential, unrealized, golden glowing and embodied in these little animals that will grow into disappointing humans like the rest of us. I am no different. But there are times, more and more, I look at Lucy, small as she is, and see the truth. She is already far from me, it's her job, someday she'll be gone entirely, even if she calls every week, even if she lives in the house next door, even if she chooses to care for Ben and me in our decrepit old age, spooning soup into my quivering mouth and looking at me with adult pitying eyes. I have lost her. I have lost the dream.

When she gets home there's another letter. She takes it upstairs and puts it, unread, with the others. There is still a little time. She opens her laptop and writes.

I awoke in hospital. Not myself wounded, but tucked uncomfortably into a green plush chair at the bedside of a figure in white. For a moment I remembered nothing, saw nothing, felt myself only to be alone with death or something like death, something still and watchful, commanding if not reverence than at least the silencing of irrelevant thoughts. Be present with your breath, it said. Then I saw the body was a man's and not a woman's and I remembered, in a single unfurling flash, hours or days before, out in the street, pushing through the trailing crowd, searching, where they might be, thinking about police brutality, some of it confirmed and witnessed—the wounded beaten in their stretchers or while handcuffed to hospital beds—and wilder rumors, of students disappeared to secret detention centers, bodies tossed in the Seine, the persistent story of a young man, a boy, run over deliberately by a CRS van, and then backed over to silence the screams, only the crush of bones on pavement audible. Practically hearing it, on a side street now back from the surge, all the shops and houses shut up tight and dark save for one, the little used bookshop on the Rue des Anglais with its metal shutters down but one door open, spilling light onto the street, still open as it had been throughout the month the rest of Paris had taken as a forced holiday, stores opening and closing seemingly at random, sugar shortages, no gas, metro stoppages, no trains running out of town, going everywhere on foot or on a bicycle, for weeks now we'd sustained ourselves selling books we no longer read, no longer needed to read, for school like normal life in the city was indubitably out, the trash uncollected, sidewalks impassable, everyone student and bourgeois alike used the center of the street to get around. All the poetry we need, Charles said, is in the streets and in our blood, the language of youth. Charles with his usual quick thoughtless charm had befriended the owner, a heavy-jowled widow whose feeling for print was entirely mercenary, and yet not untouched by a certain piety, for it had been her husband's shop, her husband who had gotten his fool self killed in the Resistance, or so she'd tell anyone who asked—guillotined by the Gestapo she said, not without a certain relish, drawing two fingers across her throat, cigarette trailing smoke like the ghost of his martyr's blood. She was a pensioner with modest needs, she insisted, she kept the store in her husband's honor, he had loved the students, had been one himself, would surely have become a professor at the university after the war, except—*snick*. And as she said this she would be assessing your stack of books with her deceptively slack yellow eye, and then quote you a price at least fifty francs less than the books were really worth, and yet the shop was convenient to our flat and she always paid cash on the spot. I never saw anyone buy anything there, only sell; she must have had a mail-order business or perhaps she was truly the martyr to her husband's memory she claimed. At any rate, Charles won her over, did her little favors, never complained about her sharp dealings, and now in the street I saw them through the metal shutters in the window looking out, and when I rapped on the grating I saw Mme. Rossignol hand her key to Charles, who opened the door and unlocked the gate and let me in. A dozen meters off the endless crowd surged by, the new old crowd, our parents' crowd, supplemented by thick-necked brush-cut youths of another order than the slim-hipped revolutionaries who had seemingly driven all other species out of the ecosystem of the Rive Gauche. They weren't even from Paris, Charles muttered, full of conspiracies; the Gaullists had bussed them in from the most benighted corners of the Republic for the express purpose of cracking heads, and the government would get no blood on its hands. Your sort of people, he said to me suddenly. No offense. I mean, the sort you grew up with. The sort you ought to be. Peasants. Creatures of false consciousness.

You know, M said, smiling slightly. Americans.

She had gotten somewhere a cut on her forehead, a superficial abrasion really, and it made her seem less rather than more vulnerable. The blood had fled her cheeks and her face was hard and angular. She wore black from neck to toe, except for a striped scarf—it belonged to Charles—that she'd knotted Windsor-style, so that she looked androgynous and natty. Charles's blood was up. We must act, he said. We have to find our brothers. Counterattack.

Mes pauvres enfants, Mme. Rossignol said, looking at Charles, his fine blond glow. She was standing as always at the high counter—there was a low stool behind her that she rarely sat upon, for when she did she and her authority vanished, inviting shoplifters. The store itself was narrow and claustrophobic with its high shelves crammed with a cacophony of medical textbooks and artists' anatomies and a complete set of Balzac and a reprint of the first French edition of Darwin's *L'origine des espèces* and a dozen copies of the first volume of *Capital* (no sign of the second or third) and the poetry of Baudelaire and *Germinal* and near the top shelf, in the back, all in a row, the most recent acquisitions, shelved three deep, books from the denuded flats of ourselves and the revolution. When it's all over we'll have to buy them back, I thought, and then Mme. Rossignol will turn the profit she's been dreaming of. But it was blasphemous to think so, and I glanced quickly at Charles and M as though they had heard my thoughts. The bell over the door rang. M had run out into the street and Charles, after a moment's gape, had run after her. Mme. Rossignol and I stared at each other, stupefied, like sailors in a ship abandoned by its captain.

They'll be killed! she said at last, as though reporting the verdict of the highest authorities.

I ran after them, pelting down the alley piled high with trash, empty boxes, bits of rubble, past the naked stumps of trees that had gone for barricades, past boarded and blacked-out windows like so many mouths of broken teeth, toward the end where light and darkness mingled and the bodies were surging past. The chant *Vive De Gaulle! Vive la France!* thumping and thundering, felt more than heard, shaking me out of the private dream that had grown to include the world and my friends. At the end of the alley was a black knight, a man on a great dark horse, his uniform absorbing all the light, a glint where eyes should be, a rock to break the human wave. M had seized the reins and was shouting up at him, her face white, tendons on her throat standing up, Charles also shouting, reaching his arm across her, to grab the reins himself or to protect her or simply in reflex. He had never looked more beautiful, his light overshone M's completely. I wanted to hear what they were saying, screaming at each other, Charles and M and the horseman, but only heard the chant. *Vive la France.* And as Charles pushed M back, snapping her grip, the horseman raised his baton and brought it down with astonishing speed, hard and forceful, onto the top of Charles's head. I heard the crack. And his face twisted upward toward the sky, uncomprehending, the blood starting to flow. And M on the ground, and his body covering her. The horse reared up against the crowd, the bridges, the sky, a figure of ancient power, something atavistic coming to claim the City of Lights for its own. I felt his silhouette over me, like I felt the crowd chanting. And then the clap of iron hooves, and the crowd surged, and he was gone. We were in the mouth of the alley, M and I, alone with Charles and the blood matting his hair and trickling through our fingers and onto the street.

Charles. You thought you understood love. But to love is to look, and you never once opened your eyes. No need to look when everyone looks at you. And you look out at everyone and see only masses and theories and most of all yourself. Your women, Charles, your women showed you everything, there was nothing left to the imagination, because it was your imagination they wanted to test, and you failed. Remember the poster, Charles, the one I helped to print and you helped to write? *I take my desires for reality because I believe in the reality of my desires.* A lover's creed. But what is it you desire, dear Charles? Can you give it a name? Revolution? Power? Or simply not to go on with things as they have been, not to go on with yourself? Yours is the heroism of the suicide, whose only faith is in the blankness that will come after blowing yours and everybody's brains out, certain that nothing will remain: *après moi, le neant.* You love nothing but the new. And that's why in spite of yourself, in spite of your broken skull, you'll live on to pass your exams, choose a career, marry. It takes the love of others to keep your powder dry. But we are drifting away.

Where was she? I remembered her leading the way after I hoisted Charles on my back, darting in fits and starts through the streets, trying to avoid further contact with cops and crowds, running for the hospital. His dead weight on my back. M looking back at me, her mouth set in a line, her eyes alive with fear, two little flames in a field of ashes. Body of Charles, the burnt blunt blur of a second head on my shoulders. Limp, leaden. His blood soaked through my nylon windbreaker, through my shirt. I don't remember anyone else in the streets, just a few parked cars and the weird gray light of the sky reflecting back at us the lights of the city we dimly remembered from the days before the riots, the lights of shops and billboards, the city as it had given itself to me in the first days: lights running up and down, peering out from the exposed skeleton of the Eiffel Tower, the spotlights throwing the facade of Notre-Dame into shadow like an African mask, or the spooky reactionary light that bathed the smooth dome of Sacré-Coeur, day and night. It was an endless stagger, not quite a run, M leading the way, reaching a white hand back toward me and me reaching out toward it with my free hand, never quite touching, silent running, blankness, sound returning only when she ran up the stone steps of the ancient building, *l'hopital*, and pulled open the outer door and held it for me, us, sweat burning my eyes, I registered with a glance once more her face, cast down and away, as I passed through the doors into the light-filled hum of the gray-green corridor, calling for a doctor, blundering through chairs, up to a hole in the wall behind which a middle-aged woman in white sat writing, looking up appalled at the bloated gasping giant filling her window, and the ruined face of Charles slack and expressionless. I held him in my arms now, like a child, an offering. And it wasn't until a noise came to answer the roaring in my ears, two identical orderlies with black grease-streaked hair easing my burden from me, directing me to a chair, Charles flying away on a gurney to triage and surgery, other patients and attendants now manifesting around me, holding magazines and books, looking at me curiously. I heard the ringing of phones and the names of doctors being paged and the resumption of small talk (a elderly woman in the chair directly behind me talking slowly and patiently and loudly, as though to a deaf person, to the much younger man next to her about the holiday she'd taken last winter in Martinique—her son, grandson, a stranger, who knew?)—as I say, it was only then that I registered M wasn't there. Perhaps she was smoking a cigarette on the steps to calm her nerves? But when I stepped back out through the doors there was no sign of her. Two men in white stood next to an ambulance sipping Styrofoam cups of coffee and I came down to them gesticulating. No. A girl? No. They'd just arrived. They were between calls. A quiet night, they said. Quieter than they'd had in a long time. They were exhausted, really. Yes, they had sympathized with the students at first, especially when the cops started cracking heads. But enough was enough. De Gaulle had called elections, what more did they want? He was the man for a crisis, even now. He stood head and shoulders above the opposition. That little Jew, what was his name, one said to the other. Cohn-something, his companion replied. The chubby little redhead. Give it a rest, why doesn't he. Give us all a rest.

I turned heavily on my heel and climbed back into the hospital. Sat down exhausted in the row of plastic chairs outside the door through which Charles had disappeared.

I am a lover of one thing, Charles. Like you I have no name for that thing, only aliases. For a long time it was art, a great imposing house at the door of which I camped out, waiting, almost glad when *les événements* came to carry me away. Then, for a little while, it was you. A man I should have hated for having everything, being everything, that I was not: money, looks, a golden tongue, above all that ease of movement, gesture, insolence. Instead I loved you, and in your own way you requited that love. For an even littler while, I loved what you professed to love: the revolution. Not because I wanted the servant to at last be the master, but only because I was an outcast, invisible, neither student nor worker, not even a peasant any more, young in a way you've never been, without the beauty of youth. I didn't love your cause, only your face, its pride and haughtiness, its cruel humor. So beautiful all the faces, all the young men and women, the faces I tried to capture in my sketchbook, many faces united in single transcendent moods of outrage, euphoria, attentiveness, like so many dogs listening to the same inhuman frequency. Faces to stand behind, faces in the grips of bodies, thousands of faces floating down boulevards toward perfect destruction and loss. Even now past the end I see those faces facing the faceless—the cops and their sticks, their gas, their guns. Have you seen these men, have you seen a man like your horseman with his helmet off? I have. He is neither young nor old. A kind of savage humor in the set of his jaw, the line of his mouth. No eyes, even without the visor, without sunglasses. If he ever had eyes he lost them in Algeria or Indochina. He fought there and committed atrocities so you, Charles, could grow your own beautiful face, like a sunflower in a jar, all of you, thousands of sunflowers, until the time came to harvest them, to reap youth, to ensure that future in which nothing happens. A sunflower like Van Gogh's, vivid with madness and joy, most alive the moment it's torn from its roots.

But Charles, there was another face, another flower, with invisible roots, arcing downward forever out of sight, inscrutable in perpetual half-light, a face neither old or new, the face of M. She puzzled you, challenged you. She gave you what the others had, but contemptuously, and she let you feel her contempt. She showed you nothing of herself that you didn't have to invent for her. On my canvas that you have not seen and never will see. Her pain makes her beautiful: in that we are guilty of the same crime, seeing that or not seeing it. It sets her apart from the world, a foreigner wherever she may be. In America too I'd wager.

A bright morning. Summer was beginning to pierce the heavy damp cloak of the long spring. The light was paralyzing, falling directly on my face from the window opposite where the still swathed form of Charles lay. And it took another moment to recognize whom the regal woman of more than middle height with her ash blonde hair in a chignon must be, standing next to a lean greyhound of a man in sunglasses and a gray mustache, both of them looking in from the doorway with fixed expressions of horror. Directed at me, I somehow felt, and not at the wreck that had been their son—for their son he surely was—in the bed there. I tried to stand, but a surge of nausea bent me double, and I sat down again.

They were in the room. It was narrow; they had to stand in front of me where I sat in the green plush chair to look at their son, so that I saw only the backs of their coats. They stood close together and yet not touching, haloed by the glare of the sun from the window behind them. I managed with difficulty now to stand, and with greater difficulty to edge past them toward the doorway, almost believing they hadn't seen me, that I might get away. But I felt a hand grip my arm.

What happened to my son? the woman demanded.

All I could see in her face—the blue eyes, the refined cheekbones, the fullness of her upper lip—was Charles. I opened my mouth and closed it.

They say you brought him in, she said. I should call the police.

It was the police that did this to him, I said.

She creased her brow and removed her hand from my sleeve. It was as though I spoke in another tongue. Her husband did not change position, but I saw his hands gripping the bar on Charles's bed, the knuckles flexing pink, then white; pink, then white. I could not take my eyes off of them.

How could you say such a thing? How could this have happened to my boy? My beautiful boy?

Standing at the foot of the bed I saw Charles's face inside its margin of white bandages. It looked small and impossibly pale, severe as the carved stone face saint. And that other face, face of a mother, identical to his but for the touch of lipstick and blusher, the plucked eyebrows, the blue eyes holding my gaze for a moment longer. Then her eyes closing, slowly. Turning her face away. Leaning now into the body of her husband, both gazing mutely, crossed shadow of the window falling on them, on the antiseptic bed, barring what would not ignite in whiteness. The cross.

Flight, then. Into the slumbering submarine streets of Paris after the revolution, the crested tide of youth, irrefutably itself, and me what I had been at the beginning, once again. A stranger.

Charles was in hospital for six weeks, as long as the Events themselves had lasted. Longer. A lot happened, nothing happened. L'Ecole des Beaux-Arts had been the last stronghold to fall, but fall it had and classes had resumed. I attended a few times to see what it felt like, then stopped because it didn't feel like anything. The young people no longer moved in invincible masses; they stood around in little clusters of three or four, talking softly or not talking, shoulders hunched, sheltering cigarettes, filing into and out of exam rooms. Men in green uniforms made the mountains of trash disappear, brought in saplings from the country to replace the uprooted trees. Work crews were everywhere putting fresh impenetrable layers of asphalt on top of the remaining paving-stones. Some graffiti was left; already these bits of brick and granite had become tourist attractions, flocked to by groups of Austrians and Italians with cameras clicking, while a self-appointed docent, subsidized by the state for all I knew, stood underneath a furled umbrella and blared the facts about the revolution that wasn't, that hadn't. The summer vacation was on; the city began, again, to empty. The concierge told me one afternoon as I came in from a rain shower that Charles's share of the rent payment had not been forthcoming, and I would have to come up with the extra francs or vacate the premises by the end of July. I went upstairs, dripping, and lay down in my wet clothes on the floor. Someone had come for Charles's things while I was out; his clothes were gone, the record turntable, the set of gold pens he'd received as the winner of a prize at lycee he'd somehow never gotten around to pawning. Of M and myself there was only my old trunk, the electric tea kettle, my paintings and sketches, and a small red suitcase which I opened and rummaged through without compunction. On top of a small collection of blouses and underthings was a stack of letters, postmarked Queens, New York, rubber-banded in a stack and unopened. I hefted them, flipped through them like the pages of a book; collectively they represented about a year and a half of steady correspondence, a letter every month or so. I held one up to the light. I sniffed it: clean paper, slight stink of ink from a ballpoint. The handwriting appeared masculine. Another lover? A teacher? Her father? I knew little of American geography but the American ambassador-at-large did not, I thought, live in Queens. She had been gone for almost a month. I heated up water in the kettle, got up a head of steam; it didn't whistle any more, no one could possibly detect my violation, or the barefaced need that led me to it. I held the most recent of the envelopes over the steam, not caring if it singed my fingers a little. The envelope's dampened flap curled upward like a lip. I sat by the window and slid the single sheet of blue paper into my palm. But I couldn't read it. It was in a strange language, profligate with accents. Finnish? Hungarian? A language that I'd never seen, or heard, or suspected that M might speak. Perhaps she didn't speak it. Perhaps the letters were unopened. It was signed *az Apád*. I stared at the meaningless clots of syllables for a while, then carefully replaced the folded letter in its envelope and resealed the flap. It rejoined its brothers in the suitcase full of similarly mute objects. There was one more item aside from clothing: a small leatherbound diary, with a rawhide strap winding it shut. I opened it. All the pages were blank.

One afternoon not long after that I climbed upstairs with a few groceries and discovered a padlock on the door to the flat, my trunk and M's suitcase standing at attention on the mat. My sketches were in the trunk, the painting of M was not. I called the concierge, got no answer that was clearer than the lock on the door: something had ended, it was time to move on. But I couldn't move on. An acquaintance from the art school took me in temporarily while I tried to get my bearings. I was no longer a student. I no longer sketched or painted. M and my picture of M, both gone. My mornings were given over to reading detective novels—my friend had long shelves full of them, in French and English—and my afternoons to wandering along the Seine or the Luxembourg Gardens. I ate comparatively little and my big belly began to hollow itself out. If I caught sight of myself in the mirror, I saw only the skull beneath the skin. I went by the old building with some money I'd borrowed and the concierge let me into the still vacant flat. The walls smelled of fresh paint. There was no sign of the picture of M, she hadn't seen it, had no idea what had happened to it, some blacks cleaned the place out, she shrugged, maybe they took it. I looked in the trash bins but too many days had passed. I heard Simone was back in town and sought her out, to see if M had been in contact with her. She had a part-time job in a handbag shop in the Marais; I found her standing in its doorway smoking a cigarette, half an hour before closing time. Simone's beauty had become more angular, an effect enhanced by what she'd done to her long hair: she'd chopped it all off into a sort of bob, poised disconcertingly between Louise Brooks and Joan of Arc. I look like a collaborator, she said laughingly, offering me one of her cigarettes. We smoked together. An older woman in a short-waisted black frock watched us from inside with her arms folded.

Don't look at that bitch, Simone said. She thinks she owns the street.

Is she a customer?

Simone blew smoke. She's my boss.

Have you seen Charles? I said after a while.

She shrugged, shook her head. Is he recovering?

I don't know. I suppose so.

What about M?

I was hoping you'd seen her, actually.

Simone shrugged again. No. I have some mail for her, though.

Letters? From New York?

How would you know that? Simone said suspiciously.

It's just a guess. That's where she says she's from.

I wish I were from there, Simone said fervently. I wish I were from anywhere else. I wish I weren't stuck in this shithole. The spiraling gesture she made with her cigarette encompassed the shop, the street, all of France. You know, he really believed that a new age was dawning, Charles did. This wasn't what was supposed to happen. There ought to be a revolutionary committee right now, with Charles on it, running the show. Rich little cunts like her (flashing her sweetest smile) pushed up against the wall and shot like the counter-revolutionary pigs they are. Now, I'm selling fake alligator bags to women just like her. And when fall comes again I'll go back to school and meet some guy like the kind of guy I knew before I met Charles. He'll want to take care of me. And I'll let him. The fucker. The poor fucking bastard.

I don't understand anything, I said, crushing out my smoke.

That's why I always liked you, Gus, Simone said, looking up at me through her bangs. You know what you don't know, unlike the rest of them. And you're gentle, and sweet. Did you ever show M that giant dick of yours?

If you see her, I said, starting to walk away, tell her.

Tell her what?

Just tell her, that's all. Good luck, Simone.

She didn't say anything until I was almost half a block away. Then I heard her shouting *Bonne chance!* ironically at my back. I waved without turning around.

It all happened like she said. She met a guy whose father owned a car dealership in Rouen, and dropped out of school and married him and moved there. They had three kids. Dropped into the stream of life that flows steadily and without interruption. No happier or unhappier, I'm sure, than anybody else. It makes me feel cold inside to think of it. As for me, I kept on living in the aftermath of an inchoate hope. A hope that had taken an improbable twinned form: the beautiful young people in the streets, the beautiful face of my American. A desire that persisted in the wake of that hope, a spiritual hangover. For one wide horizon-to-horizon moment I had kept company with beauty. I could never be beautiful myself, I knew that. Nor could I expect the beautiful, the chosen ones, to love me. It would have been better to hate them, and I did hate them. But I also loved: *je les aimais.* I adored, *je les adorais.* All the intimacy of the *tu* folded up in that anonymous plural: me and the students, me and M, our fellow Americans. That plural preserves the proper distance from the *I*: I the freakishly large, I the uncouth, I the dirty-minded peasant boy, I the secret German, son of Vichy, son of Pétain, the reluctantly claimed son of a village lawyer who could barely meet my eye when he was alive.

It was time to go home; or rather, since there was no home to go to, just as there was no glimmering future, then it was time to go on with some sort of decision about who and what I was. If not an artist then an illustrator; if not an illustrator then a painter of walls and houses and signs. This is how I brought in the little money I needed to keep overlarge body and attenuated soul together: in white coveralls, on ladders, in genteel apartments, applying layer upon layer of the subtle and inoffensive colors of the bourgeoisie: off white, pale lemon, cream blue, watered rose. My comrade and employer was Yusuf, born in Tunis, raised in Marseilles, a small and wiry man with a black widow's peak shot with an arresting streak of gray, a prominent nose hanging out over his perpetual, somehow shaggy grin, into which an American cigarette was often fixed. Mutt and Jeff, Stan and Ollie, we toured the better neighborhoods in his little Renault van, stopping always with the concierges and managers who were our true employers so that Yusuf could slip them a couple of cartons of cigarettes and a bottle of Hennessy, the price of doing business he explained to me. We rarely saw or interacted with the high hausfraus whose domestic interiors we freshened; when we did, swarthy Yusuf who was always quick with a filthy joke on the ground floor suddenly became shy and nudged me forward to doff my cap and speak, pulling unexpected rank as native Frenchman, as *le Blanc.* The White.

Make sure your man there doesn't touch anything he doesn't need to, I was told on more than one occasion by well-kept women holding their purses tightly against their sides, in their own homes. And I, playing my part, would reply Certainly, Madame. You have no occasion for worry, I assure you; he's been my faithful employee for years. Eventually I ceased to wonder at how these women could possibly take me for the employer and superior of a man twice my age. But I'm proud even now to say that my use to Yusuf extended beyond these necessary deceptions, for though a deft enough hand with a brush he would always call upon me to execute tricky scrollwork or to follow a line of molding where it met expensive antique wallpaper. I would lie almost prone on the dropcloth like Michelangelo, applying quick sure strokes of the brush, never spilling a drop, while Yusuf took one of his frequent cigarette breaks, talking incessantly of the perfidy of his wife, referring to her always with pride as a native Frenchwoman, une vraie femme and like all of them a spendthrift, whore, and liar. His imagination had been fully stocked by the Swedish blue movies he screened in his spare hours with a crowd of other painters, mechanics, and cabbies from his homeland, many of them his cousins, in a nameless sort of social club in the shadows of the housing projects of Belleville. Even now, he said, gesturing expansively, she's no doubt greeting some salesman at the door in her dressing gown, nothing underneath, while my son's at school and I'm out here breaking my back so that she can wear those fancy perfumes she likes. It's a scandal, I tell you. It would serve her right if I got one of these hoity bitches alone for once like the one who lives here. Did you see the ass on her?

The posterior in question belonged to a matron with dyed hair, sixty if she was a day, and no doubt amply supported by elastic.

You have no idea how good you've got it, Yusuf said sadly. If I was your age, the tail I'd be chasing! And catching, too. And you're educated, everyone can hear it in your voice. You could be the man of the house, a house just like this one, if you had any sense. What are you doing here, anyway?

Just because I've been to school doesn't make me smart.

He laughed: That is the truth, my friend! You speak truth!

Yusuf, I said later, as we were packing up. What did you do in May?

What do you mean?

I mean during the events.

That was a crap time, Yusuf said emphatically. Business went completely into the shitter. I stayed away from the trouble until it was over.

But how did you feel about it? I mean, what the students and workers were doing?

The workers? Don't talk to me about the workers. I am a worker. It had nothing to do with me.

Liberation has nothing to do with you?

Liberation to do what? To go where? Listen, I'm the son of a bricklayer who couldn't support his family. Instead of going out to make money, he went to the mosque, as if every day were Friday. I looked around me at my brothers and my sisters and my uncles and aunts and said, I'm not going to live like this! I came here on my own and made a business and made a life in the richest and most beautiful city in the world. Married a Frenchwoman. My kids will go to university. What more can I ask for?

But what about racism? What about what we did to your people? Doesn't that make you angry?

"We," Gustave? What "we" are you talking about?

I don't know, I said. The French. Europeans. The West.

Yusuf laughed. We had been driving in the little van and were now stopped at the Metro station where he could drop me off before beginning the climb back home to Ménilmontant.

Just names, he said. Listen, it's the end of the week. He took a zippered envelope out of his pocket and counted out my pay.

Thanks.

This, he said, holding up the barely diminished wad of bills, this is what it's all about. Money and nothing else. You ought to remember that.

I wish I could.

It'll come to you, Yusuf said, his wolfish grin restored.

One moment, I said, a thought suddenly occurring to me. A flat off the Boul' Mich. I gave him the address.

Were you by chance the one to paint it over? It would have been sometime in early July. I used to live there. Did you find anything left behind?

Yusuf shrugged. It doesn't sound familiar. But yeah, you know yourself we paint over vacated flats all the time, all the time we have to clean out the junk some deadbeat's left behind. Not always junk. I got a pretty decent hi-fi out of an apartment I was painting once.

It was a painting of a woman. Kind of modern, I suppose. A nude.

Yusuf whistled. Sure I'd remember that. No.

You're sure?

Why are you asking me? Yusuf asked, annoyed. Was she your girlfriend?

No. Never mind. I'll see you later.

I watched him drive away. I felt myself settling back into the numbness that had been my lot since even before the policeman's baton had come down on Charles's unprotected skull. M's arm reaching up, I remembered, to ward off the blow. At least, that's what I told myself I had seen.

I thought and felt nothing through the long ride home. Thought and felt nothing stopping at the boulangerie for a ham-and-butter sandwich. Thought and felt nothing climbing the narrow, flaking stairway up to the room I'd been renting since my friend's parents had forced him to kick me out—for the fall term had begun, and it was now time, as they said, to put away childish things.

I unlocked the door and stepped inside. The lights were out, of course, so I turned them on. And there she was, curled up on the ratty little rug that was one of the room's few creature comforts, knees bent, one arm thrown back behind her head, staring at the ceiling. A plastic shopping bag sat beside her.

I fell into the armchair, a white continent streaked with arabesques of blue and pink paint.

I said her name.

Hi Gus, she said, not moving from her position on the floor. It's good to see you.Charles has been released from the hospital, she added. He's gone home to his parents. I'm going home, too. But I wanted to see you first.

She knelt before me. Her eyes, clear of makeup, were brimming with tears.

I've been such a fool. And she lay her head in my lap.

Tentatively, my paint-heavy hand touched her hair.

It's all right, I said.

And it was.

Madeleine. Matutinal. Marianne, Maribelle, Maria, Mary. Monday, Monday. Murmur *martyr*, my mother. Murk, mist, *maledictum*. Murder. Marizkha, Mikhaela, Maya. Maryam. Misery makes mournful memories, must make memory-minders mad. Moths mire mullioned mouths, meadowing. Milk milks milky maids. March. More, Madame? Magda, Malika, Marcsa, Martuska. Microphone. Meridian. Mulch milching mud. Ma. Mare. My *mare*, my moon. My Manhattan, my malted, Michelangelo. Mike mechanizes mother's medicine. Medic! Magnficos macerate macaroons, make madder, my my. Maculate my minister, my messenger's misfortune. Maintains mum. Morning's minion. Madgehowlet. Maggot. Miles manufacture, missy might meddle, muffle misogynists. Mixed messages, magnified. Mastered mainsheets make miles more merry. Munificent main, maritime moment. Martha, May, Misty. Moth-eaten *mot*, makebate. Milady's malady? Meliceris? My madame's malapert. Male malpractice, mistaken malignity, maladminstered modes modify my modesty. Mother. Miss me. Musk. Many materteral maids make my mincing misses' mephitic meconium. Maladjusted missal, marshal more mummers, make mayhem, make measure. Misrule. Monumental man, moon-eyed mogul, march myriad museums Maltaward. Murder. Millennium. Millicent. Mandarins make mandamus misprised mainpernable misdemeanors. Minx. Minor minuets mimic majority matrices, madrasas matriculate minors, merry melodies meander. Madness. Mandate. More: Muriel, Margaret, Mytrle, Miranda. Magdalene. Mingled mayflies mock maypoles. Marry, my mobled mistress mutes moneyed monastics. Misunderstood, much? Master? My moment's monument. Marble. My mother mortified, moldered, massively, my me. Monitoring my mounted marshal, my maugering meager messiah, makes me mundane mostly, moth-eaten, 'maciated. Mitigates menace. Molly, molybdenum, Mara, Mavis, Maxine, Monica, Moira, Mimi, Minerva. Murk menacing mosstroopers. Midnight. Moonstruck. Monstrous. *Moi, ma mademoiselle.* My mine. Misled. Mitred. Motiveless malignity. Mythic murmuring. Molting. Mirage.

4

Miramare

NOIR. IT UNFOLDS, IT SPREADS, needing no shape to advance, unforeseeable container of itself, like this prose, like a camera set up at ankle level under a table, angled upward and left to run, to catch what catch can. "Whose point of view is that?" "Mine." They stream by, sinister men and women, pants and dresses, terrifying nostrils, the emphasis falling on unregarded surfaces, the backs of hands, heads, buttocks, pointed heels, small dogs with short legs in rapid clicking motion, the light inescapably itself, marking an ordinary afternoon in the city, any city of the sun—Rome, Barcelona, Port-au-Prince, Miami, Lahore, Heraklion, Cairo—city on the Black Sea—capable of casting long shadows before nightfall, doorways cutting themselves out of streets, noir, each walker at an angle to herself, a sense of thickness to the air, slightest slow motion, a few extra frames per second, adding new hours to the day for a second life of dreams, mosaic of the day rearranged, plotless, into fragments of color: a hand grips a knife, a father faces his son, a husband and wife play chess. Every hair on your head is counted. And a man is speaking, a man's mouth, lips full like mine, moving pauselessly, tip of his tongue flashing between white irregular teeth, the volume's all the way down but there's something like room tone, street tone, it's no void, roaring like surf (a sun city, city by the sea), tuned into a bass line, a song you danced to once in a sweating cinderblock club, white shirts gone purple in the black light on the men, flashing under dark suits, the women like suns grown old in their tight red dresses (under Ibiza, Jamaica, every deep a lower deep, clubbed) tripping limbs and heads snapped back, numb to the point of a wallflower's nonexistence, watching all this, the music no longer music, just a grind, thoughtless perceiving point, the father is lecturing, lips and hound jaws and chin and tongue wagging, the upper mandible immobile as we know, top of your attention (the frame) cutting off the windows to the soul, just a mouth's authority, fathering—but who, who is he—soundtrack blurring out what you thought you wanted most to know—what is he saying. You do not wake from this, a camera dreams its battery life away. You are alone with the others in the theater looking at a bright white screen, that isn't even white, a sort of mesh or grid or desert of such terrible purity it becomes annihilating substance, if you could feel in two dimensions, that part of yourself that's always a little ahead of the rest of you, in the eyes, in front of them, like the little space for breath between nose and mouth, visible in winter, the image of the past, its absence, retreating, red shift. It's a simple situation moments before you wake: you sit looking forward at nothing, as at the sea at night, and nothing spreads its wings behind you in transcendental light, making no shadows on the wall, and you are lying in bed, and there's a woman in your arms, and she tells you a story in which you play no part.

Dear Elsa,

I'm going to sing to you now, sing like a canary. Sing from pain. To truly sing is to open a second mouth deep inside your body; it is the wound that sings. Something deeper than memory, than images, something in the flesh. You can catch it like a disease, you can be afflicted with someone else's memories. I sang, I smoked too much, for the same reason, smoke from a bomb crater, smoke from the crematoria, smoke from the secret mouth. And do you have the same syndrome, do you remember for me who spent her whole life trying to understand her own mother's silence? I sang for my father, from a very young age, and my mother was my teacher though I thought she was dead. I was six years old and they had all been years of terror and unease, from the moment they stamped the word *Zsido* on my birth certificate to my girlhood in a dying and divided city to the chaotic postwar period in which I changed apartments three times before my father appeared one gray morning, thin as a rake, someone I only remembered from photographs, to take me away from my mother's parents, the only family I'd ever known, with the single magic word *America*, and bring me limp and stunned on the long journey through the belly of destroyed Germany that ended in the former SS barracks in the DP camp in Belsen where my father and I would live for the next three years. I sat next to him on the packed and smoky train car that first night, trembling, forced close by overcrowding and yet wanting not to touch him, this stranger with his shapeless cloth cap and death's-head cheekbones and nails bitten to the quick. To calm me he told me to sing with him, it was December so we sang Christmas songs in Hungarian, "Silent Night" and "O Tannenbaum," and the other cramped and miserable refugees in the carriage, every one of them a Jew like us, began to sing along. Then once we were settled in that bare, bleak, drafty room my lessons began in earnest—my father found me a teacher, a once-plump woman called Frau Drechsler with thick gray hair and severe black brows and deep wrinkles on her cheeks, so that her true age was impossible to fathom, to teach me the canon, in her own language which she spoke in a harsh croaking raven's voice that dissolved impossibly at the drop of a hat into the half-ruined but luminous mezzo-soprano that had made her her living before the war, she taught me the songs, the lieder and cantatas reclaimed from the murderers, of Bach, Strauss, Brahms, Schubert. I joined a children's chorus that gave concerts every Saturday when the weather was fine, and we learned English songs to please the homesick British soldiers who watched over us: "It Might as Well Be Spring," "I Can't Begin to Tell You," "Accentuate the Positive,"

"Teddy-Bears Picnic," "It Could Happen to You." Sometimes I'd give little impromptu concerts for the soldiers hanging around outside the canteen or at the main gate to try and wheedle a few chocolates from them, or a cigarette I could trade for the butterscotch candies I loved. German, English: I sang in these languages, not understanding them, but filled nonetheless with feeling, a kind of creeping deep inside, the feeling of that inner mouth coming unglued, unstuck. Even then I knew that the soldiers' English with its elongated vowels was not the "real thing"; it was the English on American radio, Hollywood English (American films twice a week in the little theater where SS officers had once brought their families to relax). I studied my future at the cinema and my father on the sidelines of soccer games, practicing his trade, his restless hustle: making bets on the outcomes of games, smuggling black market luxuries, ubiquitous on the heavy iron-wheeled bicycle he dragged into our room in the barracks at night and leaned against the door so no one could steal it or sneak in (we were lucky to have the room, cold and bleak as it was, to ourselves, entire large families were crammed into neighboring rooms, it must have been my father's activities that guaranteed our relatively sumptuous privacy), so if I had to pee in the night I had to do it in the cracked metal basin we used as a chamberpot, squatting in the harsh glare of the camp lights that the scrap of canvas that we used for a windowshade didn't do enough to deflect. Women, too, my father had his women, it's incredible to think now of desire able to survive what had to be survived, but it had, it rampaged forth, and as little flower gardens sprang up everywhere in the camp to accompany the much larger vegetable gardens, as we sang for the soldiers and sat up at attention in the camp school, so too did flirtations and affairs take place, women who'd lost children, men who'd lost wives finding each other furtively in sheds and behind bushes, no one much caring for the old proprieties, the camp's birthrate was impressive, though he never brought one back to our room I knew they were out there, my father's women, he might have been pimping for all I know, I wouldn't put it past him and I wouldn't blame him, not really, after what he'd been through. Which he never spoke of, naturally, and naturally I never asked. He was only my father, a stranger that I lived with and came to know intimately without his ever shedding that strangeness, that male difference, washing with a rag under his arms and between his legs in the pale mornings, stretching like a cat, shaking his hair out like a dog, stepping into a cloud of cologne that stung my half-closed eyes in the bunk where I pretended to sleep. He would escort me every day to Frau Drechsler in the music room of what had been the senior officers' quarters, where she presided over a battered upright piano, asking her about my progress, but never staying to hear me sing. Was it the German that pained him? He certainly spoke the language, his little smuggling business depended on it, though Bergen-Belsen by then was its own city of Jews, its own little Jerusalem, Germans still surrounded it and came into the camp, making deliveries, working construction, unembarrassed, men in stiff gray clothes who had perhaps performed similar duties before 1945, it was impossible to know for sure. My father would go up to these men with a friendly smile, neatly dressed, exchange a few low words and something in his fist, laughter. They called him the Ambassador for his distinguished air, or to mock him: he carried with him that indefinable aura of prewar grace, of unwounded Europe. He would return to our room with a knapsack full of cigarettes or a bottle of cognac or tubes of lipstick or brilliantine or soap (a prized and extremely rare commodity), even packages of condoms—I didn't recognize them of course, spilling from his knapsack onto the bed, my father said they were balloons and inflated one for me, but when someone knocked on the door he darted out with his cigarette and popped it, smiling oddly at my tears. I had no toys, my father could not or would not devote his energies to acquiring any, I had to make do with an old mop head he tied with some string and pair of mismatched buttons sewed to make the mad lopsided eyes of the mouthless dolly I carried with me everywhere and slept with, burrowed in scratchy but warm woolen blankets. Why did he bring me to the camp, life was better in Budapest, even then, with my grandparents whose faces I can no longer recall but whose love and care were like iron, doing everything they could to guard me from the truth, the tenuousness of our lives in the apartment where I was born, the ever-foreclosed possibilities of my life and the foreshortened horizon of their own lives that cracked open again miraculously in '45, the narrow escape they never permitted me to escape, living indoors almost all the time, only discovering the sun and rubble at the war's end, beginning to grow, until he appeared that day with that queer cap of his turning and turning in his hands, his apologetic but frozen smile, the words he must have used to make my grandmother relax her grip on my shoulders, letting go, then touching me again firmly to push me toward this stranger and his plan for me of a better life in America. It was liberation of a sort, school only happened for a few hours a day and my father was always elsewhere, except for Frau Drechsler the camp, strange as it may sound, was a fabulous playground, a Babel, Jews from all over Europe making themselves understood with whatever lay to hand, Yiddish or German or French or English or Hebrew or just gestures, nods, lifted eyebrows. I ran wild with the other children, some of them much older, some of them survivors (I already understood the secret but critical distinction between the remnant that had actually survived the *Lager* and those who, like me, had gone on living comparatively normal lives in hiding in their own cities and towns), we ran in fierce packs through the muddy alleys and fields of the camp, fighting other packs, stealing whatever we could, girls as young as eight smoking cigarette ends they found behind the British barracks, cursing proficiently in eight languages. All this should have taught me something of the world, but it did not. I was young and remained young, for a shockingly long time. At night I dreamed of my mother's voice—no words, just a rhythm, a tone. Her face was a benign blur, a little glowing fire in the cracked hall of mirrors of my childish memory. When I sang, for Frau Dreschler, for the soldiers, in the children's chorus, I tried to sing a memory I couldn't possibly possess.

There's no sun up in the sky
Stormy weather
When she went away
The blues walked in and met me

What did my father remember of her? What memories had he suppressed, in the silence of his breathing when he came wheeling his bicycle in long after curfew, the weight of him sagging the bunk where he lay smoking one last cigarette before dropping off to sleep? What was it that lived in him that lived somehow in me, a crack in the heart like the crack in the cornerstone of a large building that never quite collapses but only settles, day after day, deeper into the earth? My mother was a ghost to us both, a ghost in Budapest, a ghost in the camp, a ghost on the day our papers came through, a ghost on the steamer that carried us in three slow days across the ocean to New York. There I came fully into English at last, American English, the language of optimism and transformation. I spoke only English from the moment I crossed the gangplank, determined to arrive in New York an American, answering my father only in that language to his amusement and frustration. I had, have always had, as even Frau Drechsler admitted, an uncanny ear. I avoided him and the other passengers as much as I could, choosing instead to spend my time with the few American members of the ship's crew, practicing accents—the Indiana flatlands of the purser, a steward's Brooklyn twang, the black stoker's melancholy Alabama drawl. When my feet touched American soil I felt myself becoming a part of it, immediately and all at once, and it shamed me to be dragged away from my glimpse of Manhattan to darkest Queens where I found myself once again in the camp, what seemed like solid blocks of other Hungarian Jews, first in the spare bedroom of my father's cousin's two-family house on 32nd Avenue and later across the street in the bungalow of our own that you, Elsa, must remember. I wanted, more fervently it seemed than my father, whose idea it had been, to be an American and only American. I dropped the *lieder* and sang only American songs, what I heard at the drugstores and ice cream parlors: I wanted to be Rosemary Clooney, I wanted to be Doris Day, blonde and girlish and pure as ice cream, not the dark-haired dark-eyed foreigner I felt myself to be and saw reflected everywhere, the women in the grocery store and the bakery, weary waiting for the bus, jabbering away at each other in what I now thought of not as Hungarian or Yiddish but as foreign, jib-jab, nonsense. Now I no longer answered my father when he spoke in our native tongue: I sat stony faced until he repeated his question in halting, heavily accented English. At school, surrounded by other immigrant children, I gravitated toward the native born; I still remember Marianne, who was Polish but second generation, born in the USA, picking up from her the slightly dated Americanisms that tasted to me like freedom: gee whiz, gee willikers, quit bugging me, I got dibs, guy's got a DA, don't be a spaz, got a thin one?, razz my berries, that's a panic and a half. All this time the ghost of my mother was circling. It was two years almost to the day of our arrival, my second birthday as an American, when I came home on a warm breathless September day to that house, we had only moved in the previous month, into a hush, an unnatural summer silence, to find a strange brand-new looking paisley suitcase blocking the front door the way my father's bicycle had blocked the room we'd once shared. I had to search the little house, room by room, until I found them sitting there, in my own bedroom at the foot of my narrow bed, my father neatly dressed in the white shirt and natty tie he always wore when working, next to a narrow and strange woman, like an insect that disguises itself as a stick or vice-versa, wearing a gray woolen dress much too heavy for the day and a kerchief over her hair that marked her to my practiced eye as a proper greenhorn, fresh off the boat. Just sitting, the two of them, not saying anything, her eyes fever bright, his hooded, her holding a black-and-white photo of me in her bone-white hands. Untold forever her odyssey from the bright black hole she had vanished into one Budapest morning along with my father, the worm-hole she'd traveled down out of sight and memory only to remerge on a hot afternoon in Queens; though I did learn later she'd been in America already for two or three months, staying with a second cousin in Jersey City, watching and waiting for the moment, who knows what would make it right in her eyes, to rejoin our lives. She spoke no English, never tried to learn, she looked at me with enormous hopeless tragic eyes and said my name in a way that made it foreign, that brought me closer to her, it suffocated me. Mama, I said in English, it sounds the same in Hungarian, that was the nearest and only bridge I would cross. Mama, where did you come from? Mama, where did you go? I did not ask that question then, but would in the years to come, she would answer only *Az ilyen történetek nem a gyermekek számára*, such stories are not for children. But Mama, I'd say, I'm twelve, I'm fifteen, I'm sixteen, I'm a grown woman, I'm not a child any longer. I'm eighteen, Mama. But by then she was dead, no longer a survivor, and my father had a new business partner in the woman who'd become his second wife, that awful bitch, and I was living my own real life at last, an American life. In between were six years of noisy silence, Mama a pair of eyes in the kitchen, my father gone all day and into the night, cutting hair at first, trying and failing at the old schemes, two shops closed down under him until he was reduced to driving a taxi at all hours, the invisible man. Mama did nothing at all as far as I could see, apart from making me inedible lunches to take to school in the morning and preparing hot tea and peanut butter sandwiches for me to eat when I returned—though I was returning later and later, spending as much time as possible in the living rooms of girlfriends and the cars of boyfriends. One evening in particular I remember coming home to find Shabbat dinner all laid out on the little kitchen table, with roast chicken and challah loaf and all the rest. I scarcely knew what it was—Papa had come back from the *Lager* with all the religion burned out of him—and he never appeared that night. But I remember Mama standing there at the head of the table gesturing for me to imitate her, to cover my eyes and say the prayer as God's bride, the Sabbath, approached. She said it in Hebrew, I watched her, moving my lips, saying nothing. After that we just sat there, me smoking a cigarette, her with hands on her knees, watching the chicken get cold, waiting for my father. When it was full dark I stood up and told her I had a date, which wasn't true. She said nothing I could hear, though her lips moved. When I got back late that night the table was still laid with the cold dinner—Papa's coat was in its usual place and their bedroom door was shut. The next morning it was all cleared away as if it never had been, and my mother never repeated the experiment, at least not while I was in that house. The next year I went away to college. And the year after that she was dead.

Memory, Elsa, is a poor substitute for justice.

What I'm trying to tell you, my impossible daughter, is that these memories aren't even mine, so how could they be yours? Let the dead bury the dead. Don't spend your youth as I spent mine, carrying your mother on my back. Life is short and memory is long, too long—you must kill it when you can. Hate me if you must, it's better that way, you must get free of it all somehow, as I've tried to do. I don't know and can never know about my parents and what they suffered. They were ordinary people and they stayed ordinary, and I wanted to be something else. This city now, here, where I live out my last days—I look around and it seems like all the people are young or old, nothing in between. How many of them are murderers? How many the children of murderers? And how many—a far smaller number—are the children of the murdered? There's no living with these questions, no going on with them. We are what we are, here and now. You must let go of me, Elsa. Bless me and let me go.

What is the "I" that intrudes incessantly in this narrative like punctuation? If chapters were commas then readers would ride. Not Gustave, not Ruth, not Ruth's anonymous Papa. No mother writes, only M, her posthumous correspondence. Least of all poor Lamb, leading the goose chase from city to city in Europe, stoic ingénue, winding deeper and deeper into the I's conspiracy with itself. That this is my story through a glass darkly. That it's my history like a concealed weapon, maybe it's there and maybe it's not, you can't relax till the showdown comes. Pistols, heartbreak at dawn. Forget the future, forget the glaciers melting and the sleepless nights, what about a sustainable past to go foraging in, secure enough to forget? If horses could sing Bach. If I could sit across from you, close enough so our knees touched, and recite this to you, story of my own estranged and operatic heart. If people still read poems there'd be no need for novels. I must unfurl the concealing veils for a reader to guess at, to pounce. I am sitting at a cafe with all the other I's, each telling his or her story to one of the endless series of listening Lambs, all of them hatted, equipped with tape recorders, silencers, false passports, money belts. To get the story to kill the witness and make a clean getaway. Like Lamb, I am more than a client and less than human. You exist nowhere but here in the film of my persuasion. To stay you, on task, is to be an accomplice to your own vanishing. In the frame, in the Lamb-sized holes, a past appears. And somewhere Ruth, my Jewish-American Emma Bovary, is preparing to start out on her own journey, at the close of day like Athena's owl. To find a future in the Old World, to build an American hope on a heap of bones. We are not innocent, but the I can't help it. To make a self is to self-exculpate, digging deep. I carry this forward, a woman with no gender, motherless. In search of the body, corpse with a beating heart, against which I nestle, for shelter, dreaming past dawn.

There is a third figure to consider for the man who takes care of things: the enforcer, the muscle, *le samourai*, the assassin. A gardener wields his secateurs calmly, with no outward show of passion. He does not make history, he makes nothing happen that is not inherent in the existing situation. He prunes; he intervenes; he cuts short. He cannot make history disappear but he can disappear it, mark it off cleanly and boldly and without remorse. He vanishes anonymously into the mob whose face he momentarily bears or—it is the same thing—is taken up as sacrifice. He does not face, cannot be mistaken for, any justice. His aesthetic is cold in its perfections, nearly sterile. The surgeon cuts, and if the vivisected limb goes on aching, that is not his fault. If brass awakes a trumpet. Silence opens—she can hope, without admitting—a wounded life.

We took the train from the Gare du Nord and from the moment we stepped aboard I felt us new with each other, tender, she was *with* me at last, she was mine. All night in the third-class compartment she slept with her head on my chest, on my belly, while I sat upright trying not to disturb her, to cushion her tangled cloud of hair from the bumps and shocks of the slow-crawling westward train. She had spoken vaguely about our going to England, to some friends she knew in London, where we could begin anew. I would paint; she would study again, perhaps at the School of Economics. Something practical, she said. I want to learn about money. Where it comes from, where it goes. What makes it seem so real. But when we got to La Havre just before dawn she blinked against me, yawned, sat up, and said she wasn't ready to get off the train.

But this is where we get the boat to Dover.

Dover isn't the place. Let's keep going.

All right, I said. Let's keep going.

We changed trains for Cherbourg. The new train rocked us gently together, as if she were the bird and I were the nest. When I opened my eyes, it was full daylight. M was gone. But then I saw her outside on the platform, laughing at me.

Your face! she shouted. Did you think I had vanished? Like Kim Novak?

The town was dismal, somehow gray even in the

summer sunlight that fell in blinding sheets between the buildings, making me hold my hand before my eyes. M had sunglasses. Let's go! she said. I want to find the beach. Come on! And she ran. I lumbered after.

It didn't take us very long to achieve the port: a few high-masted pleasure boats, a steamer parked offshore with black smoke funneling up from it like a fresh smear of charcoal. M ran down to the quay and stared at the water. I heard her ask a bespectacled pensioner with a fishing rod, *Où est la plage?* and he pointed. *Merci!* she shouted after him, running again. I saluted him awkwardly as he watched us go by, pipe in his hand.

It took the better part of an hour for us to walk there. She put her arm in mine and we walked along the coast road, saying little, watching the sea. It was a turbulent gray day with sudden shafts of light striking out here and there, touching the pewter waves and turning them into fiery medallions that as abruptly faded. The sand I could see, below us, was gray. It was summer, but the wind was cold and I had no jacket. M, in her jaunty blue raincoat, was better equipped. Still, she walked on my left, so I could shield her a little.

La plage. The beach, when it appeared, was broad and bright. We had to descend to it, and as we did the sun broke more fully through the clouds and turned the indifferent gray expanse of sand into a radiance I squinted at. M walked faster and faster, then pulled away from me suddenly and ran. I did not run after her but continued to walk steadily as her body grew smaller and smaller, as she ran down the road and across the brush grass and into the dunes. There were holidaygoers here and there, but not very many—it was not at that time a fashionable area. Its claims to fame were historical: in 1912 the Titanic had stopped over at Cherbourg after leaving Southampton, taking on additional passengers and cargo before steaming into the night, never to be seen again. And in 1944 the D-Day landings took place not far off. Years later, I found myself wondering if this beach, what I came to think of as the beach of M, if it were not the same as Utah Beach, where the Allies had suffered comparatively few casualties in their ultimately successful effort to reclaim France from fascism. It was not and could not be, of course. All my contacts with history were destined to be fleeting if not imaginary. I knew this even at the time, and did not care. For I had M.

I had her, but she was running. And when she reached the edge of the water and did not stop, I again began running too. She ran straight into the waves, arms outstretched, and disappeared for a moment in the surf. I beat down the beach after her, passing a few scattered blankets and umbrellas. Someone was playing the Rolling Stones on a transistor radio: *I was drowned, I was washed up and left for dead....* I kicked up some sand in that direction and a few voices protested. I was over a dune and down onto where the sand was hard and flat. For a moment I did not see her. I took off my shoes and plunged in.

Gus! she was shouting, crying, laughing in the water. Gus! It was not so deep, after all, where she was standing. Gus! Her face, hair, clothes were wet. She turned from me toward the waves and shouted something at the sea.

I grabbed her by the shoulders, then by the waist, and lifted her out of the water. She kicked viciously at me, still wailing.

Finally we sat down in the sand together. A man in sunglasses and madras shorts had stood up, had begun to approach us to see if everything was all right. He saw her sobbing with head down, caught my glare, hesitated, withdrew.

For a while the sun shone on us and kept us warm, while the dune did something to block the wind. But then the clouds rolled in.

I called her name, over and over, softly. It was getting colder.

She had composed herself by this time and was staring out to sea. When she finally looked at me her smile was like that you'd give a stranger you trust not to harm you. But then she gave me her hand.

Somehow we made it out of there, in the growing chill of the later afternoon, both of us wet, chilled, with sand in our clothes and our hair. We had passed, on our way out of town, a small cluster of buildings, one of which was a hotel. By the time we made it inside the dark miniscule lobby we were both shivering uncontrollably. But M shook out her hair and drew herself up when the concierge greeted us warily. Behind our backs she pressed some bills into my hand.

Monsieur et Madame Niemand, she said to the clerk. *De Paris. Nous sommes en voyage de noces.*

C'est vrai, I said. We've had problems with our luggage, though. The rail company is supposed to send it on to us.

The clerk looked at us: the hulking, heavy-browed Alsatian and the delicate, arched woman with the American accent. He shrugged.

Sign here, Mr. Niemand. He put the key in my hand.

The room was small, on the fourth floor: a chair, a little table or writing desk, a sink, the bed. The window faced the alley, a blank white wall that reflected perfectly the mood of the sky, turbulent with clouds but very occasionally permitting a shaft of sunlight, long as a finger, to touch the earth here and there. A little rain was wetting the windowpanes. If you opened the window and leaned out, a bit farther than was comfortable or safe, then your gaze might bring you a glimpse of the sea.

Trembling, I locked the door behind us and watched her at the window, leaning out so very far, letting in a little wind, a little rain. Her wet hair clung to her shoulders and curled at her cheeks. She was very pale.

Close the window, I said.

We undressed quickly, not looking at each other, and slid into the bed, which groaned under my weight. Immediately our cold, clammy skins were touching, and then pressed together, and the cold gave way in me to a rush of heat that spread through my limbs and up into my face, so much so that in a moment I wanted to kick the covers off. Her body was very cold, until it wasn't.

I painted you, you know, I said to her. That same day Charles was hurt, the day you disappeared.

Where is it?

I don't know, I admitted. I lost it in the move.

I wish I could see it, she said, eyes tightly shut, her cold skin warming against me. Did you make me ugly? You always made me so ugly.

Holding me.

It is one thing to paint a woman, to imagine her, as an artist must imagine what he sees to make it real. It is another thing to touch her and to be touched. The imagination, which for so long has rushed ahead, is defeated by the actual, the senses. There are no words. When she was warm enough, she opened her eyes and smiled at me. Then I was on my back and she was on top of me, like I had never dared to imagine. My belly, her buoyancy. The shock of dark hair on her head, under her arms, abundant at her crotch, against the whiteness of her skin. A rose was petaling her cheeks, her throat, at her sternum. She was moving more rapidly against me. It's really happening, I remember thinking. And: I must hold on. On.

The things we remember so well: did we experience them at the time? What I remember is her face, as we ground ourselves together, rooted for the moment in the moment, the distortion of it, the tension around her mouth. Her face in the sea. Did Charles give her this face? Did I? Where did it come from, this feeling that could not last, that convinces—in the moment—that it will never be repeated?

What happened? I said softly into her ear, her head nestled against me, our bodies cooling.

I lay there in the bed, watching the light on the blank white wall turn pink and purple with the sunset, while she whispered the story to my chest. How she fled from history into history. There were no trains, she said, there was no gas for cars, only for doctors and police and the army. I stood up in the hospital room, rebuked by his sleeping face, the blank bloody bandage over his right eye, and walked out into the hallway and down the stairs and out into the street where the *manifestation* had left its long wake: trash, tree trunks, the smoldering remnants of overturned little cars. Under the paving stones: bare earth, dirt. I walked. It was late, the action was west. I went east. I passed few people as I walked, mostly small groups of twos and threes, not students, who glanced fearfully at me as though I carried a Molotov cocktail in my hands. One middle-aged couple crossed the street when they saw me approach. I kept my head down. There were no trains, but my steps guided me anyway toward the Gare de Lyon. It was closest. It wasn't even the right station for where I was going. At Ile Saint-Louis the Pont de Sully was closed: big trucks blocked the bridge and I could see some men in black uniforms standing very still, it seemed, while the lights from their cigarettes bobbed and danced like fireflies. Austerlitz then. I followed the Seine, which reflected the city lights like always. You couldn't tell what had been happening there. I reached the station and it was deserted, of course, a great hulking building. Two men stood by the entrance warming their hands by an ashcan fire. They looked at me and I became afraid. I didn't know what else to do but keep walking. I was glad for my boots. To my right the station was sliding by, the still tracks that led south and away to Orleans, the warm south, Marseille, Spain, Portugal. It wasn't the right station. To my left the river, vast and silent between silent walls. Then a miracle that I heard before I saw, down a bend in a side street: an engine. I followed. Outside an Autoprix, a small truck with engine idling. The driver came out and said something to someone inside, then reached up and pulled the metal grating down over the shop's windows and front door. He locked it and handed the lock back to someone through the grating then turned aside to light his cigarette. He saw me coming. A middle-aged man with a head like a treestump wedged upside-down on his shoulders, a gray cap squashing down the unruly roots. He smoked, watching me approach, neither friendly nor unfriendly.

I need to leave Paris, I said. I'm traveling east.

He shrugged like a Frenchman.

I'm going east, he said. Northeast, but east.

Perfect.

I rode at his side for what seemed like hours in the truck's little cab, barely exchanging a word. The radio played no news, only songs whose melodies and lyrics enjoyed ironic relations: «*Comme d'habitude*», «*Le Déserteur*», «*Cinématographe*». Wind blew smoke from his cigarettes out cracks in the windows and the engine snorted and gabbled like some sort of sea creature. He took two cigarettes out of the packet and lit them both and passed one to me: I knew some ritual was being enacted but didn't understand the rules: I took it and smoked it down to the last scraps, though I never smoked. Once I caught him looking at my legs and instinctively pulled away. *Ce n'est pas neccesaire, mademoiselle,* he grunted. His gray cheek flushed. After that I tried to move as little as possible. The heart of Paris bumped and stumbled away behind us while the sun began to make itself felt on the horizon of the bleak industrial suburbs we passed through. I saw a sign and said what it said aloud, startling him: Drancy.

Comment? the driver said.

Rien.

There was nothing to distinguish Drancy from the other cités I'd seen, nothing at all. There was nothing to see, much less to remember. But the name sat queasily on my stomach and I thought suddenly of the fat, impish face of Cohn-Bendit and what we'd all screamed at the top of our lungs two weeks ago, an eternity ago.

Nous sommes tous des indésirables, I whispered.

Comment?

Rien.

Just after dawn we crossed the Marne and the truck came to a stop on the single main street of a little town. This is as far east as I go, the driver said. Before I could respond he had opened his door and climbed out. I watched him cross in front of the windshield and around to my side of the cab, where he opened the car door and, with extreme politesse, offered me his hand. When I got down he extended his other hand, in the palm of which was folded a ten-franc note. Now it was my turn to say *Ce n'est pas nécessaire, monsieur. Merci. Merci beaucoup.*

Vous devriez avoir d'argent liquide, he said. Liquid: the word everyone had been using for cash with the banks and the American Express closed. Take it.

I took it.

Good luck, he said to me in English.

I hitchhiked. East and east. There were few motels and I didn't have money for inns. I met up with backpackers and slept in their little tents, smelling their sweat. A woman in a village where I found myself totally alone and rideless let me sleep on a pile of blankets on the cold stone floor of her kitchen with a fire grumbling under an iron pot like in the Middle Ages. A man in an Italian suit picked me up and let me sleep in the back seat of his Renault in the garage, not telling his wife. I woke up in the middle of the night and found him there with me, still wearing the suit, with a bottle of cognac. He kept talking about how all of his friends and cronies deplored the events—even out here they called them that—but not him, he thought the students were *très sympa.* Finally I put my hand into his pocket, before he could ask for more, and masturbated him, and after he slunk back to the house full of promises, I got out of the car and that garage and walked out into the night until I met yet another driver. At the border I got some strange looks from the *douanier,* who asked me repeatedly what my business was in Germany. He warned me that my student visa might be revoked if I left France now. This was nonsense of course. Already I knew from the papers I'd seen and the conversation of the men I'd met that the Events were subsiding, that the factories were up and running again. Only the students hadn't gotten the message. But I was patient and I was pretty, and they let me through. And there I got my ticket for West Berlin. And in Berlin I waited six days for a visa, to cross to the Soviet sector. Men in uniforms looking down at my passport and up at me, down and up, down and up, in a kind of official seesaw rhythm, before handing it back to me, little book of identity, and waving me through. And from the Ostbanhof another train, east, always east, to Poland. Trying to reach the house of death itself or to its threshold. I didn't look on the house, I didn't behold the gate, didn't read the words written there, their mocking embrace taking me in as they had taken my father, my mother, and later, unaccountably, returned them to life. I only saw the little town with its unspellable name, with insensible glum blond people and a hotel with no screens to keep out the blackflies and an official guide, a minder, who called herself Zlota. She had a round face and round legs and a runny nose and wore the same blue windbreaker every day, indoors and out, no matter the weather. Every morning she took me out to see the sights: farms, factories. I'd told them I was a journalist for a student paper in Paris; they wanted to support the revolution there and I didn't tell them it was already over, already lost. Every morning I told her I wanted to see the camp and she shook her head. It is not possible, she said, and screwed up her face into an apologetic look. I imagine she wrote reports on me every night while I paced the dingy room overlooking a black wall. Imagine, a room just like this one with no view except of a wall, but this wall is white and that wall was black. So black that night was no night, it was just blackness, and that's as close as I came to seeing what I'd come to see. Standing in that window which wouldn't open more than a couple of inches, staring at nothing, sometimes craning my neck as though I could see around that wall, around that building, around Zlota, around darkness, and see what my parents had seen. I didn't make it. The day before my visa was set to expire, I left. Zlota saw me to the train; I believe she'd become fond of me. She stood on the platform in her blue windbreaker, a kerchief tied over her hair to make her look like the peasant farmer's wife she was born to be. She had made me some fudge if you can imagine that—a heavy brown square of it. I looked her in the eye. I'm a Jew, I said. And then, I don't know why German would have been clearer, I said it in German: *Ich bin eine Jude.* And then: *Je suis juive.* I am a Jew, a Jewess. How do you say it in Polish? Her expression didn't change. My parents came here, I told her, on a train, with many others. Do you understand? Zlota could have been anywhere from twenty to sixty with that kerchief covering her hair. Do you understand? And they came back, I said helplessly, with the train standing there, spreading my fingers by my sides, they came back and they couldn't talk about it. No one will talk about it. And you haven't said a word. Will you speak to me? It is not possible, she said, like she'd been saying all along, like she'd said even silently riding next to me on the little diesel bus to see the sights of the province, like she'd said when she'd watched me try a little of the local brandy without drinking any herself, like she'd been saying when she asked me about the revolution in Paris and about America and Elvis Presley, like she'd been saying from the moment she'd met me on this very platform standing a little apart from a pair of bored soldiers with machine guns who'd been furnished by someone as window dressing, as reminder of what I wouldn't be permitted to see or to know. It is not possible. And then I was on the train with her chocolate on my lap, leaking through the thin paperboard to stain my only dress, watching that round silent face retreat through the window; I was sitting backwards in the compartment and so the town and the house of death fell away from me like a film running backwards that someday would have to be run forward; it is inevitable, and yet not possible, that's how I've come to feel about it. So rewound backward over miles and governments to Paris, to Charles's bedside, and further back to the sea, and now to you. And soon I'll have to get on the plane and fly back to America and pick up my life there. Because that's the only life, I see that now. I came looking for origins. I came looking for real life. But this Europe, this continent of yours. It's a graveyard. The headstones are beautiful, and there are beautiful people to tend the graves and walk in the grass. But everything's dead here, and everyone. Don't you see that?

Lying next to me, her voice and the spiral of cigarette smoke and the dry heat of her leg pressed against mine the only reality; that and the blazing rectangle of light the single window cast above our bed, showing every crack and ripple in the ugly wallpaper, sparking the dull edge of a brass wall sconce into fire. What did she discover? That she was part of something she didn't want to be a part of? Or not part of something she wanted to be a part of? I pictured it, I pictured her, east and east, through the verdant fields and charcoal-green forests and industrial parks of Deutschland, from the Rhineland where I was born to the border, FRG to GDR, shiver of the closed train, the closed faces, the arrival finally in Poland, rain and smoke, Zlota the watchful peasant at her side all day and in the night that black wall and some unimaginable past rising up in the night, in her body, in Jewishness itself, as unimaginable to me as to her, to anyone who tried to see it, feel it, standing on the border, face pressed to the icy glass, all possibilities foreclosed. It is human, I said to myself, not knowing why, it is human it is human.

We should go south, I said drowsily. To Mont St. Michel. We can hitchhike. I've always wanted to see it.

She didn't answer.

I wonder if there are still monks there. My uncle told me about a trip he took there before the war. He said at low tide you could walk where the water used to be. That it was like walking on water. That the sand there bends like a trampoline, holding you up.

She was sleeping.

I've always wanted to go. The sun died through my closed eyelids.

The two of us slept.

When the light returned she was gone. Money on the bedstand. So I had been valued to a point, I had been the one the spy loves. I had a story to tell, though I have never told it before now. Of course I looked for her, at the train station, at the beach. The concierge watched me come and go without my wife with bemusement, until I paid him for the next night, and the next. I spent the rest of the week there, waiting to see if M would reappear, knowing she would not. I slept a good deal, ate simple meals, felt not the slightest desire to paint or draw or sketch. When the money was almost gone I took the train again, east, not getting out at Paris, east and east toward home, Strasbourg, where I would eventually apprentice to a printer who specialized in tour guides and wall-sized maps for classrooms and governments. And he made me a partner, and then he died, and I married his widow, a short plain woman with a pleasant smile and nothing wistful about her, and we were in business together for almost forty years. And I was married and then I wasn't and then I was again to a woman I now never see. She lives in Venice. And I never again saw or heard from M, though I have written her letters, not knowing where to send them, until you came along. That sort of thing becomes a habit, I believe.

Dawn is making itself felt through the thin hotel curtain. The city, never fully asleep, is now not fully awake: like a big cat it stretches, squeezing its eyes and extending, tentatively, its claws. Gustave stands.

I have one last letter for her here that I should like you to deliver for me.

Give it to me, says Lamb.

You won't open it, Gustave says in a low voice.

The American shrugs. Think of it this way. At least someone will read it.

Gustave pauses, then hands it over. A plain white envelope with no name and no address.

Will you see her?

I don't know, Lamb says, tucking the letter away inside his jacket. I doubt it.

Gustave nods. He is standing there, bent slightly at the hips, cumbrous, patting his pockets as though to make sure everything is still there. Though it isn't, of course.

It's a strange story, Lamb says.

Do you find it credible?

Why shouldn't I?

Why shouldn't you, Gustave echoes. He turns his back on Lamb to look out the window at the city. What I have told you is the truth. I am nobody's father and nobody's son. There was a woman who tried to make history real, and for a moment, I bore witness. That is all.

The bulging eyes of the angel, looking back.

I have a train to catch, Lamb says, packing his things away. You won't see me again, Monsieur Lessy.

It's not you I want to see, says Gustave. The sun catches the edge of the Fernsehtum, unlimited eye of the Stasi, kitsch monument to an eastern past. It glints and blinds. The eye flares. In memoriam. In tears. Someone moving behind him, slowly, with a final purpose.

Her face.

Gustave is gone. What was he?

A full stop. A white wig. A point of view.

I didn't ask you to kill him, the new reader says into the phone. Or she whispers it, defiantly, desperately: It's not me. But there's no one there so she puts it down. The threshold. The private dick's history is indistinguishable from death. Every day grisly packages she expects in the mail. When she opens them, more books spill out, books she can't remember ordering, books on parenting, on how to stay married, books on recovering one's creativity, writing down the bones, what color is her parachute, do what you love and the money will follow, write a screenplay in thirty days. When she's out with the child and the child is sleeping she finds herself in bookstores, running her eyes across spines in the self-help section, afraid to look up and see someone she knows seeing her there. She browses the European travel books, trying to predict his movements by letter: Barcelona Berlin Brussels

Budapest. What have I unleashed, what have I asked for. An accounting. A reckoning. He is out there in the home of my mind, the place I belong, that doesn't exist, the old world. Wrecking the joint. A man with a gun. What I want him to kill is in me, this rabbit in my brain, this hamster wheel that never stops squeaking. Her daughter lies sprawled in the stroller as though she'd been dropped from a height. How can her neck stretch that far without waking her, hurting her. She sits at the café table with a bad latte and a stack of magazines, leafing through rapidly, registering only the poses of women with sleek skin and provocatively vacuous expressions. They leave a sweet smell on her hands that nauseates her. She has a couple of hardbacks, bestsellers; she flips them open and peels out the little anti-theft magnets, drops them into the basket under the stroller, stands up, leaves the coffee and magazines, and rolls on out. There are no alarms, no one stops her. The new reader is a successful shoplifter who doesn't care what she steals as long as it's printed matter. Most of the books go unread, they line the walls of their bedroom in precarious stacks. He doesn't say anything about it. She can hear him thinking: better books than expensive clothes. Better books than jewelry. Better books than a bitter wife who gives me no peace at night. It's unfair to Ben, unfair to herself. She is hiding from something, burrowed as deep as she can go in pages, but that something has followed her. The words, the sentences, are increasingly abstract. All she retains of almost anything she reads now is a certain cadence, a progression. Paragraphs are not emotional but sentences are. She takes refuge in paragraphs, whole pages repelled at a glance, turning them, black on white, under the kitchen skylight while dinner's boiling over or on a park bench or in a Starbucks or late, late at night while everyone is sleeping. She looks at the clock and thinks, He is just getting up over there. Or, He did not go to bed, he's still up, he's smoking and looking at the moon. Somewhere under the bed Rimbaud is groaning, legless spirit pushing stubby fingers through his thatch of hair. Time of the *assassins*. Time of the fathers marching to their doom. Time of the vanished M, the letter unites the lips, nipple or cigarette, something to grasp, fondle, hold. It all disappears. She moves her lips uncomprehendingly over the pale pages. There she is, at the end. There he is, waiting for her. A man can be a destiny. A woman can be on a journey without leaving her comfortable home. M. M is a murderer. M is a marauder, M is empty, M is waiting for the mail. M is alone with M. M is a queen in a castle surrounded by thorns, staring into a mirror, waiting for her breath to appear. M I miss you, M I cannot amputate. Memory.

Lucy is my daughter. L comes before M. An Elsa? Ruth? Me.

The new reader hates reading, hates its endlessness, its pointlessness, hates the jabber and the pretentious talk and sentences that are too short or too long or fatuous or have the wrong mouthfeel. To finish reading, not to stop but to finish, that's what would be truly new. To close the book and look up at the horizon or a stranger or one's husband or anything at all and to say, I'm finished. I've read enough. I'm ready to live. The flesh is happy, for I've read all the books.

M goes missing in me, makes a text, marks her place in every book I read and discard, manufactures a middle way between absolute loss and the terrifying fullness of resurrection. As long as the pages keep turning, the sentences keep coming, she is not gone. She is not here. Hers the body I come from, and will return to. Night flight, nap of the earth. The darkness demands something of me. I answer the call.

In her own living room, alone with Nadia, Ruth says, It's my stepfather, he's dead. Nadia nods sympathetically, doesn't speak, watches. Ruth covering her face. When she takes her hands away she's laughing and crying.

I killed him.

What do you mean?

I was angry he didn't try to stop my mother. From moving to Europe when she was sick. He went with her, and then he didn't even stay with her. He let her send him away when she needed him most. And he died.

If she sent him away, Nadia said slowly, how is that his fault?

He shouldn't have listened to her. He's been like that forever. He can't stand up to her. No one can.

But what does this mean, that you killed him?

I don't know. I got a call from the consul in Budapest. Apparently he was living in a hotel there. They say he had a heart attack.

I don't understand.

He died there. In Berlin.

Wait a minute. Which is it, Berlin or Budapest?

There's a man, Ruth says. His name is Lamb. He works for me. I think Lamb killed him.

Lamb gave your stepfather a heart attack?

I know it sounds crazy. It sounds crazy to me. But it's not crazy. I sent Lamb over there to find him. To find my father.

Your stepfather?

Not my stepfather. My real father. And he found him. But he wasn't what I thought he'd be. He didn't know what I wanted him to know.

Which was?

About my mother, Ruth says. Angrily thinking: *Words!* About M. So he went on. I told him to go on. I told him not to stop until he found out.

Found out what?

Where she was. He went to ask him. And he asked him, he kept asking him. He asked him too hard. And he's dead.

But your mother is dead.

She's not dead, Ruth says. She's alive. I can't explain it but she's alive. I buried her, but I didn't do it right.

Nadia holds Ruth's hand, her expression serious.

Thanks for pretending you understand.

But I do understand. I understand you have suffered a loss. The greatest possible loss.

No, Ruth says, weeping, that's not true. What you lost was much worse.

It is no use to compare losses. You have lost your mother, and not only her life. You have lost her death.

Now I'm the one who doesn't understand.

You do not have her death, Nadia says slowly. You cannot hold it. You do not believe in it. So you do not live. You are aimed like an arrow at another woman's death.

If you read about this conversation, would you believe it? Late at night, alone in the dark, just the lamp and the window and the page?

What should I do?

This man, Lamb. You must find him. You must see him. You must find out what he knows.

But he's told me everything. I have his report. It's cost me everything, my whole inheritance.

You must find out what he knows, Nadia repeats. And if necessary, you must stop him.

Stop him from what?

From killing her again, Nadia says simply.

This is a mad conversation, the new reader thinks. It's not realistic. I don't buy the psychology behind it.

This woman who resembles me, who is caught up in the melodrama of her own grief, who can't complete the work of mourning, I can recognize a little bit. But this Nadia must be a figment of her imagination, like all the others. How terrible. How terrible to be a character like that, all alone.

You're right, Ruth says. You're right.

This time Nadia lets Ruth hug her.

And that evening, cooking dinner at the stove, her eyes are dry and clear when Ben walks in the door and stops, quite abruptly.

What's wrong.

She looks at him, standing there in the doorway with his suit coat off, tie loosened, eyes baggy, attaché dangling from his left index finger. He is middle aged, she realizes. We both are.

My stepfather is dead. He died of a heart attack in a hotel. In Berlin.

My God. I'm so sorry.

Moving to put his arms around her. Lucy watches them both from her usual spot on the floor, a plastic toy in her mouth.

I have to go there.

To Germany? Seriously?

Yes, Ben. I have to settle his affairs.

Of course. Of course you do.

They watch the pot bubbling.

I'll come with you.

I don't want that.

Stepping back. Now there are two pairs of eyes watching her, fascinated yet detached in their curiosity. Only a tiny wrinkle at the corner of Ben's mouth to suggest his pain.

Why? I could help you. I want to help you.

I need to go, and I need to go alone. You can ask your mother to come help. She'll be delighted. She doesn't like me anyway.

That isn't true at all.

It is true. I don't care, it's fine for her not to like me. Why should she like me? I took her only son away from her. I lie in bed all day, I'm barely employed, I'm her batshit daughter-in-law. Bring her here for a few days, a week at most. She'll have the two of you all to herself.

But is Lucy ready to be on her own?

She won't be on her own.

The scene is a frieze. On the stove, a pot of something bubbles toward conclusion. Lucy has crawled over and has a parental pant leg in each hand, tugging, grinning. Ben, eyes pained, confused, but she can see it, she knows she saw it, that flash of relief in the thought of her going. She feels it too.

I don't understand, Ben says. He bends down to pick up Lucy, holds her close, already playing the part of the abandoned father. You haven't spoken to him since he left. You blame him for your mother.... I mean, I understand he's your stepfather, he raised you, but. Can't they just, I don't know, ship him back?

We can bury him here.

It's not Papa I need to see, she tells him.

It's not?

I need to see her.

Ben opens his mouth and closes it. Lucy looks at his face, then Ruth's. Her expression is quizzical, Ruth recognizes it. Deciding whether or not to cry.

Can we talk about this later? Ben asks, indicating Lucy with a jab of his head.

We can talk as much as you need to, she says quietly, turning back to the stove. But it's settled. I'm going.

You need to see a body? he says tightly. Is that it? You need to see the fucking body?

I don't expect you to understand.

Ruth. I'm your husband. Standing there.

You need me to go, she whispers. I know you do.

It's expensive to fly last minute, he says desperately.

It's already arranged. I got a bereavement fare. Don't worry about it. I still have some money.

Her money, you mean.

Yes. It's all I have of her.

Ruth, honey. It's not true. She loved you. I know she loved you.

It's all I have, Ruth repeats. Could you take care of her please? I think her diaper's full.

Ben has a face he will never show, and he shows it now. She turns to the stove.

Please.

He leaves with his daughter in his arms. Ruth is alone in the kitchen with the pot boiling over.

The mind is the only mirror, the mirror is the only me. Alone with herself in the dark, naked or nearly so, looking at the other body. Boobs that never sagged, belly never pooched, raveled with stretch marks. Dark eyes ringed with kohl by the single bulb, in a bathroom between Chicago and their unmutual destiny.

You should know, she says to her, you hired him.

The taut sister gives her a contemptuous look. Does she still smoke? She smokes.

I wanted Papa to be Papa, she says defensively. And you…

You wanted M not to be M.

Fingers to the glass push hard against melodrama. A bell somewhere, the air pocketing the two of them. Not undead, unborn. You must birth yourself, unaided, alone with a lethal image.

Elsa. You told me he wasn't dead.

No more are you.

No more are *you*. That's what you said, isn't it? When we were girls.

I was never a girl.

As if the dream took on flesh, married, grew older, tended fretfully its diminishing circumference, the garden, died. Leaving what in its wake. A name? A child?

Elsa. Is she alive?

Are we?

The bell again. Return to your seat. She makes a little tepid water flow over her fingers and applies it to her eyes. Outside it's night, the north Atlantic. She fastens her seat belt and tries to sleep. But she never leaves that room.

There is a woman who resembles the sentence.

My name is Elsa Ruth. I'm coming for you, M. For the name.

What Ben said to her, should have said, she dreamed that he said it, standing silhouetted in the doorway of their bedroom on the last night. *If it's true, she didn't deserve you. She abandoned you. She ran into the arms of Europe, the arms of death, away from her history, her legacy, her baby. My poor baby.* Cradling her head as she sobbed into the counterpane heaped around her like a sea. And I have recalled her to life with these letters, these facile continuations of her unwritten suicide note. We must have an end to it. To questions.

For Lamb, licensed to kill. With questions if not with kindness.

Europe. The dream of M.

The bloody middle of it.

In her carry-on is the last envelope she received from him, from Lamb, the man she has to find, has to stop from finding. The man who is murdering her past. The envelope was mailed from that city. She will track him down. He will lead me, she thinks, to M.

It's a big city, not quite walkable. She walks. In the Jewish Museum she watches Peter Lorre as M, the murderer, on trial with other criminals, pimps, whores, gangsters, as his jury, on his knees, rolling those eyes, screeching, beating his breast, repeating: *I don't want to—I* have *to! I don't* want *to—I HAVE to!* Pursued, the pursuer, murderer of innocence, his own. Lorre was a Jew. The heroic caved-in miner in the film that follows, an allegory of the workers' solidarity, a Jew. The young woman dying from an illegal abortion in the film that follows that one, a Jew. The 1930s in an endless Ufa loop that stops short of the limitless self-mutilation that is German history. She sits there for a long time, watching.

Libeskind's tower like a vertical pit, cold even in summer, not quite pitch black. Traffic sounds. Her own footsteps, soles scraping concrete. Shush of her fingertips on the metal. Straining to remember what she never knew.

Outside it's Berlin, city that was divided and stitched back together again, Western capital suturing the scar on capital's face, leaving a blank furious space in the center called Alexanderplatz. She wanders north to the hotel on Friedrichstrasse but does not go inside, turns west Unter den Linden to the Gate, joins the flood of tourists, sometimes hurrying, slipping between oblivious bodies, muttering inaudibly *Entshuldigung, Entshuldigung.* She looks at them, the Germans, their faces, trying to feel something. Was your father a…? Was your grandfather….? There are no old people in this city, she thinks, no old people at all. They were all born when the Wall came down, *der Mauer.* She has seen it in its relict state, framing the "Topography of Terror" that she knows so well from her childhood, her mother's books. The photos. She has passed through the Gate and allows herself to be pulled and pushed southward. Another memorial: innumerable stelae, a city block's worth, an abstraction in stone. People pose for photos, a dog runs to catch a ball, schoolgirls flirt. Here and there bent shoulders—there's a man in his seventies or eighties standing with his back to a pillar, with a younger man holding up his phone, shooting a video, an interview. Grandpa, what did you…? How do you…? She flashes past, her feet are burning but she can't stop walking, can't rest before Potsdamer Platz—the sun's going down—she's taken in by the crowd of new buildings, electric glitz of them, finds her way into the Sony Center where a fountain rises and people throng senselessly, under an open rooftop like fan blades coming apart. She can check her email here and does: Ben has sent her a video of him and Lucy, looking soulfully into the camera's eye. Come home Mommy. We miss you. She is tired. What am I doing here? I am looking for something and not finding it. What was that saying? Find before seeking, yes. Turn things around.

Are there any messages for me? she asks the hotel clerk. He knows I'm here, she can feel it. There are no messages.

The room is small and secret, with an interrupted view of the Spree and the turning halo of the Berliner Ensemble. I must go to Brecht's house, she reminds herself. She takes out the envelope again, again slides the disk into her laptop.

A man in a hotel room—it could be this one. His face is drawn with fatigue. What could be gray morning light has turned his skin the color of parchment. He could be anyone's grandfather.

He has nothing to tell me that I don't already know.

Lamb, she says out loud, in frustration. But Lamb does not appear, of course.

Gustave, on the screen, pinches the bridge of his nose and rubs his eyes. He looks up, off screen, into someone else's eyes. Lamb's eyes. You have heard my confession, he says. I'm sorry. I'm sorry. Then he says the name.

That's enough, Lamb says, unseen.

In my beginning is my end.

And the final convergence: to Miramare, castle by the sea, where restless spirits fly. As voices and bodies bearing our look. Ruth in white, the castle is gray, Lamb in dire cinematic black. The castle's a thrust stage that plays for the sea.

The flight from Berlin to Trieste is no longer than the flight from Chicago to Newark, as in the old days when she still had a mother to visit. She has the letters in her hand. Still jet lagged, in the bus she presses her temple against the cool glass and watches the Mediterranean flash by. The bus follows the road above the coast, high through deciduous trees, the sea is refracted below like a million dimes on an infinite skillet. Her eyes are closing when she is startled by the glimpse of an ordinary road sign reading *Duino-Aurisina*. Why did she not purchase a guidebook? But she knows, she remembers, she has a letter in hand, she finds the relevant paragraph:

Duino is disappointing and at the same time not. The ancient castle hulks high above the water on white cliffs, but you're not allowed to walk there; tourists are confined to the newer castle (newer! it dates to the 14th century) which has a big enclosed courtyard, as if the inhabitants wished to hide from the sea, or from Rilke's terrible angels. They're not so terrible to me, an old woman trying to keep the wind from blowing her sunhat off. He must have listened to the wind, walking back and forth there, until he heard... what he was prepared to hear. Life is wasted on young men, angels too. I've stood for a long time in that castle, listening. And when I get tired there's a café, of course, and an espresso sets me up for the bus ride back to town. Bernardo came with me the last time, he'd never been. Imagine living in this place all your life and never once going to see the castle where Rilke once lived. Of course that sort of thing happens all the time. But he's not an imbecile, I gave the poems to him and he's reading them. He likes the end of the First Elegy best:

> *The children who have gone ahead no longer need us,*
> *weaned from earthly things as from*
> *the mother's breast. But we who need*
> *these secrets—for from sadness*
> *springs our progress—can we be without them?*
> *Is the story false that grief for Linos*
> *first dared music to pierce our drought,*
> *so that, in shocked space, the outline of youth, almost godlike*
> *suddenly forever departed, that void vibration*
> *that now ravishes us, comforts us, and helps.*

To live in the kingdom of elegy. The present tense only an aftermath, thin consolation for the thickness of past. The decisive moments that go unglimpsed. I can show you the before, I can live the after. The event is plural and passes without recognition, passes unsurpassed. To fix it is the work of the fictional. The characters pursue the event in vain. When did she become my mother? Why did I fall in love? When did I resign my hopes?

Linos the singer, murdered with his own lyre.

She drops off her bag at the Hotel Verdi and goes straight to the address on the Via dei Piccardi, not bothering to ring the bell for number 3. She knows the apartment is empty, or let to another. But she presses the buzzer for 5, again and again, until a hoarse woman's voice answers: *Si?*

My name is Elsa Freeman. I believe that you know my mother.

Su madre?

Si, Signora.

I don't know. Suspiciously.

She knew your son as well. His name is Bernardo.

A long pause, and then the buzzer.

The apartment is spacious but dark, Signora Bruno herself a long black feather with faded cheeks done up a morbid shade of rouge. I have called my son, the Signora makes it plain to her through signs and gestures and particles of English. He will be here soon. Do have some tea, or some coffee.

Grazie. I mean, *no grazie.* I'm fine.

You look like her, the Signora announces, falsely.

Bernardo. He is old enough to be Ruth's father. He makes a courtly, embarrassed little bow and speaks rapidly in Italian to his mother, without taking his eyes off of Ruth. She shrugs. He offers Ruth his arm and says in nearly accentless English, Let us talk somewhere else. Your first time in Trieste? We will go to the San Marco, it is not very far.

The streets are narrow. Old World, she thinks, Old World. What is there in me that responds to these streets. Is it M, in my blood, speaking.

I wanted to meet you, she says when they are seated at a table in the buzzing Vienna-style café. Around her mostly middle-aged men and older with espresso cups and glasses of wine, talking and gesticulating. She hears snatches of languages that don't sound quite Italian. My mother wrote me about you.

She was a great lady, Bernardo says. Very brave. Very strong.

Is it true, Ruth asks, pausing, not sure she wants to hear the answer. Is it true that… you were her friend?

For a little while, yes.

You knew about her husband?

Bernardo is embarrassed again. He coughs and sips some water. Yes. But she was not, we were not involved in the way that you think.

It's none of my business if you were.

Yes. But I want, I think she would have wanted you to understand her. She was lonely, but proud. She wanted to meet the end alone. I was a kind of weakness, an indulgence of hers. You must forgive her.

Must I?

What she says is: I never understood her. I have tried. But I don't know why she left.

Why.

She told me once she wasn't searching for anything. I'm not looking for love, she said, or for answers, or for anything. I'm not looking for a cure for the cancer. I want to be alone for a while. Because once I'm dead, I won't be alone any more. I won't belong to me.

She said that?

Yes, it's a peculiar phrase, isn't it. She said it a few times so I'd remember it. "Once I'm dead, I won't belong to me"

To whom does she belong, then?

Bernardo lowers his eyes. I could not say. I only knew her for a little while.

She must have trusted you.

I don't know. Perhaps.

And… when she died?

There, I am afraid, I was like you. I didn't know until it had already happened. I hadn't seen her for a few days. I became worried. Then the concierge told me about the letter.

What letter?

The… the note I suppose you would call it. So that the concierge would know whom to call. Me. And then, the police. I thought it was best to let the authorities notify you. Nothing she'd said to me made me think I was, how to put this, authorized to contact you. She was afraid of the confusion it might cause.

But I knew all about you, Ruth says. She holds up the packet of letters. She wrote to me about you.

A gravely pleased look is his reply.

She is *still* writing to me, Ruth murmurs.

I have an appointment, she adds. A last appointment. I have to go to the castle, Miramare.

Why do you want to go there?

Because that's where it happened. Where it ended.

I don't understand.

Didn't she tell you? In the letter she left for you? Where she went to end it?

Eyebrows raised slightly, he looks at her, in mild shock of inquiry. She takes the envelope from her purse.

This was the first letter. Or the last letter, take your pick. Look.

The canceled stamp: a gray formal crenellation like the rook of a chess set. The address in a steady, legible cursive hand with U S A in block letters underneath it like a signature.

How do I get there? To Miramare?

You had better not, Signora.

It's the only reason I'm here.

He looks at her with his puzzled, kind, infinitely tired eyes, and shrugs in a way that reminds her ineffably of her grandfather. *So nu?*

Then you had better take a taxi. No. I have a better idea. There is a boat you can take. You will have a splendid view.

All right. Signor Bruno… Bernardo. Can you just tell me… The last time you saw her… She struggles to formulate a question that makes sense. He puts his warm, dry hand on top of her own.

The last time I saw her, he said, was here. At this very table. She sat where you are sitting now. She did not look ill, not at all. She did not wish to.

What did you talk about?

He shrugs, lifts his other hand, spreads the fingers.

She said she was going on a journey. Before going into the hospital. I thought perhaps she meant she was going to try and find her husband. I thought she was going to go north.

How did she look?

Bellisima.

But in her mind she saw that head, hairless, that body, reduced to air and bone, in a hospital bed, in a universe of plastic and taupe. Sleeping. Tiny sleeping bird with its head under its wing.

She had only to close her eyes.

Ah, my poor signora, Bernardo says. You have had a hard journey, I think.

It is almost over, she says, rising.

She sits in the bow of the motor launch that carries her, from the Grand Canale out into the harbor on a wide arc, watching the castle swing into view. Miramare, mirror of the sea. In her mind's eye the woman in gray is a mirror behind the mirror, the great glass prow of the castle where the Empress of Mexico once stood, trapped in her husband's dreams of the sea, of the name of action. In our mind's eye turning to discover Lamb, coiled in a Biedermeier armchair, hat leveled, pistol easy in his hand. The contract is about to be fulfilled. Hurry, Ruth says silently to the boatman, to the swell of land, the forest of Miramare beginning to crowd itself around them. To her own heart. Hurry, and at last.

The mistral is blowing, it renders everything dusty

and spectral, the banners on the castle's peaks whip and thrum in the wind, the ground itself seems to vibrate. It's an ordinary Tuesday in the off season. There's a man on the promontory, the great doors behind him, coat blowing behind him, black gloves on his hands, black hat pulled low, no sign of any suitcase. The boat pulls around, she watches him, too far, she can't see his face. The castle grounds are silent when she alights in the sheltered lagoon from which Maximilian and Charlotte used to sail, little pleasure cruises in the evening, she imagines, on a wooden boat with silent splendid servants, as alone as royalty can be, going out just far enough to look back on the castle and on their lives. The heavy wind shakes the layered branches of the oaks and firs. She wraps her coat around her and steps onto the shore.

In the castle foyer there are sober tapestries, a parquet floor. Ruth holds her entrance ticket in front of her. Looking around at the high ceilings, she passes into the private quarters of Maximiliano, the frigate-rooms, feeling herself as she is meant to at sea. Where is he? Stepping to the porthole window that looks out on the promontory where he was standing like a figurehead, almost crucified by the wind. He is gone. But he is here. She climbs the great stairs toward Charlotte's rooms, frozen and disintimate, past the somber portraits of dead empires. That is Franz Joseph, she tells herself, and that is Franz Ferdinand, and that is Ferdinand Maximilian Joseph, Emperor of Mexico for three years and seventy days, and this is the house that he built on the edge of his empire of tolerance, that for a while held together so many nations and tribes, that agreed for a bit to forget their grievances against each other, a peaceable kingdom, almost pastoral, that could not go on finally refusing the brute invitations of history. Where is she buried, really buried, not the anonymous plot in New Jersey they shipped the box to, where I stood with Ben and the baby and a few cousins, is she buried here, in this city, I never saw the body, I can never know her death, or what I am, till I meet her. Having climbed to the top, to Charlotte's bedroom, where the mad Empress might have sat in that uncomfortable chair by the window with a bit of sewing or simply staring, out to sea, while doctors looked after her, while a servant looked up into her face, where a cousin might have come to visit to read to her from the Bible in French, the language of her youth.

You wanted that, didn't you. To reach and out and touch her, as she was touched by others. M. You wanted to touch it, as she wanted to touch it, history in the form of two bodies, meeting.

Every second, the narrow gate.

And there, before the balcony, backlit, black figure, the man. Lamb. Her deputy, her author, her undertaker. He shines as a vampire shines, invisibly, unmirrored.

The case is closed. You shouldn't have come.

I had to come.

You had to come. The deadliness of repetition. He has been repeating her, all along.

Does he have a gun? Is that how he plans to finish the job? Bullet fired seven decades ago, from the grave of Europe, aimed forever at my heart?

His suitcase nowhere to be seen.

She's here, isn't she, Mr. Lamb?

Your mother is dead.

But she is here. She was M.

M.

The wind catches in the windows, rattles it, builds up to an unearthly revenant whine that makes them both wince. Ruth puts her hands to her ears.

What's in a name? She called me Elsa. I called her M—. But we didn't answer to those names.

Lamb holds the gun level, pointing it at her heart. He gestures with it.

Let's walk.

Out into the storm, though the sky is bewilderingly blue and clear, not a cloud to be seen being chased by the mistral up from the south, chopping the sea behind them. Into the woods, the thick forest of the park surrounding Miramare, like Little Red Riding Hood and the wolf, seeking cover for the dark deed of their story. He walks behind her, she steps carefully, watching her feet. Is this what it was like? Is this where I come from? Istvan called it the death march, but that's not quite right. It's only death if you stop.

Keep moving.

Mr. Lamb, she calls behind her, though he can't possibly hear in this wind. Lamb. This doesn't make sense. You work for me.

I work for you, he agreed. She could feel it between her shoulder blades: the eye of the gun.

This isn't my story, she says, or thinks. This is my end.

This is the end.

Every story ends in death. But my story began with it.

She stops, flinches. The air in the wood is still though she can hear the treetops tearing with it high above them. No birds. Twigs roll under her feet like marbles. She puts out her arms to steady herself.

It's the story I wanted. To feel that I had one. That there was something behind her, beneath her, a human being. If my mother died, the human being could live. I could meet her.

She turns around and says to no one, to her, to M:

I had to love you. You gave me no choice. You were the world. And I mean that literally, you had taken the world inside you, I could see it and taste it, in the lines of your face, the voice so low, your bitterness, the snap of your rage, your blame. I bore it all, I was stronger than you knew, stronger than you. I had to survive you, what you couldn't even do, survive grandma and all the wars, survive Germany, survive Paris. And now I've done it, I can call you by your right name. I can see you so clearly. I see me in your face, and I see your own face, and none of it is alien, none of it is not mine, not ours. M, a letter, a character, in writing. It's so beautiful to know you. It's so beautiful to cry for you, now that you've gone.

The woman in white, the wind peeling her, carrying her clothing away.

Bless me and let me go.

On my knees in the dirt of Mitteleuropa, where I began, to see her. In tears, smiling at the woman who lived.

A crow's cry, a black report, under the wind. Winged. To take flight.

The castle is behind her and the man she made, stumbling blind and alone through the trees, empty-handed. No camera follows him, no awkward suitcase, no body commas the ground. No grave comes near. The air in the airplane cabin is dried-out and decontextualized. Focusing on the back of the seat in front of her, a luminous white face eyes closed in concentration. The faces of her loved ones are blooming there: the daughter who needs her. The husband who waits for her. The light whole and clear in her face, all the faces, retreating and returning, mother in daughter in mother in *in*. She opens the new book, the blank book, the book of home, its wings, her eyes write her face, a woman, renamed, writing a letter, to the middle, at last.

Joanna Kramer

Joshua Corey is the author of four books of poetry: *The Barons* (Omnidawn Publishing, 2014), *Severance Songs* (Tupelo Press, 2011), *Fourier Series* (Spineless Books, 2005), and *Selah* (Barrow Street Press, 2003). He lives in Evanston, Illinois with his wife and daughter and is an associate professor of English at Lake Forest College. This is his first novel.

www.joshua-corey.com

@joshcorey

www.facebook.com/beautifulsoulnovel

SPUYTEN DUYVIL

Meeting Eyes Bindery

Triton

Lithic Scatter

8TH AVENUE Stefan Brecht

ABROAD: AN EXPATRIATE'S DIARIES Harriet Sohmers Zwerling

A DAY AND A NIGHT AT THE BATHS Michael Rumaker

ACTS OF LEVITATION Laynie Browne

ALIEN MATTER Regina Derieva

ANARCHY Mark Scroggins

APO/CALYPSO Gordon Osing

APPLES OF THE EARTH Dina Elenbogen

APPROXIMATING DIAPASON j/j hastain & t thilleman

ARC: CLEAVAGE OF GHOSTS Noam Mor

THE ARSENIC LOBSTER Peter Grandbois

ASHES RAIN DOWN William Luvaas

AUNTIE VARVARA'S CLIENTS Stelian Tanase

BALKAN ROULETTE Drazan Gunjaca

THE BANKS OF HUNGER AND HARDSHIP J. Hunter Patterson

BEAUTIFUL SOUL Joshua Corey

BEHIND THE WALL AT THE SUGAR WORKS Marc Vincenz

LA BELLE DAME Gordon Osing & Tom Carlson

BIRD ON THE WING Juana Culhane

BLACK LACE Barbara Henning

BLACK MOUNTAIN DAYS Michael Rumaker

BLUEPRINTS FOR A GENOCIDE Rob Cook

BOTH SIDES OF THE NIGER Andrew Kaufman

BREATHING FREE (ed.) Vyt Bakaitis

BURIAL SHIP Nikki Stiller

Butterflies Brane Mozetic

But They, Um Jennie Neighbors

By The Time You Finish This Book You Might Be Dead Aaron Zimmerman

Cadences j/j hastain

Captivity Narratives Richard Blevins

Celestial Monster Juana Culhane

Cephalonical Sketches t thilleman

Clef: A Manifesto j/j hastain & t thilleman

Cleopatra Haunts the Hudson Sarah White

Cloud Fire Katherine Hastings

Columns: Track 2 Norman Finkelstein

Consciousness Suite David Landrey

The Conviction & Subsequent Life of Savior Neck Christian TeBordo

Conviction's Net of Branches Michael Heller

The Corybantes Tod Thilleman

Crossing Borders Kowit & Silverberg

Crypto-Arkansas Mark Spitzer

Day Book of a Virtual Poet Robert Creeley

The Day He's Gone Paweł Marcinkiewicz trans. Piotr Florczyk

Daylight to Dirty Work Tod Thilleman

The Desire Notebooks John High

Detective Sentences Barbara Henning

Diary of a Clone Saviana Stanescu

Diffidence Jean Harris

Donna Cameron Donna Cameron

Don't Kill Anyone, I Love You Gojmir Polajnar

Dray-Khmara as a Poet Oxana Asher

Egghead to Underhoof Tod Thilleman

Elsa Tsipi Keller

Entering Yoni Space On The Pouring Pivot of My Own Lingaraj t thilleman

Eroticizing the Nation Leverett T. Smith, Jr.

The Evil Queen Benjamin Perez

Exiled From the Womb Adrian Sangeorzan

Extreme Positions Stephen Bett

The Farce Carmen Firan

Fission Among The Fanatics Tom Bradley

The Flame Charts Paul Oppenheimer

Flying in Water Barbara Tomash

Form Martin Nakell

Gadsden Rich Blevins

Four Seasons Michael Forstrom

Gesture Through Time Elizabeth Block

Ghosts! Martine Bellen

Giraffes in Hiding Carol Novack

Gnostic Frequencies Patrick Pritchett

God's Whisper Dennis Barone

Gowanus Canal, Hans Knudsen Tod Thilleman

Graphomania j/j hastain

Grass Grows Inward Andreas Neeser trans. Marc Vincenz

Half-Girl Stephanie Dickinson

He Knows What A Stick Is Russell Brickey

Hidden Death, Hidden Escape Liviu Georgescu

Houndstooth David Wirthlin

How to Walk Away Lisa Birman

Identity Basil King

Identity Collages j/j hastain

In Times of Danger Paul Oppenheimer

Incretion Brian Strang

Inferno Carmen Firan

Infinity Subsections Mark DuCharme

Insouciance Thomas Phillips

In Thailand with the Apostles Joanna Sit

Inverted Curvatures Francis Raven

The Ivory Hour Laynie Browne

Jackpot Tsipi Keller

The Jazzer & The Loitering Lady Gordon Osing

Kissing Nests Werner Lutz, trans. by Marc Vincenz

Knowledge Michael Heller

Lady V. D.R. Popa

Last Supper of the Senses Dean Kostos

Lawfully Wedded Wives Nona Caspers & Joell Hallowell

A Lesser Day Andrea Scrima

Let's Talk About Death M. Maurice Abitbol

Libretto for the Exhausted World Michael Fisher

Light House Brian Lucas

Light Years: Multimedia in the East Village, 1960-1966 (ed.) Carol Bergé

Little Book of Days Nona Caspers

Little Tales of Family & War Martha King

Long Fall: Essays and Texts Andrey Gritsman

Lunacies Ruxandra Cesereanu

Lust Series Stephanie Dickinson

Lyrical Interference Norman Finkelstein

Maine Book Joe Cardarelli (ed.) Anselm Hollo

MannhatteN Sarah Rosenthal

Martha's Mandala Martha Oliver-Smith

Mating In Captivity Nava Renek

Meanwhile Gordon Osing

Medieval Ohio Richard Blevins

Memory's Wake Derek Owens

Mermaid's Purse Laynie Browne

Miming Mink j/j hastain

The Minotaur's Daughter Rowland Saifi

Mobility Lounge David Lincoln

Modern Adventures Bill Evans

The Moscoviad Yuri Andrukhovych

Multifesto: A Henri d'Mescan Reader (remix edition) Davis Schneiderman

My Last Century Joanna Sit

The New Beautiful Tendons Jeffery Beam

Nighthawks Katherine Hastings

Nightshift / An Area of Shadows Erika Burkart & Ernst Halter

No Perfect Words Nava Renek

No Wrong Notes Norman Weinstein

North & South Martha King

Notes of a Nude Model Harriet Sohmers Zwerling

The Number of Missing Adam Berlin

Of All The Corners To Forget Gian Lombardo

One Foot Out the Door: The Collected Stories of Lewis Warsh Lewis Warsh

Onönyxa & Therseyn T Thilleman

The Opening Day Richard Blevins

Our Father M.G. Stephens

Over the Lifeline Adrian Sangeorzan

Pagan Days Michael Rumaker

PART OF THE DESIGN Laura E. Wright
PIECES FOR SMALL ORCHESTRA & OTHER FICTIONS Norman Lock
THE PIGS DRINK FROM INFINITY Mark Spitzer
A PLACE IN THE SUN Lewis Warsh
THE POET : PENCIL PORTRAITS Basil King
POLITICAL ECOSYSTEMS J.P. Harpignies
POLYPHEMUS Gordon Osing
POWERS: TRACK 3 Norman Finkelstein
PROOF Elizabeth Coleman
THE PRISON NOTEBOOKS OF ALAN KRIEGER (TERRORIST) Marc Estrin
THE PROPAGANDA FACTORY Marc Vincenz
REMAINS TO BE SEEN Halvard Johnson
RETELLING Tsipi Keller
RIVERING Dean Kostos
ROOT-CELLAR TO RIVERINE Tod Thilleman
THE ROOTS OF HUMAN SEXUALITY M. Maurice Abitbol
SAIGON AND OTHER POEMS Jack Walters
A SARDINE ON VACATION Robert Castle
SAVOIR FEAR Charles Borkhuis
SECRET OF WHITE Barbara Tomash
SEDUCTION Lynda Schor
SEE WHAT YOU THINK David Rosenberg
SELECTED EARLY POEMS OF LEV LOSEFF (ed.) Henry Pickford
SEMI-SLEEP Kenneth Baron
SETTLEMENT Martin Nakell
SEX AND THE SENIOR CITY M. Maurice Abitbol
SEXUAL HARASSMENT RULES Lynda Schor
SHADER Daniel Nester
THE SILENCE OF MEMORY Serge Gavronsky
SKETCHES IN NORSE & FORRA t thilleman

Sketches Tzitzimime t thilleman

Slaughtering the Buddha Gordon Osing

Snailhorn (fragments) t thilleman

The Snail's Song Alta Ifland

SOS: Song of Songs of Solomon j/j hastain

The Spark Singer Jade Sylvan

Spiritland Nava Renek

State of the Union Susan Lewis

Strange Evolutionary Flowers Lizbeth Rymland

Suddenly Today We Can Dream Rutha Rosen

The Sudden Death of... Serge Gavronsky

The Takeaway Bin Toni Mirosevich

Talking To The Dead Rachel Hadas

The Tattered Lion Juana Culhane

Tautological Eye Martin Nakell

Ted's Favorite Skirt Lewis Warsh

Theaters of Skin Gordon Osing & Tom Carlson

There Where You Do Not Think To Be Thinking Chuck Stein

Things That Never Happened Gordon Osing

Thread Vasyl Makhno

Three Mouths Tod Thilleman

Three Sea Monsters Tod Thilleman

To Kill a Cardinal Michael Rumaker

The Tommy Plans Cooper Renner

Tongue a Queer Anomaly j/j hastain & t thilleman

Track Norman Finkelstein

Transitory Jane Augustine

Transparencies Lifted From Noon Chris Glomski

Triple Crown Sonnets Jeffrey Cyphers Wright

Tsim-tsum Marc Estrin

Twelve Circles Yuri Andrukhovych
Vienna ØØ Eugene K. Garber
Uncensored Songs for Sam Abrams (ed.) John Roche
Up Fish Creek Road David Matlin
Venice is for Cats Nava Renek & Ethel Renek
Warp Spasm Basil King
Watchfulness Peter O'Leary
Watch The Doors As They Close Karen Lillis
Walking After Midnight Bill Kushner
Wandering Electron Lee Slonimsky
West of West End Peter Freund
When the Gods Come Home to Roost Marc Estrin
Whirligig Christopher Salerno
White, Christian Christopher Stoddard
Winter Letters Vasyl Makhno
Within the Space Between Stacy Cartledge
A World of Nothing But Nations Tod Thilleman
A World of Nothing But Self-Infliction Tod Thilleman
Wandering On course Robert Podgurski
Wreckage of Reason (ed.) Nava Renek
Wreckage of Reason 2 :
Back to the Drawing Board (ed.) Nava Renek
Xian Dyad Jason Price Everett
The Yellow House Robin Behn
You, Me, and the Insects Barbara Henning

if it had not been for massed debris, road washouts and disarranged culverts, nobody would have been able to tell where the brooks had been any more than they had before the rain.

Thus public opinion was sensitive about anything which might have contributed to the raising of the water. Around Hillville, the consensus was that it was a bad storm, yes; but if those cussed beavers hadn't put up the water in Cooney's Heath, made that old dead waterway change channels till it filled up Ame Wilkinson's gravel pit to overflow like a dish and run down the bulldozed road, not half that water would have got into the town.

Undeniably there was a measure of truth in this reasoning. The beavers, without a doubt, had co-operated with the rain and with the slopes, eroded and bare, where once a forest of trees, now destroyed, had hindered disasters of water running down. Deserts had floods, of course, and they had them in China, didn't they? But not here; nothing like this had ever been known in this place. It must have been caused by something unusual, and everybody took comfort in having something to throw the blame on. Those damned beavers. The State had better get busy. Those beavers had got to go.

After the dynamiting, when the water from the beaver pond had drained away, the wardens found what was left of Amos on the up side of the dam. Unwilling to compromise and unable to beat Them, he had joined Them.

had been knocked unconscious when, plunging into the washout, the car had turned turtle; mercifully; because, among other things, here at last was reality that would never change for better; here, for always, a corner she could not brighten.

Amos Wilkinson had disappeared; the hunt for him went on for a week in the woods adjoining the town, before the delayed winter weather set in. Then temperature dropped overnight to twelve below zero and hovered there for four days. Ponds, marshes, swamps froze deep. For a few days a man could have walked anywhere in Cooney's Heath, even over the boiling springs from which the swamp had its being and which had never frozen within the memory of man; and over the shaking bogs, which had been known to freeze, but treacherously, with breathing holes hard to tell from solid ice. But spring and bog were frozen deep now under the frozen beaver pond. Many men went through the Heath—wardens and state troopers and search parties made up of Amos's neighbors. Mack Jensen had a hunch, he said, that Amos had gone there. "Had something down in there on his mind," Mack told people. "That's for sure. Didn't say what, but said enough so I know he did."

Mack didn't say anything to anyone about Lucy's phone call to him on the morning of the big rain. He figured that the less said about that, the better. His not doing much about it when she called him hadn't done any harm, he guessed, but it wouldn't look good if people found out he hadn't; so he kept mum.

A crew of Amos's men, headed by Mack, crossed the Heath on the ice and went all over the high ground of the hummock, carrying rifles, with which, Mack said, they might clobber two-three of them wild houn-dogs, if they run acrost any, kill two birds with one stone.

They found none of the dogs, who, on the first night that ice had frozen deep enough to bear their weight, had left the hummock and all gone home, where they now slept in warm kitchens, played with children, and were fed canned dogfood from plates. The hunt did, however, turn up traces of Amos. A spade stuck in the ice at the margin of the hummock bore his name, neatly burned into the handle, and it was reasonable to suppose that the smashed flashlight found among the trees belonged to him. But there was nothing else.

"Kuh-riced," Mack said at the end of the hunt, as the party left to go home. "Look at them trees. I'll bet they're worth twenty dollars apiece."

"All of that," someone said, "to the poor devil that had to cut 'em. The dealer that sold the finished lumber'd probably git a hundred. No sense worrying your head, Mack, nobody could get at these ones."

"I dunno about that," Mack said. "Give this bog a couple weeks of zero weather, man could run trucks acrost the ice." He narrowed his eyes, speculating. "Who owns this hummock, anyway?"

"Never heard anyone did. Who'd ever be fool enough to pay money for it? Part of the old Cooney place, I guess." The man glanced back uneasily at the stand of big pines. In his opinion Mack had got pretty far off the track of what they'd come here for. "I got the confoundedest feeling," he said, "that old Ame is around here, somewhere."

"Never found him, though, did we?" Mack said cheerfully. "Doubt if we ever will."

He realized that the fellow was looking at him in a puzzled way, and hastened to fix his face and make a comment more suitable to tragedy. "He warn't right, Ame warn't," he said lugubriously. "What I think, the poor old bugger committed suicide."

He shook his head in gloom and sorrow, lowering his

voice to a note which he hoped sounded reverent. "V never see hide nor hear hair of him again, you wait see."

That was enough, that took care of that. After a mor he said under his breath, "Jeezus, what I wouldn't giv be able to git them trees."

On both points, the trees and Amos, Mack turned ou be mistaken.

The winter, as a winter, was a dead loss. Cold wea did not last; after a wet snowstorm, it grew mild again rained. While, from time to time, the temperature dro to below freezing, it did not again make ice in the sv thick enough to risk trucks on, and never did becaus the spring, the wardens dynamited the beaver dam.

They had planned at first to leave it alone, seein reason not to; at least, they had one colony of be staying put in Cooney's Heath, where they weren't dam up some brook that would flood out cellars and de orchards somewhere else. But the tropical rainstorm which upwards of twelve inches of rain was dumped night and a day, had caused over a million dollars' v of damage. Not only around Hillville, but in many towns and villages along the coast, dead brooks whos istence had been forgotten for a century, had roared life in a night, cutting highways; ripping out culvert designed to carry run-off such as no one within the me of man living had ever seen; washing away hundre yards of road shoulders; taking out bridges; comin over the outlets of cellar drains so that water rose in ments and flowed merrily through the delicate mecha of electric furnaces and pressure pumps and deep-fr not designed for that either: a flash flood, someone saic had been West and had seen one, like in the desert, v snapped its tail over the land for a night and a day dropped back to normal so fast that in twenty-four h

PART SIX Spring, 1960

Town meeting, on the first Monday in March, stirred Marvin Coles out of his winter sleep. He ran for First Selectman and was elected, mostly on his campaign promises to rebuild the old Shore Road that ran past Clementina Wilkinson's house. That road, most people felt, had been a disgrace for years, and it was a shame that nothing had been done to it before someone got killed down there. Of course, you couldn't blame town officials for anything that happened in that storm, and everyone knew how Lucy Wilkinson drove a car. The road had been patched temporarily and was as passable as it ever had been; still, word somehow seeped around town that Marvin Coles, if elected, was going to rebuild it if he had to mortgage the Town Hall. This pointed out with a certain amount of delicacy and a nice sense of timing that, while, of course, the present incumbents might have had some difficulties in raising money for the job, and no one was calling them negligent, still, the thing wasn't impossible, and who knew what might have been accomplished—or prevented—if they had extended themselves a little. This logic got around, and Marvin's ticket was elected by a handsome majority.

Tax assessing kept him busy through most of April, but at the time when he normally did, he got out his cleaned and faded coveralls, with RANDALL'S stitched across the shoulders and FOREMAN on the chest pocket, and prepared to go back to his job to resume his habits of half a century. He laid the coveralls on the front seat of his car, weighted them down with his lunchbox, got in and drove down the side road, on which his house was, toward town. As he turned into the highway and accelerated, an old-fashioned privy walked across the road in front of him.

Marvin let out a yell, yanked at the wheel and jammed his brake to the floor. His rear wheels spun on the sandy shoulder, skidded sideways; he missed hitting the telephone pole head-on, but his fenders scraped against it the full length of the car with a noise like a falling washboiler full of flatirons.

Marvin was shaken up, but not hurt; he sat there, paralyzed, for only a moment.

For godsakes, that was a backhouse! One them old-time, high one-holers. Walked acrost . . . what's the matter with me, am I crazy?

His reddened, choleric eye caught sight of a stir in the bushes by the roadside; he was out of the car and over there, bow-legged, in an instant, just in time to see a kid, a girl, scrabbling like a rabbit to get out of sight in the underbrush. On the ground, apparently where she had just crawled out of it, lay a tall shipping carton which had once held an outsize refrigerator.

That one! That hellion of Nellie Overholt's. Walked acrost the road inside of that thing—just the size and shape of a one-holer, no wonder I . . . Damn near killed me.

As Marvin realized what, almost, had been carelessly done to him, he put back his head and opened his mouth; his outrage, offered freely to heaven, made the empurpled welkin ring.

By the blistered this-and-that, he told himself, as he stamped back to his car, too much hell was being raised in this town by kids, and by that uncircumferated little devil in particular. Keep on, she *would* kill somebody, and it was time the law put a stop to it. As First Selectman, by gumpty, he guessed he could put a stop to it, too. He needed an issue, anyway, something that people could get their teeth into, to take their minds off of repairing that cussed Shore Road; and, you count up, there was plenty to add up to the reform school. There was the windows in Wickham's henhouse; there was them copper cents into the factory machinery; enough other shenanigans, and witnesses for 'em, too, all over town. Might mean tangling with Nellie Overholt, but what of it? He guessed that flapping the law in her face would slow her down. Them Overholts and Warrens was a weedy combination, anyway; look at Nellie's husband, that Billy, and Gert Warren. And this one, unto the third generation. It was about time for a clean-up; a good morals issue—nothing like it to turn a town upside down. Hoe out that house, get rid of them undesirable elements, and straighten out some of the young hellions that was headed hell-a-hooting right down the same path. Too much was enough. And too much was too much, he added, glaring, enflamed all over again, at the paint and fenders on the First Selectman's car.

He didn't get down to the factory that day.

No real hurry, he told himself; time enough when the town business slacked off a little.

Beck was caught this time, well and truly caught. She had set out sincerely that morning with Kate for school; halfway there, she had suddenly ducked into the bushes and run, paying no attention to Kate's frantic yawp that they'd be late.

It was too nice a day to go to the old-fool school; anyway, Mama wanted her to. Go to school, get your education, Mama said. That was what *she* wanted; so . . . that was what Beck wasn't going to do. Chicken-licken, the sky is falling—who cared. It hurt ten minutes and then was over. Meantime you'd had your whole day.

If old Mama-Schmama wanted Beck to do anything, then she had better let Beck do some of the things Beck wanted, not be so poison. Let her go back to see Aunt Gert once in a while; let her have some of the things Uncle Reggie brought. After all, they were Beck's things, they weren't Mama's. Mama had had them all, somewhere. The airplane suitcase, Just The Right Size For A Child, the doll, the dresses, the nylon briefs, and Uncle Reggie's Going-Away Present, the little transistor radio, made too big a bundle to be hidden anywhere in the house; they weren't there, Beck was sure; there wasn't any place she hadn't looked. They certainly weren't around now. Mama said Kate and Henry didn't have any such nice things, so it wasn't fair; and then she said she'd considered the source; and that was all she would say, but Beck was beginning to guess what. Old Strawberry Sudsworth, the one Jody tracked around with now, had a transistor radio now; he said his father had bought it at the second-hand store in Bishop; and it was hers, she knew, because it still had her initials, R. O., that Uncle Reggie had had put on in gold leaf. You could see where old Strawberry had tried to scratch them off and then stopped because it made too deep a mark in the paint. So the second-hand store was probably where the rest of the stuff had gone, too.

All right. What you were waiting for now was just to grow up. Just to get big enough.

Beck's leg was healed—not quite so limber as it would be, Dr. Garland said; but all right now. She'd limped on it good and hard for a week, a lot longer than she'd needed to, hoping Mama'd let her stay some longer with Aunt Gert. But it was no use. In the end she'd had to go home. Now she couldn't go back at all. Even Aunt Gert said, "Honey, you mustn't, not if Mama says no, it'll only make bad trouble. Wait a while, and we'll see." Well, Mama was watching like a hawk, knowing she'd go if she got a chance. Even Uncle Reggie was gone—back to New York. He'd come again, Aunt Gert had said. So far, he hadn't.

So nowhere to go except old-fool school; nothing to do. Nobody to play with—even with Jody she was all fouled up. He'd taken up with Strawberry Sudsworth whilst Beck had been sick and they ganged up on her now if she tried to horn in; so she guessed she knew when she wasn't wanted. The only thing she had on Jody, his little brother had come, the doctor had finally brought it in his little black bag; she guessed she could snicker over that, but only to herself, she couldn't tell anyone, because Dr. Garland trusted her and she trusted him; she guessed he was about the only one left she could trust now.

She schlurked around through the bushes and came up on the back lots behind the business section, and had almost decided that it might be worth while to get Run Over again, when she spotted the old refrigerator carton in the rear of the electrical shop. It was just lying there, not doing anything, so she crawled inside it. It was nice and private in there, but nothing to do; so presently she took her jackknife and made handholds in two sides of it and eye slits so she could see out on all four. At first she just stood it up alongside the highway and, from inside it, secretly cased the cars going by, Sally Spittleoffsky, the Russian Refrigerator Spy; then she got the idea. When she saw a car coming, she would lift the carton by the handholds just high enough so its bottom edges wouldn't scrape, but not high enough to show her feet, and walk it, upright, across the road. It was wonderful to watch what the car drivers would do; some of them were a living sketch, screeched their brakes, wabbled all over the road. That old Marvin Coles wouldn't of run into a telephone pole if he hadn't been so decrippit he couldn't stop his car, anyway; and he never would of caught her if her darn leg had been as limber as it was going to be.

But that old Marvin Coles had sent the Constable to see Mama. Mama said they were going to Serve Papers. There was going to be a Hearing. A School for De-something Children, she said it would probably be; but Beck guessed that was only a nicey-nicey way of saying the reform school.

Well, if none of them, Aunt Gert or Uncle Reggie or Aunt Frances or Mama cared a hoot, neither did she. At least it would be something different. Mama had gone on about it something fierce; she said Beck ought to have thought; she said what with Beck's cussed actions, there wasn't one single, solitary thing that Mama could do.

"I've told her," Nellie said, "that there ain't one single, solitary thing I can do. I've talked with that old turkey buzzard and he won't listen, in spite of his car insurance will take care of the damage, all except his fifty-dollar deductible, which I've offered to pay. Out of what little I make, three kids and barely able to keep my head above water. I don't know as I take it kindly, Gert, you getting yourself all dressed up to the nines and walking in here as if you was welcome."

The rumpus was all over town; Marvin had seen to that

and that people knew the First Selectman was taking action against the undesirable elements. Gert had heard about Beck right away; and in spite of the fact that she had plenty of troubles of her own, and Frances said they had better Lay Low for a while till that old rutabaga cooled off, Gert had come right over to Nellie's.

She had worn her baum-marten cape, which, she now realized, had been a mistake, it did look a little too rich a diet inside Nellie's, but too late to remedy it now. She said, "Maybe you are willing to set by, Nellie, and see that Little Kiddy Sent Away. But I and Reggie and Frances are not."

"I would like to know what you and that ragtag and bob-tail can do," Nellie said, "that Beck's own mother can *not.* The way you're carrying on, Gert, anybody'd think you thought you'd got some rights in it, but—"

"No," Gert said. "I only wisht I did."

"I s'pose you think you could have done better. I will tell you, nobody could, not with that youngone, who I don't know where she come from, who she takes after. Not after Billy, that limp shrimp, and the god knows, she don't take after me. I swear, Gert, you might as well *be* her mother, she's more like you'n she is like anyone, I never could handle you no more'n I can her. But I must say, if some-one'd took you and shoved you into the reform school, *in time,* something would of had to give; and if Beck ain't stopped in her tracks now, the Lord knows where she'll end up. And you have got a gall to come in here and tell me you think you could have done better!"

"I," Gert said, "would've done some things different, yes, Nellie."

"Mm-hm. And what, kindly tell me, would they of been? God knows, I've licked her. It don't do no good."

"Oh, I would never of licked her, never!" Gert said. "I would not of give her a Christmas present from the Welfare,

Nellie. And I would not of took the things Reggie give her to the second-hand store. Her having them, where was the harm?"

"What I do with my own child, bringing her up, is none of your cotton-picking business," Nellie said. She had turned bright red, not having planned to have the second-hand-store deal known. "I don't know what snoop had her nose into that to find it out, prob'ly that Frances. But—"

"Oh, no. Not Frances," Gert said. "But it's known, Nellie."

"I can't say I give a Christian damn if it is. A woman with her head hardly above water, three mouths to feed, makes it where she can and what she can, if she sees a way to extry. And I would not have my child, a child of mine, owning expensive stuff from one of your— Well, I consider the source, that's all."

"Those things b'longed to Beck, that Reggie give her. Reggie is a very nice man. A Prince. And he is not poison. I have been on the phone to him. I was on the phone to him last night for an hour."

"Well, all I can say is, you'll have a phone bill to scare the sandman."

"Collect," Gert said. "Reggie has always said that if I ever needed anything, to Make It Collect. So he is coming. He is coming now instead of waiting until June."

"That'll be a help to you, I'm sure."

"Well, it will. To get married," Gert said patiently. "Now, instead of a June wedding."

Nellie's jaw sagged. "Get married? To you?"

"Yes. To me. We would of before, only his wife only died last March. We was waiting a Reverent Time—for time to pass to make it seem Reverent, that is."

"Oh, my God! What would any— What on earth would he want to marry you for?"

"For What Reason You May Suppose," Gert said. "He likes me. Now, Nellie. All this is neither here nor there.

Reggie says if you will let us have Beck, we will take her to New York to live with us. He dearly loves children, not being able to have any of his own, from getting hurt down there during the War."

"Well, for the god's simple sake!" Nellie said. "You and your fancy man run of an idea, between you, that I'd let one of My Girls go off with—"

"Better with us than Be Sent Away," Gert said. "Now, Nellie, you have always had to Live Me Down. If Beck has to go to the reform school, you will have her to Live Down, too. Any more people going to be Lived Down, Nellie, everybody will think something surely is the matter." She fingered the clasp of her alligator bag, pulling the bag around to the front in her lap. "So you could listen, couldn't you, to the rest of what Reggie told me to say."

"No, I couldn't . . . To what?"

"I am not going to put it on the basis of Beck. You let me have her, go with me; you can have the Old Home back."

"That palace in Shacktown? I wouldn't live there if—" Nellie's eyes narrowed a little as her mind took in what had been said. Property. It was property. It could be sold, realized on. She said, staring at Gert, "So what about that Frances? According to her, she's got a say."

"Oh, Frances is willing. We are both going. She says that to stay here—uh—now, would be Small Business."

"Hnf, what was it ever but? You willing to put that in writing?"

"I already did." Gert opened her bag. "A Warranty Deed, not just a Quit Claim. I got it in Bishop this morning, and this other paper that says you let Reggie and me adopt Beck, legal."

"Well, it looks like you thought of everything."

"I did," Gert said. "Except nothing is signed, it has got to be done before Witnesses. Reggie says we will all sign when he comes, he will see about the Witnesses."

"What about the stuff in the house?"

"I Make No Mistake about you, Nellie, I knew you would hold out for what you could get. It says here, Lock, Stock, and Barrel. What would I want anyway, a Deep-Freeze, a Garbage Disposal, pack them all to Scarsdale, New York, when I have got Reggie?"

"Well," Nellie said. "I guess you know what you've got. H'm, it ain't that I can avoid seeing certain advantages . . ."

A respectable woman with a job to keep . . . a sister with Gert's reputation and a youngone headed straight for reform school—both of them out of town and well away; the Old Home, Gert's things—the Garbage Disposal; one less mouth to feed . . .

"How's *he* going to feel?" she demanded. "When he finds you ain't got nothing—that you've deeded it all over to me?"

"Reggie? Oh, it was his idea, what did you think? He has Got Plenty. A Good Job and a Ranch-Type House in Scarsdale, New York, and a Lincoln Continental, and, to boot, He Is All I Have Ever Wanted In A Man. He don't need houses and Garbage Disposals from me."

Nellie was suddenly furious. Savage. "You don't rate it, Gert! A good man with money, and the rest of us with our heads not half above water! You ain't got it coming, and it ain't no use you to think you have!"

Gert nodded. "I never made no plans on What I Got Coming, I just made plans on What There Was."

"What is that man—a plain fool? He must know what you are."

"Oh, yes, he does. I told you. He likes me. He says I'm The Prostitute With The Heart Of Gold and, I tell you, his ain't made of no Pewter. Oh, Nellie, leave off talking! I never could tell you nothing, not How It Was, nor Why I Done What I Done, not nothing, no more'n I could pound it into an ox with an ax. All there is to say is do I get Beck or don't I, and so good-bye."

"All right," Nellie said. "You can have her."

I can't do nothing with her nohow, Gert might's well have a try. It's that or the reform school, and Blood Is Thicker Than Water. What more was there to say, anyway? So good-bye.

Gert's establishment vanished overnight from Hillville. Marvin Coles, going there for the second time to rant and threaten with the law unless, found the house locked and empty.

H'm, he guessed he knew what was being tried on—them loose women hid in there, lying low, so's they wouldn't have to talk to him. Well, they'd find out what it was to be outside the law.

He banged on the front door, went around and banged on the back, and, finally, broke a pane in one of the lights beside the door, reached through and turned the key. He went all over the house, searched the rooms.

By the gumpty, if they warn't gone. Ought to have known it when he come in from the empty smell in the house. Left everything, too. Well, it had been a nice house. Too bad he'd had to close it up, the town was going to miss it. But if he knew the town, it wouldn't be long before another one started up somewhere, and probably worse, so that to close it up would be a bigger feather in his cap when he needed one. In case he did.

He was coming down the front stairs when he saw Nellie Overholt, head-on and breathing fire and brimstone.

She said, "Let me see your search warrant, Marvin Coles."

Marvin sputtered. He guessed she had him there. He drew himself up. "I am in the pursuit of my duties as the First Selectman of this—" he began.

"And I am in the Welfare," Nellie said. "Going around

to people's houses. And I know that the President of the You-nited States, which you are far from, could not go into anybody's house without a search warrant or invited by the owner. That is in the statues of the State Code of Law and I can show you the page in the book and the paragraph. What you have done, you have Broke and Entered, and there is a page in the book about that, too."

"Well, a town official can—" A town official couldn't, and Marvin knew it. He finished, somewhat ineffectively, "—do what he thinks is the right, without a lot of—of damn foolishness . . ." It was, too. What did she think? He broke into a bawl. "This ain't your property! You can't order me around in it, you ain't got a word to—"

"I have got here a Warranty Deed to this place that is as legal as the cupolow on the Statehouse roof," Nellie said. "I could have the hell arrested out of you so fast that people wouldn't see your heels vanishing over the treetops. You ain't one mite better than anybody you have Preferred Charges over or Drove Out Of Town, everybody knows you come here with the best of them. So you let me hear one word about one member of my family further, I will get out a Warrant, and it won't be no search warrant, neither. Now you make tracks. Heels towards this house!"

Marvin guessed he better. Never heard such talk out of a woman in his life. She even went so far as to bawl out the door after him, for the whole neighborhood to hear, "And you can send somebody to fix that windowpane you broke, if you don't want to hear further from me!"

Well, there! It had been some old satisfactory to tell off that pompous coot. Nellie guessed she wouldn't hear any more about his hounding Beck into the reform school, not that he could now anyway. Gert hadn't left any address—better that way, her man Reggie'd said—and Nellie couldn't even remember the name of the town, so if what Marvin's idea of the law was ever caught up with Beck, it wouldn't be because of anything Nellie could tell them. The god ever knew how Beck would end up, but that man, that Reggie, seemed to be real nice in spite of what you knew about him; and money, too—he had given Nellie a nice fat check, said it was from Gert, for letting her have that wonderful little kid to keep, and not to worry he'd see she got a Nice Education. Well, maybe he would; it was hard to say.

The thing that was hard to take, of it all, Nellie thought as she poked around through the house seeing What There Was, what Gert had left here, Beck seemed to think the world of them, even that Frances; she couldn't wait to go, had hardly even kissed her mother good-bye. Well, that was the way of it, bring up kids, slave your life out, and no gratitude, leave you without looking at you. When you'd done your best. I wasn't that way with Mama. Gert was; but I wasn't. I looked after her as long as she needed it; and I buried her, too, paid the expenses out of my own pocket. Well, Beck takes after Gert, I guess, and it ain't as if I didn't have two more of my own.

There certainly was a lot of stuff abandoned here in this house. That electric kitchen, alone . . . washing machine, stove, icebox, even a drier. If this place wasn't in Shacktown, I'd move in here myself, but there, I doubt if I could even swing the taxes on it. No. Better sell it, take the money, but it certainly would simplify my housework. H'm, a whole shelf of canned groceries, though, which I certainly can take home.

Before she left, she went over to the sink, turned on the garbage disposal, listened to it hum.

✡

Mack Jensen, a week or so after Amos's body was found, made Connie an offer for her father's house and business.

"For his share of it, that is," Mack said. "Being as I was a kind of a silent partner."

He was getting married, settling down, he told her, with an air of deadpan relish she couldn't miss—in other words, she needn't think she was the only pebble on the beach; she'd had her chance and now it was too late, he was spoken for. He produced estimates of the worth of the business—the number and condition of the earth-moving machines—the bulldozers, back hoes, power shovels, trucks—saying that he was the logical one to do this since he alone now knew the value of things. He pointed out that three of the machines had taken an awful racking in the flood, so weren't worth much; and he asked that she'd make up her mind as soon as possible because, with the season starting, he'd like to get things settled—he had a lot of work lined up.

The estimates seemed businesslike enough at first glance. Connie found one or two mistakes in addition, in Mack's favor, which might, of course, have been honest mistakes. She corrected these and then realized that, so far as she was concerned, the rest of the data might as well have been in Greek. She took the estimates to Joe. Not wanting to take up his time at the plant, since everybody there was working at top speed these days, she dropped by his house one evening after supper.

She found Joe stretched out in his armchair with his feet on a footstool and his lap full of babies. The babies were asleep and Joe was nodding; all four faces had a look of milky contentment so much the same that Connie had to smile, in spite of the fact that her heart contracted at the sight of J. J. Randall.

Oh, how you've grown, she said silently to him, as Mrs. Burrage, Joe's housekeeper, ushered her in. He had, too, and so had Cary and Gary, who were fine and fat now, though still with a delicacy of structure, a transparency of skin, that made them what Nellie Overholt called "touch-

and-go" babies. But not J. J.—nothing transparent about him. He was tremendous, solid as a railroad car. And you're almost six months old, now, Connie said to him. Aloud, she said, "Oh, Mrs. Burrage, it seems a shame to wake anybody up. Joe's probably all in; I know he's had a day. Why don't I come back some other time?"

She didn't, she realized, want J. J. Randall waked up, because, asleep, without that heart-twisting, wide smile, he didn't look at all like Ernie Grindle. He looked a little like the Wilkinsons, it was true, the slight resemblance was unmistakable, but mostly like a baby.

"I'm awake," Joe said. "I'm just paralyzed under all this tonnage, that's all. Some of you womenfolks haul it off somewhere, so I can move, I'll come to."

"Don't make out it's a hardship," Mrs. Burrage said. "You'd think, to hear him talk, that we hogtied him every night and piled him up with babies. But there ain't a one of the four of them that wouldn't squall the house down if they didn't have that snooze together after supper. Here," she said to Connie, "you take this one and I'll get the one in the middle, and I guess Joe can manage Gary." She scooped up J. J. Randall and thrust him into Connie's arms and went off into the bedroom with Cary.

Connie held him; he was easy to hold. She felt a strange sensation in her arms of lightness and heaviness at the same time; and, He's heavy, she thought, but my strength doubles to hold him; he's mine. She couldn't help it; she bent her head and laid her cheek against J. J. Randall's velvety one; it was warm and smooth, and he had a rich, powdery, vaguely sour-milk smell.

"Pss-t," Joe said in a whisper. He was scrabbling awkwardly out of his chair, with Gary balanced on one arm as delicately as an egg. "Don't wake him up, Connie, or this act of mine'll all have to be gone through with again."

She followed Joe into the nursery and laid J. J. down in

his crib, tucking his blanket over him. The crib blanket had safety pins in its corners; there were tapes on the crib slats to fasten them to. Connie fastened them.

So you won't kick out in the night, she told him. And catch cold.

Back in the living room, she handed over Mack Jensen's estimates to Joe. "I'm sorry to take your time, Joe. But I think I need some help with this. I've an idea Mack's treating me like a woman, but I don't know enough to see where."

She was surprised to find her voice casual and steady.

"Well, you are. You sure are. Thank God," Joe said, his eyes crinkling slightly with amusement. "Here, le'me see." He took the estimate sheets to the table and sat down, shuffling them apart. "Where's a pencil? You ain't got a pencil on you, have you?"

"Yes," Connie said. "In my bag."

She fumbled in her bag, found the pencil, held it out to him.

"My godfrey mighty," Joe said, taking it. He glanced at the point, pulled out his jackknife and proceeded to sharpen it into his ashtray. "Anybody's only got to look at a woman's pencil to know that it don't belong to a man," he said. He glanced at her above the small, curling shavings. "It beats me," he said, "how two people ain't related can look so much alike as you and Jay do. I see you, there, with your faces together, it took a real jump out of me. Why, he could be yours, Connie, and not a question asked."

"Yes," Connie said. "I guess he really could, couldn't he?"

She almost told him. She almost told him then and there. To have someone know; to have Joe know; to ease the ache . . . the homesickness . . .

He is Joe's, she told herself steadily. I have lost title. He's

Joe's and Joe loves him. I can't tell him and I won't. He mustn't know.

She watched him while he figured—the stub of pencil in the square, brown capable hand, setting down notes, check marks, with quick little jabs; the lined, sensible, absorbed face, with its steady dark eyes and confident chin; the wide, strong shoulders. Joe.

A man, she thought. Why do there have to be so few of them?

If you had had what was here. If you had had it before the flawed years twisted the course, muddied the springs of the love your childhood had, that your young womanhood looked forward to; the love that was in you when you began. Because it was, she thought. It is in any girl when she starts out, so much of it that she can't think of anything else; over everything—school, work, career—is a screen on which the young men move like a flowing river; their hands, their eyes, their hair, the deep sound of their different voices; and "Which one?" sounds through her waking life like a theme in music. If that could be used in trust, not wasted in conflict, beginning with the nastiness of your mother telling you, and going on through the wrestling match in the back seat of a car, and the wet mouth smelling of gin of somebody you hardly knew and who hardly knew you, while you thought, scared and sickened, Is this what it is, is this what you have to do? And, fighting the damp, clutching hands away from your thighs and breasts; before you were ready, before you knew how to handle it; in terror, remembering the gentle, informing voice, "Now that This happens every month, you'll have to be careful, dear, or you'll have a baby"; a girl, not dry herself behind the ears, getting broken in, first-hand; to what would end in Ernie Grindle; in Amos and Lucy; in the life with King Kong . . .

Joe laid down the pencil.

He said softly, "Wow!" and grinned. "Mack tell you he'd like to close this deal quick on account of, oh, this and that?" he asked.

Connie nodded. "Mm-hm. He says he wants a free hand to start work."

"Well, give it to him," Joe said. "If that's what he wants, give it to him, by all means. Of course, he can't take title till the probate gets around to settling your father's estate, but if he has it in writing that you'll sell to him, why, that'll be okay, too. Because with any kind of an outside audit, some things'll likely come out, like, for instance, he's got two bulldozers listed here, one in good shape and the other one damaged by water. Well, I happen to know your father had three, because I've been dickering to buy the third one. And with a sand-and-gravel business this size, there ought to be a lot more movable tools—shovels and stuff—that I don't find listed here; if I know Mack, they're stashed away somewhere and wouldn't show up on any estimate. He thinks you're a fool, Connie, honey."

"Yes, I know he does. Well, I would be, wouldn't I, if I promised to sell to him on his say-so, without an outside audit?"

"Nope. You'd be a fool if you didn't. Here's why. If I had even a pie-shaped slice of a gravel business in this town, right now, I'd unload it so fast you couldn't see me for smoke. Nobody's going to sell farmland for gravel pits, not in this town, not now. There's quite a number of old fields being cleared out to plant this spring, and there'll be more when the idea's had time to sink in. Seems a lot of people got tired of looking at puckerbrush, don't want to see it grow any higher. You don't find surfacing gravel just anywhere; it's mostly under the places that grow the best beans, if you know what I mean. Fields like that in time to come ain't going to be bought cheap, which is the basis of that business. So you get his offer down in writing and signed. And fast."

"So he isn't cheating me after all," Connie said thoughtfully.

"Well, he thinks he is, and he's so busy getting himself a deal that he hasn't bothered to look ahead. But he's offered you just about a fair price, and if I was you, I'd take it."

Mack Jensen, Connie thought. Taking over where my father left off. With the same elephant-hide indifference about other people's rights, and no misgivings as to his own.

She had never felt sorrow for Amos. For a while, in her grief over Lucy, she had even hated him, telling herself that Lucy was what she was because of him, an identity trampled and shapeless, an appendage to selfishness, and no more; but now, with a little time to think, she had come to see that, as Clementina had said, many things had gone to make up Lucy, not all of them Amos; and that many people who did manage to grow up by the time they were middle-aged, did not live longer because of that. You couldn't assign blame; it was useless to try. So Connie did not hate Amos now. If he had been insane, she told herself, she ought to feel pity; but Amos sick had not been enough different from Amos well—it had been only a matter of degree. She could not remember a time when he had not stamped over anything in his way, no matter whom, no matter what, his privileges twisted with a sick logic out of his religion and, according to him, God-given: Man is the master of Creation, top dog of the heap; what he wants, he takes, and is justified because he can.

You would think when the old men died, with their mistakes log-piled behind them, the young men might profit from folly obvious to fools; but if Amos were insane, then you had to wonder how much of the world was, too; there seemed to be no end to that insanity. The troglodytes circling a vicious circle; around and around and around. Amos Wilkinson giving place to Mack Jensen, his spiritual son. Get-in, get-what-there-is, get-out. And the devil take the hindmost.

A warm brown hand came down over hers and she jumped a little, startled. Joe had got up from his chair behind the desk and was standing there.

"It ain't that bad, Connie," he said. "Godsakes, nothing could be," and she looked at him, seeing the kind, steady, concerned face close to hers start to blur and waver through her tears, the rough material of his shirt dissolving to a patch of misty blue.

"Oh, Joe," she choked, and finished nothing, but leaned her head against the blue patch, feeling him there, strong as a stone, the solid rib cage under her cheek shaken with his caught breath, and the sudden hammering of his heart.

"We both had it, Connie," his voice said over her head. "Both of us, too rough to take." Held close, she heard the deep vibrations of his voice; or it was as if her body heard it, echoed it, and answered. "But time goes," he said. "It has to. We'll make it go, together."

☼

On a bright morning of May, almost June, when the new leaves were unfolding on the trees like babies' fingers; when the grass was greening and the whitethroats sang like flutes from every bush, and the nights were warm enough for a man, even an old one, to camp out without freezing to death, Everard Peterson tooken off for the stay he had long promised himself in Cooney's Heath.

A man spent the winter in jail, account of the crocodiles in human form not believing his given word, had to norate around awhile till he got back his leg muscles. Everard had been out for a month, around town, walking, hunting along the fringes of the woods. He guessed he still might not be quite up to such a long trip, but he had looked people between the eyes and into their teeth too long; he was sick of the sight. He wasn't going to stand for them no longer. He could take it easy if he had to; but bad legs or no bad legs, he was going up over the hill and down into the Heath, and he was going to stay a week. Shoot them ducks, or a nice pa'tridge or two; have a roast on a stick over a fire. Them duck aigs, too, if they hadn't been sot on too long by this time, and he guessed maybe he could find some late ones that hadn't, would go almighty good. His mouth watered at the thought.

Blanket roll on back, rifle, plenty of shells, Everard set out. For the first part of the way he followed an old woods road, so grown up with alders and hardhack that it was barely a trace. God, it was a passion the way the bushes grew nowadays. Why, he remembered when this road was swamped out, between tall trees; come down here with a team and a loaded wood sled, many's the time. For years it had been a good, passable road, part corduroy; then, all of a sudden it seemed, the alders took a-holt, and the corduroy was so rotten now that you had to go out around it, fall through you'd break a leg, sure'n God. Well, it was a hard scrabble; if you went this way, you had this road and you had to climb the hill; but downslope a ways, you could hit that old branch coon trail and save two miles. Besides, in jail all winter, he'd been looking forward to seeing the top of that hill. It was nice there.

He made it to the top, breathing hard. It was as he remembered, one of the few places didn't change. Big gray-granite ledges stuck out, warm in the sun; there was one in particular that made a seat with a back, comfortable as a armchair; plumb on the tiptop; you could set there and look off over the countryside in all directions whilst you got your breath. The seat was there; warn't nothing, no reason for the spoilers to smash that up; one thing. Everard leaned his gun against the stone, took off his cap to cool the sweat on his forehead, and sat down.

That was more of a climb than it used to be to a man, by God.

Now that was country that used to be country, once; in the old days. Slash and puckerbrush now; but off north there once had been the woods, miles of wilderness, rising and falling to the shape of the land. Black spruce and pine; hardwoods like spots of yaller-green mist this time of year, where the leaves was opening out, with patches of blue here and there in the glades to show where lakes and streams were. That was the old wild in there, in them days, the real old wild; and gorry, some old good place to go hunting in. Shoot ten deer in a night if you wanted to; once he had, just for the hell of it, shot thirteen. Shoot all you want to and leave lay what you don't want. Them was the good, old free days. Not like now. Spit now, and you hit a game warden.

Off south was the ocean, covered the whole horizon from southeast to southwest, so white with the glare of morning sun that you could hardly see the offshore islands. Hard on the eyes, that glare was; who wanted to look at salt water, anyways? Pretty, if you liked it; but the idea of working on it, fishing, made him want to cry. He had; had had to; times. But it wasn't no life for a man. He turned his back on the ocean and on the roofs of Hillville, which he could see if he looked down, west. Let that go, too; wasn't nobody there he cared to think about. Them people; taking in each other's washing for a dime a throw, as if that made them better than a man, even if they thought so. Let 'em think so; it was one thing they had to keep alive on, thinking they were better than someone else.

As for him, as for Everard Peterson, Cooney's Heath, down below there, running off miles to the east, was what he had come to see. That was a sight on a spring morning to make a man feel like a king and this rock he sat on a kind of a throne.

Come to think of it, he *was* a king down in that heath; wasn't a thing in it he wasn't smarter than and the master of. Why, hell, when a king walked around his kingdom, all the people fell down, bumped their heads on the sidewalks; and when Everard Peterson went through that swamp, by God, every living thing in it fell still—the frogs, the birds, the rabbits, the deer; just as you walked, you could hear the stillness start to grow. A bullfrog would cut off in the middle. "Ker-chunk!" he would say. "Ker-" and then stop; a bird would cut off in the middle of his song. Like they said, "Shush up, boys, the old king's coming, old Everard's coming," and sat, not a rustle, waiting to see who was going to get the little surprise.

A king? Why, hell, I *am* one. And by God, I got a pretty kingdom.

In that swamp down there, must be four miles of that pink lambkill in blossom this time of year, it was like looking into a big pink bowl. Shadbush in bloom, too, and wild cherry. A goddam flower garden, and all mine.

Not much water, looked like; be muddy, but not too, on that branch trail. He could make it all right to his old camp in on the hummock. Be damp sleeping, but he could make him a nice bed of spruce boughs. The squirrels had probably chewed up that box of oatmeal he'd left when he was in here last time; but, well. Squirrels was good eating; old Everard'd likely get his own back.

"Yah, yah, yah," said a crow from the top of a tree.

Everard didn't look around, but he grinned slightly to himself. Same crow, he didn't have a doubt.

"Well, you fly around awhile," he said under his breath. "I kind of run of an idea this'n is going to be your day."

Well, huddle up, boys, here comes the king; and he picked up his gun and went on down the hill.

In the thickets at the foot of the slope, he found he had to stop for breath again; harder coming down hill, almost, than going up; got a man right behind the knees. Pouf and phew!

The branch trail was as he remembered it; growed up some, but not too bad; not too muddy. Had to part the bushes here and there.

What in hell was that, over there, like somebody left a pile of old rags under a tree?

He moved closer, saw what it was.

A body, by the gumpty; someone's body? Now, who in creeping tarnation could that be? Whoever 'tis, he ain't a pretty sight. Been there all winter. Took a helluva jump out of me, too.

Everard looked around for a place to sit down; his heart, he realized, was pounding.

Must be one of them out-of-state deer hunters, got lost in here, died, like. Never heard about one of them missing last fall, but the way they flock the woods, hunting season, could very well one of them dropped out and nobody missed him. Tall feller. Them's about the longest thigh bones I ever see on a man.

If I'd got here last fall, I might've had me a nice leather jacket, but that ain't no good now. Wonder if he had any money on him? Well, if he did have, it can stay there, all of me. I ain't going a-poking round in that mess.

Most of folks would go high-arsed back to town, couldn't wait to get told what they found in the woods. A body, a body, a body. Gab, gab, gab. Not old Everard. Not the king. I ain't going to miss my trip for nothing. This feller's waited a long time, he won't go nowhere whilst I'm in on the Heath. Maybe he can stay right here, let somebody else find him, if anybody does. Any way I look at it, I go tell it, all I'm going to get is mixed up with cops and gawpers. Whole town'd be in here, tearing up the woods. Wouldn't be any hunting in here for months on end. And, anyway, all 'tis to me is them spoilers couldn't find nothing else in here to destroy, so they've started in on destroying each other. To hell with it.

Everard went on, into the Heath.

It was tough going, tougher than he remembered. By the time he got to his old camp on the hummock, he was wet and muddy and beat out. His camp was just about eaten out—walls fallen down, next to nothing left a man could use. But he had got him two nesting ducks, and he built a good hot fire to roast them and to dry out by; he braced up the old camp, cut himself a spruce-bough bed. But by the time the ducks were ready, he was too tired, almost, to eat. Didn't seem to feel hungry, not the way he used to. Maybe it was because it was earlier than he was used to eating supper; couldn't be only but about three o'clock; but he ought to be hungry, hadn't et since breakfast. By God, come this far . . . He ate the ducks, every morsel, forcing down the rich, gamy-tasting meat and sucking the bones. There! Show that, whatever it was, bothering him. Now for a nap till dusk, deer-hunting time, and he'd wake up fit to live with himself again. He lay down on his newly made bed, covered himself with his blanket and went to sleep.

Later he woke up with a jump.

Now, what was that? Come wide awake, all to once, as if there was something, some noise around the camp woke him up.

He listened; there wasn't a stir. Wasn't dark yet; about five o'clock, he should judge; sun way over in the west, beginning to heave down to set. The fire was out, not even smoking; he was chilled to the bone, dead cold. There weren't even any ordinary noises to hear; the swamp was as still as the inside of an egg, the yolk. Better get up, build on a fire; no sense catching pneumonia out here, that'd be a fool thing to do. That duck meat was bothering him; shouldn't of et so much this early in the spring; after a winter, and him in jail to boot, a man needed spring tonic first, maybe a nice mess of dandelion greens.

Everard sat up. The world tilted and swung. A light exploded behind his eyes, started a bright pinwheel spinning. He fell sideways, choking, his hands trying to tear away from his throat the heavy swelling, the lump, growing, pressing, so he couldn't get a breath.

What had waked him, what it was, that had sneaked up on him while he slept, made itself known. It should not have seemed unfamiliar, not to him, who all his life had seen it, many times held it in his hands—the new-dead duck, the bleeding squirrel, the beaver, the heron, the turtle; the thrush blown to shreds in the middle of its song. It was only that it was new to him; a little surprise, just for Everard.

"Yah, yah, yah," said the crow from the top of a nearby tree.

EPILOGUE

On the margins of the pond Amos Wilkinson made out of swamp land which had once been the oxbow of a running stream and had ceased to be when the Cooney boys decided that the way to get rid of manure was to dump it in the creek—Hell, you put it on the land, you get weeds, and weeds have to be pulled and that's work, and why bother when you can get just as good fertilizer out of a bag for half the trouble; the cussed stuff would float off somewhere in the spring freshet and be out of the way (only after a few years it didn't, it clogged the channel and the swamp plants grew in it like crazy)—on the margins of Amos's pond the miraculous process, interrupted, now resumed.

Shards and ashes of the burned farmhouse, bulldozed over, settled into earth, washed by rain, disturbed by frost, shone on by the sun. Fireweed took root there, in bombed-out cities called the "weed of sorrow"; it throve, thrust out a mass of purple blooms pleasant to bees and butterflies. Among char and burnt timber ends, and the rotting boles of smashed orchard trees, beetles lived, drilling secret tunnels, going peaceful ways; and under a flat, gray plank, which had once been a doorstep, a colony of ants made an anthill.

ABOUT RUTH MOORE . . .

RUTH MOORE'S life has been a modern variation of an old New England pattern. A century ago Yankee seamen spent years traveling the world, waiting for the day they would come home and stay. Ruth Moore spent twenty years in cities and crossed the continent ten times before returning permanently to Maine.

In the interval she taught school, worked as a secretary and as a publicity writer, managed a fruit ranch in California, and was associate editor in New York of a national magazine. With the publication of *Spoonhandle* in 1946, she returned to Maine and has lived there since.

Miss Moore was born on Gott's Island, a mile and a half off the Maine coast where her family had lived for five generations. She now lives in a house (partially built by herself) on Mount Desert Island where she enjoys reading Thoreau, Shakespeare, John Donne, Andrew Marvell, and Plutarch; growing vegetables and flowers; and listening to music.

Before publishing *The Weir,* her first novel, Miss Moore had written six or seven others which she threw away and five plays which met the same fate. Before writing fiction she wrote verse, and that she still likes. When asked to comment on somebody's statement that writers are lazy she replied, "I can't speak for other writers. All I know is that when I'm writing I'm busier than a cranberry merchant."

Her many successful novels have dealt with the people and the places she knows best—Maine Coast people in Maine Coast towns. But a rare gift of insight into the human predicament has given her books far more than regional significance for readers all over the world.